St. Martin's Paperbacks Titles by

CHERRY ADAIR

*Undertow*

*Riptide*

# Riptide

### CHERRY ADAIR

St. Martin's Paperbacks

RIPTIDE

Copyright © 2011 by Cherry Adair.

All rights reserved.

For information address St. Martin's Press, 175 Fifth Avenue, New York, NY 10010.

ISBN: 978-0-312-37198-2

Printed in the United States of America

St. Martin's Paperbacks edition / September 2011

St. Martin's Paperbacks are published by St. Martin's Press, 175 Fifth Avenue, New York, NY 10010.

10  9  8  7  6  5  4  3  2  1

*Riptide is for all my Facebook Pips. Thank you for coming to my Deadline Dementia parties on FB and playing along with such gusto. In gratitude, I'm interviewing more waitstaff so there'll be no waiting for service at future parties. Unfortunately, due to Certain People who shall remain nameless, closet doors have now been bricked over. Tsk. Tsk.*

*Smooches,*
*Cherry*

# Chapter 1

Trouble.

He didn't anticipate it, but Nick Cutter always planned for it. And right now the hair on the back of his neck lifted.

Good enough for him.

Eyes concealed behind both brown contacts *and* dark glasses, he stretched his long legs out beneath the table. Toying with a small cup of fragrant mint tea, he scanned the immediate area. Just because he couldn't see it, that didn't mean it wasn't here. The café was situated in the deep shade on the perimeter of a busy public square. Nick enjoyed a good meal, and since he was in control of the meeting, he'd eaten well, then pushed aside his empty plate to conclude business. The men seated across from him conversed in low Arabic, trying to come to agreement with his terms.

Two principals. Three bodyguards. All heavily armed.

Ostensibly bored, he waved a buzzing fly away from his face. He scanned the throngs of gregarious, noisy shoppers milling about the square for an indication of why he suddenly felt a brush of disquiet.

He wasn't worried that anyone would recognize him. His

disguise was solid. Like many of the people in the square, he wore a mushroom-colored djellaba, a kaftan-type robe that covered him from throat to toe. His most recognizable features were concealed behind the dark glasses and contacts. Judiciously applied makeup simulated the dusky skin tones of the majority of the people around him. And to further his disguise, his face was covered by a thick black beard that desperately needed grooming. It itched like hell. He'd had the beard for a while, now; time to shave it off.

If trouble was out there, it was for his alter ego Asim Nabi El Malamah, not Nick Cutter. Which increased Nick's sense of disquiet. El Malamah had a bad rep for good reason. Nick had made sure of it.

Nothing seemed out of place. It was lunchtime, and the old city center of the twelfth-century fortress-walled medina was crowded and off the charts noisy. The hot breeze smelled of cumin, paprika, coriander, garlic, onions, and the half-empty dishes of *tajine* on the table.

Women vying for the best produce bargained loudly, their long jewel-colored djellabas brilliant as hummingbirds in the harsh sunlight. Laughing and shrieking, their children darted in and out of the stalls and between other shoppers, adding to the noisy chaos.

Nick had metaphorically chased the two principals until they'd caught him, then intentionally priced himself high enough to make himself almost unattainable. Almost. They wanted him, they'd pay. It was a precarious call, but a calculated risk.

Calculated risks were something of his specialty. But his superpower was his extraordinary ear for dialect inflections. He was one of only a handful of people in the world capable of determining a man's history from a snippet of conversation.

He spoke eleven languages fluently, understood seven others, and even when he didn't speak the language, prided himself on his ability to pick out nuances so minute that he could pinpoint the difference in dialect from towns fifty miles apart.

His specialized skills weren't in high demand, which made the few "assignments" he accepted a novelty. He enjoyed doing his thing—which usually meant listening in on conversations at a safe distance from actual danger.

Players on the hook, Nick wanted back on board the *Scorpion,* suited up and a hundred feet deep in the ocean doing what he loved. Treasure hunting. They'd been salvaging the *El Puerto* for several months, and he was very pleased with the results. It was almost time to take his haul back to Cutter Cay.

Sooner would suit him better than later. The original "favor" he'd agreed to should have only taken an hour, tops. Instead, it had taken him three days to make contact. Now he knew what he wanted to know, and that should have been the end of it.

But the favor was different this time.

His friends had asked him to go way beyond a quick listen to ID a person of interest's backstory, a hell of a lot more. Nick had agreed to see this through to end game.

He just hoped to hell his fascination with puzzles, his linguistic abilities, and his love of a challenge didn't come back to bite him in the ass.

Like right about now.

He swiped a hand around the back of his neck as the two men continued talking in urgent undertones. They thought he was distracted, but he had ears—as his brother Logan would attest—like a bat. Najeeb Qassem and Kadar Gamali Tamiz whispered in *darija,* the informal Moroccan Arabic spoken by the locals, but the inflection was definitely Krio.

The fact that Qassem and Tamiz were both from Sierra Leone, although they'd informed him they'd been born and raised in Rabat, was not his concern. But the people he'd report this meeting to in a couple of hours would have one more piece in their intricately constructed puzzle.

And so would he, though he doubted his friends would share anything else with him. He'd baited the trap, as requested. It was past time for Asim Nabi El Malamah to disappear, and Nick Cutter to get the hell out of Dodge.

Ready to close the deal, Nick placed his cup on the table and shifted in his seat. Just then a gap opened between the shoppers, and his swiftly moving gaze snagged on a leggy brunette entering through one of the stone-arched gates. Hard to miss her killer body displayed in tight jeans and a loose white shirt among the loosely flowing djellaba-garbed people around her.

Now wasn't *she* interesting and very much out of place?

He had a thing for tall, sophisticated brunettes.

Oh, yeah, Nick thought, observing the woman as she paused to talk to the ancient man selling dried rosebuds by the gate; she was definitely his thing. Her presence here could only mean the trouble he was sensing. The old man pointed across the square. He could be indicating the nearby silk kiosk, or the jewelry maker next door to the café. The medina was so tightly packed, the old man could have been pointing to a dozen different things.

Nick's gut said otherwise.

The rose-seller was directing her to the table where he was concluding business. The woman glanced across the square in his direction, then turned back to smile her thanks, before heading his way.

Oh, yeah. Trouble with a capital T.

The only European woman in the bustling outdoor market, she stuck out like a catwalk model, and all eyes watched her saunter across the uneven stone on her high heels as though she were gliding over water. She had a loose-hipped stride that triggered carnal thoughts and turned heads. Like a heat-seeking missile, she was headed his way, her long legs drawing attention Nick didn't need.

Damn it to hell.

He didn't have the luxury of a long slow perusal. The closer she got, the faster he tried to figure out who'd sent her, what they wanted, and what her angle was. She was striking, and walked with the confident knowledge that men would look. And want.

Yeah, she was trouble all right. And out of place in the sun-drenched, noisy, frenetic medina filled with midday shoppers. Nick leaned back in his chair as she closed in.

"You know the woman?" Najeeb Qassem asked in Arabic. He couldn't possibly miss the intent in the woman's long-legged stride, or the direct path she was taking.

She had a fascinating awareness of the space around her. The square was crowded, but she didn't let anyone get within arm's length. A nifty trick that must have taken a lot of practice. She pulled it off like she wasn't even trying.

Fifty yards and closing.

"La," Nick responded shortly as he swiveled to redirect his attention at Kadar Gamali Tamiz, seated on his left. No, he didn't know her. But he suspected he knew who she was. Even though her presence here in Morocco, and specifically in the medina, made no sense.

Which made her sudden appearance in the same place as Nick Cutter suspect.

Forty yards. "The number of containers, while somewhat difficult to conceal, is acceptable," he said, his voice cool. "The price, however, is not. Getting on board undetected with all eyes on the ship will be a risky endeavor. Cutter is no fool. And while he is docked here to find more crew members, he will have his people scrutinize each new hire scrupulously."

"Our men will pass even the closest scrutiny undetected, we assure you."

Nick made to rise. "Then I suggest you use these men to carry the merchandise on board," he said with enough finality in his tone to suggest he wasn't anteing up any more than he had already. "If it's such a simple task, you don't need the likes of me to assure your prize is hidden well enough to avoid discovery."

Tamiz's fingers closed on his wrist. Narrow-eyed, Nick glanced from the man's hand to his face. Tamiz quickly dropped his hand. "Apologies for the insult, my friend. My men are merely insurance that the product stays where you place it. Simple men."

Nick settled back into his chair. "Well armed?" Thirty yards. Damn it.

"Of course."

"Good." Shit. Not good at all. Unknown, armed men on board his ship was just asking for trouble. "Your product would be valuable in any hands."

"You are a hard man to negotiate with, *sadiqi*."

"Not when the price is right." Nick kept the woman in his peripheral vision. Twenty yards. With any luck she'd pass by, he'd enjoy a glance at her ass, and that would be that. He didn't have excess time to admire the gentle bob of her breasts under her crisp white linen shirt. The hot breeze teased a few strands of her dark hair out of the severe hairstyle, and lovingly pressed the thin fabric of her shirt against her body, highlighting her mouthwatering shape.

Fifteen feet.

Her footsteps slowed. A calculated move? Or indecision?

"We would double your fee should you escort the merchandise to its final destination." Qassem, a stick-thin man in his late sixties with a sun-lined face and bottomless black eyes, leaned forward. Nick had no intention of spending weeks on board his own ship in disguise.

"Tempting. But mal de mer must limit my participation in this endeavor," Nick told him easily, watching the woman close the gap between them. She looked innocuous enough, but as he well knew, looks were deceiving. Her shiny black hair was slicked back to reveal high cheekbones, freshly glossed red lips, and a smooth olive complexion. Her eyes were hidden, like his, behind dark glasses. His gaze skimmed her body for a weapon, and his muscles tensed in anticipation. The jeans were tight, the shirt loose, and the leather bag over her shoulder looked heavy. She could be carrying an arsenal on her and nobody would know it.

He shifted so he had better access to the Sig Sauer covered in the folds of his loose clothing. "I have no desire to take an extensive ocean voyage," he told Qassem. "I negotiate only for safe delivery of the merchandise to the ship, and making sure that it is well hidden so that it arrives as safely as a babe in his mother's arms at its destination."

Nick's pulse picked up a different rhythm as the woman stepped into the shade mere feet from the table. She was close enough now for him to smell the heated perfume of her skin. Spiced peach. Sophisticated. Sexy. Exotic.

*"Excusez-moi, messieurs."* Her contralto was naturally husky. Black velvet and incense. "Which of you is Asim Nabi El Malamah?" She spoke French with intriguing and subtle layers, doing a credible job pronouncing the unfamiliar name.

Too bad Nick didn't want to hear it from her. Especially here. And sure as hell not now.

Her dialect gave her away. The second she'd said the first couple of words he knew *exactly* who she was.

Princess Gabriella Visconti.

Still didn't answer why she was there. Or who'd sent her.

People were stopping what they were doing to stare. At her. At him. At his lunch companions. She looked expensive, chic, and perfectly at ease. Not a bead of perspiration marred her perfectly made-up matte complexion in the afternoon heat. Her hair, twisted into a coil at her nape, caught the sunlight with blue-black highlights, her olive skin hinted at the Mediterranean, and her accent was layered with more than enough to pique Nick's interest. He ruthlessly tamped down his curiosity.

He knew the gist. More than enough.

"I'm busy," he told her without inflection in Moroccan French. Asim Nabi El Malamah was notorious for doing anything. For a price. But his skills weren't for the likes of her. And her contact with him, at this time, in this persona, could get her killed. Or worse.

Unfazed, she readjusted the heavy-looking leather tote up on her shoulder. "I'd like to hire y—"

"I repeat," Nick's voice was cold. Dismissive. Final. "I'm busy. Leave us, woman."

"You to transport me to a ship . . ." She waved a slender

hand in the general direction of the marina as if he hadn't said a word.

Nick ran a bored finger around the rim of the gold cup, sharing an amused glance with the men at the table. Women, his shrug said, what can a man do?

Qassem scratched his beard. "What ship?"

Her hesitation was infinitesimal before she answered. "The *Scorpion*." She turned back to Nick. "Do you know it?"

His ship? "No." Nick slouched back and lifted his cup; the metal was warm from the tea. He glided his thumb across the smooth surface and wondered what her breast would feel like under his hand. Yes, she was definitely his type. Brunette, long-legged, and sophisticated. As if she'd been fashioned especially for him.

And she wanted on board the *Scorpion*.

He didn't believe in coincidences.

Someone knew his tastes. Gold glinted at her ears, around the base of her slender throat, and around one wrist as she said pleasantly, "I'll pay you many dirhams for a few minutes of your time."

Nick glanced up, saw his own surly hirsute face reflected in her dark glasses, and said with icy disdain, "I have no need of your money." Jesus. The foolish woman had no idea what she'd just interrupted. Or did she? Was she a ladybug fearlessly walking into the web of a deadly steppe spider? Or the spider herself? He looked her up and down. Slowly. "Unless you are willing to offer more than coin?"

Tamiz laughed. The other man at the table remained stone-faced.

She frowned, or possibly scowled. Hard to tell behind the big sunglasses. "I'll give you my watch, it's a—"

"You offer a watch when I suggest a fuck? I have no need of a woman's watch. A woman? Possibly. When I have completed my business here. Wait for me at the Hotel Dar El Kebira, we can . . . talk there."

Her expression didn't change. "Your exchange rate is disproportionate to the request, Asim Nabi El Malamah," she told him dryly. "It is, after all, merely a short trip. A miserly amount of your time. I'll find other transportation."

As long as she managed it tomorrow, Nick was okay with that. The *Scorpion* sailed from Tarfaya harbor at dusk tonight. "You do that."

Her lips tightened. "I will. Gentlemen." She nodded curtly to the others, then turned to leave.

Nick reached out and snagged her wrist. "If you should find a man stupid enough to transport you to the ship, be prepared to spread your legs for him. Make no mistake, your request will imply consent, Mademoiselle."

Lips tight, she glanced pointedly from his fingers shackling her wrist back to his face. "I'll take that under advisement." Her expression read "Fuck you." She turned and walked away.

Nick turned back to Najeeb Qassem. "My time is valuable, gentlemen." He pushed away from the table, getting to his feet. "Meet my price, or you, too, must find another mule."

*       *       *

"Son of a bitch!" Bria Visconti muttered under her breath as the dragonfly-sized helicopter landed with a jarring thump on the seemingly too small helipad on the upper deck of the *Scorpion*.

Nick Cutter's boat—ship—was a megayacht, all gleaming white paint and shiny brass, and the size of a blasted football field. It was in the middle of *nowhere* between the Canary Islands and Madeira and pretty much in the middle of the Atlantic Ocean. Nothing for miles around but sparkling cobalt ocean and powder-blue skies.

Either Cutter had used the money—her family's money—to help pay for this expensive toy, or he had other investors funding his expensive taste. One thing was blatantly, conspicuously evident: He had money to burn.

Peachy. That would make her job here much easier. Bria's jaw ached from clenching her teeth for hours. She took a

deep breath, relaxing the stress from her shoulders and jaw.
She had a temper, and it had been simmering for days, but
she was determined not to let it boil over. This could be
handled in a civilized manner, and she was determined to be
cool, calm, decisive, and above all—firm.

The trip from California on such short notice had cost
her a small fortune, which she could little afford. She'd been
unemployed for a year, and this trip had wiped out her meager savings. If she'd found someone to take her the short trip
between Tarfaya and the *Scorpion* yesterday, she wouldn't
have had to spring for an expensive, last-minute flight from
Tarfaya all the way to Las Palmas. Hiring this private helicopter to take her from the Canary Islands all the way the
hell and gone out here in the middle of nowhere hadn't been
on the agenda either.

She'd been unhappy when she'd received the call at home
in Sacramento, she'd been unhappy on her flight to Morocco,
she'd gotten downright cranky when she'd realized that asking
to be transported *anywhere* from Tarfaya without giving up an
organ or her virtue was next to impossible. And she'd been
pissed beyond belief yesterday when she'd realized that the
*Scorpion* had sailed out of reach of any relatively inexpensive-
to-hire motor launch.

So much for the tall, dark, and hairy Asim Nabi El Malamah who-would-do-anything-for-the-right-price. He hadn't, he
didn't, and his laziness had cost her a lot of money. *Jerk.*

Each arduous, annoying step of this journey had ratcheted up her anger and frustration. She'd never met the
man, but Nick Cutter was already a pain in her ass. At this
point, Bria knew she'd be hard-pressed to be civil, let alone
honey-sweet.

"Almost over," she told herself. She smoothed her hair
back neatly, tucking nonexistent wisps into the chignon at
her nape before removing a small gold compact and lipstick
from her tote. Her makeup was flawless, all she needed was
a fresh swipe of kick-ass red gloss to boost her courage. One
last look. She was good to go.

She'd taken off the headset the pilot had given her in Las

Palmas and picked it up again as the rotors spun noisily overhead. She hooked the strap of her heavy tote over her shoulder, armed for battle. "You're sure there's no other ship with the name *Scorpion*?" She'd pictured a decrepit dive boat, not this multi-gazillion-dollar floating palace.

"Ask him," the pilot said indicating a man in white T-shirt and shorts running toward the helicopter. He was bowed low to prevent being decapitated by the slowly spinning rotors. Nick Cutter? Bria's heart did a little hop, skip, and jump.

*"Espérame,"* she instructed the pilot to wait in Spanish. "I will return shortly."

*"El viento empieza a soplar. No voy a esperar si mi helicóptero está en peligro, señorita."*

Oh, for—! Bria noticed the windsock thingy fluttering on a nearby pole; the wind *was* blowing, but it was hardly wild enough for concern, she was sure. *"No pasará mucho tiempo,"* she insisted.

She took the pilot's grunt as a yes, he'd wait.

The middle-aged man in white popped open the door, then helped Bria down and pointed across the deck to a glass-walled atrium nearby. Bent almost double and trying to run on five-inch heels was a nifty trick. She was lucky she didn't break a leg as they ducked under the still spinning blades.

Bria straightened and pushed open the glass door, looking around for a second to orient herself as the man shut it behind him. The noise of the helicopter abruptly cut off.

The vast room, surrounded on three sides by enormous windows, gave a panoramic view of nothing but flat water all the way to the horizon. A massive stone wall fountain—wall *waterfall*—taking up the entire far wall provided a pleasant ambient sound and reminded her she needed a bathroom.

She ran a light hand over the coil at her nape to make sure her hair hadn't fallen out of the combs. It hadn't. Double-checking was a nervous habit.

The room was elegantly, if austerely, furnished in white with touches of navy. Very "Give-me-something-clean-looking-not-fussy-money's-no-object." Sleek white canvas sofas and wavy chairs, glass and chrome, some interesting, but sparse, objets d'art here and there, and a highly polished, dark teak floor. Impersonal and expensive, and impossible to gauge the personality of the person who'd paid for it. The room was too modern for Bria's tastes, but then she wouldn't be staying long enough to care one way or the other.

Sunlight streamed through the windows, and she wished she hadn't put her dark glasses away. But she wanted to appear sincere and open when she met Mr. Cutter.

Before leaving the hotel this morning, she'd exchanged the jeans and T-shirt she'd traveled in for a figure-skimming red sundress that showed off her bare arms, had enough cleavage to distract a man, and was short enough to display her long legs to advantage. Red-soled strappy black sandals with five-inch heels made walking on a slightly bobbing ship a bit problematic, but the killer heels accentuated the outfit to perfection.

Unless Nick Cutter was gay or blind, he was going to be putty in her hands.

The man who'd brought her inside crossed the room to her side. He was in his fifties, with ginger hair and a thick beard. His unwelcoming glare wasn't in any way masked behind frameless glasses. "Is Mr. Cutter expect—" he began, just as she said, "I'm—"

"Principessa Gabriella Visconti," a deep, vaguely familiar voice said from behind her.

Bria turned around slowly. She hadn't heard the second man approaching although the floor was uncarpeted. Which was weird, because he was large and imposing, and seemed to suck up all the oxygen in the room by his very presence.

He was barefoot and half naked, wearing just the bottom half of a wetsuit. Diamond-like droplets of water sparkled in the dark hair on his sculptured chest, then ran in a straight, neat line down his flat belly to disappear under tight black neoprene.

The punch to her gut was completely unexpected. Bria had expected Nick Cutter to be in his late sixties at least. She'd pictured paunchy, dissipated. Gray hair if any. She'd pictured avuncular.

He was none of the above.

She noticed his dark hair and that he was tall, tanned, and had the long lean muscles of an athlete. She noticed the wet sheen on his skin, and the smell of salty male. But it was his striking, impossibly blue eyes that made Bria want to press her fist to the pterodactyls swooping in her tummy, and caused her breath to hitch. Testosterone poisoning, she diagnosed, feeling a little panicky.

And here she'd only brought determination and cleavage.

"You know who I am?" *Please*, Bria thought a little desperately, *please don't be Cutter*. This man had his own gravitational field, complete with tractor-beam eyes. He had an almost visible aura of raw power kept on an incredibly tight leash.

He didn't appear to be a man who'd be distracted by long legs or boobs. He looked like a man who had things to do and places to go, and she was an inconvenience. A not-that-interesting inconvenience.

"I read the papers," he said smoothly in flawless Italian, maintaining eye contact. *Okay. Not a boob man.* "You're extremely photogenic, Your Highness. Thanks, Blake," he added in English, addressing the older man hovering beside her. "I'll take it from here." He turned those extraordinary blue eyes back to her, his expression set and coldly dismissive and not in the least welcoming nor interested.

"I'm Cutter. What can I do for you, Princess?" he asked coolly, switching back to Italian. A single drop of water snaked slowly down his bronzed bicep and she had to blink the conversation back into focus.

She wasn't used to being called Princess. And she sure as hell wasn't used to a man using that tone of voice when he spoke to her. She'd done nothing to earn his—what? Contempt? Scorn? Bria had no idea what lay behind his inscrutable expression. But she didn't like it.

She waited until the other guy left the room. She heard his footfalls just fine, and her own as she tap-tap-tapped a few steps closer, hand extended. "English is fine, and call me Bria, please."

His fingers, cool and still damp from his swim, closed over hers in a polite and brief handshake. Firm. Decisive. No lingering.

Her heart jolted in surprise. One look at his polite expression told Bria he clearly didn't feel the sharp spike of electricity that she'd experienced when skin touched skin. Goose bumps rose on her arms. She took a small step back. A tactical retreat.

Fine. Cutter clearly wasn't impressed, or charmed, or blinded by lust seeing her bare, red-polished toes in high heels. So be it. Bria's tone changed slightly. "If you know who I am, then you know why I'm here."

"If you'd sent word you wanted to observe the dive, I would've made arrangements for an overnight stay. Unfortunately, with a full crew, and a large dive team, that won't be possible at this time."

Dismissed. Again. Before she'd even made her pitch. This was getting old, fast. "I'm not here to observe you dive, Mr. Cutter," she said with asperity. "Nor do I have the intention of spending any more time on board your ship than necessary."

She indicated the waiting helicopter outside the window behind her. "I'm here for a refund."

He gave her a bland look. "A refund?"

Bria felt her cheeks burn as her temper rose. Her temper was her Achilles' heel, and she'd spent most of her life learning to control it. For seven short years she'd been a pampered princess in a fairytale land. Then she'd been ripped from everyone, everything she loved, and plunged into a terrifying nightmare that had changed her life forever. She'd learned to modulate her temper over the years. And because she considered it one of her worst faults, she did everything she could not to lose it. She should take lessons in self-control from Nick Cutter.

She'd faced far worse than a man telling her no. No matter what his tone. She gave him a cool smile, even though she had a creepy sensation that those piercing blue eyes saw everything she was. And everything she wasn't. "My brother made a foolish investment. Before he throws good money after bad, I want the money he gave you returned to the country."

Nick Cutter leaned his hip against the back of a white canvas sofa. His eyes moved over her, a bland inspection that gave nothing of what he was thinking away. "You're the king's business partner?"

Not partner, nor confidante. Barely even sister, as distant as she felt from him. Her cousin, Antonio, had had to tell her of Draven's latest foolishness. "My brother made an error in judgment," was all she said. One of many since he'd ascended to the Marrezo throne two years ago.

Bria ignored the familiar fluttery sensation of panic in her stomach. How she felt about her brother's lack of financial sense was none of Nick Cutter's business. "I've come to rectify his lapse."

"Have you, indeed?" He pushed off the sofa back, one dark brow arched. "Let's go belowdecks and discuss this in my office."

Said the spider to the fly. She'd rather stay right where she was, sunlight streaming into the spacious room, the helicopter—her only means of transportation and already paid for round-trip—right where she could see it. "I'd pref—"

"I'm sure you'd like to freshen up before you head back to Las Palmas," he said over her, autocratic as hell. "Wash up, have a cup of coffee, resolve this, and be on your way?"

She didn't like taking orders. She didn't enjoy being told what she'd like to do by the man who'd accepted five million dollars from the Kingdom of Marrezo's coffers when he clearly didn't need it. No matter how hot he was.

Bria didn't get her reaction to him. She enjoyed guys. A lot. She liked their big hands, and big feet, and everything in between. She liked their tougher skin, and the smell of their cologne. She liked a nice tight butt as well as the next woman. She liked to lightly flirt, it made her feel like a woman. She liked men. Men liked her.

Nick Cold-as-Ice Cutter didn't like her. And he annoyed the hell out of her.

A situation she didn't appreciate.

Still, there was no need to be annoyed much longer, and an enormous sense of relief washed over her at his words. He was going to give her Draven's money back. Thank God.

And even though she would've preferred ironing it all out here and now, now that he mentioned it, she remembered that she needed the restroom. Another lengthy trip in the helicopter without a pit stop would be impossible. She settled her tote on her shoulder. "Very well."

Nick picked up the phone on a nearby table that also displayed a very phallic-looking statue in Carrera marble, an intricate bas-relief gold box, and a square glass vase filled with vivid red flowers. The only splash of color in the room other than Cutter's disconcerting eyes.

He asked that Khoi come to the sundeck, then put down the phone to address her again. "My steward will show you where you can freshen up, then escort you to my office. Take your time."

"I—"

Cutter didn't wait to see what she had to say. He gave her a piercing look that made her heart pound in annoyance, then he strolled out of the room, giving her a tantalizing look at his long, tanned bare back, and tight-neoprene-covered butt.

Bria didn't have time for lingering nor admiring. Not only did she have a helicopter waiting, she had to get her country's money back where it belonged within thirty days, or the bank would own the principality of Marrezo, and the small country that used to be her home would revert to Italy. In addition, she had a new job to report to the following week. Taking her time was a luxury she couldn't afford. "I've also got important things to do and places to go," she told the empty room.

She planned to speed pee, locate Cutter's office, accept a check, and be on her way back to Las Palmas within the next twenty minutes. She'd stop in Marrezo and give her cousin the money to bail out Draven's coffers. Then she'd wing her way back to Sacramento and the prospect of a fabulous job, happy as a clam to be away from the mess her brother had created. Hopefully her cousin Antonio could manage to rein

Draven in so he didn't get involved with any more wild-hair-
get-rich-quick schemes.

Treasure hunting! God, where had her brother come up
with such a crazy idea?

The only person making money from her brother's reck-
less "investment" was Nick Cutter.

# Chapter 2

"What the hell does it matter what she looks like?" Nick asked, mildly annoyed by the question from his friend, and not sure why. He'd grabbed a quick shower and changed into jeans, a T-shirt, and as usual, he was barefoot. "As the only woman on board, no matter how short the duration, she's inherently a problem. And one we don't need, especially now."

And whatever she really wanted, she'd come loaded for bear in that little nothing of a red dress. And Jesus, her legs went on for-fucking-ever. He'd told her no, and she'd looked at him with doe-like, big, brown, fuck-you eyes that promised, "I *always* get what I want, you might as well roll over now."

Jonah Santiago, the *Scorpion*'s captain and Nick's closest friend after his two brothers, had been involved with every aspect of this voyage. Up to and including what was going to be going along with Nick's favor to some friends in dangerous places.

Nick rose to close the wood-framed window behind his desk so their conversation couldn't be overheard. Then paused for a moment to enjoy the sound of the waves lapping at the hull, and the drone of the blower as his dive team expanded a new area of the wreck site. Window latched, he sat on the corner of his desk to collect his thoughts. Exquisitely carved from the timbers of a sunken British barque-rigged ship, the desk took up a large portion of the floor space in his office.

"I don't miss your hairy face at all," Jonah said mildly, leaning back and locking his hands behind his head as he gave his friend the once-over. He was wearing long white pants and a short-sleeved white shirt with his navy-and-gold-striped captain epaulets on the shoulders.

"Trust me, I was happy to see it go. My lack of grooming wasn't what I wanted to talk to you about, however."

"Right. Just out of curiosity," Jonah rocked back on two legs of his chair. "Are you pissed she showed up here now?" He was tall, broad-shouldered and dark-eyed, with wind-blown dark hair that always needed a trim. Neatly dressed in crew whites, Jonah could do with a shave himself.

"Hell yes."

Jonah's eyes danced, but he wasn't stupid enough to smile. "Maybe even a little intrigued?"

God, yes. But that had nothing to do with the who and why of what the princess was doing on his ship, and everything to do with the sexual energy coming off the maddening woman in pulsing waves. "No."

Jonah grinned. "Oh, good. I was afraid I was losing the ability to read your inscrutable expression. Her presence certainly makes the game more interesting," he threw out as the chair dropped back to all fours. He slouched in the rich brown cordovan leather chair, legs stretched out so that if Nick wanted to move about he'd have to detour around Jonah's big feet.

Nick rarely wanted to move about unless he was diving. Or having sex. He focused his mind on the former as best he could, since thinking about the princess *and* sex simultaneously was dangerous to his mental health.

Her skin was olive, fine-grained. Looked silky. All over? Yeah, he'd bet the treasure of *El Puerto,* two hundred feet down, that she felt and tasted as good as she looked. He wasn't sure he could ever look at a ripe peach again without imagining Princess Gabriella Visconti.

*Damned* annoying.

"Having millions of dollars' worth of smuggled conflict diamonds on board is excitement enough, don't you think?"

"Nah," Jonah smiled slightly, waving a fortune in diamonds aside. "Those stones might as well be ballast. The exciting part comes when the good guys arrest the bad guys, and the diamonds are confiscated. And that won't be for at least a month-ish. Pretty boring until then."

"What's your point?" Nick demanded.

Jonah grinned. "Your princess is here now."

"She's not *my* princess," he countered immediately, but the thought had merit. She could be his— No way. Trouble like that would cost more than the dive's payout. "And she'll be leaving within the hour." Nick picked up the centuries-old ornately filigreed gold box studded with precious stones they'd salvaged on day one of the most recent dive, turning it end over end in his palm. His version of pacing.

She used those long, luscious legs of hers to pace, to stride, to strut. Her long strides ate at distances as though her environment was too small for her. No matter where she went, no matter who she was with, she'd fill any space she was occupying to capacity with her beauty. With her personality. With her jaw-dropping sensuality.

Nick liked things more subtle. Over the top wasn't his way. Low key was. Which was why his brothers called him Spock. His expression rarely gave the game away. Jonah frequently teased that he was too buttoned up, that one day he was going to blow.

He didn't know Nick quite as well as he thought. Nick's emotions weren't buttoned up; they were stapled, screwed down, and then hermetically sealed. Just the way he liked it.

"Are you just going to sit there and brood?" Jonah asked after several minutes of silence. His tone casual, but, damn him, filled with laughter. "Or do you have something to share? Because even though we're anchored, and much as I enjoy watching you stew over a beautiful woman, I have better things to do."

"I'm thinking," Nick picked up a pen and doodled on the

notepad, just to give himself time to think the princess through. "Give me a minute." As Asim Nabi El Malamah, he'd negotiated an outrageous price to bring the blood diamonds on board and secrete them away. The plan was for the diamonds to stay put until the *Scorpion* docked at Cutter Cay in three or so weeks. From there they'd be transported by Qassem and Tamiz's men, who were somewhere on board, through the Caribbean and then taken to Miami. They'd be sold on the North and South American diamond market undetected.

That was the Moroccans' plan.

That plan, however, would be nipped in the bud.

Neither Nick nor Jonah liked that they didn't know which crew members were in the pay of the Moroccans. But the situation, by definition, was tightly confined. The stop in Tarfaya had served a twofold purpose: They'd used the time to replace several crew members, and he'd made contact with the diamond smugglers.

They wouldn't be going into port again for supplies, and in a couple of weeks the *Scorpion* would set sail from the dive site, the diamonds secure. The delay, and secure means of transportation, would give the counterterrorist organization Nick was involved with the time they needed to figure out who headed the diamond smugglers, and how they were getting blood diamonds out of Africa and filtering them into the American market undetected. Who the buyers were too.

That was a lot of birds with one stone.

As far as Qassem and Tamiz knew, El Malamah had delivered the containers of uncut diamonds to the *Scorpion* for them, then disappeared back into the underbelly of Morocco. And vanished *fast*. Nick knew they'd never leave him as a loose end.

Of the five new crew members Jonah had hired on in Tarfaya, he and Jonah had taken an educated guess that at least two, if not all five, of the new hires were the Moroccans' men, there to ensure the diamonds reached their destination safely.

Isaac, Fakhir, Blake, Basim, and Abdul-Jalil.

Everyone else on board was pre-Morocco, and had been with them at least a year, if not longer.

Still, no matter where or when any of the crew were hired, everybody had been thoroughly background checked. *Everybody.* And even though they knew some of the recent hires belonged to the Moroccans, nothing in their usually rigorous background checks had indicated anything untoward.

Which meant that some of the new hires had gotten sophisticated new identities.

After several minutes of companionable silence, Jonah asked, "So what's your plan?" He leaned back in the chair, stretching his arms up with a laziness that belied the amused gleam in his eyes. His captain was enjoying the hell out of this.

Nick shook his head. "No plan, yet. I have to decide what I want to do with her."

That laughing gleam intensified. "May I make a suggestion? Or five?"

Nick didn't need the help. "No," he said evenly, proud that none of the agitation simmering below the surface colored his tone. The plush red-and-black Turkish wool carpet muffled his steps as he crossed his office, stepped over Jonah's feet, and replaced the box carefully on its mahogany shelf.

The room smelled pleasantly of old paper, Gurkha's premier, Louis XIII Cognac-infused cigars, and fresh salt air. Nick's office was filled with history. Old charts, notebooks, maps, hundreds of books, and small, priceless artifacts found on various dives throughout the years. The space was crowded, aged, and just right. Unlike the rest of his ship, which was sleek, modern, and minimalist, this cabin could've existed, exactly as it was, centuries before. It was the place he felt most at home.

He crossed to the window. The back fin of the helicopter sitting on his landing platform was just visible from this angle. The princess had to have spent a great deal of time and money tracking him down and hiring the helicopter. So she couldn't be all that hard up for cash.

"Question is," he mused, "take her at face value? Or lump her into the current situation?"

"Justifiably paranoid, all things considered." Jonah's words came slowly, as he mulled. "But don't you think she's too . . . well, obvious to be part of the diamond thing?"

Obvious was an understatement.

Nick dismissed the easy answer out of hand. "That might be exactly the point," he said. "Why else would she be here? She's either been sent to keep me distracted for the duration or the king wants a close eye on me." And his money.

"Then whoever sent her didn't do their homework on you," Jonah responded mildly. "It would take much more than a great pair of legs to get past you. You juggle ninety-six things at once, and make it look like you're only focused on one at a time. And even that one thing looks like it bores you into a coma." Jonah gave Nick a crooked smile and swiveled in his chair.

"It's uncanny," Jonah continued cheerfully. "You're not a guy who's easily distracted. Okay, let me rephrase that. You're not a guy who ever gets distracted. Focus is your middle name." His lips twitched. "*Spock* is your first name."

"Multitasking," Nick said, unruffled by the neat assessment. He shot a quick glance at his multifunction watch.

Jonah rolled his eyes. "The point is, anyone could tell you that having a beautiful, sexy woman shoved under your nose while you pretend you don't know a fortune in diamonds is being smuggled on board your own ship is a waste of everyone's time. Especially yours." He paused. "Unless you think you can learn something from her."

"I don't believe I said she was either beautiful or sexy." Although she was both. Sex appeal shimmered around her like some kind of hallucinogenic drug. Nick picked up an antique jewel-handled letter opener, sliding his thumb across the sharp edge. "She could be a modern day Mata Hari."

"See, paranoid is all well and good, but let's not get certifiable," Jonah said wryly, scratching his stubbled cheek. "Look, whatever she is or isn't, you can handle it. She might be exactly who she claims to be."

"Which is?" he asked, curious for Jonah's take on the matter. He half-expected "sex-kitten" to be at the top of his captain's list.

Jonah disappointed him. "A concerned sister to one of your most prestigious investors."

"Maybe," Nick allowed. "Hell, probably. You're right. One way to find out what she really wants is to keep on eye on her." The thought unsettled him, and he tossed the letter opener to the desk with a metallic clatter. "I don't mind the cloak-and-dagger distraction, but the situation could go from sunshine to shit in a heartbeat."

"Come on, Nick," Jonah braced a foot against the bottom of the desk to slow his lazy swing. "Any dive could wind up the same way."

This was different. "I can't afford unknowns in this particular equation," Nick told him, running a hand over his freshly shaved jaw, glad to have gotten rid of the scratchy beard. "For the duration, there are only two people on board that I trust. You and me. And until I'm told that the operation is over, I'm inclined to treat everyone else as suspect." And as hard as it was to swallow, that included people who'd worked for him for years.

And a certain leggy princess, whose presence was already irking him and she'd only been on board for ten minutes. A woman didn't travel halfway across the world and dress to kill on behalf of her brother. "Even though I find it damned coincidental that she sought me out in the medina yesterday, I can't *logically* connect her to the Moroccans. But I'll find out what the connection, if any, is. What's the point in having contacts in low places if not for this kind of shit?"

Jonah's lips twitched at Nick's wry response. "She might be unexpected, but she *is* royalty and they have a whole different way of thinking," he pointed out, not unreasonably. "The king did invest several mil with Cutter Salvage. It's not out of the realm of possibility that he'd send a family member, a good-looking and smart family member, to keep an eye on his investment."

"Sounds like the guy is having investor's remorse." That happened every once in a while. Diving was an expensive business. Sometimes, an investor got scared he'd lose his cash to a dry dive. Taking treasure from the sea was a gamble. The thrill ran in Nick's veins whether he scored or not. Sometimes it didn't pan out. When his brother Logan talked to investors, he always drove that point home so that there would be no misunderstandings.

Cutter Salvage had a no-back-out policy.

Jonah shrugged. "So he sends his kid sister to watch the pie."

Nick's annoyance flared as he followed that thought. "Doubt it," he finally said. "Why would the king want to withdraw his investment before we finished the salvage? Not when he stands to make millions on his return." He leaned back in his chair. The sun beat through the window and painted a white square on the surface of his desk. "I don't think so."

"Steal the pie?" Jonah offered.

That one made Nick slant his friend a wry eyebrow. "And haul it out . . . how?" he asked. In the two and a half months they'd been salvaging the Spanish ship *El Puerto,* they'd found millions of dollars' worth of gold and silver, and a veritable treasure trove of gemstones. "The money's wrapped up in gear and equipment. Think she can hide it in her purse on the way out?"

"All right, fine. Call the king and ask," Jonah suggested reasonably.

"Did that." And Nick had known before he called what the response would be. Logan had told him a month ago that King Draven Visconti rarely answered the phone, and seldom returned calls. Up until a few minutes ago, that hadn't bothered Nick in the least. He liked being left the hell alone while he was working. Especially by his investors. "His people told me he was unavailable, he'd get back to me."

"There you go." Jonah cupped the back of his head in his hands, reminding Nick of his younger brother Zane at his most annoyingly cheerful. "Not like you don't know how to handle a needy woman. Explain the intricacies of what happens before a payout is made, and let her fly back to wherever. Seems pretty cut-and-dried to me."

"Unless—" Nick exhaled, clearing his mind of the emotional clutter. He had all too much of that at the moment, and he needed to zero in on the meat of the matter—and what had been bothering him since he'd first laid eyes on the princess in the medina where she didn't belong.

"Pretty farfetched that she's connected to the diamonds, you must admit—"

Nick agreed, except— "What's my type?" he cut Jonah off.

"I haven't noticed in the last year."

Nick refused to crack a smile at his friend's jab. He was fully aware of how long he'd been without a woman. He'd been busy.

"Okay. Okay. Intelligent? Great legs? Brunette?"

"That's the princess. In spades. And just maybe someone did their homework well enough to know that."

Jonah was giving him the look again. The one that suggested Nick was overanalyzing himself into paranoia.

Bullshit.

Nick turned back to the window, memorized the numbers on the helicopter's side. He'd check it. Find out where it had come from, who'd chartered it, and how it had been paid for. It might not yield any information, but then again, it might. "If good King Visconti wants his money back, why not ask himself? And make no mistake, Logan made the terms crystal clear from the outset as he always does. Why send his sister? Why now? And, for Christ's sake, her tracking me down in the medina yesterday?"

"Not *you*, buddy. The dastardly Asim Nabi El Malamah. Perhaps she's just trying to impress her brother with her dedication to the task he's given her."

"Didn't we just get done assuring ourselves that she's intelligent?" Nick asked dryly.

Jonah waved that away. "Clearly, your parents should have given you a sister instead of two lunkhead brothers. Placate her and send her on her way." Jonah's lips twitched. "Or take the scenic route and frisk her, then send her on her way."

"I don't trust her." He had no reason not to trust her, Nick thought. It was *himself* he wasn't trusting as far as the princess went. Fortunately, in a few minutes he'd send her on her way and never see her again.

"You know what they say. Keep your friends close, and your enemies even closer."

"You just had to quote Machiavelli in *The Prince*," Nick told him, amused.

Jonah smiled. "I thought I was quoting Michael Corleone from *The Godfather*."

"Him, too." Nick scrubbed a hand across his freshly shaved jaw. "The big question is, if Visconti did send her, what's he playing at?"

"I presume that's rhetorical," Jonah answered, reaching over for one of Nick's very expensive cigars, bringing it to his nose and rolling it between his fingers as he took an appreciative sniff. "He got the contract, knows we have to take everything back home to be sorted, et cetera, therefore he's also aware that nothing can be divvied up until after we get back to Cutter Cay and Brian."

Brian Donahue was Cutter Salvage's head marine archeologist and a stickler for dotting I's and crossing T's. Nothing was leaving until it was researched and meticulously cataloged.

"Might be years." *El Puerto* was Spanish, but had sunk close to Portuguese waters. There was already a lively debate going on between the two countries as to who would benefit from this salvage.

"Maybe they think they can waltz on board whenever they choose and pick up a chest of coins and jewels as their share?" Jonah offered, circling again to the concept of a thieving princess.

"I'll explain how it works to her," Nick told his friend.

"What does a princess do in this day and age anyway, besides pose for paparazzi?"

"How the hell should I know? Preside at balls? Cut ribbons at dog shows?" Nick shrugged. "I do know she doesn't live on Marrezo. Hasn't for a long time. I've asked my 'friends' to check her out. Accent says Marrezo as a young child, but that's layered with a rural town outside of Paris, a trace of Chicago, and quite some time spent in Northern California."

"Yeah?" Jonah pointed the cigar at him. "Northern California is pretty vague, pal."

"Sacramento."

"Better," he allowed. His version of yanking Nick's chain. "What the hell is a princess from a minor Mediterranean country doing living in Sacramento of all places?"

Nick shrugged. "Logan ran the usual background check on Visconti to ensure he was good for his investment." The Cutters never took on an investor unless they knew who they were and where the money had come from. "According to the report, twenty some years ago their respective bodyguards spirited the prince and princess out of Marrezo after a political coup went wrong. Terrorists killed their parents and took over. Hell of a gruesome bloodbath, and both children were believed to have been killed when the castle was overthrown."

"Very medieval and Goth." Jonah put the unsmoked cigar back in the humidor on Nick's desk. Neither of them smoked. "I presume they were split up so they wouldn't be found? They must've been pretty young when they fled."

Nick nodded. "She was just a little kid. Taken on a circuitous route through Europe, then to the U.S. Visconti was somewhere around twelve—and taken to South Africa. That's all I know, I didn't follow the hoopla in the press when he made his triumphant return. What do you know?"

Jonah gave him an arch look. "The whole media circus of his return from the dead, and his hasty coronation were on the front page of every paper, at the top of the hour on every newscast from Singapore to Siberia a couple of years ago. Hard to miss."

Nick threw him a glance. Jonah was a news junkie, and read a dozen news aggregators a day when he gave himself time to bury himself on his computer.

"Under his steadying influence, Marrezo's economy seems to be in the black for the first time in two decades," he reminded Jonah.

"Presumably she gets a cut?"

And . . . bingo. Maybe not. Was she here to finagle a cut? If she was, the princess was going to be in for one hell of a rude surprise. Nick shrugged as he flipped open the notepad on his desk and scribbled down the numbers off the helicopter, even though he'd memorized them a few minutes ago. "If she does or doesn't, it's a family matter and none of my concern."

"Harsh, dude." But Jonah's tone lacked sting. He got to his feet. "Good luck with your princess."

"She's *not* my—" Nick caught the twinkle in his friend's brown eyes and gave him a level stare. "Send her in on your way out." He ripped the page off his notepad, folded it in half, and handed it to Jonah. When Jonah cocked a brow in inquiry, Nick added, "She's right outside."

"Ears like a bat."

"So I hear." Nick watched him cross to the door, then warned, "Hey, Jonah? We still have two weeks at anchor before we head home. Treat everyone—without exception—as a suspect until we know who are us, and who are them."

Jonah paused with his hand on the brass handle to look back. "There are people on board I've known since I signed on two years ago. Most of them guys you've known for longer than that. You really think—"

"I think that everyone has secrets." Nick cut in smoothly. "And money, this kind of money, is enough to motivate even the most loyal employee. Watch your six at all times."

"I hear you." Jonah opened the door and stepped aside to let the princess into the cabin. "Ma'am," he offered cordially, then slipped out behind her and shut the door.

She looked as beautiful and put together as a fashion

model as she paused just inside the door, bringing with her the heady fragrance of hot summer nights. The princess's makeup was perfect, hair meticulously pulled back. Her eyes were large, dark, and long-lashed, her nose straight, her jaw stubborn. A striking—hell—*stunning* face. Instinct suggested that the exquisite exterior package was a thin veneer over a gypsy soul.

"Take a seat." Nick gestured to the chair Jonah had just vacated. Principessa Gabriella Ilaria Elizabetta Visconti's bare legs, long, tanned, and looking extremely smooth and stroke-able, flashed beneath the flirty hem of the clingy red dress as she crossed his office. Discreet gold flashed at her wrist and ears, and her black hair was slicked back. He wondered how long it was, and if it felt half as smooth as her skin wou—

She was nothing more than a royal pain in his ass, he reminded himself. A pain in his ass with an agenda that might very well affect the safety of his crew and dive team, and the outcome of his little side dealings.

Instead of sitting, she rested her hands lightly on the back of the chair. Nick could almost feel those long red nails scoring his back as he pumped inside her. Thank God nothing of his thoughts showed in his expression. His body approved the thought, however, and he was damned grateful he was sitting behind his desk.

"Thanks for your hospitality, but I have to run," she demurred, her sultry gaze matched her sultry smile. I'm female—you're male, that look said. Her husky voice stroked his ego and libido both. Exactly as it was supposed to, he had no doubt. Unimpressed, he didn't bat an eyelash. Zane, his younger brother, a born flirt, could charm a snake into making itself into a pair of shoes without breaking a sweat. Nick had plenty of practice not caving to a winning smile.

The princess knew to the last eyelash flutter exactly how sexy, desirable, and beautiful she was. He was completely, utterly unaffected—Who was he kidding? He'd have to be made of stone not to be affected by her blatant sensuality.

Didn't mean he had to take the bait and act on it. But, damn, she was making him work for sanguine.

"Sit anyway," he suggested silkily, his tone making it clear it wasn't a suggestion. "We're not royalty, but we're civilized people on the *Scorpion*." He eyed her steadily, trying not to notice the curve of her cheek, or how the sunlight, shining through the window at his back, put her in a spotlight of gold. Everything about her was vibrant and vivacious and so fucking *alive* it hurt his eyes.

Her crimson lips tightened just a fraction at his subtle dig and he could see her inner conflict. Add that the princess didn't like being told what to do to her not liking to be told no.

After a brief hesitation, she sat down, sliding one silky-smooth leg over the other. A barely there sandal, with ridiculously inappropriate high heels, dangled from her red-tipped toes.

Smoothing her hair back with one slender hand, she gave him a steady look from those big, guileless brown eyes. Her hand dropped to her lap. "I'm sure you're a busy man, Mr. Cutter." A hint of annoyance lay just beneath the surface of the words. "If you'd cut the check, I'll be on my way."

She had sexy feet and it took a moment to gather his thoughts enough to return his attention to her face. She smiled sweetly, showing almost straight white teeth. Her eyeteeth were a little crooked, taking her exotic beauty to an all new level; a difference that Nick was hard pressed to identify.

The small imperfection was probably charming to another man. But he didn't have time to be charmed. He had plenty enough distractions in his life already. He wished she'd leave so he could remember to breathe.

He wasn't enchanted by her smile. Or her bare toes. Or— He found his gaze fixated on her silky legs for the second time, and dragged his attention back to her face. Where it belonged. "Check?"

Her smile slipped. "The refund of my brother's investment?"

He'd seen feet before. Plenty of feet. He'd felt the drum of heels in the small of his back, he'd felt soft soles surrounding his dick—

*Don't go there.*

The fact that he liked her feet was his problem. Which made it hers by default. His eyes narrowed. "The salvage operation is still ongoing, Princess. The artifacts have to be taken to Cutter Cay for cleaning and appraisal. After that, the Spanish will get their take. I suspect Portugal is going to want a finger in the pie as well. We're talking months, if not years, before there's a return on the king's investment."

That smile melted, and she straightened in her chair so subtly that he wasn't sure she realized she'd done it. Shoulders settling as if gearing up for a fight, she said crisply, "I wasn't asking for a 'return,' Mr. Cutter. I want a *refund*."

"Impossible."

She blinked. *"Impossible?"*

"The salvage business isn't an ATM machine." He waited a beat. "Princess." A flicker of her lush lashes told him the way he said it grated. "On a salvage, it's always a crapshoot if there's any return on the investment at all."

Nick already knew their investors—all of them—were going to be very happy, and he and his dive team hadn't finished the salvage, much less had everything cleaned and processed. An educated guess put everyone's profits at a conservative 600 percent return. *Conservatively.*

Not that he'd share that information until all Brian's I's and T's were crossed and dotted. Maybe it wasn't any of her business. Maybe she was scheming to make off with her brother's money after all.

"What do you mean?" she demanded.

"I mean," he said evenly, "that your brother knew the risks when he made the investment and handed over the check."

"My God." Her skin suddenly looked pale against her dark hair. "The risks? Are you saying you haven't recovered anything in all these months? That Draven has lost his investment?"

What? He frowned. "No, I'm telling you that the dive

isn't completed, and that everything we do retrieve has to be taken back to our archeologists on Cutter Cay before proceeding." Like he'd said already. "Until then, your brother's investment is not in the form of liquid assets."

She looked horrified, appalled down to her manicured nails. "It was five million euro!"

"A hefty sum," Nick agreed.

Bitter chocolate eyes flashed and the expertly applied makeup failed to hide the heightened color in her cheeks. "How long will that take?"

Nick shrugged. "Six months. A year. Maybe more."

"That's unconscionable! Haven't you found the shipwreck you were looking for?"

"We found her."

"Then what's the da—" She caught herself and finished in a more modulated tone. "What's the problem?"

Nick repeated what he'd told her—in Italian.

Her chin tilted, and her expressive eyes darkened with annoyance. "I understood you perfectly well in English, Mr. Cutter. I'm neither brainless nor deaf. I understand the process of provenance. But if a portion of the *El Puerto*'s treasure has already been retrieved, then I'll take Marrezo's share now, and save you the time and trouble of returning Draven's investment to him later."

"No." He said it without a fleck of emotion. Cold and controlled. Reluctantly fascinated by the fact that the cooler he became, the harder it appeared for her to contain her temper. Nick found watching it unravel fascinating. If looks could kill he'd be a dead man.

"Wha—"

"*Naheen. Ngo. Saan.* Do you have a language preference for the word no, Your Highness? If so, I'd be happy to use it."

Color high, teeth clenched. She recrossed her legs impatiently. Pissed, but not moving until he gave in.

"I'm not leaving empty-handed."

"Hard to swim carrying plastic buckets of gold coin."

"I won't be swimming, Mr. Cutter."

"Yes, you will." As if on cue, the whop-whop-whop of helicopter rotors cut through the ambient splash of waves against the hull. "That sound you hear is your ride leaving."

# Chapter 3

Bria hadn't heard the helicopter before Cutter mentioned it, but now that she did, she shot out of her chair as if jet propelled. Just in time to see her ride back to civilization swoop down, and then lift out of sight. "That—" *Scum-sucking, bastard.* "I told him to stay. I paid him to *wait*."

"Hire him out of Las Palmas?"

"Yes."

"Notoriously unreliable." He didn't look even mildly sympathetic.

Lord. Could this trip get any worse? "Apparently." Bria sank back into the chair. Her eyes rose to his. "Now what?" The question was more for herself than him.

Not a flicker of reaction to her plight. He couldn't be pleased to be stuck with an uninvited guest, but his expression was impossible to read. "Apparently you're stranded, Princess. Inconvenient."

God, yes it was. "Not really." She leaned back and re-crossed her legs. Slowly. With the sunlight streaming in behind him, it was difficult to see his expression, but Bria suspected there was none. He wasn't gay; she'd bet her first paycheck on it.

But he was also completely unimpressed.

A challenge for sure.

She had to take a few rapid-fire beats of her heart before she could sound casual and unfazed as she mentally scrambled to regroup. "Since I'm not leaving empty-handed, his departure works out just fine." Like hell. Other than a couple of changes of underwear, jeans, a couple of shirts, and only two pairs of shoes, she was on board a ship, in the middle of nowhere, with just the skimpy clothes on her back. When this was over, her brother was going to owe her *big*.

"You have a Plan B?" he inquired politely, looking at her from those arctic eyes.

He wasn't just good-looking, he was drop-dead, fantastic-looking. Those eyes . . . Still, he had zero charm, less than zero warmth, and sub-*sub*-zero interest.

The man, Bria thought, looking for any sign of emotion and seeing none, was an iceberg. What made him interesting was, presumably, the ninety percent he was hiding. Or maybe he wasn't hiding anything. Maybe what she saw was *exactly* who Nick Cutter was.

Intriguing. No, she scolded herself. Not intriguing at all.

He was clearly stratosphere-wealthy. And he was arrogant.

The arrogance was his problem. His wealth was convenient, he could simply write her a check.

She barely had a plan A, but she adjusted quickly. "I'll just stay until you give me what I came for," she said, striving for cheerful calm. She barely managed either, but gave herself points for effort.

"Unwelcome and uninvited?"

Her good cheer almost slipped its moorings. Bria had a sudden flash of herself lunging across his big fancy desk and beating him to death with his fancy humidor. While satisfying—until she got arrested for murder—it wouldn't get her what she'd come for. Marrezo's damned money.

The money her people desperately needed, money that Draven had recklessly invested.

Her lips curved in a smile. "Mr. Cutter, I've spent half my life being unwelcome and uninvited." A bit of a stretch, but he didn't know that. God. Was he wearing colored contacts to make his eyes that extraordinary cold sapphire blue? But then dropping her gaze to his Sean-Connery-in-his-James-Bond-prime mouth wasn't any less disconcerting.

Bria had been attracted to men before— No. Not like this. *This* took physical attraction into a whole new stratosphere. The unfamiliar sensation—heat, excitement, heart-racing-pulses-pounding-hyperawareness—was something she'd *never* felt before in her life. Odd, since she found him annoying as hell. Interesting, because the sensation was exhilarating.

Bria lifted her gaze to an inch left of his ear. Better. "Believe me, this won't be much different. I don't eat much, and I won't take up a lot of space. You won't even know I'm on board." And then her point, delivered with a brilliant smile. "But if you want to get rid of me, pay me what you owe my brother, and I'll make arrangements to leave."

He took so long to answer, and was so still, Bria wondered if he was considering tossing her through the window behind him. Still, she schooled herself not to be the one to break the silence. Her small smile didn't falter as she awaited his response. Every breath she took during this meeting was directed toward getting her brother's money back. Her country's money back. Her reaction to him was none of his business.

She was holding on to her temper with everything she had, bound and determined to remain cool, calm, and in control, be it by a thread.

She'd never wanted something to be over with more than this meeting with Nick Cutter. She felt like a cat with its fur being repeatedly rubbed the wrong way.

Thousand and one.

Thousand and two.

Thousand and three.

After what felt like an eternity, he stabbed a button on the phone. "Khoi."

She kept counting. Thousand and fifty.

Neither said a word until there was a rap on the door, and

the skinny guy who'd brought her down earlier popped his head inside. "Boss?"

"Do we have any empty cabins?"

"No, boss."

Those extraordinary blue eyes focused on her. "Apparently there's no room at the inn. Sorry."

Which he clearly wasn't. Bria waited to see if his next words would be the offer to share his bed. But Nick Cutter wasn't that crass, nor that interested.

She wasn't going down without a fight. "There are plenty of sofas in your sunroom," Bria told him, undeterred. Cutter might be an ass, but he was unlikely to toss her overboard. "I'll sleep there."

"I can make arrangements . . . ?" The steward's voice came from behind her.

"See if anyone's willing to be inconvenienced, and will move, to accommodate the princess." Cutter's eyes, which had remained disconcertingly on Bria through the whole exchange, narrowed. "Happy?"

"Ecstatic," she said dryly. Really, the man had the personality of a sloth. In a coma. "Should I go with Khoi, or wait here?"

This was all sideways. She had a gift for making friends, real friends. Friends that she'd retained for most of her life. She was a hardworking, tax-paying, bargain-shopping fashionista who just wanted to go home to Sacramento and start an exciting new job.

After she procured Draven's damned money.

Was that too much to ask?

"Go with Khoi, and wait . . ." He waved a big hand dismissively, as if he didn't give a damn where she slept. "Wherever he puts you to wait until a cabin becomes suitable for your occupancy."

A personality-less, *rude* sloth. Bria got to her feet. "Thank you," she told him sweetly, charmingly, trying to be—well, all right, if not friendly, then at least civil. "I won't get in your way."

"That remains to be seen." His tone assured her he had no such foolish hopes. "Las Palmas charters has one chopper. I doubt they'll make another trip out here tomorrow, when they have dozens of tourists willing to pay top dollar for short trips."

"I'll call them and ask."

"No need. I'll fly you back to Las Palmas myself first thing in the morning."

"*You'll* fly me?" That sounded way too suggestive and she cleared her throat. "On what?" The *Starship Enterprise*? A broom?

"There's a helicopter on board."

*Of course there was, silly her.* "Great. Thank you."

"This isn't a free ride, Your Highness. You'll work for your keep."

Bria started to feel not that damned friendly. He could cut the attitude anytime now. Her pulse raced; she felt the heat in her cheeks and reminded herself to modulate her tone. Losing her temper now would be really, really stupid and give him the advantage. Wasn't going to happen.

"I'll be leaving first thing in the morning," Bria pointed out. "Surely you don't expect me to work for my supper?"

"If you're here longer than twenty-four hours, I'll put you to work."

*If it's longer than twenty-four hours, I might kill you and toss you over the railing of your fancy ship, Mr. Spock.* "Doing what exactly?" Her studied, mild tone didn't telegraph the screw-you she was feeling. For God's sake, what did he want her to do? Swab the decks for the privilege of dinner and a bunk?

If she suspected for a second that he had a pulse, let alone a sense of humor, she'd think he was teasing her. He didn't. He didn't. He wasn't. She didn't think.

"Whatever you're capable of doing, Princess. Is there anything you do well, other than making poor choices of footwear and barging in where you're not welcome?"

Poor choice of footwear? So he had noticed her shoes.

Score one for the pissed-off princess.

*Ass.*

"As soon as I'm settled," Bria said sweetly. "I'll sit right down and make you a list."

\*     \*     \*

The steward took Bria back to the upper deck sunroom and left her with a glass of iced tea and a plate of warm brownies while he went off to arrange accommodations. She had a feeling if Cutter had his way—and why wouldn't he? it was his ship—the little Vietnamese steward would stuff her in a broom closet and Nick Cutter would lock the door.

Surely there had to be some room on this huge yacht. Bria took a sip of the cold lemon-kissed ice tea. She should've thought this through a little better, she admitted as she sat in a surprisingly comfortable chair. It was just a knee-jerk response to her cousin's frantic call telling her what Draven had done. In essence, he'd mortgaged the country.

Her country. Or at least, their parents' country. Draven had only been the ruler for two short years, and he'd borrowed more than he needed. Worse, more than he could pay back.

Bria had used up a chunk of her savings to hop a last-minute flight across the continent, across the ocean, and across the fricking globe. Sacramento to New York, New York to Paris, Paris to Rabat, Rabat to Tarfaya, and from there to Gran Canaria where she'd charted the helicopter from hell. All in all, she'd crossed several time zones and had been traveling for three days with a single damn carry-on.

She was tired, and not up to her fighting weight. Especially when it came to the likes of Nick Cutter. She took a chocolaty bite as she looked around. Just a cursory glance was enough to tell her the man probably had fifty million euro in his wallet as walking around money.

Okay. Maybe not, but he certainly could access Draven's money before the salvage was complete, couldn't he? At least as a loan against returns if nothing else.

She sighed and closed her eyes. Just for a second. Under the sound of the relaxing trickle of water in the wall fountain was the throb of a large engine, almost like the ship's heartbeat. It might've been relaxing if she wasn't about to jump out of her skin with nerves.

What would happen if Draven didn't pay the banknote in thirty days? It hadn't even been a possibility an hour ago. She'd been so sure Cutter would be reasonable. Now everything going to hell in a handbasket was a very real possibility. Could the bank take Marrezo lock, stock, and barrel?

That's what her cousin Antonio was terrified would happen. Their people had been traumatized, terrorized, and ousted from their homes for twenty years. In the two years since her brother had returned and been crowned, things had started to change. Crops were planted, vines pruned, families had returned to homes long abandoned. What would happen to them if the island kingdom reverted to Italy?

Bria tamped down the rise of fury at her brother's crazy get-rich-quick scheme. Investing in treasure hunting? Draven might as well have gone to Monte Carlo and thrown away five million euro at the blackjack tables.

As much as she tried to convince herself that he was doing his best to hold everything together while he tried to rebuild the country, she was furious that he'd taken such a wild risk with the borrowed money.

There was some jewelry left . . . It was his and his wife Dafne's to do with as they wanted. Sort of. No. Not sort of. Not even a little. Regardless of what she'd told herself, none of it was reassuring. The priceless gems belonged to the country.

Bria buried her face in her hands. Diamonds and gold weren't going to help rebuild the people's homes, or pay off that balloon payment for the loan he'd gotten when he first went home. For that, Draven needed cold, hard cash.

But for God's sake, treasure hunting? How simple would it be for Nick Cutter to claim that no wreck had been found? How would Draven know? And even if Cutter did admit that treasure had been found, how frigging simple to not declare all of it?

"Might as well wave my lovely new job bye-bye," Bria muttered under her breath. She'd call. See if the company would hold her job for— How long? A week? A month? Until she was ninety-frigging-two?

She was a damn good publicist, but in this economy, and in Sacramento? They could find a dozen good publicists that they liked just as well from the Bay Area alone. Damn it. She'd really wanted that job. Had been thrilled and excited after being unemployed for almost a year to finally find a job. Let alone one doing something she loved.

She'd blown the last of her savings on this wild goose chase, she was still unemployed, and she was stuck in the middle of nowhere on a boat with a man who looked at her as though she were as useful as a china teacup in a . . . salt mine.

She got to her feet and walked across the room to stand at the window. She placed her hand on the sun-warmed glass. The sunset was a splashy, and quite spectacular, magenta and tangerine symphony. The sinking sun was a perfect ball of fiery red in the center. The colors rippled and danced across the surface of the water like the colorful skirts of flamenco dancers.

An ache formed in her chest as she looked out over the vastness of the Mardi Gras–colored water. She was the only person who could save her country. She had to get that money from Nick Cutter. To that end she could take anything.

Even the disdain in his cold blue eyes.

"I am Basim," the darkly good-looking steward told her when he materialized in the sunroom half an hour later. Unlike the slight Khoi, whom she'd liked, this guy was short and stocky like a wrestler, and didn't have a deferential bone in his body.

"A cabin has been made ready for you. If you will follow me, *mademoiselle*?"

Bria was taken aback when he led her to a round glass

elevator instead of stairs. She shouldn't be, she realized. The difference between a man and a boy was the price of his toys. Nick Cutter had some very nice toys.

He had excellent taste. And, she reminded herself irritably, Marrezo's money with which to indulge himself. Which meant he could, if he chose to, return Draven's investment. It hadn't been her idea to stay on board the *Scorpion,* but now that she was here, she would gladly take advantage of the situation. She would get the money back—she just needed to figure out how.

Basim smoothly answered her casual questions. There were about twenty people on board—all men. The name of the captain was Jonah Santiago, not Cutter. Odd. He didn't even captain his own ship?

The miniscule cabin Basim showed her was in the lower deck crew's quarters and so small that the steward remained outside in the corridor as she entered because there wasn't room for both of them inside. The freshly made-up bunk took up almost all the floor space. Fortunately, the cabin had its own bathroom.

"All the comforts of home," Bria told him cheerfully as she tossed her heavy tote onto the narrow bed. She'd slept in worse places. "I hope I'm not actually kicking someone out?"

"It's nothing." Basim's oval, liquid eyes watched her closely, making her slightly uncomfortable. Which, she was sure, he'd been ordered to do by his boss. After asking if there would be anything else, he said in lilting English, "Dinner is being served out on the sundeck, *mademoiselle.* Would you like me to wait?"

"No. Thanks. I'll find my way."

Bowing slightly, he slipped away like smoke.

Bria, not given to claustrophobia, still found the space too confining and quickly freshened up. She took the combs out of her hair so it fell to her shoulders, absently finger-combing the slightly wavy strands into submission as she dumped her purse on the bed. She sighed. "Hard to come up with anything creative and fashion forward with this." She hung up what she could, unwrapped a who-knew-how-old mint, and shoved everything else back into her tote.

Cutter could make her life extremely uncomfortable if he chose to. She hoped he didn't choose to. She'd grilled Basim like a cheese sandwich on the way downstairs. Twenty crew members—all at her service, he'd said diplomatically. She sincerely doubted it. Bria crunched down on the stale mint as she stripped off the red dress and hung it up in a closet only large enough to hold three hangers.

"I'd bet my favorite discounted-fell-off-the-designer-truck Jimmy Choos that Nick Cutter didn't extend that offer," she told the tiny space. Usually a good judge of character, she found him maddeningly hard to read. He was so enigmatic she couldn't get a bead on him at all. Which, unfortunately for him, made him a challenge. And being in the public relations business, Bria thrived on challenge.

It's not as if she had anything else to do for a while.

Basim had informed her that besides the captain and Nick and the crew, there were five scuba divers who went down every day to bring up the treasure. She was ecstatic with that piece of information.

Less than ecstatic with her reluctant host, she took out the pencil and sketch pad she was never without, and did a quick sketch of Nick Cutter glaring at her from behind his desk, then another quick one of the first time she'd seen him. Wet suit slung low on his hips, water beading on his chest—a curve here, and shadow there.

Yes. In a few lines and smudges, she'd encapsulated his arrogance, implied the striking color of his eyes, and she was surprised to see that she'd captured the sensuality of his stern mouth, Obviously having studied it without being aware that she was doing so.

"It's *you,* all right."

Bria shook her head and tucked the pad back in her tote.

Even if she could barely feel the movement of the ship, her high-heeled, red-soled sandals, while fabulous, would get her nothing more than a sprained ankle on board. Although he'd mentioned her shoes, it had been in derogatory terms, and he hadn't exactly fallen all over the sexy footwear. Or anything else for that matter.

Thank God she had a healthy ego.

She changed into her jeans and white, scoop-necked T-shirt, which she turned backward to show a little cleavage just in case, then switched her footwear to lower-heeled wedge sandals that she'd worn to travel in. Now her eyes would no longer be on the same level as Cutter's mouth.

"A good thing," she assured herself. Because his eyes were that piercing I-can-see-into-your-brain blue, it had taken awhile to notice his mouth. Which was pretty damned spectacular and very tempting, except for the things he said with it. Things like no.

His lips were well defined, and very sexy.

"Down girl," she reminded herself as she slicked on red lipstick without looking in the tiny mirror by the door. She didn't need to see herself; she knew exactly what she looked like. Pretty girls were a dime a dozen. Her looks were genetics and nothing to do with her. Her figure was good in clothes, and a little meaty without them. Not too many people had seen her without them. Her legs were her best feature and she played them up in the highest heels she could find without getting a nosebleed. She loved fashion, buying all her clothes at discount stores; she had a knack for making them look designer.

She was a public relations professional without a job, a princess without a place in her own country, and a sister trying to bail her brother out of a massive mess of his own making. *And* she was stuck on a ship with a man who looked at her as if she was hamburger when he was looking forward to Chateaubriand.

How Nick Cutter perceived her was immaterial, she reminded herself firmly.

She was there on a mission. A short-term, extremely serious, deeply personal mission for the people of Marrezo.

When her transportation had flown away, it had given her a reprieve, and a few more hours to convince him to see things her way.

All bets were totally off.

"There's not a thing in the rule book that says it's illegal to use flirtation as a tool of negotiation, is there? No, there isn't." After spritzing a light mist of fragrance on her throat and wrists, she slid the keycard Basim had given her into the back pocket of her jeans, leaving the cabin with a spring in her step and a glint in her eye.

Bria's sense of direction was good, which was fortunate, since she didn't see a soul as she bypassed the circular glass-and-wood elevator and took the stairs all the way up to the sundeck.

Through the large windows, she saw Nick standing in the middle of a group of men by the rail. Just seeing him made her heart speed up. The man was potent. And not interested, she reminded herself firmly.

*Not. Interested.*

The movement of the luxury ship was barely perceptible. She could be in any boutique hotel in the world. The sound of the waterfall as it spilled in a tinkling, sparkling fall over chunks of rough-cut white marble was a soothing counterpoint to her racing pulse. Bria found it interesting that her body reacted to Nick Cutter exactly the same way it would react to extreme danger.

Unfortunately, the flood of flight-or-fight adrenaline was accompanied by a hormonal surge of oxytocin.

"Analyze it on the way home," she told herself out loud in the vast, empty room. Just because she saw something she wanted, didn't mean she should have it. She'd wanted the dancing red-gold flames in a fire pit when she was five, too. Fortunately, wiser heads had prevailed, preventing her from being badly burned.

"Think fire." A good "safe" word that would help her through the next few hours.

It wasn't fully dark yet, but a few lamps around the room cast a warm glow on the white furnishings. Out on deck, strings of white lights moved with the slight dip and sway of the boat. The backdrop of the last glimmer of the sunset smudged the horizon with salmon and lavender. The scene was picture postcard perfect.

Bria slid the door open and stepped out on deck. The sultry evening breeze, after the air-conditioning, wrapped around her in a welcome embrace and brought with it the mouthwatering smell of barbecuing meat. The men turned as one, and the animated conversation cut off mid-word.

There seemed to be a lot of them, but a quick headcount assured her there were only seven guys drinking beer and staring at her as if she were an alien life form. Well, six stared; one was supremely disinterested.

"Princess Gabriella Visconti." Nick stayed where he was, his hip on the rail, and indicated her with his beer bottle. "You met Jonah earlier. Pierce, Levine, Mikhail, Burke, and Olav."

She turned to smile at the guys. "Bria, please." She shook hands and tried to fix names and faces using the same techniques she did when working a room at any client event.

Pierce: Slight, freckly redhead. Levine: Bald, tattooed biker-type. Mikhail: Russian Norse god with big, very white teeth in a darkly tanned face. Burke: Dark skin, sun-bleached hair, predatory gaze. Olav was as tall as Nick, with beautiful white-blond hair and hands like hams. She presumed the tall guy with epaulets and a winning smile who had come out of Nick's office earlier was Jonah.

They all looked to be in their thirties, all fit and tanned. T-shirts, shorts. Barefoot. Outdoorsy. And interested as they clustered around her. Someone offered her a drink. Beer. Bottle was fine, and he went off to retrieve it from a nearby cooler.

She slid a glance at Nick. He was still by the rail. Wondering how he could weight her body? She was ultra-aware of him watching her. Maybe she was hyperaware of his gaze because his eyes were such a vivid and startling blue. Or maybe, she acknowledged, it was the strong pull of his disinterest that attract—intrigued her.

*Fire.*

She accepted a frosty bottle from Pierce, whose blush obliterated all his freckles as he smiled at her. That fair skin must be a big problem on board ship. She smiled her thanks, and turned the smile to the other man beside her. "Jonah, nice to actually meet you." She held out her hand, inviting Jonah to acknowledge Nick's lapse in manners. "You captain a beautiful yacht."

Jonah's eyes glinted with amusement as he lightly kissed her knuckles, European style.

"Ship," Nick clarified in clipped tones. So, her shoes and red dress got her nowhere, but insult his ship by calling it pretty and he actually winced.

"What's the difference between a yacht, a boat, and a ship?" Not that she gave a flying flip, but these men were all on one, and the question was meant as a conversation starter.

Nick answered before anyone else. "You can fit a boat inside a ship, but you can't fit a ship inside a boat." He drank from his beer as he turned to look out over the water.

Fabulous. He'd just stopped the conversation with his generic answer and surly tone.

Jonah smiled. "Nick designed the *Scorpion*. And I'm the lucky man who guides her through smooth waters."

"Who steers in a storm?" Bria asked with a teasing grin, sending a pointed glance at Nick's back.

Jonah laughed, offering her his arm, then led her to the large round table. "Me."

Olav, who was about to sit down himself, pulled out her chair, his expression telegraphing his appreciation. Bria didn't flatter herself. As the only female on board, she was also the only game in town. Several of them, including the very attentive Jonah, were attractive. She had no interest in male companionship. Okay. A lie.

*Fire.*

She wasn't here to find a fling, temporary or otherwise. All she wanted was Draven's damned money . . . Until she got it, her life was on hold.

"Where do you live, Princess?" Levine asked as Khoi and

Basim served a simple dinner of enormous barbecued steaks, baked potatoes, and a salad.

"Bria," she corrected warmly. "Sacramento, California." She placed her palm over her wineglass as Basim paused beside her chair with a bottle of wine. "No thank you, Basim."

"What do you do there?" Jonah handed Olav the basket of bread.

Bria picked up her fork. "I'm in public relations." Currently unemployed and possibly destined to stay that way.

"The princess has come to make sure her brother gets an instant return on his investment," Nick told the others, his tone conveying exactly what he thought of that.

"Ah." Olav drank from his bottle of beer.

Mikhail smiled sympathetically, his teeth blindingly white against his suntanned skin. "That isn't how it's done, Princess."

Damn. He was already rallying the troops to his corner. Bria shrugged, disarmingly breezy. "There's always an exception," she said lightly, cutting into the king-sized-bed–sized steak that mooed on her plate.

"Nobody, not even Nick, gets his share until we're done." Pierce, the freckled redheaded said, sounding apologetic. "We aren't done with *El Puerto* yet."

"To great dives!" Jonah raised his bottle and the rest of the table cheered.

Bria glanced up and her gaze tangled with Nick's. Her fingers clenched around her utensils as an almost physical lightning bolt shot through her body. Just from a look, for goodness sake. Thank God she was leaving in the morning, because that was about all the time she could hang on before she did something she'd regret the morning after.

Blissfully unaffected, Nick gave her a bland look in return, then turned to talk with Burke, seated beside him.

"The more treasure we salvage, the larger everyone's share." Levine, a short, skinny guy ran a hand over his shaved bald head. His smile, like Mikhail's, telegraphed his sympathy.

Seemed everyone had to wait.

Bria lifted one shoulder. "I'm not asking for a profit, just the king's original investment returned."

"And you've already gotten the answer six ways from Sunday." Cutter told her shortly.

"Then I'll keep asking until I get the answer I like." Bria said hotly. The man was infuriating, and the cooler he became, the hotter her temper got. Better than lust in this instance.

Flies. Honey. She reminded herself. Damn it, even her toes were clenched in her sandals, making her great-grandmother's antique gold wedding ring dig uncomfortably into her toe. She had to put her fork down because she was gripping it hard enough to bend it.

The table had gone quiet, eyes darting from her to Nick and back again like spectators at a tennis match.

"As I said," Bria calmly picked up her bottle of beer. "I'll be leaving soon enough." She sipped. Cold. Bitter. Just like Cutter.

Nick sipped from his own. "Perhaps you didn't pay the pilot?"

"I told you. Both ways." Bria kept a lid on her annoyance with a great deal of effort. The man was absolutely maddening.

"Charter out of Las Palmas?" Jonah asked. Was he smiling behind his beer? "Notorious for cheating their customers."

She smiled, every inch the poised confident princess she wasn't. "I'll contact them in the morning and have another pilot come and get me." *After I've sat on Nick Cutter and he's given me Draven's money back. Only perhaps without the sitting on him bit.* The visual *that* stimulated made her palms sweat, and her heart thud uncomfortably. A chemical reaction, she reminded herself. She drank from the bottle. She took another sip to cool down. It didn't work. She was still annoyingly hot and bothered.

She added *chemical* to her danger word.

Nick Cutter was a chemical fire.

How the hell, Bria thought crossly, rolling the chilled

bottle over her hot cheek, could someone so damned cold be so hot?

"Oh, I'd *hate* to inconvenience you," she told him cheerfully, putting the bottle on the table to pick up her fork. "I don't mind waiting a few more days for the commercial charter." If she wasn't gone by lunchtime, she was either going to toss his unconscious body overboard or seduce him. Perhaps the one before the other.

Nick's incredible blue eyes glinted as he asked blandly, "*Where* did you say you work, Princess?"

\*      \*      \*

Despite Nick's efforts to embarrass her and put her on the spot as far as her employment went, Bria had quite enjoyed dinner. The silky feel of the warm night air and the smell of the ocean were soothing, even if Nick's glances were not. His dive team, as a whole, were charming, and friendly, and their tales of various dives fascinating.

She flirted lightly with Jonah, who was seated beside her. But she suspected he was no more interested in her than Nick was. The long hours of travel and stress were now catching up with her, and she'd excused herself before dessert was served. She was ready to turn in. Ready, she had to admit, to not be "on."

She needed some downtime. Time to decompress.

In spite of its size, the *Scorpion* was easy to navigate. Bria used the stairs instead of the small elevator just to get a little exercise. The honey-toned, wood-paneled lower deck corridor was well-lit, but kind of spooky and quiet as she walked it alone. It was fairly early, so she presumed the crew were finishing up their day's work, or having dinner of their own, since there was no one around.

She had a feeling she'd be tossing and turning and cursing Nick Cutter's name when she got into bed. He was a potent guy for all his chilliness. Just because he didn't appear interested, didn't mean she felt the same way. He might be as annoying as hell, but there was some unidentifiable pull of sexual tension when he looked at her, which made her blood course through her veins like fizzy champagne.

Fantasy and imagination mixed with heightened aware-, ness.

No doubt about it. There'd be a lot of tossing and turning tonight. Her need for sexual satisfaction would have to be a solo flight. She was already uncomfortably aroused and he hadn't so much as touched her. Bria rubbed the goose bumps on her bare arms as she walked faster.

Potent stuff, Nick Cutter.

A man dressed in the white shirt and shorts indicating he was a crew member came around the corner as she was sliding her keycard out of her back pocket. He looked vaguely familiar, which was unlikely considering where she was. Really, he shared all the traits of everyone else on this boat: suntanned skin, easy athleticism. White shorts. White T-shirt.

Though his attention was on the piece of paper in his hand as he walked toward her, he glanced up as she got closer. He started to smile a greeting, but his eyes widened with surprise and the smile died. His steps faltered as, clearly shocked, he gave her a startled look. "Principessa?!"

*"Buona sera,"* Bria smiled. *"Ti conosco?"*

He shook his head and his prominent Adam's apple bobbed as he swallowed. *"Sono in ritardo per il lavoro. Mi scusi."*

He looked Greek, but spoke fluent Italian without an accent. The Italian press had had a field day with the Visconti's return home. He must recognize her from her pictures splashed all over the news.

As he hurried past her in the narrow space, Bria noticed the gleam of sweat on his forehead. He looked ill, and she turned to offer her help, but he was gone. Boy, he must've run like hell to disappear down the long corridor so quickly, or slipped into a nearby cabin.

It had taken her a long time to get used to casual recognition from strangers. Getting one's face splashed all over the news had a way of stripping away a girl's anonymity.

She turned the corner and found her cabin easily enough.

Inserting the keycard, she rotated her tense shoulders. A hot shower, a little manual stress relief, and a good night's sleep would make a world of diff—

The sharp blow to the side of her head came out of no-where.

# Chapter 4

Stars sparked in Bria's vision. She hadn't heard a sound. Pain radiated from her shoulder as she was slammed hard into the unlocked door. It swung inwards with her weight. Staggering to maintain her balance, she had to do a quick two-step to stay on her feet. She managed to turn in time to block the second blow with her forearm.

She got a blurred image of black hair, dark eyes, white clothing, but the force of her attacker's fist sent a painful vibration along the bones of her arm and the pain distorted her vision.

She didn't scream. Maybe he expected her to. Instead, she went in for the attack as she'd been trained to do from childhood. Fists, knees, elbows. Marv had taught her well, and diligently. Her assailant didn't expect her to strike back.

Her palm slammed up under his jaw, knocking his head to the side. Vision still swimming, she met her attacker's stare dead-on.

The guy from a few minutes ago.

He launched himself at her, and through the pulsing pain at her temple, it was as if he moved like a strobe-light. "What—" was all she managed, blocking another blow and trying to center herself so she was ready for his next strike.

Heart pounding and her hearing dimmed, and trying to

shake off the disorientation and disbelief of the surprise attack, and the very real menace behind it, she fought hard. Krav Maga, a martial arts discipline that emphasized simultaneous offense and defense maneuvers, had been developed in Israel from street-fighting skills. There were no rules, and even if there were, Bria didn't give a damn. She fought back with everything she'd been taught to do for just this kind of attack. She targeted his most vulnerable points—eyes, jaw, groin, knees. She struck fast and randomly, so he didn't know what she was aiming for until she'd done the job.

She grabbed his hair, pulled him closer, and kneed him in the balls; he screamed. She raked her nails down his cheek missing his eye by fractions of an inch. Then did it again. Not missing the second time. He screamed in pain.

*"Ma io non sono qui!"*

He wasn't . . . there? He looked very much there to her. Bria didn't try to figure that out because he was bound and determined to get her off her feet. She dug in her heels, but he shoved her farther into the tiny cabin. The back of her knees hit the mattress, and she grabbed his T-shirt to remain upright. Was he trying to rob her? Rape her? Kill her?

She held on, bringing her knee up hard and fast, no easy feat when she was unbalanced. Before her knee made contact a second time, he punched her in the chest. The blow knocked her sideways and she crashed onto the bunk, hitting the top of her head against the wood-paneled wall. Her breath left her in a grunt of pain.

One of her arms was pinned under her body, her own weight keeping it immobile, but she scratched and fought with her free hand, trying to arch her hips away from him as he climbed onto the bed, his body looming over her as he grabbed her wrist so she couldn't slash at his face again.

Blood dripped down his cheek in four distinct nail gouges.

Realizing she hadn't made a sound to alert anyone she was in trouble, Bria screamed at the top of her lungs.

He tried to cut off her cry with a vicious blow to her cheek that hurt like fire and made her eyes water. He wrapped his hand across her mouth and jaw to shut her up as she kept on screaming. He was small and wiry, but heavy as hell as he flung his leg over her hip to straddle her waist, holding her in place. He ground his knee into her free arm, and his weight almost wrenched the arm she was lying on out of its socket.

Bucking and struggling was useless. He had her pinned like a butterfly by sheer brute strength and his hands were wrapped around her throat, cutting off oxygen. His fingers tightened until Bria saw sparkling black dots in her vision.

She struggled to bring her knees up behind him, but nothing dislodged him. She had the sensation of sinking beneath black water, her vision and hearing smothered into nothing . . .

"What the *fuck's* going on in here?!"

Bria gagged as the assailant's weight was instantly yanked off her. Uncomprehending, she dimly watched him fly through the open doorway, to crash against the far wall out in the corridor.

The small cabin dimmed around the edges as, dizzily, she struggled to draw air into her constricted lungs.

Her world was suddenly filled by piercing blue. "Are you going to pass out?"

"T—" *Trying not to.* Bria attempted to form a coherent word, but nothing came out. Nick's face faded for a second, then came back.

"Shit! Jonah? Get some guys down here ASAP. The princess has been attacked." He cupped her cheek. His fingers felt cool. "Stay with me."

Right. She closed her eyes and drifted.

*       *       *

Nick carried the princess to his cabin on the upper deck, his heart pounding hard and furious from the jolt of adrenaline. She was conscious, but barely. She remained limp in his arms, her cheek pressed against his chest, bruises turning dark about her throat, her hair a midnight fall over his arm. She didn't say anything as he moved quickly through his ship. He didn't talk with the few people he passed, instead communicating with Jonah through a lip mic. He'd never been more pleased that they'd chosen a Bluetooth to communicate throughout the ship. It saved a hell of a lot of time.

"I hope he broke his fucking neck when he hit the wall. Has he said anything?" Nick demanded grimly when Jonah let him know he was down on the lower deck. He felt the rapid thrum of Bria's heartbeat where her chest pressed against his. At his words her arms tightened around his neck, stirring the scent of peaches that clung to her skin.

"Unconscious," Jonah said grimly in his ear. "Mario's going to secure him in a closet in the engine room until we figure out what to do with him." Jonah's voice was as grim as Nick felt. He hesitated, then spoke quietly. "Was she raped?"

Nick owned the ship, but he wasn't the only man on board with a deep sense of responsibility to the passengers and crew. As captain, Jonah was just as culpable as he was. Which was exactly why Nick had filled him in on the whole diamond-smuggling scenario.

"Halkias better hope he kept his dick in his pants," Nick told his friend, his voice savage and low. He didn't like how fragile she looked lying in his arms, eyes closed. A fairy-tale Snow White. God. He didn't like this one fucking bit. "Have two of the men make sure he stays where you put him. I'll be down to deal with him shortly."

His arms tightened around Bria's rib cage, right beneath the gentle swell of her breast, and under her knees as she shifted in his arms. Her naturally husky voice was more so as she croaked, "Put me down, I can walk."

"Shut up."

His head steward, Khoi, waited outside Nick's suite. He opened the door the minute he saw them, his eyes shadowed with concern. "Tea, boss?"

Nick didn't know what the hell she'd need. Not to be attacked in a place where he was responsible for her safety was probably a start. God damn it to hell. "Tea would be great. Leave it in here."

He strode through his office and into the suite, where the

stars winked through the octagonal skylight over the neatly turned down bed.

"Please put me—" Nick set her gently on the edge of the mattress. "Oh!" Her face was pale, her eyes very dark as she put a delicate hand to her throat. Her manner, her dress, her go-to-hell attitude, all spoke volumes about who she thought she was. But her long-lashed dark eyes as she looked up at him were filled with vulnerability.

She'd lost her shoes somewhere along the way, and she rubbed her bare feet together as though she needed some sort of physical comfort, even if it was only from herself. For a moment, he stared at her toes with their flashy bright red polish and sassy gold toe ring. Damn it all to hell. He dragged his attention away from her slender feet, and from the brink of doing something damned stupid, like wrapping her in his arms and burying his face in her midnight hair.

Fuckingfuckingfucking hell.

Why would a man whom they'd hired a world away, and a year ago, try to kill a woman who'd barely been on board four hours? It made absolutely no sense.

Logic dictated that the attempt had something to do with the diamonds. But he'd only made contact with Najeeb Qassem and Kadar Gamali Tamiz in the last week. Agreed to bring the diamonds on board twenty-four hours ago.

Still, they'd seen her at the café. Perhaps recognized her . . . ?

Maybe. Wouldn't that mean she wasn't involved with the diamonds?

Or maybe it meant she was, and was an outside player they didn't want horning in on their territory?

A long shot by any stretch of the imagination.

But *why* was she attacked? That was the question.

Hell, none of it made sense.

But for the Moroccans to get to the Greek crew member hired almost a year ago on the Ca Mau province salvage? It was a big leap, and just didn't add up.

A sexual assault made more sense. Stunning and sexy as

she was, Gabriella Visconti was also the only female on board.

"Were you raped?" Nick kept his tone noninflammatory with a great deal of control. He'd already noted that her jeans were still done up, now he saw the lacy edge of a nude-colored bra peeking from the scooped neck of her white T-shirt. The relief he felt was profound.

She shook her head, causing the silky black fall of her hair to spill like ink over her shoulders. She winced at the movement and massaged the darkening fingerprints at her throat. "No," she whispered. "I think he had something else in mind."

"Like what?"

Her eyes met his. "Like trying to kill me."

"How did you manage to piss off someone after only being on board a few hours?" Nick asked lightly, studying Bria's face. Maybe it was a gift—she'd gotten his back up in the first twenty seconds. Quite a feat.

She gave him an arch look. "Funny."

*Savage* was closer to how he felt. "Do you need a doctor?"

"I'm angry as hell," she said crossly. "Not hurt."

Her color was high, and her eyes glittered with unshed tears. Yeah. He got that she was furious. But he saw too that she'd had some of the bravado scared out of her. There were dark bruises now marring her beautiful skin. He'd prefer to see her mad rather than terrorized. He suspected she had a temper and wondered, if not under *these* circumstances, under *what* circumstances she'd let it rip.

Experiencing one of her tempers would probably be similar to being hit by a tsunami.

His brothers teasingly referred to him as Spock. Emotionally detached. Unflappable. Extreme displays of emotion made Nick want to run, not walk, to the nearest exit. Always had. But right now, rather than have her sitting so still and withdrawn here on his bed with this dazed look in her eyes, he'd welcome her losing it.

Cry. Scream. *Anything*.

His control was bone-deep.

The princess was hanging on to it tooth and nail with everything she had.

"Start from the beginning." He'd get a lot more detail from Halkias when he interrogated the deckhand—none too gently—later.

"The guy passed me in the corridor." She smoothed her hair back in a nervous tell. "At first I thought I knew him, he looked a little familiar."

That surprised him. So this was personal. In a way, that was a relief. A relief that she wasn't involved with the Moroccans after all and he wouldn't have to turn her over to his friends at T-FLAC who knew how to handle terrorists. "His name is Cappi Halkias."

She was already shaking her head gingerly. "I don't know him, I just thought I did because he looked a little like my nail guy."

"What's a nail guy?" Nick asked, puzzled.

She held out a slender, lightly tanned hand and showed him her red nails, and the three woven gold bands on her middle finger. "The guy who does my nails."

He was more interested in the dark bruises marring the smooth skin of her forearm. She'd blocked a heavy blow. Several. "A manicurist?"

"Manis and pedis, yes." She paused, and added dryly, "The guy who attacked me isn't my nail guy."

That she'd been injured on his watch infuriated him, but damn, he was unaccountably amused by her. He rolled his hand, motioning for her to get on with the story. Because amused by her or not, the situation wasn't funny in the least.

"I thought perhaps he was sick. He looked—"

He waited a few beats, then prompted, "Looked?"

She blinked, the distant glazed look in her eye refocusing. "Jumpy. Nervous. Sweaty." She shrugged. "Odd I guess. I was going to ask if he needed help, but when I turned around he was gone. I presumed he'd gone into one of the cabins. I unlocked the door and he jumped out of nowhere. He hit me here." She touched two fingers to the red mark on her temple. "I went flying. He grabbed me, wrestled me to the bed, jumped on top of me and tried to strangle me. That's about it."

No, Nick thought with cold fury. That wasn't it. He might not want Bria Visconti on board, but he was still responsible for her safety. "Do you need anything?" Other than the bruises, which were bad enough, she didn't appear to have suffered any physical damage, but emotional damage was sometimes harder to recover from.

Emotional damage was so far out of his comfort zone. He'd rather break the man's face and call it good.

She dropped her hand to her lap. "I suppose a bodyguard would be redundant now?"

"Not unless more than one person has it in for you, Princess. The man's locked up." And then, because he couldn't help himself, he added pointedly, "You should've brought your own guard with you."

She didn't fight back. Not even with a look. Unaccountably, that worried him more than the bruises did. "I don't have one anymore. I live in California and nobody cares about my pedigree as a princess of a small island nation when they have movie stars about."

A hint of fire flashed in her eyes as she added, "Has anyone told you just how warm, fuzzy, and charming you can be?"

"Not today."

"Not in a lot longer than that, I bet," she told him with asperity as she started sliding off the bed.

Her feet gingerly touched the wood-planked floor, and Nick gently wrapped his fingers around her upper arm as she teetered. "Where do you think you're going?"

She had muscles under the velvety soft skin. He found himself stroking his thumb across tawny satin, then dropped his hand. She was steady enough, and he'd be better off not touching her again.

The feel of her under his hand was addictive. He stuck his fingertips in the front pockets of his jeans.

She tucked her hair behind her ears. "If the man responsible is securely locked up, I'm going back to my cabin."

"I think it'd be better if you stay put until I see what he has to say for himself."

Her lips, bare of lipstick, tightened. Her lower lip was fuller than the top one, and Nick had to force himself to get a grip and not lean in for a taste. The princess would probably resort to violence if he made a move on her. Especially now.

Sometimes Nick envied his younger brother Zane's savoir faire. His brother was so charming, he charmed himself.

Nick knew who he was, and who he wasn't. Hitting on a woman who'd just been attacked, a woman he wasn't sure he trusted, was out of the question. More so because like it or not—and it was a big fucking *not*—she was under his care for the duration.

She gave him a narrowed-eyed look, as if she'd read his mental gymnastics. Crossing her arms, she rubbed her hands up and down her biceps. The movement almost covered the fact that she was still trembling. "What am I supposed to do while I'm waiting?" she demanded.

The spiced peach scent of her skin tantalized him and he clenched his teeth. "Whatever you were going to do in the crew quarters."

A flare of amusement darkened her eyes. "Take a shower and go to bed."

If Nick read that brief spark correctly, she'd been primed to seek sexual satisfaction alone in that narrow bunk. A glutton for punishment, he indicated the door to the bathroom. "Shower."

She had very expressive eyebrows, which were at the moment telling him he was insane. "The bathroom door has a lock," he told her shortly in response to what she didn't say. "Make yourself at home. I'll be back."

"How long?" she asked, suspicion lining every facet of her gorgeous—fucking hell—*bruised* body.

He heard the steward enter the adjoining office, followed by the rattle of china. "I'll have Khoi stay outside the door until I get back." It wasn't perfect, but it was reassurance. Of a sort. "Grab a shower, have a cup of tea, or have him get you a Scotch. Relax. You're safe here."

He'd make damn sure the situation with Halkias had been an isolated incident.

\*        \*        \*

"Jesus, Jonah. Not five minutes ago I assured her she was safe, and now you're telling me Halkias managed a Houdini and escaped?"

The captain didn't look any less furious than Nick was feeling. "He had help. And I have all hands searching for him."

"Let me guess, the same fucking hands that helped him get away?"

Jonah gave him a pained look. "We don't know that."

"I know that," Nick told him, his voice cool. "I want to see his log, his CV, and his hiring information. Now."

"I hired him myself on the Vietnam trip last year," Jonah ran his hand around the back of his neck, cleary frustrated. "His performance has been exemplary from day one. No drinking. No fights. No indication of any sort of drug or mental problems. And in such close quarters, someone would've reported to me if there was any evidence to the contrary.

"Your princess did a number on him, I have to tell you, Nick. She beat the sonuvabitch bloody *and* broke two of his fingers."

Nick raised his brow disbelievingly. "He must've gotten into a brawl before he attacked her."

"No. She attacked him right back," Jonah said admiringly. "Her Highness inflicted a heap of hurt on the guy, *and* he's twice her size."

"Shit. None of this is making any sense." A Ninja princess? That put yet *another* question mark against what the hell she was doing on board.

"I hear you. I have all his info in my office. I'll go with you, then start taking statements."

"Let's get this done." Nick grabbed the SAT phone from its hook. "I'm calling Max Aries and having him send someone here to escort the princess wherever she wants to go first thing in the morning. Under armed guard if necessary."

Considering Aries was the one who had pulled him into this dangerous game with the diamond smuggling, that seemed reasonable. The princess wasn't supposed to be part of it.

He dialed. Aries picked up on the second ring. "Aries."

"It's Cutter."

Aries was nobody's fool. "You're taking a risk calling me," he said shortly, his voice tense on the line. "What's happened?"

Nick told the T-FLAC operative about the princess, the attack, and the Houdini dude.

"Disappeared?" Aries demanded.

"Like smoke." He had a big ship, but this was ridiculous.

"Hang tight."

Jonah raised his eyebrows at him as Nick dropped the mouthpiece away from his lips and stared up at the ceiling. "Anything?"

"He's checking," Nick said shortly.

He didn't have to wait long. The line clicked over. "Preliminary intel turned up no connection between the diamonds and the princess," he said shortly.

Nick hadn't really believed she was involved. A few weeks in the company of counterterrorist operatives and he saw conspiracies all around. "Good to know. Come get her. Keep her safe until this situation is done."

"Sorry, Cutter. I know you want her off the *Scorpion,* but she's safer on board until you find Halkias."

"Leave her where she's already been attacked?" Nick asked, his tone downright frigid. "That makes no fucking sense."

"It gives us time to run intel on Halkias. See if or what the connection." Aries continued, unruffled.

"A safe house in *Paris* would do that."

"All I got for now. I want things contained. If we swoop in now to claim your princess—"

"She's not—" He bit off his retort. Damn it, she wasn't *his* princess.

"The princess," Aries corrected without a hitch, "then

the whole operation is blown to hell. We can't afford to spook the tangos, you got it?"

Yeah, he got it. Nick disconnected and narrowed his gaze at Jonah. "Until they figure out the who and the why—"

"Yeah," his friend cut him off. "I got the gist. They don't think this has anything to do with Tamiz and Qassem or the diamonds?"

"Nope. Do you?" When Jonah rubbed his hand over his jaw and shook his head, Nick said, "Neither do I. Let's find the son of a bitch and ask him."

# Chapter 5

But the Greek couldn't be found. The whole damned crew, even the salvage team, once they learned the princess had been attacked, got in on the hunt, scoured the ship from stem to stern, and then repeated the search again, and then again. Nick temporarily called it off.

Bria was locked safely in his cabin, Khoi standing guard outside. She'd stay there until Cappi Halkias was found and detained. Had she gotten rid of the itch? In his bed? The thought made Nick's heartbeat pick up the pace. "She's probably asleep by now," he told Jonah when his friend yawned pointedly. "I'll bunk in here with you."

Jonah grinned. "Interesting."

"That we're both tired and need a few hours shut-eye before we start our day?" he asked flatly. "Yeah, real interesting."

Jonah made a sound like a gameshow buzzer. "Wrong. One, I notice you insist on calling her the princess, instead of Bria."

"So, what?"

"And two, that you have a beautiful woman sleeping in your bed, and yet you'd rather sleep with me," Jonah added, his grin widening.

Nick resisted the urge to swat the back of his friend's

head. "Don't be ridiculous," he muttered. "She's banged up, and needs her rest. Why disturb her when I don't have to?"

*Why disturb* me *if I don't have to?* Nick thought irritably.

"I think not, pal. She's your princess, not mine. If you're too chicken to go to your own cabin, then take the one she vacated down in the crew quarters."

"Basim's back in there." He presumed.

"I refuse to share my cold and celibate bed with you. And no. You can't sleep on the chair, or the floor, or in my bathtub either."

"Jonah—"

"No thank you," Jonah cut him off. "Handsome as you are, it'll be a cold day in hell before I let you be the warm body in my bed." He pulled his T-shirt over his head, and started on the zipper of his pants, giving Nick a meaningful look. "Get lost, Cutter." He jerked his chin at the door. "I want at least a few hours of sleep before the fun starts all over again."

Son of a bitch. Some friend he turned out to be. Nick exited Jonah's suite and walked toward his own cabin via the deck. It was a hot still night. The breeze had died down, and the sea was black and calm, scattered with glittering pinpoints of shimmering starlight dancing on the surface.

The faint savory smell of their barbecue dinner lingered, kissed with the ever-present salty balm of the sea. Wavelets slapped the side of the ship like the applause of mermaids.

Nick shook his head at his fancy as he paused to look out across the water, his fingers curled around the wood railing. He loved the quiet. Loved the solitude. Loved the heartbeat of the *Scorpion*'s generators throbbing calmly beneath his feet as she lay at anchor.

She was hovering protectively over a wreck that, while not breaking new ground as far as artifacts went, was going to net everyone involved a healthy chunk of change. Bria's brother was going to be able to buy ten islands when he got his payout. She'd be happy about that. She might not be happy about how long that would take, but good things came to those who waited.

Was she awake in his bed? Had she found satisfaction?

The idea of climbing into musk-scented sheets, with her, sleepy and satiated, gave Nick an erection. He sucked in a draft of warm night air, trying to ignore the raging hard-on.

Like his captain, Nick needed some rest. He could sack out on one of the sofas in any number of public spaces on board. Plenty of them.

Neither of them would sleep long, if at all. His friend was too good at his job for that. He'd be in his office pacing, probing, trying to figure this out. Bria's attack had happened on his watch, by a man he'd hired. And that man was gone. Lost on two hundred feet of ship in the middle of an ocean.

He wouldn't get far.

Nick's fingers tightened around the smooth wood of the rail, a rail that Halkias had spent the better part of that day polishing. How and why had the man gone from diligently doing his job day after day to attempted murder?

What was he missing? It seemed to Nick that if there were dangerous elements on board, then the diamonds were at the heart of it. The Moroccans had paid a lot of money to have them smuggled aboard. And with good reason.

They'd seen Bria at the *medina* and she'd inquired about the very ship they were using to carry their uncut gems out of the country. Easy to consider—very seriously—that they might assume that was too damned many coincidences.

Or, *they'd* set up that scenario at lunch the other day, and they were the ones who'd hired her to come on board and keep an eye on their investment. The fact that the princess was exactly the make and model of women Nick favored, and that she'd sought him out in Tarfaya, where he just happened to be closing the deal with Tamiz and Qassem, was also suspect.

He shook his head. It was a possibility, but his gut said she had absolutely nothing to do with the diamonds. He trusted his gut. Sometimes a coincidence was just a coincidence.

He knew the crew and his dive team were taken in by the

perfect ass and long slim legs wrapped in skin-tight denim, the clingy T-shirt and tantalizing view of cleavage, and the long dark fall of her hair that swung about her shoulders. Hell, had he been a less thoughtful man, he could have succumbed to the temptation too. She was just his type all the way down to the little gold toe ring she sported on her shapely right foot. So he couldn't blame them.

Sure, there was no doubt she was who she claimed to be. But was she the concerned sister of the king of a small country, who was trying to stabilize himself financially, or was that a convenient ruse to get her on board where she could keep him distracted for the duration?

His alter ego, El Malamah, had carried the blood diamonds on board, then disappeared. Nick Cutter, owner of the *Scorpion,* didn't know anything about them. But did Principessa Gabriella Visconti?

He pushed off the rail and strode silently down the dew-beaded deck to his cabin. Question was, was she an innocent victim or a cleverly chosen plant? Because, goddamn it, now that he was mulling over all the imaginable scenarios, it wasn't out of the realm of possibility that the "attack" had been nothing more than a carefully staged ruse to bring her even closer to him physically. His gut notwithstanding, he couldn't completely discount the possibility.

He shoved open the door to his office to see Khoi and Basim, playing cards. They jumped to their feet. Nick glanced at the closed door to his suite. "Everything okay?"

Khoi nodded. "The princess asked for nothing, and has been quiet, boss," his chief steward informed him as he gathered the playing cards and returned them to the box, then put them away in their thirteenth-century Chinese lacquered box on the bookshelf. Jonah had hired him on a couple of years ago in Vietnam, and he'd quickly climbed the ranks. The man had the uncanny ability to know what Nick wanted before Nick knew himself. An excellent trait in a man whose duties covered your modern day butler's.

"I took the liberty of having someone procure clothing for the princess from the storeroom," he said now, looking around to see if there was anything else he needed to do before departing. Satisfied, he looked back at Nick. "A selection is being laundered. And I will personally ensure that the clothing is delivered here when she wakes."

"Good man." His head steward was on the ball and had thought ahead to what Bria might need. Even before Nick knew she'd be on board for a few more days.

They kept odds and ends of clothing in the storeroom for just this reason—when a guest found themselves light on luggage. Most of the collection was swimwear, but he presumed there'd be other items of clothing left behind by the occasional female guest.

After the men left, Nick locked and bolted the main door, then went through to his suite. A single light burned beside the large comfortable chair by the window, leaving the rest of the cabin in shadow.

The princess was curled up on the easy chair, head bent at an uncomfortable angle. She'd scavenged the *MENSA International Journal* off his nightstand, and it was spread open on her lap.

Nick felt a strange twist of emotions as he looked down at her. He couldn't leave her like that, and the fact that she'd put him in the position of having to touch her was annoying. Slipping his arms under her, he shifted her so her body naturally rolled into his arms and against his chest. Been here done this, he thought, trying not to inhale the intoxicating fragrance of her skin as he carried her to his bed.

She'd showered, and her hair was still a little damp and smelled like his shampoo. But not. On her it was sensual; on him, it was clean. Hell. The feel of her in his arms had given him an erection the moment he'd touched her. More likely it had never gone away.

Obviously she had no intention of seducing him, or she wouldn't have gotten dressed. There was a white toweling robe behind the bathroom door that he'd never worn that would have looked dynamite against her tawny skin . . .

No. She was smarter than that. Stripping would be too overt. Too obvious.

Christ . . . she was good.

Or was he paranoid?

The covers on his side had been thrown back as if a princess had slept restlessly, then gotten out of bed. Nick lowered her carefully to the crumpled white sheets. She mumbled in her sleep as he straightened her legs. He considered removing her jeans so she'd be more comfortable. Decided he was insane and opted for her being uncomfortable, and him being comfortable not having to share a bed with a semi-naked siren.

She was hard enough to resist when she was wide awake and fully clothed.

Crossing the room he turned off the lamp, plunging the cabin into predawn darkness before going back to the bed. Toeing off his shoes, he lay down on the wrong side. It was a huge bed, with plenty of room to leave a wide gap between them, but tonight it felt too damned small. Stacking his hands under his head, Nick stared up at the canopy of fading stars beyond the octagonal skylight as the sky gradually lightened to pewter.

He closed his eyes and forced his breathing to become slow and even as he concentrated on falling asleep. He didn't need much—a couple of hours would suffice, but he needed at least that to be in top form.

Just as he was drifting off in a hazy relaxed state, she rolled over against him, flinging an arm across his chest. His breathing snagged as her nose nuzzled against his arm. His eyes snapped open. Hell.

Trouble.

Warm breath tickled his skin, cool silky, peach-scented hair slid over his arm, and his entire body participated in the feel and smell of her. Every muscle tensed as he tried to extricate himself from her light but invasive hold.

He knew she wasn't asleep. Her breathing had changed, the relaxed state of her body wasn't quite as relaxed as it had been moments before. Did she have no boundaries? Yeah, they were both fully clothed, but they were still prone, and in his bed. Strangers.

Cat and mouse?

"Hi," she said softly.

Nick glanced down to see her sleepy eyes looking up at him through a tangle of silky black hair. His heart did a triple axel. "I thought you were asleep." A man could hope. He found himself fingering a silken strand that clung to his fingers when he tried to release it. Static cling.

"I am." She scooted up a little higher so the crown of her head brushed his chin. "Did he tell you why he did it?"

Nick hesitated. No need to tell her—yet—that Halkias had escaped and was still missing. "Not yet."

"He will. Just freeze him with your eyes."

He'd heard that before. Didn't bother him any. His brothers had good reason to call him Spock. Emotions were messy, and inconvenient. "Did King Draven send you to me, Bria?"

"God, no. He's not going to be happy I'm here at all. But I have to do something."

She sounded sleepy and sincere, which made her good at what she did, not necessarily honest. "Did he use your money to invest with my company?" If her brother had stolen what she believed to be hers, she'd want the money back. And he'd have to find a way to give it to her. God. Was he grasping at straws? Hoping like hell her story was the truth?

Her version of the truth anyway.

Her laughter curled around him like sunlight. "I've been unemployed for almost a year, I don't have any money. He only went back to Marrezo two years ago. Contrary to what Draven wants the world to think, our country is in deep shit right now. In fact, if there's a layer below deep shit, that would about sum up the situation." She sighed sleepily, and her breath tickled his throat.

Goose bumps rippled down his arms. "When Draven went back to claim the throne, there was no industry; the vineyards, after twenty years, were a complete mess, so no wine. Nothing left. It's been dire. He managed to get a short-term loan, but that's due in thirty days. Not," Bria said bitterly, "that he told me any of this. He left that to our cousin Antonio to do."

"He didn't indicate to Logan that he was having financial difficulties, Bria. Are you sure?"

"Positive." She yawned. "Who's Logan?"

"My older brother. He's CFO of Cutter Salvage." At the moment, anyway. The Cutter brothers maintained a standing bet: whomever hauled in the greatest find would get to be CFO until the next biggest find came along.

Nick didn't want to win it. He never did. He left the paperwork to his brothers and let them duke it out.

"He and your brother struck the investment deal a year ago," he added. "Logan is savvy as hell, he didn't get the impression this was a last-ditch effort to repay a banknote or anything else. Logan is a bloodhound when it comes to financial backgrounds, Bria, something would have popped up."

"Obviously Draven wouldn't want anyone to know he was on the brink of bankruptcy. Worse than that, even." Her soft breast brushed his arm as she shifted slightly. "I guess he thought the salvage would pay off in time."

"What happens if the loan isn't repaid?"

"Marrezo reverts back to Italy."

"Not the bank?"

"In this case, Italy *is* the bank," Bria told him. "If we default on the loan—" She huffed out a frustrated breath, which drew his attention to her breasts. Nick forced himself to maintain eye contact. But her darkly troubled, big brown eyes were a distraction too.

"With a blooded Visconti on the throne, we've got rights, but only barely. We've always had to pay a tithe to Italy anyway, but add a gigantic loan on top of that?" She shook her head.

"But that tithe wasn't paid for twenty years between the time you left, and your brother went back, was it?"

"Yes, it was. Sort of an automatic withdrawal went into effect. But that fund was depleted by the time Draven got back. Marrezo was in arrears. He secured the loan . . ." She spread her elegant, expressive hands. "And here we are."

*Yeah. And here they were. Both of them wanting something they weren't going to get.*

"Like colonialism, but at least we get to do our own thing until we fail to pay. It's a centuries-old agreement, but valid. I checked."

"Would that be so bad?"

"Would it be so bad if America reverted to the Indians? Or England, maybe?" she asked rhetorically. "There are families who've lived on the island for twenty-five generations, Nick. There's been a King Draven Visconti for five hundred years. So, yes. It's important that the continuity of the country be maintained."

Nick shifted uncomfortably under both the silken weight of her body and the new information she had given him. "Even if I wanted to, I can't return your brother's investment," he told her, not for the first time. "It, combined with the financial backing of our other investors, was used to purchase equipment and hire specialized personnel. Until the treasure from *El Puerto* is processed, nobody gets a piece of the pie, because there isn't any."

She was silent for a moment. Then, softly, she began, "Couldn't you—"

"Nobody," he told her emphatically, closing the conversation cold. There was more riding on this salvage job than just the salvage and the financial windfall that would come down the road. Aries had told him emphatically, and in no uncertain terms, that nothing could be allowed to jeopardize the safe transportation of the diamonds to Cutter Cay, so they could follow the trail and close it for good.

The value of the diamonds could be counted in the millions of dollars, which was nothing compared to the devaluing of legal diamonds through the United States and South America if this smuggling and laundering operation wasn't stopped.

Thousands died in the bloody diamond trade and thousands more would die if the counterterrorist group didn't put a stop to one of the largest smugglers of conflict diamonds in Africa. The same people who were selling weapons bought from the purchase of the diamonds to warring factions in Africa. Hence the name blood or conflict diamonds.

He hated to draw a comparison, even in his own mind, but the stakes were a hell of a lot higher for the diamonds than the itty-bitty country whose fallback was Italian sovereignty.

Bria's breasts rose and fell against his arm as she sighed, the sound of resignation. "It was worth a shot," she murmured, then fell silent.

Nick listened to her breathe, but he knew she wasn't going back to sleep. He counted her breaths, counted the pulse of blood in his jeans, and bided his time.

Finally, she stirred. "Fine. I'll go home and hope to God my cousin can help Draven work out the financial problems. I don't want to take you away from your diving. I'll just contact the charter company and have them send another pilot out to pick me up. Maybe they will be able to send someone tomorrow. Besides, I paid both ways. The pilot had no right to leave me stranded."

"We can discuss it later." She wasn't going anywhere until he got the green light from Aries. "Maybe you'd like to hang around and see what a dive entails."

No good deed goes unpunished. He was damned if he did, and damned if he didn't.

"Yes. Maybe . . ."

His fingers absently combed through her damp hair, teasing the scent of sun-drenched peaches and his own mint soap from the silken strands, and he changed the absent to intentionally. *Let's see just how far you'll run with this, Princess.*

She licked her lips, more nerves than seduction, but it had the same effect on his already aroused body. He turned toward her, knowing he was playing a dangerous game, but here in the semidarkness, it didn't seem like such a bad idea.

He touched his finger to her chin until she tilted her face up, and met his eyes. "Did you pleasure yourself in my shower, Princess?"

Her cheeks got sweetly flushed. "No."

But he could see she'd thought about it. "Did you do the naughty in my bed?"

She looked him right in the eye, and murmured huskily, "Of course not."

"Liar."

She drew in a thin breath, and her lips parted to say . . . something.

Perfect.

Nick fisted her hair and crushed his mouth down on hers.

\*    \*    \*

Bria closed her eyes and kissed him back with everything she had. The desire to taste him was all-encompassing, and she didn't even think about resisting. She'd burned all day wanting to know if Nick Cutter melted, or stayed icy.

He went from frigid to a rolling boil between one swipe of his tongue and the next.

The hard ridge of his impressive erection nudged her hip. They were both fully clothed, and having him so near and yet so far was frustrating, maddingly so. Bria wanted to feel skin on skin. She wanted him to touch her intimately. She wanted her hands and mouth on his body—everywhere.

Lord. She wanted *his* mouth on *her* everywhere.

Maintaining the kiss, she rolled on top of him. He spread his legs, cradling her body hard against him, then curved his large hands around her jean-covered bottom to press her against the ridged length between them.

She kissed him ravenously, nothing held back—a first for her. In response, his fingers tightened on her butt. Heat swept through her at every point of contact. She jerked her lips from his, panting, gasping for air. He pulled her head back down to his.

Breathing was overrated.

She touched his face as his mouth slanted over hers. He used his teeth. She nibbled back. His tongue swept the roof of her mouth, she waited her turn impatiently. He pushed all her buttons and she reveled in it. His hard chest felt wonderful pressed against the softness of her breasts. Her nipples were painfully hard, and she rubbed herself against him like a cat in heat.

He murmured low in his throat, and slid his fingers down the back of her jeans.

She never had been able to resist playing with fire. Her childhood nickname had been *Fiammetta,* fiery one. For temper more than temperament at that age. But she'd always been hot-blooded and curious. And she didn't resist the temptation. Tightening her arm across his chest, she fisted her fingers in his shirt.

The kiss was raw. Powerful. A riptide that dragged her under without a struggle.

Impulse had let her forget she was horizontal in the man's bed. The instant his firm lips touched hers, she knew she was out of her league. Way out.

*I'm in deep, deep trouble here,* she thought as her brain went hazy and her heartbeat spiked into the stratosphere. Oh, my God. The man could kiss.

This was no first kiss, no subtle invitation, nothing as polite as a tentative exploration between two strangers. No. This was shockingly hot, wet, and dizzyingly carnal. Nerves sizzled the instant their lips met. She breathed in his breath, tasted greed in the lavish use of his tongue and teeth. He nipped her lower lip, then laved it with his tongue before sweeping it into her mouth again.

When Bria stroked her tongue along his, his chest vibrated with a low, feral growl. One minute his forearm was a steel band across her back, his fingers tangled in her hair; the next, he said her name in a hoarse whisper.

Not "Princess." Not that insufferable "Your Highness." Gabriella.

Twisting her so she was sprawled beneath him, Nick's arm tightened around her as he pressed his knee unerringly to the wet place between her legs that ached for it.

The ferocity of his unleashed hunger startled her with its intensity, shaking her all the way to her toes. He knew exactly what he was doing, and he commanded the kiss, taking her little experiment from zero to a hundred and fifty in one second flat.

She wanted his kiss more than she'd wanted anything in her life. And she moaned as his tongue swept between her teeth, sleek and hard and searching. She slid her fingers through his dark hair to cup the back of his head, mirroring what he was doing to her.

His mouth fed on hers until she forgot to breathe, couldn't reason. She went blind and deaf, her entire being focused on where their mouths and bodies were fused together.

The hard length of his erection ground against her hip, and she arched her hips to get more . . . She started tugging at his shirt. Pulled at her own. She wanted skin, damn it—

Panting as if she'd run the two-minute mile, Bria had to drag in a shuddering breath. She blinked. The cabin was much lighter now than it had been what felt like seconds ago.

"Come back here," he murmured thickly, capturing her lips again with another drugging kiss.

What was she doing, what was she doing, what the *hell* was she doing? Reason slammed into her like a bolt of lightning, a blinding flash that harshly illuminated her situation.

She yanked her head away, and felt his ragged, uneven breath against her damp lips. "Stop," she managed. Her heart was beating so fast she could barely tell one hard thump from the next. Her skin was sheened with perspiration, and her lips stung.

If he pressed that knee a little harder, she'd come right then without any further assistance. "Please. D-don't move."

This was nothing like the mild pleasure she'd experienced before, hands-on or solo with her vibrator. Those sensations had been easy to walk away from unscathed. Not Nick Cutter's kiss. The whirlpool of lust she felt—was still feeling— scared the living crap out of her. It was too much. Too explosive.

For a guy who'd given the impression of having zero emotions, hell, barely a frigging *pulse,* Nick's kiss was nothing short of electrifying. Bria's girl parts had melted from the combustible heat of his mouth on hers alone.

Potent stuff.

He went predatory still for a moment, then lifted his head.

"Stop?" His eyes, his amazing azure eyes, narrowed fractionally on her face. His fingers flexed on her ass.

"I'm sorry." She was shockingly aroused, her taut nipples rasping against his chest even as she could barely drag in a breath. She was *this* close to a climax and shook, trying to resist the urgent pull of it. "I can't do this." Thank God her brain was in charge, because her body was begging for more, more, more. Anyone else, and she would've fluttered her eyelashes, smiled, and lightened the situation so she could walk away without a backward glance. Or apologized for leading him on and defused the situation. All the while leaving the guy's ego intact.

Nick Cutter wasn't that guy.

"You started this," he pointed out, his voice was cool, unaffected.

She'd realized the moment their lips touched that she'd made made a tactical error in her attempt to see if he was cold all the way through. But that hadn't stopped her from kissing him back. That hadn't stopped her from touching him. Or rubbing against him.

Bria's heart was knocking uncomfortably. Her body buzzed and throbbed and a strange euphoria racing through her bloodstream made her dizzy. She was wet in places that usually took concerted foreplay to make damp. "I know." Very slowly, she uncramped her fingers from the back of his head before he got any more confused. Or angry.

She couldn't make her body move any more than that. Not for a minute. Or ten. "Sorry." Oh, God, she sounded like some dim-witted Victorian virgin. "But I only met you a few hours ago! I—"

"You don't go to bed with men you don't know?"

"N—" She bit her tongue, the tongue he'd been nibbling on with devastating effect a heartbeat before. She didn't owe him any explanations about her somewhat limited love life. Not only wasn't it any of his business, it wasn't the point. She could have told him a version of the truth: For a moment I lost my mind, thinking I might've died, and was looking for a little human connection, a little confirmation of life.

And, be honest, it was a foolish experiment.

Except this wasn't the time for that kind of brutal honesty. The man was a stranger.

The orgasm started to ebb unfulfilled. It was a night for that. Her brain screamed get away from the man for God's sake! But her body, her traitorous sex-starved body couldn't comply, because moving right then would set off a domino effect.

"I don't usually have people trying to strangle and kill me. I don't— Never mind. I just don't."

There was no excuse. She couldn't even lie to herself. She'd needed warmth to hold the flutters of fear at bay. She'd wanted to see if she could elicit a spark of . . . something. A little heat, anything to staunch the cold feeling inside. And what she'd done was set a match to a forest of dry kindling.

When Nick Cutter warmed up, it was overwhelming. She needed a moment to regroup.

# Chapter 6

Nick rolled onto his back, lifting his hands in surrender. As if. She already knew him better than that. He did nothing to hide the erection straining at his zipper as he cupped the back of his head and watched her with hooded eyes and a stern mouth.

Tingling, throbbing, *pulsing,* Bria swung her legs off the mattress, then sat there, back to him while she tried to calm her manic heartbeat and slow her breathing. She fought the urge to bury her face in her hands.

His voice cracked the silence. "Are you a virgin?"

She couldn't help laughing. If her lips weren't swollen, and her heart racing, she would've sworn from his tone that he hadn't kissed her senseless three seconds before. "A woman asks you to stop, and you presume she's frigid?"

"A woman crawls all over me, and I presume she wants to be fucked. Did you take the edge off before I got here, Princess?"

She thought she had. She hadn't. She glanced over her shoulder to stare narrowed-eyed at him. "Wow. That was unnecessarily cold, even for you."

"I don't do warm and fuzzy."

"You don't even do tepid and downy," she retorted, mimicking his cool tones. She slid to the edge of the mattress and dropped the foot necessary to get off the high bed and stand. She combed her fingers through her tangled hair, re-adjusted her clothing, and called it good. If she didn't blow-dry her hair, it returned to its curly state, which was why she kept it long and slicked back. From Nick's expression—if a tic in his jaw could be called an expression—he was not impressed by the Wild Woman of Borneo look.

What a shame. He wasn't worth spending an hour blow-drying her hair for. "Is it too early to call the helicopter company? If it's all the same with you, I'll just use the phone in your office and see how long it'll take someone to get out here."

"Called them before I came in." He stacked his hands behind his head. Long, lean, and confident of his sex appeal. And why not? "They're having some mechanical issues," he continued, smooth as silk while she was trying to keep her skin from catching fire from being in the same freaking room. Unfair. "They'll call when they have a chopper certi-fied for flight."

Oh, no, no, no. She had to leave.

Now.

He was way out of her league. He'd eat her for breakfast and use her bones as toothpicks if she allowed this to go any further.

She had to put a stop to it.

"How long do they think that'll be?" she asked, hoping the desperation wasn't evident in her voice. She looked around for her sandals, trying to hide how freaked out she really was. *I'm good with people*, she told herself silently as she found one shoe near the chair and the other under the bedside table.

Nick Cutter wasn't people.

She presumed he wasn't enjoying the view of her bottom wiggling out from under there. Rising, she pressed her fin-gertips on the mirrored surface for balance as she slipped her shoes on.

"A day." His expression—big surprise—was inscrutable. "Two at the most. I told you I'd take you."

"Now?"

"Maybe later today."

"What time?" she demanded desperately, shoving her un-tucked T-shirt back into her waistband. God. Even the brush of her own fingers on her skin set little licks of flame dancing across her nerve endings.

"When it's convenient for me to leave my ship and my dive team."

The only option—other than wild monkey sex right then—was to run. About ten miles should dissipate the worst of her unfulfilled arousal. She headed for the door.

"Where are you going?"

Anywhere! "I'm hungry," she lied. "I'd like breakfast." The fact that what she really, really wanted right then was hard, driving, mind-blowing sex was out of the question. Apparently cold fusion was alive and well inside Mr. Ice Cold. If one short make-out session affected her this way, Bria was damned sure anything more would leave her in ashes on the sheets.

She liked being in charge in the bedroom. Nick clearly wasn't the kind of guy who'd lie back and enjoy the ride.

He studied her through half-lidded eyes, barely a glint of blue in the ambient light leaking through the glass ceiling. "Ring for Khoi," he told her. "Tell him what you want."

She half turned, her fingers on the door handle. "I'd rather go and eat with the others."

Was it her imagination, or did that gleam in his eyes intensify? Was he laughing at her? No way. The man didn't know what humor was.

"Then feel free to invite them here," he said. "You're not leaving this cabin until I find Halkias."

That stopped her in her tracks. Her hand dropped from the door handle and she turned slowly to face him. Twenty feet of floor wasn't enough distance. "Find him? Find—" She swallowed before her voice rose another octave. "I thought Jonah had him locked up somewhere!"

He shrugged. "He managed to escape. Don't worry. We'll get him. Just hang tight." His calm nonchalant tone alone pissed her off.

"Hang tight," she repeated, acid and—damn it—fear rising in her throat and obliterating—thank God—the last vestiges of lust from her overstimulated girl parts. "With an attempted murderer wandering around out there?" Bria rubbed the sudden goose bumps on her upper arms. "I wish I had a gun."

He got off the other side of the bed. Standing, he unzipped his jeans, oblivious to the massive erection tenting the front of his black boxers. For a moment Bria's eyes were riveted on the wedge between the open teeth of his zipper. Her already manic heartbeat accelerated, and a film of perspiration sheened her skin. Her fingers actually twitched with the need to touch him. *There.* Hot, silk-covered steel. Everything female inside her responded to that blatant show of maleness.

*Gimme!*

Fire, she reminded herself. Fire. God help me. *Fire!*

Apparently fear *didn't* make a dent in how her body reacted to his.

Nick's jeans dropped to the floor. He kicked them, caught them in one hand, and tossed them on the chair by the window. "You'd shoot yourself in the foot," he said, as if unaware of her gaze fixed to the black swath of material covering his crotch.

She blinked, jerking her eyes up to his face. "That's insulting on so many levels," she snapped. "I lived with a professional bodyguard for twelve years. There isn't a gun I can't load, clean, or fieldstrip." She let that sink in for a moment before asking pointedly, "Do you have one I can borrow?" Living with a paranoid, ever-vigilant bodyguard gave a girl some kick-butt skills.

Of course, no one had tried to kill her in, oh, twenty years. Not until she'd come on board the *Scorp*—

God. Now he was pulling his khaki T-shirt over his head.

Nick tossed it—without looking—onto the chair with his pants. He had the body of an athlete, a swimmer. Satiny bronze skin stretched over long lean muscles. The dark hair on his chest arrowed down to his shorts.

Bria's mouth went dry. She suddenly felt faint. Lust poisoning.

Unfazed, Nick gave her that maddening bland look that made her blood pressure spike for a whole other reason. "There's no need to have a loaded weapon on a ship."

"There are a *hundred* reasons to have a gun on board." She told him tartly. "What if pirates attack?"

"They'd want treasure. Or money. Which you don't have."

True. "I could defend myself in my own cabin if I had a weapon," she pointed out. Early morning sunlight, weak and more gray than golden, limned his body. It outlined his broad shoulders, the curve of his waist, and highlighted the hair on his long legs.

She tried to avert her gaze, she really did. But it was impossible not to notice that he was large and . . . robust, for want of better words. She could barely think them, let alone say anything with her tongue glued to the roof of her mouth to prevent her from doing something incredibly stupid.

Like pull those black boxers off him. With her teeth.

She had to get away from Nick before she leapt across the room to tackle him into bed. God, her nipples ached. She could just imagine his broad hands covering them, kneading her flesh, shaping them for his mouth—

*Fire.*

"And risk you damaging the ship with a wayward bullet? I think not, Princess." He held up a hand and pierced her with his cool, assessing gaze. "You're staying in this cabin. With me. And if you don't want to finish what you started," he gestured downward, drawing her gaze toward the flash of skin showing in the front of his boxers, "then I'm going to hit the shower."

Speechless, Bria stared as he stripped off the black boxers, tossed them onto the chair with the other items of discarded clothing, and padded supremely naked toward the bathroom. He glanced back at her over his shoulder, that bottomless blue gleam taunting her. Inviting her. Sucking her in.

He smiled a tiger's smile. "You're welcome to join me."

*       *       *

"I worked on this sucker all night," Jonah said the second Nick walked into his office half an hour later, his hair wet and slicked back. Unlike his own office, Jonah's was all sleek, modern glass and high-tech, with not a book or ancient knickknack in sight. It was as though their inner sanctums had split personalities. A shrink would have a field day trying to interpret what their respective environments said about each man. And their friendship.

A shrink, Nick thought with annoyance, would have a field day analyzing his reaction to one Princess Gabriella Visconti. He'd never lost his head to a woman, or been shaken to the core by dizzying lust, *ever*. Nick liked sex. A lot. But he hadn't had sex in almost a year.

There hadn't been time, and when the inclination struck, he took care of himself.

Deprivation would explain it.

Hell, he couldn't swallow that big a lie. Even from himself. His unbridled passion for her—harder and faster and hotter than any momentary lust he'd had for any other woman, ever—rocked him to the core. He was immune, damn it. Until her mouth brushed his. Then all bets were off and the rules changed.

His personality wasn't an act, it wasn't a persona. Cool, unemotional, and detached was who he was. A leopard didn't change his spots. But, holy hell. He'd forgotten himself completely. Lost his head completely. She brought out emotions that he didn't know lived inside him.

For those few minutes when their mouths were fused, Bria was everything. Nourishment. Air. Life.

Possibilities.

Nick tasted her even after he'd brushed his teeth several times while he showered. He smelled peaches on his skin, even though she'd worn nothing but his soap. Her taste and smell surrounded him like an invisible hallucinogenic drug.

He'd lost his fucking mind.

"Do you have something more important on your mind than what I'm showing you right here?" Jonah asked, an edge to his voice that Nick had never heard before. "Because, pal, we have a serious situation on our hands. And no," he snapped, as Nick frowned, "I can't do anything about the focus. Someone fucked with the feed from the surveillance camera on the main deck. But take a harder look."

Pleased, no, ecstatic for the distraction, Nick narrowed his gaze at the monitor. "What am I looking at? Blurry, blurrier, and blurriest?" The deck surveillance cameras were strategically placed for a three-sixty view of the surrounding area. There for a variety of reasons, mainly to monitor for piracy, and a boat called the *Sea Witch* and her thieving redheaded captain. The feed was usually clear enough to read the name on a boat two hundred yards away.

These images were useless. Impossible to ID a shape as human, let alone any details.

"Two men. Here," Jonah touched the screen. "And here. A third . . . here."

"I'll take your word for it," Nick said, shaking his head. "I could have gotten better pictures with a disposable camera. Hell, I could have drawn a better picture—in crayon."

Jonah, who looked like hell, his dark hair standing up around his head like a mad scientist, was not amused. The expensive surveillance equipment was one of his many babies on board. Nobody messed with it. And clearly, someone had. He was not a happy camper.

Nick wasn't either.

Jonah leaned his hip against his sleek, black glass desk. "Blurrier," he told Nick tightly, "is Halkias."

The pale, elongated blob was suspended in midair over the dive platform, and Nick only knew it was the dive platform because it was marked as camera number five. There was a field of black, and three, ghostly cigar-shaped blobs. Two upright, one in flight. "Jesus, someone tossed the son of a bitch overboard. It doesn't look like Her Royal Pain in my ass, but I wouldn't put it past her." The woman had lethal skills. Especially when she kissed.

Without her hair sleeked back in the sophisticated coil, she looked wild and sensual. The tangle of glossy curls around her shoulders made her look as though she'd climbed straight out of bed after hours of manic lovemaking. Her bee-stung mouth told the same story.

He'd fucking kissed her for less than seven minutes. A lifetime—

"Nick?"

"What?" he snapped. Jonah had just said something he'd missed because he couldn't keep his mind off the pain in his ass princess.

His friend sank into his chair and rubbed a hand across the dark stubble on his jaw, brown eyes troubled. "The last time I saw him, he was very much alive, Nick. Unconscious, but alive."

"Yeah." Nick folded his arms over his chest, glaring at the blurry video still. "I was kinda hoping I'd broken the son of a bitch's neck when I pulled him off her. Someone saved me the trouble and aggravation. Either they killed him, then tossed him, or they just tied him up and tossed him. Shit, now, instead of one homicidal maniac on board, we had three? Have you called this in?"

"That's the second bit of bad news."

Nick sank into Jonah's guest chair. "Christ. Are we going to put this farce to music? Now what?"

"I figured you'd want to contact Aries before we contacted the authorities." Jonah slid a piece of paper across the shiny surface of his desk, and Nick reached for it. "Instead of answering, he sent us this encrypted e-mail. I took a wild guess as to the content. You give it a shot."

It only took him a few minutes to decode the message. He and Aries had knocked this code out months ago. "Son of a bitch."

"What'd it say?"

"All communications from the *Scorpion* are being monitored," Nick paraphrased as he crushed the note in his fist. "The signals are being triangulated between Rabat, Freetown, and Dubrovnik."

Jonah raised his eyebrows. "Morocco, Sierra Leone, and *Croatia*?"

"I doubt the trace is originating from any of those cities," Nick said, glancing at the high-tech equipment nearby. This "favor" had gone from mildly entertaining cloak-and-dagger to murder, too damned fast. The stakes had been raised by players unknown, and Nick was no longer amused or interested in playing spy.

"So." Jonah exhaled. "Now what?"

"Aries says 'business as usual' as they close in on the principals from their end." Nick scrubbed his jaw. He needed a shave. "We have sixteen innocent people on board who didn't sign up for a God-damned murder mystery cruise."

"What do you want to do?" Jonah asked. "Head back to Tarfaya? We could claim engine trouble, unload everything and everyone, and be short of both the diamonds and the men responsible for killing Halkias."

Nick gave the idea serious consideration. It certainly had merit. Reluctantly he shook his head. "I can't do that."

"Nick—"

"Hundreds of thousands of men, woman, and children are being killed by weapons purchased with money obtained through the sale of blood diamonds," he said tersely. "We're the only lead Aries and his team have to this group of sellers. Our participation in this will put a stop to much of that, which is why we agreed to do this."

"Tragic, but hardly our responsibility, Nick. The crew and divers trust us— Fuck." Jonah slammed a fist against the arm of the chair. "Trust *me* to keep them safe on board. You own this ship, but as captain, the buck stops with me."

"Officially, yeah. The buck does stop with you. But I was the one who made the pact with the devil." Nick pocketed the message, unwilling to trust the sanctity of his own goddamn garbage bins anymore. "Christ, Jonah. I'm sorrier than hell for dragging you into this mess."

His friend shook his head soundlessly.

Nick stared at the floor. The situation was a mess, and he had to fix what he could. "Our crew comes first. Take the men you know you can trust and use the chopper to fly out of here." Nick looked up. "You're a shit pilot, but you should be able to get to Las Palmas in one piece."

"I'm not sure that's the answer." Jonah didn't rise from his seat, and the set to his jaw told Nick everything he needed to know about his friend's opinion on Nick's orders. "We both knew the risks of transporting multimillions of dollars' worth of diamonds. I opted in without question because what's happening in Africa is criminal." He rubbed his brow, his tone weary. "But now we know there are murderers on board. We can't tell the crew. We can't call the authorities."

"And Aries has tied our hands." Nick was torn between what was right for the world and what was right for his ship. He'd made a choice, but now people on the *Scorpion* were being attacked. He couldn't just sit back and do nothing. "I'll stay on board, finish the transfer. You keep your name clear."

Jonah gave a mirthless laugh. "Think I'm going to leave you to have all the fun? Hell, no." This time there was a glimmer of humor in his eyes. "No guts no glory, Cutter."

Nick frowned. He was the one who'd offered to help the counterterrorist operative. Not Jonah. And having his friend put his life—hell, any of their lives—at risk because he'd wanted a little excitement in his life didn't sit well with Nick. "You didn't sign up for murder."

"Neither did you," Jonah replied, "but that's what we've got."

Nick blew out a frustrated breath, then stood and clasped his friend's shoulder. "The only way we're going to protect our crew is if we find those bastards first. Have you fixed the surveillance camera or is this the grainy crap we'll be getting for the duration?"

"Working on it." Jonah paused. "Have you given any more thought to your princess's involvement?"

Nick knew the taste and texture of her mouth, and the silk of her hair between his fingers. He knew just thinking about her gave him an erection. And he knew, damn it, that he didn't like losing control like that.

But, no. He didn't know anything else for certain.

He was starting to think nothing about this trip was what it seemed.

"I don't entirely trust her," Nick told him, pleased to notice that his modulated tone hadn't changed to the imbalanced frenzy he felt just thinking about her. "That said, I'm not willing to throw her to the wolves if she's an innocent."

"Interesting. *I* don't get the criminal vibe from her," Jonah said with a shrug. "But I'll follow your lead."

"Appreciate it, buddy." Nick hesitated, jamming his hands into the pockets of his jeans. He didn't get the vibe either. But he had to have *something* to deter him from jumping her at any, and every, opportunity. "I wouldn't have agreed to do this if I didn't believe it was the right thing, no matter what Aries wanted me to do."

And one princess with a sexy mouth wasn't going to distract him from staying the course no matter what chaos she caused.

"I know," Jonah said, watching him soberly. "Aries and his people are closing in. Once they have that sewn up, they'll round up whatever bad guys are on board, and things will be back to normal before we dock at Cutter Cay. A matter of days for that to happen, right? Doing our part in this will make a difference." Jonah sounded more comfortable now that they'd cleared the air and he felt back in control.

"It's a plan, then. We'll stick to our schedule, and while we're doing that, uncover who on board is our murderer." And why Bria had been targeted by Halkias. "In the meantime, it's business as usual. Consider everyone on board a suspect. Everyone."

"Right."

They were scheduled to remain at anchor in this location for another two weeks. But plans had to change. Nick got to his feet. "Let's tighten two weeks to one, then we'll head to Cutter Cay at top speed, agreed?"

They shook on it. Then they went to Nick's office where he unlocked the safe and handed Jonah a weapon and a box of bullets.

They weren't without skills of their own.

\*      \*      \*

Nick had instructed Bria not to leave the cabin under any circumstances until he was positive all signs of danger were past.

A lovely sentiment. But after an hour in his suite—no matter how luxurious and white it was—she needed air. She needed human contact. She needed, damn it, not to be pacing as she analyzed those mind-blowing kisses. Or staring at the bed where he'd practically had her salivating after his hard body.

She expertly applied makeup so she looked naturally sun-kissed and not made-up at all, which always took longer. Then judiciously applied concealer to the bruises on her throat and arms.

She sketched the view from the window. Water as far as the eye could see. She sketched Nick—first, with his head on a platter, which amused her, then one of him smiling, another of him scowling, and then one of his expression right after the kiss. *That* was an interesting one. And interesting that her pencil remembered more than her mind's eye.

He hadn't been as unaffected as she'd first thought.

Tossing down the drawing pad, and in need of more aggressive movement, she stalked from one side of the bedroom to the other. Seven times.

She made the bed.

She paced to the window. To the door.

Looked at the pictures in a magazine.

Went to the bathroom.

Reapplied her lipstick.

Did a sketch of the *Scorpion* and another of the man who'd attacked her. Then paced some more.

Fortunately, the steward had saved her from her own insanity, calling through the door between the suite and Nick's adjoining office that he was leaving a selection of clothes on the chair for her.

She'd collected them immediately and spread them out

on Nick's bed. A bright cornucopia of designer labels. The real deal, not the knockoffs Bria was used to. She plucked up a white one-shoulder sundress made from fine linen. It looked as though it would fit.

It did. After winding the red sash from the dress she'd arrived in around her waist a couple of times and tucking in the ends, she shoved her feet into her wedge sandals, and left the cabin with her tote, which contained everything she owned. Nobody stopped her.

The boat was a hive of activity, and it was easy enough to inquire from the guy polishing the glass on the elevator where she'd find everyone. Near the dive platform on the aft deck. Good. She'd have a chance to see just what it was that Nick wasn't willing to share. Bria settled her sunglasses on her nose as she stepped out onto the deck, and almost knocked over the freckled guy with her heavy purse as he was walking over to the nearby cooler for a drink. "Sorry. Miles, right?"

"Yes, ma'am." She shook her head when he offered her the soda he'd just dug out of the ice. He was wearing blue-and-green board shorts and had a wet towel slung around his neck. Big globs of white sunscreen streaked his entire face and body, but he was as red as a boiled lobster despite the SPF protection.

"Are you— Did he— You seem okay."

"I'm fine. Really," she assured him when he gave her a worried frown.

"Perfect timing then," he told her, his smile shyly inviting.

"For breakfast I hope," she said, returning his smile as her tummy rumbled.

"Nah. To see what Olav and me brought to the surface just now. It's the most amazing— Come on. You have to see this." Endearingly oblivious that he still had zinc oxide on his fingers, he grabbed her hand and hauled her along in his wake.

All the divers were clustered around something on the table, but the only man Bria saw was Nick. Like the others, he wore a swim suit—black—and was bare-chested. And delicious looking. Her pulse picked up the thudding rhythm of some sort of machine nearby. He was like a giant magnet.

Her body felt charged, drawn toward his muscled strength, and it took everything she had to keep her mind firmly in line.

No touching. None.

*Fire. Hot.*

He glanced up as she approached, his chilly blue gaze going from her face down to her hand clasped in Miles's.

Conversation subsided.

One look at Nick and Miles let go as if her hand had suddenly burst into flames. He was certainly red enough for contact burns, but his embarrassment wasn't nearly as intense as her annoyance at Nick, who raised one supercilious eyebrow.

"After last night . . ." he trailed off suggestively, his voice husky and intimate despite their surroundings. He walked—stalked—over to her, leaving three feet of deck between them. Crowding into her personal space.

Instead of backing up, Bria lifted her chin and met his gaze through her dark glasses.

God, was he going to kiss her again? Here, in front of his men? After she'd told him no?

Looking up at him, she held her breath. He was close, but he didn't touch her. "I thought," he said, lowering his voice so that it sounded even more intimate, "I told you to stay put and wait for me."

It was a neat trick to imply that they'd spent the whole night in each other's arms instead of just a few minutes followed by an autocratic and emphatic order to, "Keep your ass in here until I come for you."

Miles sidled away, his ears glowing redder.

She tilted her head to meet Nick's eyes, dead on. Fearless. "Nobody stopped me."

"I thought your good sense would do that."

Did he sound . . . annoyed? Bria wanted to grab his wrist and take his pulse to be sure. "I don't like being confined," she told him, forcing her steady gaze to lock on his. Not that he could see her eyes hidden behind the dark lenses.

But since she was 98 percent sure that Nick could read

minds as well as leap tall buildings, all while annoying the hell out of her, and almost making her climax with a kiss, she was pretty sure he could see the expression in her eyes just fine.

"Didn't bother you last night," he said, just loudly enough to carry.

He might as well tattoo MINE on her forehead. She shot him an under-her-lashes naughty look, and leaned in close, spreading her zinc oxide sticky fingers on his muscular chest. Then murmured in a stage whisper, "Are those mink-lined handcuffs always attached to your bedpost, *tesoro*?"

"No." He moved forward to brush her lower lip with his thumb. His casual touch set up a blaze of chain lightning throughout Bria's entire body. "Those were just for you." He paused, a fraction, and added with more silken heat in his tone—his eyes—than she could handle, "*Bella.*"

"Okay, you two." Mikhail slapped a beefy hand on Nick's shoulder, breaking the odd spell that made Bria feel as though she and Nick were the only two people on the boat. Hell, the entire freakin' ocean. "Give us a break. We're all celibate here."

Just like that, the heat she thought she'd read in Nick's eyes was gone. Switched off like a light.

Oh, she wish he hadn't done that. Because now Bria was determined to see it banked again, just to prove her point.

# Chapter 7

"I'll take you back down to our cabin," Nick told her.

Oh, no way. *Her* rules. "That's sweet of you, honey," she said cheerfully, giving his white-streaked pecs a friendly pat. It was a mistake touching him because it affected her more than it did him. Bria retracted her hand as casually as she could manage. "But Miles wants to show me what he and Olav salvaged this morning."

The men stared at the back of Nick's head for so long, she wondered if he could feel their gazes drilling into his cold, alien mind.

His lip twitched. Or was it a trick of the light? "Fine."

The men cleared a space so she could see what everyone was so excited about. The simple waterlogged wooden box, about the size of a modern-day briefcase, wasn't impressive, to say the least. It looked as though bugs had been feasting on it for a long, long time. Was it filled with priceless jewelry? A fortune in gold? Seaweed?

It could be anything. Curious, and swept up in the mystery and intrigue of one little box, Bria asked eagerly, "Can you open it? What's inside?"

Olav removed the top of the box with care. "It's a medical chest, probably owned by the physician on board the *El Puerto*.

Six centuries old, and see here?" He pointed. "This is a bleed-ing cup. This here is a surgery hook. Amazing, ya?"

"Wow," she breathed. "Incredible." Hyperaware of his every move, she knew without turning that Nick had come up right behind her. She felt the heat of his half-naked body radiating all the way down her back, and his energy force field enveloped her, causing her heart to pound and her palms to sweat. Being annoyed by him was exhilarating, she thought with a smile that—if he could see it—was sure to annoy him.

"The most fascinating thing is here, in my opinion," Miles said, his face even more flushed, not from the sun but in excitement. "We think these small boxwood and tin con-tainers contain tablets of some sort."

Bria glanced up in surprise. They were awfully small. "Stone writing tablets?" Amazing, considering they'd been living on the seafloor and buried beneath the water for six hundred years.

"No," Mikhail told her, his grin splitting ear to ear. "We think pills. Medicine of some sort, that would've been dissolved in water or wine to treat any number of com-plaints."

"Or melted and applied directly to the skin," Miles added.

"Maybe both," Olav offered. "The containers are sealed well, so the tablets should be dry."

"Open one so we can see," Bria suggested, enraptured with the idea of six-hundred-year-old medicine.

"No." Nick splayed his hand on her hip and leaned in over her shoulder so his breath fanned her cheek. "The en-tire medical kit is an archeological coup. This find is too unique and valuable to contaminate by exposing the con-tents to air."

Disappointment filled her. A split second before the heat of his hand at her hip speared through her belly. Her blood. Her girl parts sat up and took notice, and did a hopeful, happy dance.

*Fire.*

"We'll preserve everything as is and send it to our lab for analysis," he continued, talking now to his team over her head. "Brian will need a microscopic amount for the FTIR machine to identify all the organic compounds. He'll do advanced DNA analysis and whatever other tests are required to get the full picture. Until then?" His breath stirred tendrils of her hair at her temple as he tilted his head a fraction, this time to look down at her profile. It took everything she had to remain still. Not turn her head and see if he was close enough to kiss. "Sorry. We wait."

Bria let out a sigh of disappointment as Nick straightened, circling around her to run his hands over the small case. She had to remember the end game, here. No matter how intriguing, how was an old suitcase of pills going to bring in any cash? "Will you sell it? It seems like a lot of work for very little reward."

All eyes swiveled from the case to her, but it was Nick—of course—who read her freaking mind. His eyes cool as the ocean water they'd dragged the box from, he said, "It's not always all about money, Your Highness."

"Do you dive?" Stan asked eagerly, vying for her attention and oblivious to the undercurrents. Maybe she was the only one who was aware of them, Bria thought, glancing around.

"I could take you down to se—"

"The princess has things to do belowdecks," Nick cut in, his tone brooking no argument. "Maybe ano—"

"I do," she said, cutting *him* off with enormous satisfaction. She bestowed a thousand-watt smile on Stan. "And I'd love to see the wreck."

Nick slid a restraining arm across her shoulders. "After our calisthenics last night," he said suggestively, dangerously smooth, "maybe you should lie down. Or soak in the hot tub before doing anything strenuous." His touch ignited sparklers of prickly heat on her bare skin.

She raised her chin. "So sweet of you to worry, schnookums." She didn't appreciate his innuendos, but she could hold her own. And then some. "Swimming will be a lot less . . ." She gave him a meaningful sideways glance from beneath her lashes. "Let's say exerting, than going back to your cabin. A swim is just what the doctor ordered to keep my muscles limber."

His eyes flashed blue warning.

She upped her smile. Just for him. "Stan and I won't be long. Will we, Stan?"

He shot her a big grin in return, his bald head catching the sunlight so it looked as though he was wearing a metal beanie. Bria had always had a soft spot for guys who shaved their heads. Marv, her bodyguard, had shaved his head for as long as she'd known him.

"I'd like to go with you. Won't take more than an hour," Miles promised.

"I'll run down and change," she all but purred as she saw a small muscle flex at the corner of Nick's mouth. Finally. A reaction.

Good.

Toying with Nick was like prodding a tiger with a stick, then pulling its tail when it turned around snarling. Scary, but God, something about needling him was exciting as hell.

His fingers tightened at her shoulder. "I'll go down with you, then."

Whoa, no way. "That's sweet," she said quickly, brightly, intentionally misunderstanding. "But Stan asked first."

"To my cabin." His lips curved into a knowing slant. "To change."

Even worse! The whole point of this was to get away from him. "I can find my own wa—"

His fingers dug into the ball of her shoulder, and his forearm was a yoke across her neck as he lowered his mouth to her ear to add in a carrying murmur, "I don't want you out of my sight. Darling."

She gave up, keenly aware of the number of eyes drilling holes in their little performance. She gritted her teeth through her smile. "Then let's go."

There was a certain amount of safety in numbers, but she wasn't being given a choice. Short of diving in her dress—not likely—she had to either go with him to change now for a few precious moments out of his reach, or forfeit diving at all.

Fine. She shot an all-encompassing smile at the group. "Thanks for showing me your treasure, guys. I'll be back in a flash, don't do anything fun without me."

Nick's pace didn't shorten, and he didn't let her go, forcing her to move faster as they went through the sunroom, sliding the door closed behind them. Basim and Khoi were cleaning, one pushing a vacuum cleaner, the other polishing chrome and glass. Nick shifted his grip from her shoulder to the back of her neck under her hair, propelling her across the large room with silent determination.

"Don't," he warned in a harsh undertone as she tried to break free, his fingers tense at her nape as they stepped into the elevator.

"I'm perfectly capable of walking on my own," Bria told him, her temper and—oh, yes! sexual awareness—simmering on a low rolling boil. She could handle him just fine. One hand tied behind her back. She just didn't want to.

Okay. That wasn't strictly true, she acknowledged. She didn't quite know how to handle a man who kept his emotions under such tight control. The real problem, she realized uncomfortably, was that she didn't know how to handle a man like Nick Cutter. A man who refused to be handled.

She grabbed his strong wrist. "You're hurting me," she told him tightly. His implacable hold didn't hurt at all. Not even a little, a nifty trick, because despite the pain-free grasp of his long fingers she couldn't break free.

And he knew it. "No, I'm not."

"I don't need to be restrained. And I don't need assistance to walk." She tried to peel his fingers up one by one. He used his other hand to dislodge her effort.

"Someone made an attempt on your life six hours ago," he reminded her, shoving her gently through the curved glass door as soon as it slid open. Her wedge sandals wobbled precariously, and she obeyed his unyielding directions rather than let him drag her out onto the upper deck level where his office and suite were located. He would too.

"You said you'd find him," she began, and clicked her teeth together as he spoke over her.

"That someone is now dead himself."

Bria's steps faltered, and goose bumps of buried fears roughed her skin as the game she was flirting with became deadly serious. "He's dead?"

"We have video from our surveillance cameras. He was thrown overboard an hour after he attacked you." Nick met her gaze, implacable as ever. "So instead of fighting me, how about we do things my way and keep you alive?"

"God." It had been a long time since she'd had to be constantly on the alert for danger. After Marvin had spirited her away from Marrezo, it had taken her years to learn how to live without seeing shadows around every corner, hear whispers behind every door.

Marvin, bless his heart, had never stopped seeing assassins behind every shrub. Even years later when it was obvious no one was coming after her.

Yet now, with this new wrinkle, Bria felt the familiar itchy feeling between her shoulder blades. As if a bull's-eye had been painted on her back. Two violent acts in a matter of hours in such close confines couldn't be put down to paranoia. And she didn't need her guardian's voice in her ear to remind her coincidences like that shouldn't be ignored.

One, maybe. She'd rationalized her recent attack to make it fit the current scenario. A random act of violence. But that didn't gel anymore if someone had killed the man who'd tried to kill her. The whole thing added a new level of confusion to what she already felt.

She realized she'd been staring at the floor in front of her. Nick hadn't said anything, allowing the silence to stretch until she was aware of her own heartbeat in her ears. Of his grip firm and steady at the back of her neck.

She frowned, straightening her shoulders. "So," she said slowly, "someone liberated him from wherever he was locked up, then just threw him overboard?" She didn't wait for the obvious answer, adding tersely, "Let me go, please. I won't be manhandled, especially now."

"Yes, you will," he said, and caught her arm with his other hand as if guiding her in a dance. Only they weren't dancing, and he wasn't letting go. Not even to cross the circular lobby. "Especially by me," he added, low voice tight with . . . what? Anger? Determination?

Damn it, he was impossible to read.

She set her jaw as her shoes rasped against the floor. Beside her, Nick's bare feet were silent as a cat's. He pushed her ahead of him down the wood-paneled hall, toward his office. And his bedroom. Bria's internal thermostat flipped to high.

And because thinking of an attempt on her life seemed much safer than thinking about the bed in Nick's room, she tried grasping at straws. "Maybe," she said hopefully, too brightly, "this has nothing to do with me. Do you have any clues as to why any of this happened?"

"Not yet."

She almost felt sorry for whoever was going to receive the punishment Nick's frozen tone implied. Almost. But, she realized as they approached the end of the corridor, she had a more immediate threat to contend with.

Ignoring his cabin wouldn't make it go away.

She tried to slow her steps. Anything to delay their progression. She was not going back into that bedroom with him. She'd gotten away fairly unscathed the first time. She wasn't going back for a second helping of Nick Cutter.

Just because he warmed up to tolerable under certain situations didn't mean she liked his attitude the rest of the time.

He frog-marched her into his office, and once more, she was struck by how much it looked nothing like the rest of his sleek, modern ship. She could live in here. It was cluttered, a little dusty, and filled with warmth and personality and color. Completely unlike the man who was gripping her neck as if he were about to do a Vulcan mind-meld.

Nick kicked the office door shut behind him, then spun her around to sandwich her between his hard, practically naked, damn him, body and the cool glossy mahogany.

Her temperature shot to a hundred and fifty.

"We have unfinished business," he said softly. "Princess."

Oh. Hell. No.

She was almost eye level with his mouth. Her gaze snagged there for a second. Another. Then slid up to meet his laser blue eyes head-on. "No, we don't." She was pleased she was still able to command a level, no-nonsense tone with him.

"Yes." Slowly he slid his hand from the back of her neck, eased it out from under her hair—making the sensitive follicles stand to attention—then spread his fingers across her throat where her pulse throbbed a crazy beat. "Yes, we do."

Bria flattened her hand on his chest to hold him at bay. Big mistake. Huge. His chest was bare, hot satin against her palm. Her fingers involuntarily curled against solid muscle covered by crisp hair.

Like petting a live wire.

She shoved as hard as she could. She might as well have been shoving the ship itself, because he didn't budge. And she didn't have anywhere to go. She frowned up at him. "I already told you no."

"You panicked," he countered, the self-assurance of his voice making the temperature in her blood spike.

God, yes. But she didn't want him to know that. The knowledge would give him power. Bria made a rude noise. "I did no such thing."

"Freaked out like a virgin."

"I can assure you," she said, responding to his taunt with a lift of her chin and slitted eyes, "I'm not."

"Let me guess." His thumb stroked a maddening line along the sensitive skin under her jaw. "Two lovers. One in high school, who was as inexperienced and inept as you were, one because you wanted to see what sex between two consenting adults was like, but he was too selfish to do the job properly."

Close enough. She swallowed hard. "Wrong," Bria denied stoutly as he lowered his head. She made a feeble attempt at shifting her mouth out of his reach, but her nanosecond of triumph turned to a small moan as, instead of kissing her,

Nick put his open mouth on her bare shoulder. A shiver traveled under her skin as he lightly bit down.

"I've had dozens of lovers," Bria lied, not daring to move, hoping to brazen this encounter unscathed. Her nipples tightened under the thin linen of the dress as his teeth raked across her shoulder. "I'm a princess. We're mad for lovers." Her mind fractured beneath the hard edge of his teeth. "Not," she added tartly, "that it's any of your damn business."

He pushed several strands of her hair out of his way, and she felt the heated wetness of his tongue as he tasted her skin. He slipped his other hand around her waist, his hand curving up between her shoulder blades. "You're on my ship."

"So what? You think that entitles you to special privileges?" Surrounded by the heat of him, overwhelmed by the fresh-air smell of his skin, Bria kept her head upright with effort. Everything in her wanted to arch her throat to give him better access.

She didn't dare.

"News flash," she continued, aware it came out more breathy than she'd intended and powerless to help it. "You do not have a feudal system on board. And just because I'm the only female, doesn't mean you can pull rank and claim me as your own sexual plaything."

The very thought of that gave Bria a fresh case of goose bumps.

His lips moved against her skin as he said, all too freaking rationally, "Officially, as captain, Jonah has rank." His damp mouth traveled slowly up the straining cords of her throat. "But yes," he whispered against her ear, making her internal organs clench.

Bria blinked. "Yes, what?"

"Yes, Princess, I'm pulling rank."

"That's outrageous!" Her indignation would have sounded more sincere if her voice hadn't gone up several octaves, and her pulse skidded into overdrive. "I didn't want you to kiss me, why would I sleep with you?"

"Oh, there won't be much sleeping, I promise."

Oh God, oh God, she was so out of her depth, she could feel the water closing over her head. "Excuse me. Don't I get a vote on this?"

"Of course," he said nibbling her earlobe. The small nip was hard enough to sting. The way he sucked it, smoothed the small pain better, made a whole raft of other sensations suffuse her body with pulsing heat. Her fingers curled defensively against his chest.

His lips moved up to her temple where she knew he'd feel the manic racing of her heart. "Now?" he murmured. "Or later?"

Damn it. It was impossible to think clearly when he was moving his mouth like that. "Now or later?" she repeated blankly.

"Right. Now." He swept her up in his arms. The room spun.

Bria punched his shoulder. "Put me down." He strode through to the bedroom. And the bed. She punched him harder. "I'm warning you, Nick—" She shrieked as he dumped her from a dizzying height onto the freshly made bed, where she bounced gracelessly.

He straightened. "There's a killer on board," he told her, his tone uncompromising as hell. His eyes pinned her to the bed. "Until I can ensure your safety you're to stay put. Here, Princess." He turned his back and walked to the door.

Bria scrambled to her knees. "I can protect myself, you egotistical . . . jerk!" Grabbing a book off the bedside table, she hiked back her arm and let it fly. It missed him by two feet and fell to the floor. She grabbed the other book and launched it after the first. He turned, hand on the door handle.

Just in time. The second book, bigger and heavier, hit him squarely in the middle of his chest. He looked from the projectile to her. "Childish."

"Really?" Bria huffed out a furious laugh. "And not two seconds ago you wanted to have wild monkey sex with me!"

"Wild monkey sex? Sounds intriguing, but I don't recall making that offer."

With an infuriated growl she threw the small stone dish holding his watch and a few coins. Everything scattered on the wood floor between them.

He shook his head and arched a condescending brow. "My father gave me that watch for my twenty-fifth birthday."

She bared her teeth. "My father was murdered right in front of my eyes when I was seven." She looked around for something else to throw at the son of a bitch, rat fink bastard. Finding nothing, she rolled off the bed in a flurry of white sundress and bare legs and sprinted toward him. "You're violating my civil rights! And I won't tolerate being kept a pris—"

He slipped through the door, slammed and locked it before her race across the room could stop him. "Damn you!" she pounded both fists on the solid wood surface. "Get back in here, you— You—" There weren't words vile enough. Her voice rose. "Damn it, Nick Cutter. Open this door immediately!"

"Calm down before you hurt yourself," he said, his voice muffled by three inches of polished wood. "I'll be—"

"Open the door and tell me to calm down again to my face!" she yelled, temper flaring white-hot. "Go on, I dare you." She slapped her open hand on the door, which only made her fingers sting. "Nick, I'm warning you—"

To no avail. She heard the outer door of his office snick shut.

He'd gone. Just walked out.

She screamed out her fury and frustration at full throttle.

Then again, because yelling made her feel better.

She swore in Italian. At the top of her voice. But it wasn't very satisfying. She only knew two curses. She knew three in French and she let those fly, multiple times. Then she gave English a shot.

Eventually, she got tired of yelling.

Muttering every swear word she knew in whatever languages she hadn't exhausted yet, making them up when her twisted fury couldn't find an apt enough outlet, Bria paced the room. To the bed.

She kicked off her shoes. Bastard.

That hadn't been heat he'd shown her, it had been mirroring back what he thought *she* wanted to get her to do what *he* wanted.

Bria stormed to the window. That made some sort of convoluted sense. To the bathroom, where there were all sorts of breakables to throw—but knowing Nick, she'd be on her hands and knees cleaning up shampoo and debris until every shard and sudsy bubble were gone. Marv had made her do it enough times that she knew the drill.

She left the pristine bathroom to storm back to the door, where she pounded on it with both fists. "Bully!"

Her hands hurt. Finally, Bria walked to the chair by the window and stared out at the beauty of the sunlight sparkling on Cutter blue water. Growling low in her throat didn't do anything to assuage the temper eating at her hard-won—and so easily lost—calm. She sucked in a ragged breath and yelled to her absent jailer, "You can't keep me locked in here forever!"

Could he?

Spreading her fingers on the window, Bria acknowledged that she was having a meltdown. She needed to get a grip. But damn it. She was so . . . so . . . furious—and worse! Aroused.

She heard Marv's voice in her head as if he were in the room with her. "You're never gonna catch a man if you lose your temper like that, honey," he'd said, over and over. "You gotta learn to control yourself."

Thinking about the man who'd been like a father to her for most of her life made tears sting Bria's eyes.

Someone had tried to kill her. All right. Fine, she could work with that. Her fingertips pressed against the cool glass as she stared fiercely out over the water. She could practically hear Marv's answer; she knew exactly what he'd say: Cutter put you somewhere safe while he worked it out.

Fine. She was somewhere safe. She got that. But she didn't need her foster father's kind, gruff words to know what the real problem was. It wasn't some unknown killer that had her twisted up inside.

"You're scared all right," she murmured, resting her forehead against the glass and closing her eyes.

But it was *Nick* who scared her.

"He's too . . . complicated." A cipher. Unreadable. Not controllable.

A challenge. Her lips curved as she thought about what Marvin might say. He's a real man, honey. Not one of those nonthreatening, easily-led-by-the-nose types you always go after.

He—that is, her subconscious had it right. Marvin's voice or not, she realized that was exactly the problem. No, not the problem . . . The lure. The draw, the—the spark.

Nick kept people at a distance with his cold, hard shell. Bria kept them at arm's length with a sunny, flirty persona that hid the scared little girl, afraid of abandonment, inside.

Deep down she felt like a sham, from her polished toes to her manicured fingertips. She'd been trying to figure out who she was since she was seven and on the run.

Her parents' death had traumatized her, and she still had nightmares. For the first seven years of her life, she'd been raised to be a princess. But that lifestyle had been abruptly shredded.

Marv had taught her everything he knew. And he'd known a lot. She could fieldstrip a variety of guns. She knew several forms of martial arts. But he'd also made sure she had all the skills necessary to be a princess, should she ever be called back home to Marrezo. She could talk as easily to a head of state as to a sick child in a hospital bed. She could ride, play tennis, and play the piano. She spoke several languages.

She was accomplished, secure in who she was as a woman, and confident. But Bria didn't need a shrink to tell her that even with all that she was afraid to love. Because eventually, somehow, some way, fate had a way of stepping in and ripping away everything important.

When she was a child on the run, taken away from everyone and everything familiar and loved, all she'd ever wanted was to go home. To go live with her brother, to be the princess while he was the kind and strong king of their people.

But that was never going to happen. Draven wasn't the idealized hero of her childhood anymore. He was a man she didn't know, and didn't feel any connection to. With his massive weight gain, there was nothing familiar about him at all. And really, why would there be? It had been twenty years, after all. She wasn't the same person as she'd been when she lived on the island either.

Besides, she thought with a sigh of resignation, the fact of the matter was that running a country was hard freaking work. Between their people and his demanding wife, there was no room in Draven's life for her.

The warmth, the closeness, the protection he'd given her when she was a child, was absent in the adult version. All that remained was an unfeeling, self-absorbed man bent on pleasing the wife who dreamed of being the next Grace Kelly—beloved queen of a small country.

A twinge built in her chest. Her eyes popped open.

"What is wrong with you?" she demanded, knowing full well she was talking to herself and beyond caring. She shouldn't be thinking like this. It was disloyal. Like her, Draven had grown up knowing his place but barred from it. They'd been raised half a world apart. Of course they were strangers.

But it didn't make the loneliness any easier to bear. Or Nick's high-handed behavior any easier to tolerate.

"Oh, woe is me," Bria said with self-deprecating humor. She rested her head on her stacked hands on the cool glass, and squeezed her eyes shut again. It blocked out the beautiful water, the sparkling sunshine, but an image of her stone-faced tormentor rose sharp and crystal clear behind her eyelids

"God!" she muttered. "He's infuriating."

But . . . She understood why.

Even being raised by a bodyguard, Bria realized she still thought like a princess. She always got what she wanted. But Nick stood firm. He wouldn't let her boss him around.

In some small part of her brain, the part not sizzling with temper, she realized that Marv would've liked Nick Cutter.

He'd never tolerated liars, and he'd never allowed Bria to lie—especially to herself.

And she was really good at doing just that.

"I just wanted to see if he was really as cold as he appeared to be," she groaned.

Her little experiment proved that he wasn't. He'd called her bluff. And as Marvin would have told her, "You've got your nose bent out of shape 'cause someone didn't play the way you wanted. So what are you going to do about it, honey?"

Didn't play the way she'd wanted? "From pucker to DEFCON five in two point five seconds," Bria told the invisible, and sorely missed, Marv morosely. "Yes, I'd say so."

She needed a plan.

# Chapter 8

Nick and Jonah sat on the aft sundeck near the hot tub, beer bottles in hand, feet crossed at the ankles and propped up on the rail. Nick had showered and changed in Jonah's cabin, then borrowed clothes from him because he hadn't wanted to disturb Bria by going to his own cabin.

Jonah had laughed his ass off, and clucked annoyingly.

Their one-a-night drink was another similarity the two men shared. Both of their fathers had been alcoholics.

But that's where their history diverged. Nick's father had been a womanizer in addition to his ability to drink his weight in rum, while Jonah's father had been a hands-on parent and faithful husband despite his liking for too many beers.

Which was probably why Jonah was as well-adjusted as he was, Nick thought absently as he looked at one of the few men he trusted without reservation. The blended and familiar smell of chlorine, hops, and ocean salt was a calming way to finish the day, which had taken Nick through an unfamiliar kaleidoscope of emotions.

Relaxed as he might pretend to be, even to himself, Nick felt . . . ruffled. "See the silver bars from this afternoon yet?" he asked his friend. The king's ransom in silver bars that he and his team had spent the better part of the day bringing to the surface was in excellent shape. The cache had been located to the southeast of an already established scatter pattern. A pleasant surprise.

"Olav said some hundred and seventy bars. Weighing what? A hundred pounds apiece?" Jonah leaned over and gave a fist bump. "Nice job."

"Investors will be happy." Nick had worked his ass off all day, diving, hauling. Things he did every day of the week with intense pleasure had suddenly become busywork, so he didn't think of a certain pair of snapping brown eyes and wild gypsy hair.

The only damned problem was . . . Hell. She surrounded him whether he was with her or not. Her ripe peach scent lingered in his shower, in his office, down the corridors. There was no escape on confined real estate in the middle of the ocean.

Jonah turned to look at him, lowering his sunglasses to make eye contact. Disregarding Nick's foray into neutral ground, his friend said plainly, "You know you can't leave the princess locked up in your cabin forever, right? There's sure to be some inconvenient international laws against it."

"It's debatable if I'll have a cabin left after this morning's meltdown." Nick shrugged, keeping his tones cool, detached. "She's got quite a temper for someone with a royal pedigree. Thought the personality was supposed to be bred right out of them."

Jonah grinned. "Imagine being married to a woman like that." He rested his half-filled bottle on his flat belly. "Man, you'd never know what day of the week it was, with that one. Up. Down. She'd turn you inside out."

Nick took a long pull on his beer. The whole thing sounded like a too-familiar kind of life that he'd rather avoid. His father, the original Casanova of the Caribbean, had been a stellar example of why marriage, or even long-term relationships, weren't of any interest.

He shook his head. "I shudder to think." Nick stared out at the water. A small splash indicated a fish coming up for an evening snack. A few lazily drifting cotton candy clouds floated aimlessly in the hard, bright blue bowl of the sky.

A great diving day—marred by thoughts of an infuriating woman. Nick was not happy to have his relaxation spoiled by images of Princess Gabriella Visconti. He rolled his head to look at his friend. "Ever been in love? Like seriously, until-death-do-us-part in love?"

Jonah looked out over the water. "Once."

News to Nick. In the two years he'd known Jonah, they'd talked about just about everything under the sun and found more similarities than differences. Up to and including being the same age and having birthdays three days apart. But this was one subject they'd never broached. "What happened?"

Jonah brought the bottle to his lips. "She got away," he said into the glass, and drank.

Nick was silent. What did a man say to something like that?

"What about you?" Jonah countered, his side of the conversation clearly closed. Fair enough. Obviously an unpleasant memory.

"In love? Hell, no. In lust? Oh, yeah." They both grinned and toasted each other.

"Why do you think that is?" Jonah asked. "Seriously. Why do I still have a jones for the woman who . . ." He took a slug of his beer without finishing the sentence. "And why don't you commit? Ever think about it?"

"Not if I can help it." Images of his mother's tear-stained face leapt to mind. Marriage hadn't been the best thing for her or his father. It seemed to cause more hurt than anything, especially when one person wasn't honest. Everybody lied. It was human nature.

"I wish you could've known my father," Jonah murmured, staring out over the water. "He was— God, he was an amazing man. Even as a small kid, I'd watch him with my mother, and I'd think, damn! I want that."

"I'd look at my parents," Nick told him without inflection, "and I'd think, Jesus, I *never* want that." The lies. The betrayals. The subterfuge.

Jonah shot him a concerned glance. "You aren't your

father. You know that, right?" There was an edge of frustration in his voice. The same conversation they'd had over and over. Jonah was always trying to make fathers out as the greatest thing since salvaging, while Nick stood firm in his opinion that an absent father made the best father. One of their few disagreements, and something they revisited now and then whether it needed rehashing or not.

"That's only because I purposely set out to be everything he wasn't from an early age," Nick said, acknowledging his success with a grim little toast.

"What about Zane and Logan?"

Nick took a long pull from his beer before answering. "Zane did his damnedest to emulate our father in every way, and Logan— Shit, Logan, being the oldest, had his own unique way of dealing with things. Lone wolf doesn't even begin to cover it."

Jonah grew quiet. Contemplative. As if he wanted to say something, but couldn't. Nick knew the feeling. It was part and parcel of being the calm, collected brother. Predictable, cool under pressure. Spock.

Sometimes there were things just better left unsaid, which is why he appreciated Jonah so much. Their silence was comfortable. The close confines of the *Scorpion* had accelerated their friendship over the last couple of years. They had similar temperaments, so their friendship was easy. Uncomplicated.

"But now Zane has Teal. She's the component he was missing, right?" Jonah placed his empty bottle on the deck beside his chair, then folded his clasped hands over his belly. "I've always envied the closeness you and your brothers have. Now you've made room for Teal to come into your inner circle. Family, you know? More of it. It's a good place."

Nick didn't miss the wistful note in his friend's voice. Jonah was an only child. Nick couldn't imagine his own life without his brothers. "We're damn lucky," he admitted. "We kept each other on an even keel during the worst of times, and we're really close still. Always have been."

His friend expelled a breath. "You have no ide— Oh, for

crap's sake!" Jonah sat up from his slouch, jerking his head to indicate something out on the water. "Look what Poseidon just dragged in!"

The dark hull of the *Sea Witch* clung to the wavelets like an ominous shadow, backlit by the white-hot ball of the descending sun, which had lost none of its intensity as it set. "How are we so lucky that she's hitting us twice in as many months?" Nick demanded.

The redheaded captain of the small craft was a thorn in Cutter Salvage's side. She was a pirate, a sneak, and a flat-out thief. She snuck into their sites after dark, pilfering pieces they'd marked for later recovery. Expensive. And, invariably, annoying.

Didn't matter where in the world Nick, Logan, and Zane might be, the *Sea Witch* would always show up, usually sooner than later. If they weren't on a salvage, she targeted one of their other ships. Relentless, she always knew where they were, and how long they'd be around, like she had Cutter-sonar.

Nick rested his head against the high chair back. "She's a small yippy dog who always runs like hell with the choice treats," he said, unruffled despite his moment of ire.

Fire flashed in Jonah's eyes. "Those 'treats' are valuable. I keep telling you we should go over there and take back our shit!"

"Zane went on board the *Sea Witch* awhile back. Said she has our stuff all over her boat, like trophies."

Jonah leaned forward—about as jumped up as he ever got, which was just the way Nick liked it. "Let's go get it back. How about right now? She'll be diving, ripping us off, while we take back what she stole last time."

Nick frowned as a woman with long red hair, wearing scuba gear, came out onto the *Sea Witch*'s narrow deck. She waved, then got ready to dive. Idiot for diving alone, he thought without heat. But she wasn't his idiot to worry about.

While annoying, the Sea Bitch—as Teal called her—wasn't equipped to steal anything too large. She pilfered a few small, sometimes valuable, items, but the Cutters usually managed to scoop her on the really good finds. The stuff they marked for later, the kind of stuff the Sea Bitch made off with, was yet to be anything jaw-droppingly inspired. She was more of a nuisance and irritant than a financial liability.

"She'll help herself just to annoy us, and be on her way," Nick said, dismissing her out of hand. "We have bigger fish to fry." Like a fortune in blood diamonds and a murderer somewhere on the loose.

"By not prosecuting, you're encouraging her, you know." Jonah pressed a hand to his belly as his stomach rumbled loud enough for Nick to hear it.

"Her time will come." Nick glanced at his watch. "Go grab a snack. Khoi won't start serving for another hour." He swung his feet down from the railing, and stood.

"Where are you going?"

Nick's lips twitched. "To see how long a princess can keep a mad on."

\*          \*          \*

Bria kept her eyes fixed on the door as it opened.

It wasn't a tentative, checking-to-see-if-she-was-waiting-for-him-loaded-shotgun-in-hand kind of motion either. Nor was it the kind of caution displayed by a man not quite sure if she'd gone rabid and feral and torn his pristine white-on-white-on-white cabin to shredded confetti.

Or, for that matter, if she'd taken rescue into her own hands and smashed the large picture window and swum to frigging freedom.

All things she'd considered.

But no, none of that appeared to faze Nick Cutter, the rat-fink-son-of-a-bitch-violator-of-civil-liberties, who strolled in as though all was right with the world and not a damn thing had gone on in this cabin five hours earlier.

He looked his usual annoyingly calm self.

Bria's plan to mimic his *sangfroid* and take over the driver's seat went out the window the instant her traitorous body remembered what it felt like to be kissed by those arrogant lips.

Her pulse accelerated, and her mouth went dry. Worse, all her girl parts responded to even the *memory* of his sex appeal, and suddenly craved things she'd never been that excited about wanting before.

*Stop it!*

Her silent reprimand didn't help.

He'd changed out of the swim trunks that bared every delectable inch of him earlier. Still barefoot, he was now wearing soft, worn jeans and a white cotton V-necked sweater with the sleeves shoved up his tanned forearms. Effortlessly sexy. He stuck his fingers casually in his front pockets and leaned a shoulder against the doorjamb between the office and bedroom.

"Ready for dinner?" he asked pleasantly, looking at her with those shockingly blue eyes that made the hair on her body stand to attention and instantly tightened her nipples.

And ruined her resolve.

With nothing else to do, she'd showered earlier and had made do with air-drying her hair, which was now a dark, glossy, completely out of control cloud around her shoulders. She'd had plenty of time to play with her makeup, and she'd gone whole hog. Smoky eyes, vibrant red lips, a spritz of her travel perfume.

She'd chosen a short, turquoise, strapless bandage dress that was a little snug, but worth asphyxiating for when Nick's gaze lingered on the swell of her breasts. She imagined she saw his pupils dilate. And if they didn't, he'd slipped into an open-eyed coma. She felt some of the power between them shift back into her court.

Bria had weapons he hadn't even *seen* yet. Uncurling her legs from under her, she slid off the bed. Slowly. "Ready and willing." She smoothed her hand down the curve of her hip. "In fact, I'm *starving.*"

Basim had brought a rolling rack of freshly laundered clothes with a lovely lunch of chicken and fresh fruit at noon. Clearly a lot of women had come through the revolving doors of the *Scorpion*. Khoi had delivered a wicked and decadent wedge of chocolate cake and a diet soda at three.

But it wasn't *food* she wanted a bite of.

Bria needed to be back in control. Needed it. She wanted Nick's head on a platter, with a rosy apple in his mouth. *After* he'd written her a very large check.

She'd decided in the last few hours that if Nick *wanted* to, he *could* absolutely return Marrezo's money. Clearly his company was fiscally sound. There were other investors. There must be money available for emergencies. This was an emergency.

He had Draven's money. *Marrezo's* money.

She urgently wanted it back.

She was going to get it back if it killed her. Okay, wait, someone had already tried that. She rephrased. She'd get the money back by hook or by crook.

Then she'd leave before she was burned to a crisp by blazing hot ice.

She was not running, she'd assured herself repeatedly all afternoon. Not necessarily running, but certainly at a brisk walk. Metaphorically, since they were in the middle of the Atlantic Ocean.

Five minutes before he opened the door, this had seemed like a good plan. Now she could clearly see the holes. Her version of control was superficial at best. His was bred to the bone.

"You've been busy," he observed, his voice Sahara dry as his eyes flickered over the room.

Bria had chosen to convert some of the vibrantly colored clothes into luxurious pillow and lampshade covers. The glaringly, mind-numbingly boring white bedroom had been transformed with pops of color and texture. She'd done it to annoy him, but she liked the end result.

She bent from the waist to pick up her red-soled sandals, then, hooking the sling-backs over one finger, sauntered over to him. He turned to stone as she came close enough to see that telltale little nerve twitching at the corner of his mouth.

Control. She had it.

But for how long?

She put her splayed fingers on his chest for balance, feeling the steady drum of his heartbeat beneath her palm. Taking her time, she lifted a bare foot and slipped on one sandal. "I hope you don't mind. I did a little decorating while I . . ." Fumed? No, too confrontational. "Waited," she finished mildly.

She shifted to put on her other shoe, which brought her closer to his chest, and almost eye level.

He didn't move. His chest was rock solid under her touch. If it weren't for the hard throb of his heart beneath her hand, he could have been a statue.

"It's certainly . . . interesting," he said, his voice quiet. Leashed down. He was staring into her eyes, not at the bright splashes of color behind her.

"Isn't it?" She smiled up at him happily. "Amazing what a few cut-up designer dresses, a stapler, and some Scotch tape can do." His eyes flickered. "Khoi wouldn't give me more than that, so I used my nail scissors," she continued, gamine bright. "What did he think I'd do with a real pair? Cut my way out of here?"

Small supernovas flared in the blue of his eyes. "I wouldn't put it past you."

"Shows what you know," she replied, smile widening. His gaze snagged on her mouth. Kiss Me Red. *Would he?* "I don't take stupid risks, Mr. Spock. I get that there's a killer out there somewhere."

Well, she took risks. Just not *stupid* ones. This wasn't stupid. This was . . . practical. Necessary. People were depending on her to tamp down her temper and get the job done.

And she could keep telling herself that as she stayed where she was, fingers splayed over his arctic-freeze heart. "I appreciate the sentiment behind you keeping me prisoner in here while you looked for the bad guys. I really do. But," she poked him in the chest with her finger. "Don't ever, *ever* lock me *anywhere* again."

His eyes narrowed. "What did you call me?"

She stayed where she was, breasts so close to his chest

she could feel his body heat, face tilted up to his, their mouths only inches apart. She tasted the beer on his breath, smelled ocean salt on his skin, saw a flicker, just a flicker of heat in those cold blue eyes.

Then the heat was gone and she wondered if she'd imagined it.

A really, *really* stupid plan. So sometimes she did take stupid risks. But calculated stupid risks. Okay, sometimes she didn't think at all when she lost her temper. Bria took a step back, dropping her hand from his chest. A tactical retreat. Because while *he* wasn't affected by their closeness, she *was*. "Mr. Spock. The impassive Vulcan in *Star Trek*—"

His lips quirked. "Yeah, I know who he is. My brothers call me Spock."

"Good grief!" She forgot to be sensual. Abandoned it, really, and tossed her hair behind her shoulders to get it out of her face. "You're like this with your brothers too?"

"I'm like this with everyone, Princess." And what an apology it *wasn't*. "It's who I am," he added, as if she hadn't gotten that memo.

Her lips curved. "From when you were a little baby?"

Instead of answering, Nick reached out, sliding one big hand around the back of her neck. No Vulcan mind-meld necessary, he just pulled her inexorably back against him like a magnet drawing metal filings.

She licked her lips, then wished she hadn't as his eyes ignited with blue flame. Uh-oh! Somehow her arms ended up wound around his neck. Lungs constricted with anticipation, she could barely breathe as her ultrasensitive breasts brushed his chest.

One hand still in his front pocket, he raised the other to her face, brushing his thumb lightly across her chin. "I knew when I first saw this chin that I was going to have problems with you." Raw desire and dark need flared in his eyes.

His hair was cool and silky beneath her hand, his scalp hot as she combed her fingers through his hair. She loved the heated depth of his smoldering blue gaze. She loved the way her nipples ached and her girl parts did the happy dance to see him.

She rubbed her nose across his tight, slightly bristly jaw. And because she could've sworn he shuddered, did it again.

Tilting her face up she said huskily, "*I* like to think I'm determined."

"You're determined to play with fire, aren't you?"

She was. Until just that very second. Only as her knees turned to jello, she forgot that too. "Maybe you're the one playing with fire." Damn. That didn't sound in the least threatening. It sounded husky, and wanton, and needy. She dragged in a shallow, shaky breath.

He smiled. "You look stunning in this dress you're almost wearing." The look he gave her almost incinerated the dress right off her body.

Meeting his fathomless gaze she raised her chin. "Do *not* kiss m—"

His mouth slanted on hers. So much for taking control. Okay. Fine. It was just a kiss after all. People kissed every day of the week. It was no big deal. Instead of his lips on hers, she decided to think about the Sapphire Grotto on Marrezo. The startling color of the water on the cave's walls, the smell of humid—

Bria's mind went blank. Her imagination fractured into a thousand pieces as his lips moved over hers, and all she could do was stand on her toes, tighten her arms around his neck, and hang on for the ride as her nerve endings flooded with sensation.

His heat was there beneath all that daunting self-control. His fingers skimmed her cheek and tangled in her hair. His other hand was busy too. His cool palm skated up the back of her warm thigh, inching up the fabric of the short dress as his fingers skimmed higher. Bria felt the whisper of his fingertips as they brushed against the edge of her thong. His hand slipped under the sheer ribbon at her hip to glide across the globe of her bottom. A slight bit of pressure, and she was flush against the hard length of his erection.

Fire wasn't even the start of the sensations pooling hard in her belly, through her veins. Bria whimpered and melted into him. He tasted so good, and she craved more. Had been craving more since the first kiss. She met the sweep of his tongue with her own. She opened her mouth wider, and his fingers tightened on her butt as he sucked on her tongue.

Shimmering washes of sharp heat swept through her from her head to her toes as Nick made a sound low in his throat when she tangled her fingers in his silky dark hair and kissed him as if she'd be graded later. The sound he made resonated at the juncture of her thighs. Moisture pooled just inches from his exploring fingers.

Somehow he'd turned her so her back was against the doorjamb. He pressed against her, pulling her more tightly against him. Bria was enveloped by him. By his heat, and the heady male scent of his skin. By his arms, his so-sure hands, everything that was Nick Cutter.

The bed, she thought, her brain muzzy and crazy with lust. Only a few steps behind him. If he'd only . . . Disoriented, she blinked as Nick dragged his mouth from hers. "What?" The word slipped out before she could muzzle herself, sounding so damned needy, she could have kicked herself.

He slid his hand out of her hair, stroked a finger across her damp, swollen mouth. His eyes blazed with molten heat as he said smoothly, "Let's eat."

Oh, for God's sake!

# Chapter 9

Bria slid onto a chair, casting an appreciative glance over the small, intimate table. "This is beautiful." Her voice still carried echoes of husky sensuality.

Nick pushed her chair in, inhaling the succulent ripe peach scent that drifted from her golden skin. His gut clenched, and the throbbing ache in his still-too-damned-aware erection wasn't subsiding. He walked around to his own seat before he gave in and bent her over the good china.

Her soft mouth, free of lipstick, looked bee-stung from his kiss, and the pulse at the base of her throat pounded hard. If that didn't indicate her arousal, the hard buds of her nipples, pressed against the thin cloth covering them, did.

She hummed her appreciation of the meal before them. A simple lobster salad, wine, French bread. He hadn't requested candlelight, but Khoi had provided it. Nick almost blew out the flickering flames, but he liked the silken, impossibly soft, look of her skin as the flames danced in the warm zephyr of the breeze.

No romantic music; his head steward would've been keel-hauled for that. Just the soft susurrus of the waves against the hull, and a faint, almost imperceptible bass from the movie the guys were watching in the media room behind the sun-room.

"You like lobster?"

Her dancing eyes, long-lashed, melted chocolate, innocent as sin, met his. "On a night like this? What's not to like?" She made that soft humming sound again. It curled through Nick's blood like mind-altering smoke. She made no effort to conceal that her nipples were hard beneath the thin horizontal bands of her dress, which was the pale turquoise of the water of his favorite beach back home at Cutter Cay.

He gritted his teeth, grateful that his own arousal was efficiently hidden by the table.

"Glad you approve," he said, pleased at how calm he sounded, all things considered.

Set for two, the table had been placed on the sundeck near the hot tub, a favorite vantage point of Nick's. The water shimmered crystalline blue, illuminated by a single underwater light. Strings of small, round, milky-white bulbs, strung on invisible cords, swayed slightly overhead in the breeze. He couldn't have painted a more romantic picture if he'd orchestrated the setting himself.

He'd merely told Khoi dinner for two on the sundeck. Where it was in no way private to anyone glancing through the picture windows.

What was her game? Did she *have* a game? He considered that as he sipped the wine he didn't want. Yeah. Everyone had a game.

Some more dangerous than others, he knew.

He didn't peg her as the easy-come-easy-go type, but twice now she'd taken part in a heated kiss. Heated, hell. Inferno of a kiss. Skin-searing, nerve-peeling, mind-numbing kiss, the kind that made him forget things like "logic" and "rationality" and "common fucking sense."

But it wasn't an act. She'd been affected too.

Still, it wasn't his goal to toss her into his bed. He'd instructed Khoi nothing romantic, but it was hard to beat a warm breeze, the rock of the water, and a waning crescent moon sparkling on the waves for romantic, no matter who was looking at it. He took the cloth-wrapped bottle out of the ice bucket and topped up her glass.

Nick had absolutely no interest in food. Bria looked as wild and exotic as a gypsy with her thick, shiny hair in a messy tangle of curls around her bare shoulders. It was all he could do to keep his hands off her.

The game had changed, but he couldn't pinpoint how, or where, or even why. All he knew was that his old rule book was worthless when it came to Gabriella Visconti.

Her dark eyes still looked a little dazed, fever bright as they darted over the table, the ocean beyond, the deck—everywhere but at him. It was impossible for her to hide the hard, telltale throb at the base of her throat or the flush that made her skin glow.

Steam from the hot tub drifted lazily in the almost still air, the shifting lights adding another layer of mystery to the deck along the shadowy perimeter.

Bria glanced around. "Where is everyone? Did you lock everyone else in their cabins too?"

He ignored her none-too-subtle dig. But it certainly helped his bruised sense of control. "Having dinner, and watching an Indiana Jones marathon."

She tilted her head, and a few long tendrils slipped forward over her shoulder. "Why aren't you in there with them?" she asked, her eyes finally meeting his.

*Score one for me,* they flashed. He almost cracked a grin. She thought a direct question to put him on the spot was a win?

Nick couldn't quite figure her out. Was she the sophisticate she appeared to be? She certainly oozed class and sophistication. A royal beauty.

He narrowed his eyes. A royal pain in the ass, is what she was. And yet he'd stake his share of the dive that she wasn't as experienced in the bedroom as she wanted him to believe.

Unless *that* was a ruse to keep him occupied while the Moroccans skulked about his ship doing God only knew what.

Christ, what was the real answer here?

He smiled at her across the table. "Why would I watch a movie when I can get to know you better?"

"Get to know me better, huh?" The sarcastic lilt to her voice let him know the gloves were off and it was game on. She picked up her fork, toying with it a moment before tipping her head in that way she had. It slid her hair over her bare shoulder, outlined the curve of her throat in moonlight and muted deck lights.

She'd covered her bruises. Around her throat, smudged on her upper arms. But Nick knew the location of every one. He didn't have to see them to remember that she'd been brutally attacked under his watch.

"All right." She cradled the stem of her glass. Red fingernails turned him on. He imagined them digging into his ass as he pumped into her—"Nick? Where'd you just go? What do you want to know?"

Where the hell to start. How about the way she'd taste on his fingers? Nick tamped down the heat, dragging his gaze from her slender, red-tipped hands, back to her face. "Tell me about growing up as a princess."

Her jaw shifted faintly, and he wasn't sure if he'd hit a memory or a nerve. "Other than some high points," she said, readily enough, "I was pretty much like every other privileged child. Spoiled, pampered . . ." Her eyes lit with a sad sort of sparkle as she added softly, "Loved."

Dangerous ground. He reached for his wineglass and asked, "Wasn't there responsibility to go with the crown?"

Her bare lips curved into a smile that hit Nick in his solar plexus. Sweet, teasing, and completely without artifice. "I was only a princess for seven years, so I never wore a crown. Not a very long time to get all the hand-kissing, baby-shaking parts of my duties learned." Her dark eyes caught the moonlight, and her smile widened, exposing those slightly crooked eyeteeth that he found ridiculously charming.

That smile . . . Nick wanted to feel it around his dick. He wanted to crush that explosion of gypsy hair in his fists, and— His grip tightened on his glass, and he set it down before he cracked it. "Seven years," he repeated, aware it came out tense. "Before your parents died and changed things for you. Who took care of you after that?"

Her smile slipped at the mention of her parents' death. "It's complicated." She lifted a shoulder. "Marvin Ginsberg was my personal bodyguard, and he raised me."

Nick pushed his plate away with his thumbs, far more interested in Bria than food. "Marvin . . . *Ginsberg*?"

"I know, right?" Her smile, dangerous enough, returned, this time shaped into a conspiratorial grin that had Nick's pulse skyrocketing. "His real name was Mauro, but everyone called him by his American father's name, and it just stuck. He was more a Marvin than a Mauro anyway." She rested her elbow on the table, propping her chin on her hand. It did mouthwatering things to her cleavage that was practically spilling out into her salad, and Nick forced his eyes to remain on hers.

"His mother was Marrezan and lived in Pavina," she continued. "So Marv had lived on Marrezo off and on most of his life. He was my—" She shrugged slim, bare shoulders as she removed her elbows, curling her slender fingers around the stem of her glass. Her generous, kissable mouth curved gently, and her eyes softened.

"Your?" Dampening down the chaos of his thoughts, he made a fist beside his plate as he had the tactile memory of cupping her smooth ass in his palm. His erection felt as though it would be there for a while.

The smile slipped, leaving her looking sober and too vulnerable. She picked up a chunk of lobster in her fingers and dragged it through the mayonnaise, ate the bite, swallowed. He couldn't look at the movement of her throat because even that gave him carnal thoughts. He'd call Aries first thing in the morning. Insist she be allowed to leave.

Wiping her fingers on her napkin, oblivious to where his thoughts were, she continued. "He was everything to me, from seven to twenty-three. Bodyguard, mother, father, protector. He taught me a lot. About everything."

She reached for another chunk of lobster, ignoring her fork. It was the most sensual damn thing Nick had ever seen, watching her eat with her fingers with such obvious enjoyment. In silence, she focused on her salad for a few minutes.

The silence was comfortable, for *her,* filled with crackling, high-octane sexual tension for him. She didn't try to fill it, which was a pleasant surprise. Most women would've. Instead, she ate with relish, companionably quiet. But every bite she took meant he had to look at the motion of her lips, her teeth, her tongue. His control was already hanging by a thread.

He drank from his water glass, ignoring the wine, looking over the dark ocean to rest his eyes for a moment. The *Sea Witch*'s lights were out, but he could see her blacker-than-black outline out there a few hundred feet off the port bow. The moon painted a milky road across the midnight surface of the water.

Would have been nice if life could paint such clear and obvious paths to follow. But that wasn't how it worked. Things were more intriguing if they weren't so clear-cut and defined.

He'd always found liars particularly interesting as human studies. Fortunate, because in his experience, they were thick on the ground. The why-and-why-not of them was what made his hobby with T-FLAC so fascinating. Especially since he didn't play in that dirty water very often. He enjoyed the challenge a liar presented. The better the prevarication, the more the challenge. It had, he knew, started with his own father, the king of misdirection.

A man who lied to his own wife and sons was a hell of a puzzle.

Bria's fork clinked against her plate. "Okay," she said slowly, "I know I was expecting an expression north of frigid, but you have a scary look on your face right now." Her tone was light, but she pointed her fork at him like a weapon. "I hope you aren't armed."

As a matter of fact, he *was* armed. He had a Sig Sauer tucked beneath the lightweight sweater, in the small of his back. He'd instructed Jonah to do the same. Having her out of the bedroom out in the open was a risk. He schooled his features. "A trick of the light," he said softly, indicating she continue eating.

She cocked a dark eyebrow at him. "Sure it is," she said, but half under her breath.

He almost grinned. Saucy woman. He leaned back, cradling his glass. "I've never been to Marrezo, what's it like? You went back for your brother's coronation a couple of years ago, right? How has it changed since you saw it last?"

Even as he peppered her with questions, he realized he wasn't just making conversation. He really wanted to know about this woman who agitated him more than any woman had done before. About her life, her home. Her past.

Bria circled the foot of her glass on the crisp white tablecloth beside her plate. "My life as a child was idyllic. I was surrounded by people who loved me, in a country where I was adored. So if I paint Marrezo gold, that's where the bias comes from." Her eyes crinkled at the corners as she gave a gentle laugh.

"It's the third smallest monarchy in the world after the Vatican and Monaco. Surrounded by deep blue waters of the Tyrrhenian Sea."

"Sounds charming," he said, not because it was poignant, but because he saw how her face lit when she spoke about her childhood home. And he liked hearing her talk.

Her smile went crooked. "Oh, it is. Idyllic and beautiful and a strategically perfect place for international terrorists to set up shop."

"Why?"

She raised her hands to represent imaginary borders. "It's small," she explained. "Like, really small. In the scheme of things, Marrezo was just one of hundreds of tiny voices in the European Union. It's situated between Sardinia and the west coast of Italy, which is a great staging point for, well . . ."

"For terrorist activity," he supplied when her voice trailed off.

She nodded.

He watched the emotional play of her features, saw the subtle way her eye muscles firmed into studied matter-of-factness. She could recite it all she wanted, and he respected her aplomb, but he could tell the memory still weighed on her.

"So what happened?" he asked, both to watch her as she spoke and to fill his own ignorance on the subject.

She was right. Marrezo was tiny. Barely a blip on the world's radar. Given the island country had created Bria, that didn't seem right to him. The birthplace of such a vibrant woman should matter more.

But maybe that was his bias talking.

She took a sip of wine. He didn't push her, watching the fascinating play of studied detachment, resignation, sorrow, and pride as she considered his question. Then, quietly, she took a long, deep breath. "We had no warning. My mother had just read me a bedtime story—"

He watched her over the rim of his glass.

"She'd just tucked me in when we saw flames reflected in the windows. My mom was nobody's fool." Her smile flickered in and out like a light. "She screamed for Marvin, who grabbed me. As he carried me through the secret passages of the palace, we saw my father fall. Thrown from the top of the stairs . . ." She shuddered, rubbing her bare arms. "I knew in that instant that my mother and Draven had been killed too. My entire family had been wiped out in hours. I was the only one left."

Nick couldn't imagine what it must have been like for her, seven and terrified.

"I remember the glow, mostly," she finally said, studying her wine as if it held all the answers. "The palace was in flames, both towns were burning. The sky was orange with it, and thick with the smell of smoke, like a really demonic sunset. People were screaming, and attempting to run, or swim, or paddle away as fast as they could."

"Then what?" he asked when it seemed like she'd stare at her glass forever.

Her eyes lifted, and he was relieved to find them clear. Not a tear in sight. "Marv took me to the Sapphire Grotto a few miles away. He left me there, raced back to help . . ." She paused, her fingernails tapping gently against her glass. The gentle clink of crystal punctuated the silence like a tiny bell. "I waited in the cave," she said calmly, "hiding way in the back until Marv returned the next night. He had a boat, and he rowed all night to reach a small fishing village on the coast."

"Horrific." Even for an adult who might have had a hope in hell of understanding what was going down. Zane had been with their father when he'd had his heart attack and died. It was still hard for his brother to talk about that day. To a little princess, it must've seemed like the world was ending.

The door to the media room opened, and the chatter of automatic gunfire riveted her attention for a moment before it was once again muted.

Bria sighed, then raised her chin, and her eyes met his. Direct, bold. "Nick, I'm not telling you this just to share something," she said, her husky voice firm. "I'm telling you because what happened forged who I've become. You keep calling me 'princess' like it *means* something, but I'm not a princess. No matter how many times you call me one, it's just a . . . a mask. A title, a word. I don't *feel* it." She tapped her heart. "In here, I'm as American as apple pie."

She was anything but the girl next door, no matter where or by whom she been raised. "You've got the princess walk down."

To his surprise, she laughed. The sound slid into his skin, into his jeans, and squeezed. Christ.

"Show me a confident woman who doesn't."

"That's it?"

She shrugged. "I was catapulted into full-blown reality at a young age. As long as I knew him, Marv was paranoia personified. We were on the run for a long time. He taught me how to protect myself. I can fire almost any kind of gun, and I'm a fourth dan black belt in Krav Maga."

Nick's eyebrows shot up, this time in surprise. So she *had* been responsible for beating the crap out of Halkias. Good for her.

"In other words," she finished, her tone even, "to feel safe, I want—no, I *need* to be responsible for my own safety. Marvin made sure I would never feel powerless again."

She put up a slender hand as if he was about to argue. He wasn't.

"After I got mad at you for imprisoning me today, I got where you're coming from," she assured him. "I really do. You feel responsible for me while I'm on board your ship. I appreciate it, and I'll accept that." And without waiting for him to get a word in edgewise, she continued firmly. "But by the same token, you have to understand that not being allowed to take some control of the situation scares me more than having an unknown assailant around, and being locked up terrifies me."

He got it. Hell, Nick was impressed by her candor and composure. "Fair enough."

Her eyes widened. "Really?"

Before she got too cocky, he added, "But you can't wander around alone. Not until we catch the men who killed Halkias, and get to the bottom of why you were targeted in the first place."

"Fair enough," she repeated, all too quickly. "I'll take one of the crew, or whomever you can spare—"

*Hell, no.* Nick shook his head. "Either you're with me, or Jonah. Twenty-four/seven, Bria, 'round the clock. Until we prove otherwise, we're the only ones I trust."

She hesitated, clearly puzzled. "Is that paranoia," she asked, "or do you have a reason?"

"Reason."

He watched her processing his curt nonexplanation, her index finger grazing back and forth over the tines of her fork. "Will you tell me why?"

"No."

"Will you at least arm me?" she demanded, setting the fork down with a chink on the edge of her plate.

Amused, and yes, impressed as hell that she could tamp down her curiosity and take the practical approach. He held back a grin at the frustration sharpening her tone.

She was . . . fiery, exotic—*tropical;* he was cool, boring, and *temperate.* Problem was, the princess's fire was melting the ice inside him at an alarming rate.

Nick gave her a bland look. "Do you promise not to shoot me by accident?"

"I swear. I won't shoot you . . ." She hesitated for half a beat before her succulent mouth curved into a wicked smile. "By accident."

Nick caught a glimmer of simmering heat in Bria's faux-innocent big brown eyes. Heat that could drop an unsuspecting man at fifty paces. His gaze dropped to her mouth. No shiny red lipstick now, just natural, sweetly curved pink. Kissable. Delectable—

*Ah, shit.* The desire between them was tangible, but she'd made it clear that the teasing was one-sided. She'd drawn a line in the sand, and since the intense attraction he felt for her wasn't in any way logical, Nick wasn't going to cross it. A smart move. He had enough shit on his plate. More important, she was a guest on his ship.

She was in no danger from him unless she gave him the green light. His desire to leap across the table and screw her to the deck notwithstanding. He cupped the bowl of his wine glass, turning it idly between his fingers.

Who was the real Princess Gabriella Visconti? The genuinely concerned sister who'd do anything to get back her brother's investment? Or the sophisticate who knew how to deflect passion like a pro? Either the princess wasn't as experienced as her flirting led a man to believe, or she was playing a dangerous game.

It was fucking hard to stay on his toes when she'd had him off balance since they'd met.

Innocent or not, the image of Bria wielding a gun was erotic as hell. Picking up his glass, he leaned back. "I have a nine-millimeter Bersa in the safe. Know how to use it?"

"Yes," she said sweetly, as if she hadn't just finished telling him she could fire just about anything. "Thank you."

"Your bodyguard must have his hands full with you."

Bria let out a slow exhale, and the light dimmed in her far-too-expressive eyes. "Marvin died of a stroke four years ago. I miss him every day."

"Tough to lose a parent. No matter how old we are."

"He wasn't— Thank you. Yes, I considered him that way." She smiled. "Are you close to your parents?"

The loss of his own father hadn't been as cut-and-dried. A lot of resentment there. A hell of a lot of unresolved issues that would never be addressed. "Both died. My mother when I was a kid, my father a couple of years ago. Close to her, not as close to him." He drank some wine. "So, what do you do when you aren't a princess?"

She laughed softly, the sound like a warm caress over his skin. "I've been unemployed since my last company folded a year ago, but I have a job lined up. Not starting the new job immediately has turned out to be a blessing in disguise, because I'm sure they wouldn't like it if I went off for who knows *how* long to get Draven's situation handled. I'm supposed to start next week. This is an amazing opportunity with an international public relations company in Sacramento. I hope it'll be waiting for me when I get home."

She'd risked a dream job to save the country her brother seemed intent on ruining. "Princesses can't be that thick on the ground."

"I omitted that little detail from my résumé," she said ruefully. "Not much I can do about the situation from here; I'll deal with it when I get back." She nodded to the steaming hot tub. "When was the last time you sat in there and looked up at the stars?"

For a man who had no imagination, it was sure getting a workout tonight. Because the minute the words left her lips, Nick instantly got a Technicolor, 3D image of Bria floating naked in the water. He took a sip of icy wine. "A while."

"Thought so. I can't imagine you wasting your time stargazing."

True. "Want to go in?" And now he was back to imagining her naked. He shifted, suddenly uncomfortable. Again.

"Do you mind if I put my feet in?"

Why didn't she just offer to strap a dive tank to his ankles and toss him overboard? Trying to keep breathing normally in that situation would have been less difficult. She was wearing a strapless dress, a skimpy thong, and no bra.

He leaned over for the bottle and refilled his glass; hers was still full. Because all he could think of now was her peeling that scrap of a dress over her head . . . "Hmm."

His self-control eroded blink by blink, smile by smile. His fingers flexed in memory of cupping the firm cheek of her ass; a memory he did *not* need to be savoring. He lifted a hand, wordlessly offering her the hot tub, deck, table—fuck, the whole ship. She was tying him into a Gordian knot without even trying.

# Chapter 10

Bria jumped up from the table. Kicking off her shoes, she crossed the few feet to the hot tub, then sat down and dangled her legs in the hot water, humming a little as she made herself comfortable. She leaned back on her arms, which arched her back enough to showcase the delicate, feminine curves of her plump breasts.

Nick chugged half his wine. Didn't do a damned thing to cool him off or dull his libido. Diving overboard might be the only solution. "What was it like going home to Marrezo after all those years?"

"Good . . . Weird," she chuckled, which sent a vibration directly to his groin.

"Other than many of the buildings and the palace, nothing was the same. Pretty much everyone had fled when the terrorists arrived, with little more than the clothes on their backs. Homes had been abandoned.

"The men who took over the island weren't farmers, or vintners; they didn't do much of anything that we could see. For twenty years they drank to excess. When our people returned, they found literally thousands of booze bottles *everywhere*. And they partied, and shot the hell out of anything that stood still."

"How were the terrorists ousted?"

"I wish I could say Draven rode in on a white horse and saved the day. But that wasn't the case. They'd had squatters' rights for twenty years, and they just gradually moved away over the years until none of them were left. Eventually the few people brave enough to venture back contacted family and friends, and tried to resume their interrupted lives.

"Not just the country had changed. I'd changed. Draven had changed. He was barely thirteen the last time I saw him. It was a complete and wonderful shock to learn he was alive and well and back home about to be crowned."

"How did he find you?"

"Oh, he didn't," she looked over at him, and gave a little shoulder roll. "Nobody knew I was still alive either. Marvin made sure that I was hidden—safe. I heard about Draven's triumphant return in the news, and called the palace right away." She shot him a rueful look. "After a thorough fact-finding check, I was invited home for his coronation. It was . . . oh, just spectacular. The people were so happy to have the family back."

He tried to focus on her words, not on her smooth, bare legs and feet splashing lazily through the water. "And your brother? Was he happy to have his family back?"

"Of course. We both were—are. Getting used to the adult version has been a little odd," she confessed. "The last time I saw him he'd had a growth spurt, and he was taller than our father, but skinny." She smiled. "His ears used to stick out like a baby elephant's. I teased him unmercifully."

"Siblings usually do," he murmured. He found himself leaning forward, as if he wanted to get closer to her, and deliberately resettled in his chair.

Her breezy smile hinted at old sadness and it hit him like a punch in the chest. "Anyway, he's grown up," she said lightly, "and raised far from home. Being king after being gone so long must be incredibly difficult for him. He doesn't have much time leftover for family. I'm worried about his health. He's put on a dangerous amount of weight over the years. He's an insulin-dependent diabetic, and his blood pressure is through the roof . . ." She shrugged unhappily.

"He doesn't take good care of himself, and Dafne—I'm afraid she's going to love him to death."

"You can't lead someone else's life."

Not looking at him, her lips curved. "So true."

Nick turned in his chair, the better to watch her as she stared up at the sky. He didn't know what made him say it, but he found himself wanting to ease some of her obvious distress. "This salvage investment is going to pay off big, Bria. You don't need to be concerned that your brother will lose his investment."

"The money will be too late, I'm afraid. Unless Draven pays off the bank in thirty days, Marrezo reverts back to Italy."

She hesitated, clearly chewing over her next words, and he tilted his head. "What?"

"Well, to be honest," she mused, "I think he's so busy trying to make everything right, he gives the impression that he doesn't care. But I think that's just because he's so over-whelmed with everything he has to *fix* and change back to how it was. Before—"

Nick frowned. "Would it be a bad thing for the country to be absorbed back into Italy?"

She considered the concept for a moment, tilting her head back to look at the stars. It bared the line of her shoulders, glistening now as steam from the hot tub condensed across her olive skin. "Not precisely. It's just that Draven is throwing away the family legacy so foolishly without so much as a whisper of effort. We earned that land in the Crusades, and it's been held by a Visconti for twenty-five generations."

He could respect that. Legacies weren't always what they cracked up to be, but at least he and his brothers had inherited their father's love of the ocean along with Cutter Cay. "Would you go back and live there? Help run the place?"

"That was Marvin's dream for me," she said, raising one bare, gleaming foot from the water. It dripped as she wiggled her red-painted toes, light glinting from her delicate toe ring. "He spent years making sure I was equipped to do just that. But, no. I could only be the heir presumptive. If Draven had died in the massacre, our cousin Antonio would've been crowned."

"Good guy?"

"The best," she said immediately, and only the fact that she was talking about family kept Nick from suffering a sudden, irrational spike of jealousy. He covered it by retrieving a towel for her from the small cupboard beside the hot tub and tossing it to her.

"But my life isn't there anymore, anyway. I'm more American than Marrezan. Draven's wife and I don't exactly see eye to eye, either," she added wryly. "I want to help him untangle this mess he seems to have gotten into, but I don't see myself ever living there."

The hot water had warmed the peach scent of her skin, making it drift on the wisps of steam swirling around her and driving him half insane. Even though having sex with Bria out here was not going to happen for a multitude of excellent reasons, Nick turned his head to glance at the dimly lit windows of the nearby sunroom. Anyone inside could see them out here quite clearly. Which had been exactly his reason for having his staff set the table where it was.

He looked back at her. "Is it as financially unstable as you think?"

"I think it's worse," Bria said soberly. She crossed her ankles and lifted them slowly, watching the water drip off her feet. "Antonio is Minister of State. He's stayed in touch with me on the matter." She hesitated again, then sighed as she admitted, "This isn't the first crazy get-rich-quick scheme Draven's tried. It's about number five.

"The country was in dire straits when he took over two years ago, but Antonio swears that there was money secreted away, and that Draven should never have gone to the bank in the first place." She raked her hair off her face, clearly frustrated. The dark silky strands fell about her back and shoulders like a shiny black cape.

Where had the five mil come from? If it was a bank loan, Draven couldn't pay it back until his investment paid off. "So what's the issue?"

"In the last twenty *months,* my brother has been chipping away at Marrezo's funds at an alarming rate in an attempt to see his investments grow."

Nick knew this story all too well. "Let me guess," he interjected, hauling his chair closer to the tub. He sat again, leaning back and stretching his feet out, crossed at the ankle. A mere foot from where she perched on the edge.

She slanted him a wary glance.

"He's lost everything," Nick predicted.

"Investing with Cutter Salvage was a last-ditch effort. Just another scheme."

Nick shook his head, not liking what he was hearing. No wonder she was so damned eager to get the money back. "If he could go the distance, he'd recoup his investment sixfold," he told her. "Six hundred percent. This dive will pay out big." As every Cutter salvage usually did. He, Logan, and Zane researched their wrecks well. They left very little to guesswork. All their risks were calculated.

"But you said it'd be a year," she said softly.

Nick didn't have anything to say to that. There was nothing to say; the truth was the truth, and she knew it already. He drummed his fingers against his wineglass. "Do you think that if he's handed five million euro tomorrow, he'll use it to pay off the loan?" And have enough leftover to run his country until what? The vines started producing in seven years?

She was quiet for a long time. Then, her expression pensive, she lifted her troubled gaze to meet his. "I honestly don't know."

*       *       *

Despite his frosty demeanor, Nick was surprisingly easy to talk to. Perhaps because she'd shared very little of her background with her friends, who just knew her as Bria. That fiery unemployed Italian girl who was looking for a job.

She'd told Nick more about her life than she'd told another living soul. Nobody in Sacramento knew or cared that she'd once been a princess. And why should they? That wasn't who she was in California. It wasn't really who she was in Marrezo either.

And what had she found out about him? Nothing she didn't know already. He was good. He could have made it as a spy if he ever gave up salvaging shipwrecks.

She got up from the deck and grasped the towel beside her, careful to keep all the parts Nick had already touched covered. The dress, short enough, had to be tugged down to cover another inch of thigh.

The conversation had given her a glimpse, a *tiny* glimpse, into another part of Nick Cutter and she wasn't sure what to do about it. One thing was certain—she'd keep her lips to herself from now on. Stretched out, his hands clasped lightly on his flat belly, he looked the picture of relaxed. She, on the other hand needed to move. To do. *Something.*

She dried her legs and feet.

That testosterone poisoning thing . . . "I don't suppose you have a tennis court on board?" God only knew, the *Scorpion* had everything else.

He cocked a brow, not shifting from his languid stretch. "A fully stocked gym. But it's almost midnight, Princess. Bit late for exercise isn't it?"

Bria enjoyed a good, sweaty run when she was stressed, and she was *extremely* stressed. Wondering just where Nick intended for her to sleep tonight wasn't helping. A gym would be great. Sweating off the intense unwanted attraction she felt toward him before they went belowdecks would be greater.

It wasn't Nick and his intentions that bothered her. She was pretty sure he wouldn't force himself on her. Pretty sure.

It was herself she was worried about.

"Would you mind?" She asked because if she went there, he'd have to go too. She wasn't going anywhere alone until the killer was caught.

"Not at all." His easy acquiescence surprised her. "Let's go down and change."

They went down to his cabin. Her brightly colored pillows were stacked on the chair by the window. She couldn't ignore the bed, which had been turned down on both sides. Bria's heartbeat escalated, and she felt perspiration prickle her hairline. For a moment, her feet were stuck to the floor as her mind filled with images that made her hot and sweaty, her heartbeat racing alarmingly.

Oblivious, Nick went into his walk-in closet and came out carrying his clothes and a pair of tennis sneakers. "Aren't you changed yet?"

Bria scooped up shorts and a tank top and darted into the bathroom. For a moment she leaned against the closed door, her hand over her skittering heart.

This was going to be awkward and uncomfortable, and possibly embarrassing. For her. Clearly Nick didn't have a problem with any of this.

Fixing her hair into a ponytail to keep it off her neck, Bria came out of the bathroom wearing borrowed white shorts and a lime green top. On her feet, brand-new running shoes that had been delivered with the clothes.

Nick was nowhere in sight. The bed didn't look any less inviting now than it had three minutes ago. Her heart went into jogging mode and she hadn't even *stretched* yet.

"In here," Nick called from the other room. Bria went through to his office, found him waiting for her, dressed in black shorts and a ratty old gray T-shirt that stretched over his ripped torso like a glove. The sleeves had been torn off and exposed his biceps. This wasn't a man who got his killer body from gym workouts, though; those muscles came from exacting physical labor and hard work. Her tongue stuck to the roof of her mouth.

"Ready?"

Not even close. "Sure."

They took the stairs back up to the sundeck. They passed the media room. The door was open, the inside dark. The movie marathon was over. They were alone on the sundeck. Lovely, Bria thought, feeling a little panicky.

Nick pushed open one of a set of double doors and led the way into the gym, turning on the lights. It was state-of-the-art, with every conceivable piece of exercise equipment one could need or want. Several large flat-screen TVs hung strategically on three walls; the fourth was all glass that overlooked the helicopter pad and the water beyond. Now it reflected the two of them in a mirrored sheet of black.

"Pick your poison," he said, gesturing as if he offered her a banquet.

"Treadmill." There were two, side by side.

Nick turned on the TV and glanced over his shoulder. "Country road? Running track? City streets? What's your pleasure?"

A safe, quiet cabin all to herself. It was good to want things. "Country road." God, she'd never been this jittery, this hyperaware of a man, in her life. It was if she'd inhaled his pheromones and now her female antennae were fine-tuned to his frequency.

Silly. She knew nothing about the man. She wasn't even sure if she trusted him. She'd spilled her guts over dinner, and he'd barely shared a snippet about his own life. Was that his way of interrogating her in a social setting?

Yes, she thought, turning her nerves and trepidation about her sleeping accommodations into righteous indignation. That's *exactly* what he'd done.

His blasted boat. His blasted rules.

She did a few stretches. It didn't matter how long she ran, eventually she'd have to stop and go to bed. But for now, nobody was touching anybody else, and she could let her defenses take a well-earned rest as she tired her body, and recently awakened libido, out.

The image on the screen brightened to a bucolic, tree-lined dirt road, with fields on either side. The sky was blue, birds tweeted, and a light breeze kissed her face as soon as she stepped onto her treadmill. Cool. Very cool.

She warmed up slowly, then sped up to six miles per, passing two grazing cows and an oak tree. She was silent, focused on her breathing as she listened to the sound of bird-song and the thud-thud-thud-thud of her and Nick's sneakers hitting the rubber belts. She couldn't see him running beside her, but Bria was all too aware of him beside her, and if she shifted her gaze, she could see their reflection in the midnight black windows across the room.

Which was a quick way to earn herself some road rash. *Focus on your pace.*

After two miles, she was barely aware of him beside her; after five she almost forgot he was there. Somewhere around mile seven, she caught his reflection in the window as he pulled his T-shirt over his head while he ran. He used it to mop his face and chest, then tossed it on the floor.

Great, now she couldn't *not* watch him run with his shirt off. God. She was already hot and bothered, and seeing his muscled torso gleaming with sweat and his rock-hard six-pack shift with each pounding step made her light-headed. Bria forced her eyes back to the screen.

They ran up hills large and small, forded shallow streams, and ran across fields of yellow wildflowers, then met up again on the dirt road. All without a word.

Good. She'd spilled her guts enough for one night. Nick Cutter now knew more about her than anyone else on the planet.

It was an odd feeling.

She sucked in air as they rounded a bend. She was breathing hard, sweat pouring off her. She was running harder and faster than she was used to, and the killer pace was getting to her. The alternative—going back to that cabin, and the turned-down bed—made her speed up a little more. She pressed her palm against the sharp stitch in her side.

"That's enough." Nick's curt voice cut the companionable silence like a knife.

They'd run, flat-out, for well over an hour. Bria's shorts and tank were glued to her body, her hair was sticking to her sweaty face and neck, and she was breathing hard. Her heartbeat synced with her pounding footsteps. *Thud-thud-thud-thud.* "I'm. Good. To. Go."

Nick flipped a switch somewhere, and the peaceful country road, happy cows, and tweeting birds cut off mid-hill. He grabbed her arm to steady her as she stumbled at the sudden cessation of the visual. The treadmill was still moving.

Already annoyed at his domineering behavior and doubly so at being grabbed when she was hot and sweaty, Bria shook him off. His fingers slipped from her arm as she resumed the rhythm of her run.

Her temper, simmering since she'd left California and the prospect of a new job to fix her brother's mess, spiked. Unfulfilled sexual tension added a layer on top that she was finding unmanageable, to say the least.

"I . . . usually . . . run . . . for . . . two . . . hours," she huffed. Mostly because she'd been unemployed and trying not to end up weighing seven hundred and two pounds from eating all day.

"And I usually run for none," Nick told her, rubbing his face and hair with a white towel. "Time's up, Princess. It's late. Let's go to bed."

Exactly her point for running like a madwoman in the middle of the night. But in case he hadn't gotten it yet—"I'm . . . not . . . sleeping . . . with . . . you!"

"Who has energy for sex after you wiped the floor with me?"

She knew *she* hadn't—he was barely perspiring and he wasn't panting. Both of which she was.

"I still have running energy in me," she panted, putting on a little more speed, but she was flagging and she knew it. Could have, *should* have stopped fifteen minutes ago.

That cool, not quite condescending tone of his bugged the hell out of her. She'd be damned if she gave in just because he told her to. "Go ahead and go down," she said between breaths. "I'll be fine."

Bria got that there was a killer on board, she got the sense in not being anywhere alone until the man was caught. She got it. Got it. Got it. But at this stage of the game, she'd almost rather fight off a determined attack—which she knew how to handle—than deal with Nick Cutter's chilly attitude, which she didn't.

He was a freaking ice-capped volcano. A dormant one.

All stone and hard edges on the outside, nothing but molten lava underneath. Not quite still enough to be empty, not nearly emotional enough to erupt.

He confused her, aroused her, and frigging *annoyed* her. She couldn't figure him out and was too emotionally drained to try. And she sure as hell didn't want to test that leashed control in his bed.

She was a pressure cooker ready to blow. Nerves. Stress. Yes, fear too. If he just didn't touch her, she could try to get a grip on the roller-coaster emotions she was feeling.

He didn't share her reserve. Without warning, he grabbed her around the waist and hoisted her clear off the treadmill. She gave a little scream of surprise.

"Time's up." The machine stopped as he swung her out of the way of the controls and set her on her feet.

The muscles in her legs vibrated, and her heart pounded hard enough for her entire body to shake. Between one manic heartbeat and the next she realized she'd been hanging on by a thread all day. Him grabbing her like that—him touching her when her antennae were already short-circuiting, kicked her over the edge. Her outburst after he'd damn well locked her in his cabin all freaking day hadn't done anything to relieve her overall tension.

Dinner had lulled her into a false sense of thinking that she had the upper hand.

This wasn't the first time today that she'd felt out of control and so furious she could chew nails.

The man was infuriating!

She. Just. Lost it.

With a shriek of outrage, a surge of adrenaline, she lunged at him. "Don't tell me what to do!" Balling up her fist, she punched at the wide target of his chest as hard as she could, so angry she couldn't see straight.

He rotated sideways, just enough to make sure all she hit was the outside curve of his arm.

"Calm down," he said coolly, his voice soothing enough to pump up her fury by 20 percent. "You're going to hurt yourself."

Bria dashed her forearm across her mouth, wiping away the sweat on her face. And gave him a hot look that should've melted him to the carpet. "I'm going to hurt *you, figlio di troia*!" She hit him again; this time her fist skated off his gleaming shoulder. It was rock-hard. Her knuckles stung, which made her madder still. She danced around him, fists raised like a boxer.

"Stop bullying me!" Jab. "And man—" Punch. "—Handling—" A Thai kick to his ribs had his eyebrows winging upward. "—Me!" she finished, all but frothing as her temper spilled out like the volcano she'd silently accused him of being. "Go to hell, you—you *estupido*!"

She went for a knee to his groin. He shifted out of the way, and his blue eyes turned molten. Ignoring every danger sign on his face, she hauled back a foot and kicked his shin.

He flinched this time, as the tread on her sneakers rasped against his bare leg. "Gabriella, s*top*." His hand shot out—Oh, God, she'd pushed him too far!—but instead of a blow, he merely placed his palm in the middle of her forehead so she couldn't get any closer.

Her momentary fear flipped to another spike of fury. *"Callate el osico, gordota,"* she spat, struggling to reach him, arms swinging.

Nick suddenly laughed. "Shut your snout, fatty? Is that the best you can come up with?"

Her mouth opened and then closed. "You don't like my insults? How about this?" She swung for him. Everything Marv had taught her went out the window. Everything. Particularly the discipline.

Nick damn-him-Cutter had frozen that right out of her.

She saw herself, crazy and out of control, and it scared her that Nick—God *anyone*—could make her forget herself and be *this* angry. The hard pressure of impending tears built up behind her eyes. *Calm down. Calm down.* Damn it, she'd rather hit him than let him see her cry.

Her emotions had nowhere to go, and his stiff-armed stance—his control when she couldn't corral her own—infuriated her. No matter how she shifted to get out of his way, how she tried to get close enough to his body to maim him, she couldn't budge that impersonal hand on her forehead. She sank her nails into his strong wrist. That didn't move him. She tried kicking, but her toe just missed.

Already exhausted beyond her ability to get a grip on her emotions, Bria only kept trying to grab him, hit him, kick him. She needed, she needed . . .

His eyes measured her, his reach keeping her at arm's length. She gave a hoarse cry of anger and frustration. "You make me furious!"

The idea didn't seem to bother him any, as he said calmly, "I see that."

Bria dropped her arms, then stood there panting, her forehead braced by Nick's palm, tears stinging behind her lids. It was all he needed. In a lightning-fast move, he grabbed her around the waist, hauled her tightly back against his chest and carried her across the large gym.

Even more enraged at the assault, Bria fought him every step of the way. "Put me down! Damn it, Nick, I'm warning you—"

She dug her nails into the steel band of his forearm, which was cutting off her breathing and holding her immobile against the solid, implacable wall of his chest. She was helpless, and she *hated it*. Tears of fury ran down her cheeks and into her mouth.

Crying made her even madder.

He kicked open a door, and she shot out her foot, wedging it against the doorjamb to prevent him from hauling her inside. Logic, reason, just barely managed to find a place inside her head. "Whatever you have in min—"

He twisted his body, wrenching her sideways so her foot lost contact with the frame, and carried her, kicking and screaming, into the dark room. A wedge of light streamed through from the gym, but she wasn't looking at the freaking *décor* as he hauled her inside.

"Whatever it is! I won't do it!" *Whatever it is.* "Do you hear me? I. Will. Not. Do—"

He kicked the door closed with a loud thud, leaving them in complete, disorienting darkness.

No amount of writhing and bucking dislodged his firm grip around her waist. He carried her like a— Like a bag of *cat food!* "Let me g—"

The sudden sound of rushing water surrounding them cut her off as if it were a gunshot. He was going to force her under an ice-cold shower to calm her down? *As if.* Bria got a new surge of mad, and fought harder.

Without warning, she was dropped to her feet and swung around. "Stop manhandling m— Oomph!" Unsettled, her back met a cool, wet wall, and her teeth snapped together between one word and the next.

His mouth came down, finding hers unerringly in the pitch blackness.

# Chapter 11

Despite the dark, a red mist swam before Nick's eyes and his whole body seemed to expand as he blindly pressed Bria back against the wall of the steam shower. The enveloping heat released the hot, ripe peach scent of her; the same damn scent that had filled his brain all day, taunted his libido, and teased his own dormant temper.

This fiery Italian princess drove him bat-shit crazy, and Nick wanted her more than his cool, rational, Scorpio brain could handle. It was all too fucking much. The Moroccans, the Greeks, the diamonds, and the killers. Her. The wanting and not taking. The needing and not having.

The playing it safe and sticking to a game plan. Only he'd never planned on *her.*

"You have two seconds to tell me no," he told her, barely recognizing the thickness of his own voice. "After that, all bets are off." He'd thought sensory deprivation might calm her down. He'd had no idea how it would do the exact opposite to him.

Well, fuck—

Yeah. Well, *fuck.*

He wanted to rip off her shorts and have her right there, right then, standing against the wall of the steam room. Instead he kissed her as he'd been itching to do all day, while he waited for her answer. His tongue flicked against hers, and when he deepened the kiss because—Christ, how could he not?—her lips clung. Her nails not so gently scored his chest as she shifted against his imprisoned erection.

He used his teeth and his tongue on her mouth, and he skimmed his hand up under her skimpy tank top. Her skin was hot, damp and impossibly soft as he cupped the plump mound of her breast and rubbed his thumb over the hard peak through the thin wet lace of her bra. She moaned.

"One," Nick rasped, his voice hoarse.

"That's what you think," Bria said fiercely. She combed her fingers through his hair. She kissed him back, fiery and ferocious, giving no quarter and expecting none in return. Her response detonated a bomb inside his chest, making his heart thud and his dick so hard it hurt to breathe. Fuck it, he didn't need to breathe.

"No, Princess." Nick curved his palm around her damp breast, shoving the lace cup of her bra aside so he could feel the soft weight, the satin skin in his palm. The hard pebble of her nipple pressed into the center of his hand. And when he pinched it between his fingers she flung her head back gasping for air. "That's what I know."

The sweet smell of steam didn't mask the heady fragrance of her arousal. The muscles in her neck flexed as she swallowed. "You can count until you turn blue in the face, Cutter. I don't like being told what to do. By anyone," she snapped, even as she shuddered against him.

Nick kissed her sweaty throat, her jaw. He took his hand out from under her shirt to yank the clingy, damp fabric over her head, then unerringly found the front clasp of her bra and freed her breasts.

He wanted to see her naked, but Jesus—feeling her half naked in the darkness was almost more than he could bear. "I can't stand hysterical women," he shot back. Pressing her breasts together. He feasted on one taut nipple and then the other. She tasted of salted peach.

The soft, sexy sound she made low in her throat was breathlessly needy. She arched her back, pressing herself to his mouth. Everything male in him responded to her feminine cry.

His body radiated heat, perspiration ran off his skin and sheened hers, so that their bodies were all but glued together. Worked for him. His teeth found an interesting cord on her throat, which made her wriggle and arch against him as he bit down around it.

"You forgot to count," she gasped triumphantly.

Nick hadn't forgotten. "Two," he said tightly, and she moaned as if he'd done more than just seal the next few minutes. Hours. Hell, it wouldn't be nearly enough.

"You make me absolutely *furious*," she whispered roughly, her nails scoring his back.

"I know what I make you. Hot and bothered." His voice wasn't as cool as he wanted. He rocked against her, skimmed his hand around to the waistband of her shorts. Found the button, slid down the zipper. He remembered what her thong had felt like earlier, bits of ribbon and sheer nothing—God.

"Oh, please!" She bit his lower lip. "Don't." Licked the sting, then bit harder. Then punctuated each word with a stinging bite wherever her mouth could reach. "Flatter. Yourself. I. Just Spent. An hour running flat-out! I am *not* attract—"

He slid his hand into the V of her open shorts, felt the delicate fabric of her thong, and the soft nest of curls hidden beneath the thin barrier. He pushed the thong aside and touched her humid heat. Soft, slick, responsive.

Bria pulled her sharp teeth away from his shoulder to hum deep in her throat. After several seconds of frozen anticipation, her hand slid down, and her questing fingers found his zipper. It took awhile to release him; he was painfully rigid, making liberation difficult for both of them.

She was as wet as he was hard.

"Liar," he said, smiling against her mouth, then kissed her hard again. Like him, she didn't wait to shove his shorts down and off. She pushed her hand into the available space. Her fingers closed around him, and Nick jerked with intense pleasure. Need, lust, *want* gnawed at his nerve endings like teasing licks of flame.

"I am not helpless."

"Thought never crossed my mind." He slid his fingers into her wet mound, and in response her slender hand wrapped around him, gripped even tighter as she gasped and arched.

It was as good an invite as he could've hoped. He teased his way inside the damp seam, slick with her juices. Nick's thumb glided over her clit, finding the places that made her shudder and whimper.

"Two-second warning's up," he said from between clenched teeth, her busy fingers driving him to mindless distraction.

He felt the start of her climax ripple as her internal muscles clenched around his fingers. Her orgasm shuddered through her, around his fingers, filled the steamy air with her musky fragrance as she arched off the wall, pressing against his hand, her sharp white teeth clamped down on his chest.

Her fire fueled his ice-melt. Need clawed at him as steam swirled invisible ghostly fingers around them.

"You don't play fair," Bria panted, already half gone on a second orgasm. He slid another, then a third finger inside her tight sheath, and her body clamped on, holding him there where she needed him. He used his thumb and brought her to another hard and fast climax.

It pissed him off that he wanted her so much that he'd lost control somewhere along the way. Everything she did ratcheted that need and made his lack of control worse. "Who says I'm playing?"

This might take the gnawing edge off, but it would never be enough to satisfy the lust that intensified every time he touched her, hell, every time he looked at her.

He licked her salted-peach throat, then nibbled across her jaw as he shoved down his shorts and boxers one-handed, kicked them away. Then he tackled what was left of Bria's clothing, yanking down her shorts with one hand and bringing her to another small climax with the other.

"More," she demanded, sliding both hands around his waist, curving her palms over his flexing ass, and digging in her nails to pull him closer.

\*     \*     \*

"More what?"

Water pounded tile, sending up droplets of warm spray against her ultrasensitive skin. Not that Bria could see where the water was coming from, surrounded as she was by steamy blackness. Nick's large, hard, very naked body pinned her against the wall, his breath hot at her ear. "More what, Princess?"

She could barely manage a shuddering, "Mmm."

"More of this?" He ran his teeth not so gently down the arch of her throat. "Or this?" He flexed his fingers inside her.

From the cleft of her body, where his fingers moved, to her very soul—the next climax rolled through her like a tidal wave.

*"Yes,"* she panted, unable to catch her breath. Not letting go of the firm globes of his ass, she used a little pressure from her extended arm to hold his hand more firmly against her where she needed more than his damned fingers.

He was torturing her with his attention to detail, when she needed it hard and fast and *now,* damn it.

Closing her eyes was the trick to finding her balance in the onslaught of sensory overload. The forced darkness made everything more intense. And her heart was pounding so hard with anticipation she barely heard the driving pulse of the water.

His teeth raked across her lower lip, then bit. Before she could figure out if that'd hurt or not, his tongue swept inside her mouth, and for several minutes he kissed her with bruising force. Her heart skittered, not with fear, but with unbridled lust. She whimpered, a harsh sound of need, and her arms tightened around his waist. Her fingers flexed on the hard muscles of his ass.

His penis was a hard, urgent length against her thigh, and she tried to shift her hips and legs to accommodate him.

He didn't comply. No matter how she shifted and twisted, he focused only on kissing her—drugging, incendiary kisses that chased every rational thought clear out of her brain and left it as dark as the room they were in.

Only when she was gasping for breath, a low moan caught in her throat, did he lift his head, leaving her lips wet and throbbing. Wanting more. "Did you think your temper would turn me off, Princess?" His words were cool. Ironic.

*Infuriating.*

"Don't—" *Call me princess.* She swallowed the words before they escaped, even knowing that from him, it was a derogatory term. And right then she needed something less combative. Less angry. All Nick. She tried for reason, even though rational thoughts seemed light-years out of her reach. "I lose my temper sometimes." The taut muscles she was holding flexed enticingly. "It wasn't personal."

He pushed an inch away from her to run a string of burning kisses down the middle of her throat. "I think you're wrong. I think it was *very* personal." His voice vibrated against her skin as his open mouth moved down her arched throat. His cool silky hair tickled her collarbone as his lips skimmed the upper swell of her breast. "I think you had your little meltdown to hold me at arm's length because I wouldn't accept your charming offer." She sucked in a breath to argue, only to lose it on a strangled sound as he added, "Which bruised your ego."

"I didn't—!"

His lips closed over her nipple, and she jerked in response. Bria's hands fell away from his behind and skated up his sides—he shuddered—up his chest—he jerked—and slid over his shoulders. He sucked the hard point of her nipple into the hot cavern of his mouth and swept his tongue over the puckered peak.

Bria grabbed his hair, her fingers fisting in the strands. Her back arched away from the wall as he used his teeth to score a shuddering reaction from her that coursed through her body with liquid heat.

"Talk about ego," she managed. She had to pause to drag in a shuddery draft of steamy air as his thumb found her clitoris and his fingers went impossibly deeper. She stood on her toes to lessen the impact.

It didn't help. Not at all. "I d-didn't make any offers." It came out less sure as she tugged at his hair to relieve some of the unbearably exquisite sensation on her breast. He licked and kissed and brushed his evening beard against her hyper-sensitive breast, molding it, shaping it to his hand like a master sculptor.

He sucked hard and her knees went weak. Her head thumped on the wall as she tried to regain her equilibrium, but she was under sensory assault.

"A woman can ki—" His mouth moved to the other breast, Bria combed her fingers through his hair, holding. Wanting. Craving. "Stop it," she insisted, but it was only a ragged sound. She struggled to shape the words. "A woman can kiss . . . a man and not have to . . . fall all over herself to go to b-bed with him!"

His free hand slid around her waist to mimic what she'd been doing moments before. His strong fingers clamped on her ass cheek as he trailed a fiery, nibbling, licking, path down the center of her sensitized body. "You weren't the one to say no, darling."

She felt the heat of his breath against her damp mound, and saw sparklers and fireworks as he twisted his fingers inside her. He inhaled deeply, and she knew he was smelling her. Her arousal, her need.

She swallowed hard. "I said no, *tesoro*," she told him, barely able to stand, let alone talk. "I said no very firmly."

"You said no, but your body said yes."

"Ha! Well, now I'm clearly saying yes. And my body is saying hell, yes, too. How perfect is that for everybody? What are you going to do about it?"

His laugh puffed his hot breath against her belly. Then she felt the warm wet glide of his tongue licking a straight line from her navel down into the damp curls at the juncture of her thighs.

"I think," he said, his voice muffled but still strong as he sank to his knees in front of her, "that you—God, you taste like hot peach pie." His voice was low and more vibration than sound. His stiff tongue found her swollen clit and sucked until Bria nearly leaped out of her skin.

"Please—" There was nowhere to go, nowhere to run. She closed her hands over her breasts and squeezed as he slowly withdrew his fingers. Her body protested, clamping down hard. She moaned low in her throat. Her hands tightened over her own breasts, pinching her nipples between her fingers as a hard shuddering ripple started at the epicenter and started traveling though her body with tsunami speed. Need clawed at her.

"Please what?" she heard, his breath warm against her damp curls.

"Nick, just . . . *Please*." She reached down to tug at his hair. But he was happy where he was, and wasn't about to be motivated to move anywhere else.

And if she had to wrap it up, here and now, she knew that was the most infuriating thing about Nick Cutter. He did what he wanted, when he wanted. After *slow* deliberation.

He was all about the journey, and damn it, Bria wanted to *be* there already.

He stroked his tongue inside her, made a humming sound that electrified every nerve in her body. She put her hands on either side of his face and pulled. Finally, his head lifted, leaving the warm hot center of her body cold. "Too much," she told him brokenly, barely able to breathe with the intensity. "Later . . ."

He said nothing.

He slid his wet mouth up her sweat-slicked, steam-drenched wet body, his hands and teeth driving her mad. "Nick—" Her lips sought his, and she tasted herself on his mouth, which spiked her temperature even higher.

He lifted his head, close enough that she still felt his hot breath on her damp skin. "I think you're used to poor fools falling at your royal feet." His voice was thick, and for a moment Bria had no clue what he was talking about, or why he was talking at all, for that matter.

"I think no man in your life has ever had the audacity to

look behind those innocent big brown eyes, and know just how devious that quick mind of yours really is." His voice was far from steady now, and a long, long way from cold.

Bria slid her hands up his slick wet chest, enjoying the tickle of his crisp hair, and the tensile strength of his satin smooth skin pulled taut over muscles tight with tension. She put her mouth against his jugular, where she could feel the frantic throb of his pulse.

"Every move you make is calculated to drive a man insane." His voice was low and harsh, his skin vibrating beneath her lips with every breath. Every word. "Your eyes say fuck me, and your mouth says stay the hell away."

"I'm leaning toward *do me* right now," Bria managed on a broken laugh, a hairsbreadth from imploding. "You still seem to be having an issue with it. How about if we analyze this after we're done?"

"Who's to say when we're done?" He closed both hands on her hips, pulling her against his erection. The pressure there straddled a line between pain and pleasure. His fingers skimmed down her thigh and he scooped his palm under her leg, pulling her against him. But he still wasn't inside her where she wanted, needed, him. "You're playing with fire, Gabriella."

"Yeah?" she arched against him. "Show me your fire, Mr. Spock. Double dare you." Bria's smile was replaced by a gasp as he jerked his hips and plunged inside her to the hilt.

She shattered instantly, her cry echoing through the steam. Nick went still.

It took her a wild, frenetically charged moment to regain her sense of self. And realize he still hadn't moved. "I need a minute," she managed thickly.

Really she did. It was only the delicious weight of him pinning her against the cool wall that kept her upright, because she was utterly boneless. Every climax had rolled through her like an express train on a never-ending loop. One after the next until she was limp.

"Time's up," he said immediately, making her laugh weakly.

"That wasn't even a second."

He rubbed his chin on the top of her head. It was both soothing and maddening, especially since she could feel his body trembling with leashed tension. He dipped his head to nuzzle her ear. "Are you still pissed off?"

She shook her head slightly, and that alone was a tremendous effort.

"I've never met a woman who sheds anger as fast as you do."

He didn't sound annoyed. Bria smiled against his shoulder. "It's a gift." She licked salt off his skin, then took a little bite because as exquisite as his lovemaking was, she didn't like being kept waiting that long.

He jerked, causing his body to leap inside hers, and rested his forehead against her own. "You know that thing about never being taken to a second location?"

"What are you going to do? Kill me?" Her voice sounded languid and husky. All the temper had been pleasured out of her. She rested her cheek on his chest as her internal muscles contracted around his penis.

The sound he made wasn't a word.

"It'll be easy," she murmured, brushing her lips across his collarbone. The hard length of his penis moved eagerly within her, yet he made no move to change positions. Merely wrapped his free arm around her and stroked her hair.

"Nothing's easy with you," he told her.

"Well, I can't move," Bria said lazily. Well, she couldn't move outside. Inside, her body was still pulsing and throbbing and contracting around the part of him he had buried deep inside her.

*"La petite mort,"* he murmured against her temple.

She smiled, turning her face against his chest and inhaling the salty male fragrance of his hot skin. "The little death? Sounds about right."

When his chest moved, an amused sound easing out with a breath, Bria's eyes widened. Had Nick Cutter just *laughed*? "It's a horizontal surface."

She didn't have spare energy to frown her confusion. "What is?"

"That second location."

She liked the sound of that. "Soft?"

His fingers slid around her chin, trapping her face still for his lips to glide once more over hers. Firm, teasing. Tempting. "Best I can do is a wood bench," he said.

"We could go downstairs . . ."

He kissed her again, this time harder and more urgently, reminding her why leaving the steam room wasn't in the cards. He was still inside her when he carried her across the room, still inside her as he followed her down onto a horizontal surface, still inside her when she convulsed, and screamed his name.

She didn't notice how hard the *bench* was.

# Chapter 12

Bria came out on deck, Jonah at her side. She wore white shorts that exposed the long tanned length of her spectacular legs, and a purple top that bared her shoulders. Every movement she made was naturally seductive, and the guys all turned to admire the view.

Doesn't bother me, Nick thought, glad his eyes were covered with sunglasses. Let them look their fill. He was the man who'd kissed, licked, and tasted every inch of that view for hours. He'd made love to her in the steam room several times, in the gym with all the lights on, and again when they'd managed to drag themselves downstairs. They'd fallen into bed, sworn they didn't have an ounce of strength left, and then she'd touched him or he'd touched her . . .

His entire body clenched in anticipation of doing it again.

Miles and Mikhail had just pulled up onto the dive platform, and Bria went over to greet them. Olav, suiting up to go in with Burke, offered to show her what was in the bins. He watched her face light with interest.

Miles scaled the ladder to take her over to the tubs and gave Nick an absent wave, all his focus on the princess.

She peered into the plastic bins filled with seawater and loaded with artifacts to send back to Cutter Cay. Murmuring to Miles, asking questions, totally attentive to the man's answers. It was a knack Nick supposed came from her PR experience. His team ate up her attention.

Looking up, she shaded her eyes. "Did you find anything interesting today?" she called out. Miles and Mikhail hauled their baskets up onto the dive platform.

"Some pretty good stuff," Olav yelled back, giving a big friendly smile. Which she returned, bright and warm and so filled with delight that Nick stared for a moment. When Bria smiled, people automatically smiled back. It was like a chain reaction.

"We'll show you. Give us a minute here."

Nick took a soda out of the cooler and exchanged a serious look with his friend. He cocked an inquiring brow.

Jonah shook his head. Nothing untoward had happened between him fetching her from Nick's cabin, and the trip down to the main aft deck, where the dive platform was located.

In fact, Nick thought, grabbing a chair in the shade and stretching out his legs, nothing untoward had happened in the last twenty-four. They were still no closer to finding out who the killer or killers were.

Other than a missing body, two killers on the loose, a sexy princess screwing with his equilibrium, yeah, Nick thought—everything had pretty much returned to the natural rhythm of the salvage. Dive in teams, catalog and photograph what they brought to the surface, and pack everything away to preserve the coins and artifacts until they got home to Cutter Cay.

They'd already recovered a king's ransom in gold and silver bars and coins, some valuable pewter flatware, and some very nice jewelry, mostly gold and emeralds. Olav and Nick had found a conglomerate-encrusted sword a few days ago, covered with precious stones. Valuable and more important to Nick were the ancient artifacts they salvaged. Like the medical kit. The historical value, the understanding of the past, was more valuable to Nick than money. Because anyone who didn't understand the past was doomed to repeat it.

His father had issues with impulse control. He'd wanted. He'd partaken. Daniel Cutter hadn't learned from history how that affected those around him. He'd made the same mistakes over and over again because he couldn't keep his dick in his pants. He'd ruined his marriage and fucked up the happy life his three sons had deserved and had a right to expect.

Nick watched Bria throw back her head and laugh at one of Burke's stupid jokes. *Thank God he had a firmer grip on his impulses.*

Jonah looked out over the water. "*Sea Witch* gone?"

"Looks like," Nick told him absently, watching Bria's easy rapport with his dive team. "As far as I can tell, she didn't get away with anything too valuable this time."

"Woman's a menace," Jonah muttered, referring, Nick presumed, to their nemesis the *Sea Witch*, not Bria. "What are you going to do about tomorrow's drop?" he asked, following Nick's gaze as he watched Bria describing something to the guys, her hands flashing as she talked.

She'd been strung tight the night before. Nick leaned back in his chair, cupping the back of his head in both hands as he stretched out his legs. Her easy laughter made his gut clench. But then her temper seemed to have the same effect on him.

It had been quick to ignite, yet just as quick to disappear.

This morning when he'd left her to dive, she'd been her normal cheerful self. And eager and enthusiastic to make love again when they'd woken to find themselves wrapped around one another like they were on a sinking raft.

Bria accepted a tube of sunblock, and ordered Miles to turn around so she could smear his back with the white lotion. Idiot was beet-red, would peel, would burn again, and the cycle would continue. He imagined her hands, slippery with lotion on his back. His front . . .

"Yo? Nick? Tomorrow flying to Las Palmas for a drop-off?" Laughter laced Jonah's words. "I understand the princess is poetry in motion, and all things delectable, but would y—"

"That sword is secure," Nick cut him off, then sent his

friend a sharp look. "Don't get any ideas. She's taken for the moment."

"Pissing in corners are we?" Jonah raised a brow. "Alrighty, then. Warning unnecessary, but heeded loud and clear." He took two chilled bottles of water out of the cooler and tossed one to Nick, who caught it without looking.

Popping the cap, Jonah drank deeply, his eyes on Bria laughing and joking and looking hot enough to tempt the Pope. "Not that you want to hear my thoughts on the matter, but do you think that was wise? She could've been sent to distract you by the Moroccans, right?"

"If that's the case, then their fiendish plot can be considered a success," he answered, sounding as unconcerned as he felt. Mikhail checked out Bria's cleavage as she bent over to look at whatever Levine was showing her. Nick felt an unfamiliar, completely irrational surge of . . . What the hell?

*Jealousy?*

*This* was a first.

He glanced at Jonah, then shook his head when his friend grinned. He'd lost his mind, and they both knew it.

He chugged the cold water, then chased it with the rest of his soda. "It was worth entertaining the thought, but honestly? I just don't believe that's the case anymore. We talked at length last night. She has a job waiting for her back in the States. A life there. It would be a real stretch to imagine she has anything to do with the Moroccans a world away. She just happened to be in the wrong place and the wrong time, is all."

"Fair enough. But that doesn't explain Halkias's attack."

"Only two logical reasons come to mind. One—it was a random act of violence because she's female. The other, less savory reason, would be that it's because she happened to be in the medina that day, and someone doesn't want a witness to that meeting."

"All the more reason to get her off the ship." Jonah pointed out.

"I hear you. As soon as I can. Trust me." Nick folded his arms on the table. He didn't like being told what to do on his own ship. Didn't like it at all. It was only a few more days, though. In the meantime, he'd enjoy what time they had together.

"She's like Chinese water torture. A man can only take so much before he cracks."

"I'll jump in and save your ass if I think you're going down a second time."

"Don't!" he said tersely. He'd go down a second, a third, hell a fourth time. Until she was writhing and squirming and—

Hell. "The jewelry, sword, and pewter aren't going anywhere," Nick finished, and went back to Jonah's original question. He was scheduled to take the chopper to Las Palmas to send some of the more valuable pieces to Cutter Cay by courier. The rest of the bins and their contents would remain on board for the duration.

And in the hold, millions of dollars' worth of uncut blood diamonds were almost undetectable, hidden in plain sight in water, in the plastic tubs stacked ten-deep. But he wasn't going to make that trip this week. Aries had maintained radio silence. Nick had to sit tight, nobody on or off the *Scorpion* until further notice. The fact that they'd roughly estimated his treasure's worth at around three million bucks was immaterial.

But since they had millions of dollars' worth of uncut stones on board, right now the find was just another number.

"Aries wants us to stay put," he mused. He didn't like the thought of Bria staying any longer than she had to on a ship where people were trying to kill her. It was ludicrous. Dangerous. And exactly the point. He'd ferret them out. "It can wait a day or two."

Bria climbed up the ladder, nimble as the sprinter she was. All that running she did showed in the long lean muscles of her truly spectacular legs, displayed to perfection by the white shorts. She smiled at them both as she approached the table. "Burke and Olav invited me to go down with them." She gave him a challenging look. "Do you have a problem with that?"

"Jonah doesn't want to dive." He gave her a pointed look. Himself or Jonah. Those were the only two options. Jonah was captain this morning, and had dressed the part in his whites.

In all honesty, his friend loved to dive and took every opportunity presented to him when he wasn't running the *Scorpion*. But Jonah would forgive him this one. "I'll take you."

She looked at Jonah, who put up both hands and schooled his features, but Nick knew the interplay between himself and the only woman on board amused the living shit out of his pal.

"I can't dive this morning," Jonah assured her, struggling not to smile.

Nick glanced at his friend. "Don't you have a ship to run?"

Jonah saluted. "I do. I absolutely do. Gotta run and do important ship shit."

Bria turned big brown eyes on Nick, her lips curving in a smile that wriggled its way into his chest like a burr. "Then I guess you're the designated diver."

He swung his legs off the chair and got to his feet. "Let's go find you a suit." He figured they'd both be head-to-toe in wet suits, tanks, masks, flippers. Cold water. An hour when he'd be forced to concentrate on something other than how she tasted. "Ever dived?" he asked as he escorted her to their—*his* cabin and waited while she found a swimsuit in his dresser in a drawer he was sure had held some of his old T-shirts.

She had a handful of red as she headed to the bathroom to change. "I've had lessons, and gone down maybe half a dozen times on vacations."

"Why're you leaving?" he asked, leaning against the doorjamb between his office and bedroom. The room still smelled of sex, the bed invitingly rumpled with the covers and sheet thrown to the floor from their morning marathon. "I've already seen every delectable inch of you."

She shot him an arch look. "Because when you see my inches, you get distracted, and when *you* get distracted, *I* get distracted. And I'd really like to dive," she finished demurely, making him laugh.

"Don't happen to have your PADI dive book with you, do you?" he teased. She was probably exaggerating her experience by half, but they wouldn't stay down long, and since he'd be watching her like a hawk as it was, might as well do it underwater.

"It's in my other purse," she shouted, going into the bathroom and firmly shutting the door. "I'll give it to you later."

Nick shook his head, feeling as light and dizzy as if he'd inhaled helium.

Carrying a towel over her shoulder and wearing what, on any other woman, would be a modest red one-piece swimsuit, Bria looked mouthwatering. On her the simplicity of the garment only served to showcase, well, *everything*. The high swell of her breasts, the curve of her waist and hips, and her long, long golden brown legs.

Nick found himself torn between praying Aries's call would come through soon—and praying that it didn't.

They went down to the dive platform. The sound of the blower, moving the sand below, was loud enough to make hearing difficult. A slight, hot breeze danced across the sunlit surface of the water as Nick chose suitable gear. "We'll do a circuit of *El Puerto* and I'll show you some of the artifacts we've yet to bring up."

She smiled. "Awesome."

He walked her through a safety check, explaining the gear and making sure she knew how the respirator, goggles, and buoyancy compensator worked, then handed her a wet suit. She pulled the black neoprene over her red bathing suit and it hugged every delectable curve like a second skin.

"You're going to need a weight belt," he said matter-of-factly, eyeing her slender body form analytically to judge what weight she'd need. His dick eyed her form with a completely different agenda.

Pulling a belt from the gear storage, Nick pulled four of the small bullet-shaped weights off it with a little more force than necessary, and readjusted the buckle to fit her snugly. Circling his arms around her waist, he lifted the heavy belt over her hips, which required that he touch her. And even though it was in the mid-eighties, and the sun beat down on the deck, she shivered and slanted him a heated look.

He raised a knowing eyebrow. "Something the matter, Princess?" She was so beautiful she hurt his eyes.

Amusement flickered as she shook her head. "Tell me what we're going to see down there."

"First finish suiting up." He set up her BC, fitted with tank and regulator, in front of her. "Follow my lead, grab it, swing it up over your head, then put your arms through and latch the buckles."

She eyed him with a wry glance. "I've dived before," she reminded him.

Nick slung his BC into place. "*El Puerto* was on her way back to Cadiz from Cartagena and Potosi with tons of gold and silver and precious stones."

Bria huffed as the heavy BC and tank landed on her back, but her eyes lit up at the prospect of gold, silver, and gemstones. They'd be a lot brighter if she saw what the *Scorpion* was storing in the hold. "Was she caught in a storm?"

"Battle with a Portuguese warship." The black neoprene hugged her body from neck to ankle. Extremely distracting.

"Ah. A battle at sea. Exciting stuff."

"*Terrifying* way the hell and gone out here. I'll show you the cannon from both *El Puerto* and the Portuguese galleon *São Juan Poinsat*. They're practically side by side, which has made this salvage fascinating. Ships fought close together then, and the captain of *El Puerto* probably lashed the ships together as they tried to do in those days, so his soldiers could board and fight hand-to-hand."

"They sank together?"

"Yeah. *El Puerto* due to half a dozen direct hits from the *São Juan Poinsat*'s cannonballs," he explained. "I'll show you where they hit. The ships probably struck simultaneously, and that was the end of both of them, lost forever to the hungry sea. Until now."

Mikhail came over to hand Bria her full face mask with integrated regulator and communications system, and said to Nick, "No current this morning, visibility forty-five meters."

Nick adjusted the straps as he fit the mask around her head, and silently cursed as his dick twitched in response to the smell of her hair.

The sooner Gabriella Visconti was off his ship the better.

He wasn't used to—didn't damned-well *like*—this constant barrage of unwanted emotions. Every time he was anywhere *near* her, Nick felt as though he was caught in the blower's high pressure jets—tossed this way and that on the seafloor at high speed.

Not only didn't he like this excess of emotion, but get a hard-on in a wet suit and *everyone* would see it. With any luck, Aries would make contact while they dived. Feasibly he could be flying the princess to Las Palmas within hours.

For some annoying reason, Nick didn't feel the relief he'd hoped to feel at the thought of getting rid of her.

The sex was good. *Incredible.*

But out of sight, out of mind would make for a calmer, less frenetic libido. He took a deep breath. Yeah. Once she was gone, his body would be back to being his own.

But for now he felt possessed, out of sorts, and horny.

"To communicate, just press the button here." Taking her hand he helped her fingers find the send/receive button on the side of her mask. He stopped touching her as quickly as possible. His reaction to her, he knew, was pheromone based. But, Christ—he'd never, ever felt this way in his life.

It was unnerving, that's what it was.

"Works up to about six hundred feet, just like a walkie-talkie. Ready?"

Eyes big and bright behind her mask, lips curved with excitement, Bria nodded.

Her smile set off an insane chemical reaction in his brain, and he found himself grinning back as he secured his own mask.

Together they dropped off the dive platform, then followed the shot line from a slight surface chop through clear blue water. Visibility was excellent, and Nick pointed out the wrecks below. Because he'd studied both galleons in detail, he knew exactly what they'd looked like, but to an untrained eye, the pile of worm-eaten timbers on the seabed looked like nothing but coral-covered lumps.

"Hear me okay?" he asked through the underwater communication headpiece. She gave him the thumbs-up. "Just push the button and talk normally, I'll hear you just fine."

"Look at the turtle!" Bria said excitedly a few minutes later. Her breathy excitement as it reverberated through his head gave Nick his first underwater erection.

# Chapter 13

They stayed where they were, hovering in the water, maintaining their position easily and almost silently as the turtle paddled lazily by. Five smalltooth sand tigers cut through a shoal of tiny neon dottybacks. The sharks hovered for a moment in the midst of the swarm of blue, orange, and yellow, then flashed through the shoal and disappeared into the blueness beyond the hulk of the *El Puerto*. The dottybacks moved as one in a sweep of color in the opposite direction.

Bria did a graceful pirouette to watch them go, the bubbles from her regulator spiraling over her head. Her eyes smiled behind her mask. "Breathtaking."

Yeah. She was.

The light diminished the deeper they got, turning the underwater world around them into shades of blue. The darkened outline of the wrecks showed up against the light golden-sand seafloor.

The *São Juan Poinsat* rested a hundred yards away. He took Bria by the Portuguese wreck first. Little remained, so it was hard to tell what it had been. The timbers that hadn't yet been consumed by worms were burnt and twisted beyond recognition.

"Wow," Bria said through the microphone in her mask. "What happened to this one?"

"*El Puerto* carried *bomba*, ceramic fire pots crammed with flammable material. They'd throw them at the sails and rigging of an enemy ship. So while the Portuguese were firing at the Spanish ship, she was burned beneath their feet."

"A hideous way to die," Bria said soberly.

There wasn't much left of the warship, and he turned her around toward the *El Puerto*. The once magnificent galleon lay on her port side, at a sixty-degree angle to the sand, bow first. Nick touched Bria's shoulder, then pointed at the massive gaping holes running the length of her hull. "That's one of four direct hits below the water line from the Portuguese cannons. She sank fast."

"Can I touch it?" Her genuine excitement pleased him.

"Sure."

He followed as she dove down to the wreck and watched as she lightly brushed her fingers along the ragged edges of the hole in the hull. He'd done exactly the same thing when *he'd* first seen her.

"Do you know if anyone survived?"

"Out of the thirteen hundred people on board the two ships, five were picked up by a fishing boat the next day."

"That's good. Good that there were people who could tell what happened. Hopefully they were able to contact some of the families . . ."

Nick shook his head.

"What?"

"It happened four hundred years ago, in time of war."

Bria shrugged, giving her fins a little flip that stirred up some of the sediment. "Right. Well I'm sure the families must've been relieved to get news. Even if it was bad news."

"Right," Nick said dryly.

She reached over and punched his arm. "Cynic." Bria glanced around, clearly fascinated by the myriad species of fish swimming lazily about. They didn't seem concerned that they had humans on their home turf.

"There are the guys," Bria pointed. Burke and Olav were shadowy figures filling their baskets fifty feet away. "Before we head back up, can I see what they found?"

"Sure. Everything is pretty close to the wreck. There isn't a big debris field because the ships were so close together, and sank fast. They broke up on the way down. Hitting the seabed did the rest." Nick dived down five feet, and shot back to her side after picking up something from the sand. He handed it to her. "Here."

As she clearly had no idea what she was holding, Nick thought it intriguing that she looked as happy with a gnarly chunk of conglomerate-covered coins as she would if he'd handed her the multimillion-dollar jeweled sword in his safe.

"Coral?" She ran her fingers lightly over the gray clump, then lifted her shining eyes to his. Nick felt the weight of that happy look like a blow to his chest. Christ. How could she be anything other than what she professed to be? There didn't seem to be a deceptive bone in her body. Which was illogical. Everybody had something to hide. And everybody lied through their teeth if it was in their own best self-interest.

She could be excited by the novelty of it all.

Or she could be calculating the value of the salvage and her brother's investment.

"Coins," he said. "Hand-hewn, individually struck coins like these were once the most converted and widely traded money on earth." And in the *Scorpion*'s hold were several hundred thousand more exactly like them.

Nick kept her by his side as he swam the length of the *El Puerto*. Paraphrasing, he pointed out things he thought might interest her, and enjoyed her enjoyment of something he loved to do. He saw everything through Bria's eyes, and was himself seeing everything with fresh eyes.

A yellow grouper darted right in front of them, and his hand shot out as, startled by the sudden movement, she jumped back. The fish slipped out of sight behind the shattered remains of the forecastle, and three stingrays cruised by, unconcerned.

"What's he putting in his basket?" She pointed at Olav, hard to see at this distance. "More coins?" she asked eagerly.

Nick knew which section of the grid they were working in, so he knew what they had. "Silver bars." He swam closer,

Bria at his side. "They weigh a hundred pounds apiece. They've been in a wood crate, but the crate was eaten away by toledo worms. The bars maintained the shape of the box they were being transported in."

The two men continued working and Nick described what they were doing, until Bria seemed to be losing interest. He touched her arm and headed back to the wrecks.

"Is there gold as well?"

"A ton of it," And that wasn't just the expression. Nick had researched the little-known ship well. It had taken a lot of doing because there was so little written about it. But his gut hadn't steered him wrong. The Spanish ship was described in the obscure records as being filled with gold from the New World, and he and his team hadn't been disappointed. "We know the ship was in Potosi because of the reals we found scattered all over. They have the identifying full cross with lions and castle visible." A hundred and forty million dollars' worth at a rough estimate.

From the stern to forward section, shoals of emerald green parrot fish congregated over the Portuguese wreck then rose with Nick and Bria as they headed back to the *El Puerto*.

Nick circled the Spanish galleon, pointing out things he thought would interest her, then indicated it was time to surface.

"Ten more minutes?" Bria asked, like a child begging to stay up after bedtime.

"Sure, I'll show you where they stored the *bomba*." Nick wished to hell he hadn't thought of that analogy as they did another circuit of the wreck. Because now all he could think about was a kid with Bria's smile and his eyes.

\*      \*      \*

Nick ran a towel over his chest and watched the guys fawning over Bria. God, she was damn sweet. Physically, she was everything he was attracted to, and then some. But her physical attributes, as spectacular as they were, and as many as there were, were not what had him in a twist.

Her awe and excitement were contagious, and he'd enjoyed the dive more because of her reaction. She was so excited about what they had seen, so proud of the small cluster of conglomerated coin she'd refused to let go of all the way back to the surface.

Tossing the damp towel on his chair, he picked up his watch from the table, strapping it on while he watched Bria laugh with his team. He picked up the Bluetooth he was never without unless he was underwater. Or engaged in wild bouts of lovemaking. His lips twitched. Damn, she was . . .

Hooking the device in his ear, he was surprised when it immediately beeped. Not Aries. He touched his earpiece to activate it. "Your chickenshit surveillance camera's working suddenly?" he teased Jonah.

He. *Teased.* Jesus. It was a new him.

"Where's Bria?"

Eyes instantly searching the area for danger, Nick straightened. "Ten feet in front of me, we just surfaced from a dive. Why?"

"Secure her in your cabin." His captain's voice was grim, and urgent. So much so that Nick grabbed the loose shirt he'd worn early to conceal the Sig Sauer and was already walking toward Bria, the weapon in his hand, hidden under the drape of the shirt over his forearm.

He scanned the area again, a slow, intense sweep. Port to starboard. Back again. "Talk to me."

Bria, Miles, Mikhail, Stan—laughing, sunlight sharply sparkling on calm water. The dive platform, crowded with plastic tubs waiting to be taken down to the hold for transportation to Cutter Cay—

Everything looked normal. But shit! Jonah's tone set off warning alarms and suddenly it didn't *feel* normal.

"Come to the forward hold," Jonah said in his ear, his tone serious. He hung up.

Bria was many things, but obtuse she wasn't. The moment Nick called out to her and she looked at him, she ran across the dive platform. He met her at the top of the ladder, taking her hand to haul her up beside him. He handed her a towel as they walked. Fast.

"What's happened?"

"I don't know. But Jonah needs me, and I want you locked in our cabin until I know what the hell's going on."

"Okay." She slipped her cool hand into his. "Let's go."

As soon as they were in his office, Nick opened the safe and removed a Bersa. He handed it to Bria. "Do you really know how to use this?"

She hefted it in her palm. "Yes."

"Keep it with you until you leave this ship." He took the time to hand her two more clips from the safe and made sure she hadn't been BSing him about knowing how to use it as he made her load it while he watched.

"I don't give a shit who wants in." He pulled his shirt on and tucked the Sig in back of his waistband. "Me or Jonah. That's it. I don't give a fuck if the ship's on fire or blood is pouring under the door. You stay in here until one of us comes for you. Got it?"

"Yes, sir." She spread her fingers on his chest and gave him a little shove. "I'll be fine. Be careful. Go!"

Nick went. He took the stairs at a flat-out run, and within minutes was at the only closed hatch in the hold. He rapped. "Jonah? Nick."

The door was yanked open. Jonah, a Beretta in his hand, looked grim, and Nick's adrenaline spiked even further. He took in the neat stacks of seawater-filled plastic tubs lining the walls and forming a center island four-deep. In three carefully marked containers were the blood diamonds, submerged beside a fortune in gold coin.

*Shit!* "Someone got the diamonds?" It was all he could think of. If so, they were still somewhere on the ship. Other than Bria, nobody had come or gone in days. For a nanosecond, he considered that the diamonds could've been passed from someone to Bria, and Bria to the helicopter pilot, who had left in an all-fired hurry . . .

A left-field possibility, but his gut told him that hadn't been the case.

"No. I checked, which was how— Come this way." Jonah led the way through the passageways between the bins.

Nick smelled death before he saw it. "Oh, Christ. Who is it?"

"Fakhir. Hired on as cook's helper in Tarfaya two days before we sailed."

"I'm not even going to hazard a thought that it was natural causes? Yeah." At his friend's dark look, Nick shook his head. "Thought not. What the hell was he doing down here? The only people who know the bin numbers are the two of us and the Moroccans."

He and Jonah had agreed that the fewer people who knew the exact location of the stones, the better. There were perhaps a thousand containers on board. Finding the ones containing the diamonds would be like looking for a needle in a haystack.

The Moroccans' plan was to give that information to their men on board . . . *When we reach Cutter Cay,* he thought. It was too soon!

The stench got worse as they walked through the maze of containers, stacked neatly almost to the ceiling in places.

"He's right over here." Jonah had to jump over the man's sprawled legs to get on the other side, clearing space so that Nick could see him.

"Christ." Fakhir was half sitting, half sprawled, legs extended on the floor, death-glazed eyes wide open. His white T-shirt and shorts were saturated with dark, partially dried blood.

His throat had been slashed from ear to ear by something very, very sharp.

"Alfonso keeps his kitchen knives sharp, but not *this* sharp."

Fakhir's throat had been cut clear through to his spine.

Grisly. Gruesome.

Fucking unacceptable.

Nick looked around. Within two feet of the dead cook's helper was bin number 579 C. Containing diamonds.

"Agreed," Jonah said, his voice edged with anger. "Looks

surgical. I searched around while I was waiting for you, didn't find the weapon. Fortunately, we keep this area spit-polished and old-maid neat, otherwise it'd take us a year."

"I hate to break it to you, pal," Nick told him grimly. "But it *will* take a year. The weapon could be in any one of these bins, and until we dump everything out, we'll never find it." Three months of hard work? Not going to happen. At least not right now.

"Good point." Jonah pointed to bin number 579 C.

Nick nodded. "I noticed. And it's no coincidence. Secure this section of the hold. Nobody in or out until we can contact Aries and see how they want to play it."

"What about Fakhir?"

Nick glanced at the body. "Aries will have to get his ass here and take care of this." Anger flickered through him. Raw. Savage. "I sure as shit don't want a killer on board any more than I want a corpse stinking up the place. This second murder is a game changer. I won't tolerate any of our crew being harmed. Fuck Aries's request—"

*"Order,"* Jonah muttered tightly.

Nick sliced a hand through the air, as if he could wipe the whole fucking mess away. "Fuck his *order* for radio silence. Get him on the horn. I'm done with this crap. He and his people are going to have to get their asses here ASAP and clean up their own mess. Let's get this guy somewhere where no one will trip over him until then."

Jonah raised a dark brow. "A friend will help you hide a body?"

Nick eyed the man who knew him as well as his brothers. The man he trusted with his life. His secrets. "That sums it up for now. Problem?"

"None."

"There's that old walk-in refrigerator next door with all the crap we need to get rid of. You were right. It *will* come in handy. We can put him in there, until Aries and his team come and get him."

Jonah blanched. "That thing barely works, which is why we stuck it down here."

"Yeah, well, I don't think he's going to mind if the temperature isn't consistent," Nick observed dryly. "Stay put, I'll go turn it on and make sure no one else is around."

Nick slipped out, gun in hand. If anyone came down here for any reason, he'd think about explanations then. Request or order, he had to get Bria off the *Scorpion*.

Now. Right fucking now.

He didn't like not knowing what was happening on his own ship, and he didn't like dead people popping up unexpectedly. All he knew was it would be impossible for him to concentrate on finding answers when his brain was fogged with thoughts of sex with the very mind-blowingly hot princess. Or worry that she'd be next.

The thought of her death made Nick sick to his stomach.

Now he wanted her off his ship even more than he had before.

Stalking at a fast clip down the corridor toward the storeroom, he thought it through calmly and rationally. He'd personally fly her to Tenerife and put her on a plane back to Sacramento. She'd start her new job, be safe, and forget him.

Except that this house of cards had started falling when Halkias tried to kill *her*. Nick wondered—had Halkias's murderer done in the cook's helper too? Or was there yet another plot twining beneath his feet?

Bottom line? His instincts told him to get Bria off the *Scorpion* while a killer ran amuck. But if he sent her flying across the world alone, what if she *had* been the target? What if someone followed her back to California? Who would protect her then?

Halkias could've had the hots for her—and rapists weren't necessarily murderers. He ground his back teeth together in frustration. It was all moot with Halkias dead. So far they had neither motive, nor suspects. Was Fakir one of the men who'd tossed Halkias overboard? Or was he yet another victim? Had the same person who killed Halkias killed Fakhir?

Damn it to hell.

He was damned if he did, and damned if he didn't.

Was Aries right? Were calls to and from the *Scorpion*

being monitored? Or was Aries manipulating him, and his ship, for his own agenda?

"Fuck them all." He'd take the chopper to Las Palmas or Tenerife, and contact Aries from there on a public phone and get the answers to all his questions.

Nick pushed open the door to the storeroom, felt for the light switch, and walked into the large, crowded space. Even if the operative sent an escort for Bria, depending on where he *was*, it could take valuable hours, if not days before Nick was sure she was safe.

It would be quicker to take her to Marrezo.

Under the guise of returning her idiot brother's investment, Nick could ensure that she stayed in the royal palace, where she'd be securely guarded twenty-four-seven. If he pulled the money from his personal bank accounts, nobody would be the wiser.

He wended his way between deck chairs, tables, and broken lamps until he saw the old walk-in refrigerator in back and plugged it in. It rattled, hummed, and settled into an asthmatic drone. Good enough.

He went back to inform Jonah that he was going to escort Bria to Marrezo, right after they moved the body.

\*     \*     \*

Nick had threatened her with working for passage. Bria grinned. Although the idea had appeal, she presumed he hadn't meant on her back. She needed something constructive to do. Preferably something that allowed her free rein and not confinement in the cabin.

There was still a murderer on board. But with the Bersa, she was confident she could protect herself. Still, Nick's order that she not be alone anywhere without himself or Jonah was sound. She wasn't going to have a too-stupid-to-live moment and skydive without a parachute.

Having no idea what had alarmed Nick, she was not willing to fill her brain with a thousand different alarming scenarios when she couldn't do anything to help.

She was good at making lists. She'd had a year of unemployment to fill, and no money to travel. Her lists had lists. Putting aside her sketch pad—she'd been adding mythical creatures to liven up the uninteresting view of flat water as far as the eye could see—she picked up the gun he'd given her and got off the chair by the bedroom window.

Nick had left the connecting door to his office open and she went in there for a change of scenery. Her bare toes sank into the soft wool rug, and she enjoyed the explosion of colors and textures lacking on the rest of the ship. It smelled great in his office too. Like tobacco—although she'd never seen him smoke. Slightly musty from the old manuscripts and charts all over the place, but mostly the scent was Nick, and smelling Nick made her feel flushed on the outside and fluttery on the inside.

She liked the sensation. A lot.

She put the gun down where she could reach it and went around his giant desk to push open the large window. Air conditioning was great, but the warm, salty tropical breeze would at least give the illusion that she wasn't locked in.

He'd asked that she not use his computer or his phone, which Bria thought a bit high-handed. But as it was his stuff, and as such he had a right to ask her not to mess with it, she found a nice rollerball pen in a container in his desk drawer, and took a sheet of paper from his printer.

Curling up in his chair, she started to work out a list of anything she thought she could do on board. The big leather chair smelled of him. Crisp and clean and intrinsically masculine. Nothing frou-frou about Nick Cutter. No colognes or scented body washes. Just clean skin and male. Incredibly sexy.

1.

She closed her eyes to think about her first priority. But instead of coming up with some duty that Nick didn't realize was vital to the running or whatever of his ship, she thought about what his mouth tasted like.

Which wasn't getting the list written. She opened her eyes and did a quick sketch of his sexy mouth on the edge of the sheet. Then got serious and wrote—

2.
Nothing came to mind. Her pen eased to a new line.
3.
4.
He had a staff of fourteen—oh, damn—thirteen, now that Halkias was dead. Everyone seemed extremely efficient, and everything on board ran like clockwork. She doubted he'd want her swabbing the decks. But since she needed to add something, she wrote—
5. Swab decks.
She knew how to clean, and was good at it.
4. Maid service.
She clicked the pen a couple of times and chewed her lip. Did a few lines of his eyebrow. Wrote—
3. Sort artifacts from dives.
That was good. There were still a lot of bins on the deck. Things had to be moved around so same-as-same were together. She could do that with a little instruction.
2.
Nothing . . . Click. Click. Click.
She glanced at the dark computer screen. She'd love to check her e-mail and Facebook . . . Send a message to the McMan of McMan and Tate who was expecting her to show up to work soon. If she was really quick, he'd never know. Bria reached out to turn on the computer, then jumped as the door to Nick's office opened and he strolled in.
"Was it serious?" she asked, because God only knew, she couldn't tell from his poker face what was going on in his head.
"Nothing Jonah and I can't handle." He removed the Sig from under his shirt and laid it on the edge of the desk next to the Bersa. "I've given it some thought, and I've reconsidered my position on refunding King Draven's investment."
She blinked for a moment as the words sank in. Then she smiled. "Thank you, that's wonderful!" Gratitude was her first thought. *Oh, my God, it's worth five million euro to get rid of me,* was her second. "What made you change your mind?"

His features were inscrutable as his powerful shoulders flexed. "I hate to think that centuries of history and tradition will be broken by one man's desperation."

"That's amazingly generous of you. I know Draven will be grateful." No, he wouldn't. Her brother would rip her a new one for interfering with his scheme, and probably remind her for the rest of her natural life that she'd lost him a fortune.

It was worth it to get the loan paid off and her country on an even keel, however. Times were going to be tough. But it could be done. Draven just had to stop throwing good money after bad.

"Can you do it on the computer?" she asked, casually folding the piece of paper she'd been doodling on into quarters as she slid off his big comfortable chair. "Or do you need to send a bank draft? I'm not sure how these things work. It's a large amount . . ."

"We'll deliver it together."

Stunned by the suggestion, Bria paused as she was rounding the desk, tucking the piece of paper in her back pocket. "You want to go with me to Marrezo?"

He nodded, his blue-as-ice eyes trained on hers. "Sure. Grab your stuff. I want to leave right away."

Bria hesitated, her inner senses straining to pick out something, anything for a clue here. When he made a decision he wasn't kidding around. He was practically shoving her out the door. No, not *practically,* he *was* shoving her out the door.

The man was running scared.

Her conflicted emotions turned over into sympathy. And a flicker of annoyance. Did he think she was that easy to get rid of? After last night? After this morning?

She perched on the corner of his desk. "Let me get this straight. You have a demented killer on board. You don't pay out early to investors. You know my brother is— Well, let's just say not exactly fiscally responsible. And—" She almost pointed out that she had a loaded weapon an inch from her hand. "And you're in the middle of a dive."

"*Tail end* of the dive," he corrected, as if she hadn't just outlined everything before it. "I won't be gone long. Jonah will take care of things until I get back."

"Ah." Sympathy edged to anger. And hurt. "We'll leave together and you'll return alone." She hopped off the desk, shaping a sunny smile she was far from feeling. "Got it."

His startling blue eyes narrowed slightly. What? Had he expected another scene? Bria wasn't going to give him the satisfaction. "It'll take me all of ten seconds," she said, keeping her voice breezy, and was rewarded by his eyes narrowing a little more. "I didn't have much to start with, after all. I'll separate out what I came with, of course."

He said nothing, and she walked to the door between the rooms in silence before turning. "Did you call the charter company to send a helicopter? Or would you like me to do it?"

He folded his arms over his broad chest. "I'll fly us to Tenerife, then grab a flight from there to your island."

# Chapter 14

The five-seater helicopter appeared to be state-of-the-art, with every bell and whistle under the sun. It had been tucked, like a small white praying mantis, under the heliport on the sundeck.

Nick was an excellent pilot, but then Bria expected nothing less. He was focused and serious as they flew the thirty-five minutes from the *Scorpion* to Tenerife's North airport. "Can your cell phone get international?" Bria asked through the headset. "I'll call my brother and let him know I'm on my way with the money."

"It's in back. You can call when we switch planes at Tenerife."

Bria tried for tact. "I appreciate you doing this, but I insist on paying my own airfare to Marrezo."

"We're not going commercial. I've chartered a jet. It'll be quicker."

And of course he had. She hoped to God they were holding her job, because she'd used up all her savings getting here. Maybe Draven would— No. He wouldn't and she wasn't going to ask. Still, she wasn't going to let Nick throw money at her. "Then I insist on reimbursing you once I'm back in Sacramento."

"I don't want your goddamned money—" he snarled,

surprising her with his vehemence. He caught himself, features settling into that Cutter implacability again, and he said mildly, "Fine. We'll square up later."

Wow. Bria glanced at his profile as he flew low over the small island of Tenerife. Was that a little zing of temper? How interesting. Her? Or whatever his captain had alerted him to? Probably the latter.

She stretched her legs out as much as the space allowed and asked, "What was so urgent with Jonah, Nick? Is whatever it was why you didn't even give me time to find my shoes before we lit out of there?"

He studied the breathtaking expanse of blue through the windshield as he answered, "I'm returning your brother's investment. Isn't that what you wanted?"

"Yes. And that still doesn't answer the question. You could give me a bank draft or whatever, and I could drop it off on my way home. Home to Sacramento."

"I want you to stay with your brother for a while."

She frowned. The idea had no appeal whatsoever. "Why? And what's a 'while'?"

His fingers flexed on the controls, but his tone was still even as he said, "Until matters on board the *Scorpion* are resolved to my satisfaction."

She shook her head. "Still isn't an answer. What happened?"

Nick paused.

"Don't lie to me, Nick."

She watched the decision slide into his blue eyes moments before he said flatly, "Jonah found another crew member dead. His throat was cut."

She put her hand to her throat. "Who?"

"Fakhir."

"Chef's helper brownie-guy? Buck teeth and cute smile?" She squeezed her eyes shut. "Oh, God, Nick—why? I don't understand. Why would anyone want to kill him, he was so sweet and shy . . ."

"Your brother will have top security guarding him and the palace. Stay there until I tell you not to."

Her eyes popped open, half blinded by the light but pinned on his hard expression. "That's pretty damned autocratic of you," she told him. "I'm not your responsibility. I can defend myself—remember? Besides which, you haven't proven that this has anything to do with me. Perhaps the two incidents *are* related, but I didn't know Halkias, and I only talked to Fakhir a couple of times. I didn't know *him* either. So, connected somehow, probably—but not connected to *me*."

Nick's jaw tightened.

She took a deep breath. "Therefore, no one is going to follow me across the world to my little condo in Sacramento to assassinate me." She glanced down as they skimmed low over the airport, and pulled her bag into her lap. Taking out a lipstick, she uncapped it, holding the wand in her hand without applying it.

Still Nick said nothing.

"What happened to those two poor men, as hideous as it was, has absolutely nothing to do with me. I work in public relations, not some secret terrorist group or whatever. Which means I can go on my merry way back to Sacramento without some ninja special-ops type coming after me." She paused. "Unless you can prove otherwise?"

*       *       *

His gut wasn't proof.

Interesting that she'd bring up spec ops. What did a publicist know about shit like that? Nick was saved from answering as he responded to the tower's landing instructions. Within minutes, he landed the single-engine Robinson lightly on the tarmac, its two-bladed main rotor spinning overhead. Constructed from advanced composites, aluminum alloy sheet and chromoly steel, the R66 was Nick's latest toy, and with a cruise speed of 120 knots per hour, it had gotten them to the airport, and Bria off the *Scorpion,* in record time.

He felt better already.

They unbuckled and got their bags, then climbed out and headed toward the waiting car. The tarmac was sweltering hot, and there was absolutely no breeze, yet he could smell the earthy peach scent of her. Sunglasses covered half her face, and her lips were a bright, glossy cherry red.

He knew exactly how they tasted. With or without gloss.

The waiting driver immediately whisked them to another part of the airport where a pilot and a sleek white Lear jet waited on the runway, the engine idling so that they took off as soon as they were buckled in.

They were the only two passengers in the luxurious eight-seat cabin. It was a four-and-a-half-hour flight to Marrezo. Nick went to greet the flight crew, then sat across the aisle from Bria and fastened his belt as they taxied down the runway.

He intended to sleep the whole way. Or pretend to sleep. It wasn't a stretch; they had barely slept the night before. Not that he was tired, and God only knew the princess looked bright-eyed and delectable despite the lack of sleep.

"Have you ever been to Marrezo?" she asked, curling her legs up on the seat, and resting her jaw on her palm. The sun shone through the window beside her, spotlighting her dark hair, and the stubborn line of her jaw.

Nick laced his hands on his belt and closed his eyes. "No."

"Would you like me to t—"

"I'm sleeping."

"You're an ass," she muttered under her breath, quietly and without heat.

Nick bit back a smile as she rustled around in her tote, pulling out a pencil and pad.

\*     \*     \*

She didn't talk, but that didn't mean she didn't bother him. Her pencil scratched across paper. She talked softly to the flight attendant, and exchanged entire life stories over a soda. Bria's PR background obviously kicked in as her story was drastically edited, and she merely offered that she was just friends with him. No mention of being a princess. She sketched for a while, got up to use the head, came back. Nick felt those big brown eyes scanning his face, but he didn't open his eyes. Not even when he felt the whisper-light brush of her fingers over his hair.

She returned to her seat across the aisle. Leather creaked as she settled in, and after a couple of minutes, he heard her breathing change as she fell asleep.

He rolled his head and opened his eyes. Curled up comfortable as a cat on the wide, plush leather seat, she looked exactly what she was. A sleeping princess. Her dark hair a wild gypsy tangle around her shoulders, her soft red lips parted, and her long, dark lashes cast intriguing shadows on her flushed cheeks.

He wasn't sure about his fairy-tale lore. Was she the one who'd had to be kissed to waken her? Or the one who'd kissed the frog?

Amusement warred with intense arousal. Every minute that he wasn't buried inside her was merely foreplay. He'd been in various stages of erect from the second he'd first seen her in Tarfaya.

Watching Gabriella sleep hurt Nick's chest. A hard, unfamiliar achy sensation. He pressed his fist to his sternum. Probably heartburn from eating a large breakfast and then tumbling back into bed with her for another manic bout of lovemaking this morning.

Ache aside, he watched her sleep for another hour before he succumbed himself.

*     *     *

Bria's lashes fluttered, and she stretched before opening her eyes to find Nick watching her. She knew what she looked like first thing in the morning; waking after a too-short nap couldn't be much different. She'd have crazy bed-head, sleepy eyes, and an urgent need to pee.

She stretched luxuriously, arms over her head. Unselfconscious, she combed her fingers through her hair as she

sat up and swung her bare feet to the plushly carpeted floo
"Was I snoring?" She felt around under the seat in front oi
her for her shoes.

The stern lines around his mouth eased. "Like a buzz saw."

She shot him a horrified look. *"Seriously?"*

He shook his head. "You sleep like a well-fed cat. You were practically purring."

She cast a quick look to the door behind which the flight crew were seated. Then gave him a sultry come-hither glance. "I could purr more."

"We'll be landing in twenty minutes," he told her dampeningly. Too bad, because his eyes told another story. Blazing, *scorching* blue. Bria was lucky his look didn't cause her to burst into flame.

With a wicked smile, she rose and crossed the narrow aisle between their seats, then curled up on his lap. The hard length of his erection under her was impossible to miss. "Oh, you *are* happy to see me," she said, delighted with her discovery. He couldn't be that eager to ditch her, after all.

She wrapped her arms around his neck. "Only twenty minutes?" She nuzzled her lips to the underside of his jaw. He needed a shave. She liked the rough stubble, she like the way it softened the hard line of his jaw and accented his mouth, which was delectable in ninety-seven ways. "Then we shouldn't waste a second." She touched his cheek, encouraging his mouth down to hers.

He tangled his fingers in her hair, his face so close she could see the hundreds of colors that made up the extraordinary blue of his eyes. Turquoise, indigo, cobalt—

"You like to live dangerously, don't you?" he whispered against her mouth.

*Not until I met you.* "Twenty minutes," she repeated, a shaky breath. How long was he going to stay on Marrezo with her? A couple of hours? One night? "Do you want to waste them chat—"

He covered her mouth with his, his lips firm as he lazily explored her mouth, coaxing and languid. As if they had all the time in the world to explore each other. They didn't. Bria's eyes stung with unshed tears of frustration. She combed her fingers through his hair, and pressed her aching breasts against the rock-hard wall of his chest, wanting to climb inside him. Wanting to hold him to her and not let go.

His tongue flicked against hers as he deepened the kiss, which just made her ache more.

Sunlight streamed inside the cabin, changing direction as the small plane banked. *No. No. No.*

She gasped, moaned in abject frustration deep in her throat, and his legendary cool disintegrated. She could feel how much he wanted her. Not any woman. Her. Gabriella Ilaria Elizabetta Visconti. No one else.

No one had ever wanted anyone as much as she wanted Nick.

With a guttural sound of passion, his fingers tightened in her hair as he slanted his mouth to devastating effect. Her head fell against his shoulder as she gave way under the onslaught, reveling in his sudden loss of control.

Her nipples ached for direct contact, and she pressed her breasts firmly against his hard chest. That didn't ease anything. But then every part of Bria's body hurt from wanting him so desperately. He couldn't touch her, or hold her, or make love to her hard or fast enough to fill the throbbing emptiness engulfing her.

He tried. His tongue pushed into her mouth, slid against hers, not teasing so much as tasting. Tempting. His lips were warm and wet against her own, and she sucked in a surprised gasp as he dug his thumb into her cheek. Just by the corner of her lips, coaxing her head back. Her face up. He deepened an already carnal kiss until the world spun and she forgot about the flight attendant.

About the time they had left. Or didn't have.

Until he cupped her cheeks to tug her gently away from his mouth. Her lips clung for a moment more. "We just landed."

Dazed and breathless, she lifted her head to stare uncomprehendingly out of the window at the tiny stone building that served as Marrezo's airport terminal. She hadn't felt the plane touch down.

The terminal had originally been a centuries-old stone farmhouse. The modern flight control tower had been added to the back of the house some sixty years ago, making the terminal look oddly surreal. They deplaned with the flight crew and walked inside.

The waiting room sported two ancient sofas, a battered, yellow Formica-topped coffee table, and a 1970s Coke machine. Taking up a large portion of the back wall were a pair of elaborately framed, faded prints. Portraits of her parents in their royal robes.

Her gaze slid away. Seeing her parents made her heart ache. The originals used to hang over the fireplace at the Palazzo. They had not been destroyed by the fire, and Draven had exchanged them for portraits of himself and Dafne. She didn't understand why he'd done it. She wished he'd left things as they'd once been. But he was the new, and he'd gotten rid of the old as fast as possible.

But since she wasn't going to stay, it wasn't her right to say anything. Now that he was king, she'd opted to keep her "temperamental opinion" to herself.

Two men ran from the office to greet them. The older gentleman's face paled as he realized who she was. "*Principessa* Gabriella?"

The younger man's eyes widened, and he took a nervous step back. "We didn't know you were coming! We would have alerted the press, had refreshments waiting—"

Bria winced inwardly, but smiled with enough charm to ease the men's apprehension. "No need to stand on ceremony," she assured them quickly. "This is a quick visit to see my brother."

The younger man blurted, "But, *Principessa*, the king, he has gone to Roma!"

She glanced at Nick, who said quietly, "The palace is still staffed I'm sure."

"Probably." Draven had so many bodyguards and servants it was no wonder the country was bankrupt.

The older man rubbed the back of his head. "*Principessa*,

would you give me an autograph for my granddaughter? She dreams of being a princess someday."

She'd had that dream, too, once. Bria waited, smiling gently as he fumbled to fish a pen and a sales receipt out of his pocket for her to sign. Then scrawled a quick note for the little would-be princess. "Would you please take the flight crew to the hotel in Pescarna?" she asked the younger man who was standing at attention beside his boss.

There was only one taxi on the island, and the owner was notoriously absent when anyone needed him.

The younger man glanced from Bria to Nick, who lifted a brow in inquiry. The kid flushed and turned back to her. "We would be honored. Will you require a ride, *Principessa*? We will, of course, take you to the palace first."

"No, thank you. I'll call and have them send the car."

The terminal was locked up with all due haste, and the pilot, copilot, and flight attendant were whisked off, squeezed into a dilapidated pickup truck with strips of silver duct-tape holding the doors shut.

"From private jet to a 1980 pickup in the blink of an eye." Bria smiled and waved as the old truck drove sedately across the tarmac, leaving the two of them locked outside the tiny terminal building.

"I'm impressed," Nick told her, his dark hair ruffled by the wind's fingers. He didn't have his sunglasses on, and the sunlight on his face made his eyes look liquid and not in the least bit mysterious.

"With what?" she asked, dragging her gaze from his eyes to his mouth. She'd felt his mouth on every part of her body . . . Would she feel his lips again before he left?

A tendril of hair fluttered against her cheek in the warm, gentle Mediterranean breeze.

Nick was his usual inscrutable self as he studied her face for several seconds, then reached out and caught her hand as she was tucking her hair back up into her ponytail.

Her voice was husky as she repeated, "What are you impressed with?" A little shiver zinged through her as his fingers lingered for a few seconds on her ear before he dropped his hand. She had to keep her mind off sex before she jumped him out on the tarmac. "The efficiency of the Marrezo International airport staff?"

"You." His voice was low and tinged with appreciation. "In your element."

"I don't belong here."

"Coulda fooled me. You smiled and were gracious, you signed an autograph for a kid you don't know, and you ensured the crew had a place to stay. You practically charmed the teeth out of everyone. *Principessa*."

For the first time saying her title, Nick's voice held a note of respect instead of mockery. She held the scent of the island inside her lungs. "It's surprisingly good to be here again."

Marrezo smelled different than anywhere else on Earth. There was a magical tinge of pine and ocean, and the earthy scent of freshly turned ground in the nearby vineyards. She imagined she smelled tomatoes bubbling for tonight's dinner, and the robust red wine Marrezo used to be famous for and would be again with this return of Draven's liquid assets.

"While I find the historical aspects of the tower and the old farmhouse absolutely riveting, do you have a well-formed plan for us too?" Nick stuck his hands in his front pockets, a twinkle in his eye. "No rush. Just checking."

A plan? "Oh, damn," she said suddenly. "With all the chaos, I forgot to borrow the phone." But walking the couple of miles into Pavina, on such a beautiful day, with Nick by her side, was appealing. "It's a short walk, do you mind?"

"Nope. How about you in those heels?"

"I can do a ten-minute mile in them if I have to." Or take them off, as she'd done walking the streets and countryside of the island as a child. "There are two towns on the island. Pescarna—ten miles *that* way—is a fishing village. Pavina is that way, and is where the palace is located. May I borrow your phone? Mine won't work here, I don't have international calling on it. I'll just let them know we're here, and we can get going."

Nick handed her his phone, and Bria dialed as they walked across the single runway toward the tree line.

He studied the quiet lone tower over his shoulder. "I'm presuming this place shuts down when those two go off like that?"

Bria laughed and nodded as the phone rang in her ear. "We— They get one flight a week. *Maybe*. Silvio, the older man, has the radio with him all the time. They come when they're needed."

"Cushy job. Is there dental with that?"

She shot him a curious look. "Marrezo takes care of its people—including health care. They get paid a stipend, really. And live comfortably enough through fishing."

Nick nodded. "Now that's something I understand. A rod, a reel, and a cooler of beer on a sunny day."

"It's a simple life. Not exactly diving for treasure."

He arched a brow. "Or working in California?"

Bria turned away rather than say anything. She'd been surprised when Nick had told the pilot to return the next day. But even twenty-four hours wasn't nearly long enough. Still, she was grateful he wasn't getting on the plane to fly back to the *Scorpion* right away.

The phone continued to ring. Home. Bria felt an emotional tug in her chest. No matter where she was, no matter how long she'd been away, or how much she felt she shouldn't intrude on Draven's world, Marrezo would always be home. There was just too much of it wound into her earliest memories, memories of her parents, to think of it otherwise.

Finally, a man answered. An under-butler she presumed, since Draven liked all the pomp and ceremony that went with his title. The man asked her to hold, and a few moments later her sister-in-law, Dafne, came on the line.

"Here in Pavina," Bria responded when Dafne asked where she was calling from. "We just landed at the airport. I have a friend with me and we're walking. We'll be there in about twenty— No, really." She rolled her eyes at Nick. "It's only— Right. We'll probably be there before he takes the car out of the garage. Okay, fine we'll meet him on the road, it's too hot to stand around— No I wasn't, yes, I'm sure in some circles it *is* extremely rude just to drop by, but I'm—" she wanted to say *family,* but instead finished, "I'm here anyway."

She handed Nick back his phone. "Lovely woman," she said, straight-faced. She hitched her tote higher on her shoulder and strode off toward the road. Nick fell into step beside her. The air smelled pleasantly of pine. She inhaled deeply again—as much as the scent carried welcome childhood memories, it also whispered of betrayal and death. Time away hadn't erased the bitter with the sweet as she'd hoped.

"Don't get on with your sister-in-law?" he asked, sliding her heavy tote off her shoulder and hooking it onto his own.

She smiled her thanks. "She thinks she's Grace Kelly, only prettier, classier, and much, much richer. Unfortunately for Dafne, she's *not* any of those things. Times four.

"Queen Dafne is sending a car. I might add that *a* car would also be *the* car. If you have a thing for cars, be prepared to be impressed, because she's a beauty, even by today's standards."

He smiled, causing her train of thought to vanish in a curl of smoke. "I know a thing or two about things of beauty."

Bria smiled up at him. "So do I."

He shook his head with a laugh. "You are something else, Gabriella Visconti. Tell me about *the* car."

"A 1959 Silver Cloud Rolls-Royce that has been in the family, according to Dafne, for ten generations." Bria grinned.

"Since a generation is considered to be about twenty-five years, that would make the car pretty old," his voice was Sahara dry.

"Math isn't my sister-in-law's strong suit," Bria said lightly, so damn happy to be walking with Nick Cutter down the road toward Pavina in the sunshine that she could barely stand it. She refused to think about even an hour from now. Right now, right this second, here and now, with him beside her, and his long strides accommodating her shorter stride, everything was absolutely perfect.

"The car actually belonged to my grandfather, and then my father. So I guess it was the family ca— Ouch!" Bria hopped on one foot, her heel caught in a crack of the cobbled road.

"Here," Nick said impatiently. "Take my hand before you fall and break your neck." Without waiting for her response, he laced his fingers with hers.

She was used to walking in heels, and not worried about falling, but holding Nick's hand as they walked was an opportunity she wouldn't miss for the world. Not now, when every step toward the palace was a step farther away from being with him. The smell of his skin, intensified by the heat, melded with the smells of home, becoming imprinted on her synapses.

The dark green of the pine forest ran all the way down the right-hand side of the road. On the left, rolling hills of grapevines grew in symmetrical rows as far as the eye could see. As a backdrop to the lush green vines, Monte Tolaro rose to a flat-topped peak that seemed to touch the sky.

"You look like your mother."

"Thank you," she said quietly, his words touching her deeply. "I aspire to be what she was."

Nick raised a dark brow. "Queen?"

"God, no!" Bria flashed him a quick smile to take away the sting of her sincere but hot denial. She loved the feel of his palm brushing against hers as they walked, and the way his fingers were laced lightly through hers. "Although I was wondering if I was going to become queen-sized if I hadn't gotten the job after a year's unemployment.

"I have to admit, when I came home for Draven's coronation, I was shocked to see him again because he was so heavy." Heavy was an understatement; her brother would be considered morbidly obese. "Dangerously so, I think."

"Not something you have to worry about. But you're a woman who would be desirable no matter what size you are."

Bria hefted her chin. "I wasn't fishing for a compliment; genetics are responsible for how I look. My mother always told me that looks would fade, but integrity lasted forever.

My mother was the kindest, most intelligent woman I'd ever known. She was amazing."

"She sounds like it."

"Is your mother . . . ?" Bria looked up at him as they walked.

His eyes remained on the road ahead. "She died when we were kids. I was about six. Car accident. Drunk driver."

She squeezed his hand. "I was seven. It hardly seems fair. I'm sorry, Nick."

"I only have vague memories of her. Most of them fraught with something my father did or didn't do. Their marriage was . . . rocky to say the least." He paused and Bria warmed as he trusted her enough to continue, "She'd taken Zane and Logan and me to live with her mother in Portland. Dad didn't like it, and took us back to Cutter Cay."

"She died before she could get you back. Poor woman." Bria tsked.

Nick's steps faltered. "How did you know that?"

"She loved the three of you enough to try and take you to a safe place," Bria offered quietly. "If your parents had an acrimonious marriage, or even frankly if they didn't, she would've fought tooth and nail to keep the three of you with her. You needed your mother." She indicated they move over enough to walk in the shade. "She knew that. Death is the only thing that can separate a mother from the children she loves."

"She was killed while the lawyers battled it out."

The ancient stone wall of Pavina was visible ahead, and Bria slowed her steps, not wanting this moment to end. "What kind of man was your father?"

Nick shrugged his broad shoulders. "He was what he was. We had a good life on Cutter Cay. He taught us everything we know about sailing, about the salvage business, but love— Not sure he knew what that was about. He wasn't faithful.

"Logan and I worried that Zane would fall into that familial pattern, but Ace met someone, and that seems to be that."

"Zane fell in love?"

"Oh, yeah. He met his match in Teal."

"He's happy."

"Ridiculously so."

She smiled. "You must be happy for him."

"I am. I'm . . ." He huffed out a breath. "I'm relieved. We all remember what it was like. The lies, the bullshit. The drinking. Tell me a happy memory of *your* parents."

"God, I remember the family picnic the month before it all hit the fan. My parents, Draven and me and all five of the dogs crammed into the Rolls. It was the best day of my life." She heard the husky, half-longing note in her voice and she cast him a sassy look before things got too deep, too fast. "Until a week ago, anyway."

He lifted his sexy mouth in a half smile.

"We drove to the caves up there in the foothills where the mountain overlooks the sea." She pointed to the peak rising thousands of feet into blue skies dotted with smudges of soft gray clouds.

"It's spectacular."

"There's a lake inside the cavern, and hot springs. It's pretty amazing. Draven threatened to push me down the tunnel that drains the spring waters of the lake into the sea. I wasn't allowed to swim there." She smiled. "I think my mother believed he'd do it too. Thirteen-year-old boys aren't fond of seven-year-old sisters. Do you have any sisters? You never said."

"Just Zane and Logan. Although . . ."

"Although—?" She glanced up at him. Pausing to memorize his features, the way the sunlight shone in his dark hair, the way his eyes were suddenly speaking volumes, though she wasn't understanding what they were saying. On the other hand, this was Nick Cutter; he could just be squinting against the sun.

"That sounds mysterious," she said lightly, swinging their joined hands as they walked.

He didn't say anything for a minute and she glanced up at him to see if he was regretting telling her intimate details about his family.

After a moment when she thought he might not say

anything, Nick let out a breath. "Some high-priced New York lawyer called Logan awhile back, claiming to represent a guy who says he's our long lost brother."

"Interesting." The ancient stone walls of Pavina came into view again as they rounded the next curve, and Bria slowed her steps a bit. "Did you know you'd lost a brother? How's it possible to lose a brother?"

He didn't seem excited. "It's a scam to cash in," he said flatly. "Cutter Salvage has been doing extremely well the last couple of years."

"You don't believe this guy is who he says he is?"

"We'll have plenty of questions if he ever shows up. DNA will be just the beginning— Christ." His voice dropped in awe as the car rounded the bend in the road. "I'm in love."

# Chapter 15

*If only.* "I thought you might be, hence the warning," Bria told him sternly. "Don't drool on the seats, or Dafne will make you walk."

She didn't grab at him when he let go of her hand, although she wanted to. The magnificent car, silver paintwork polished to a platinum sheen, slowed and stopped on the edge of the road.

The driver jumped out, still hastily buttoning his black jacket—a ridiculous pretension in this day and age and in the heat. Beaming and bowing, he opened the back door with a flourish. *"Buon pomeriggio, Principessa!"*

*"Buon pomeriggio,* Enzo," Bria said with a smile. She'd met him briefly two years before. His wife was Dafne's something-or-other—whatever the unfortunate woman did for her sister-in-law, Bria figured she didn't get paid nearly enough. She motioned for Nick to get in. Let him do the sliding. *"Stai bene? Come sta la tua bellissima moglie?"* she asked the driver.

His eyes widened with delight that she'd remembered his wife. *"Sta molto bene, grazie per esservelo ricordato, Principessa."*

Bria grinned when she saw Nick stroking his hand across the butter soft, beautifully preserved dark green leather seats.

She slid in and Enzo shut the door with a solid, expensive thunk.

For such an enormous vehicle, the Rolls had been built to carry only two passengers, and Nick was close enough for her to feel the brush of his elbow against her bare arm. She smiled. Nick was checking out the polished exotic-woods interior as if he'd been handed a map to the location of Atlantis.

"Left-hand drive," he murmured, caressing the seat back in front of him. "Six cylinder in-line configuration, cast iron cylinder block, aluminum alloy cylinder head—"

Because the road was so narrow, with the forest on one side and vineyards on the other, Enzo had to drive all the way back the way they'd come, to the airport, to turn around. Bria crossed her legs and leaned back, enjoying Nick as he enjoyed the car.

"Let me know if you two would like a moment alone," she said with a laugh. A silly little pang plucked at her heart. Her father would've liked Nick Cutter. Obviously her brother did. He'd invested a hefty sum with him. But what would her mother have thought? Would Nick have been too emotionally detached for her taste? Sometimes Bria wondered if her parents being gone had been one of the reasons she'd never thought about settling down. She just couldn't imagine a wedding without them.

For the rest of the trip Nick and Enzo talked Rolls-Royce in rapid-fire Italian.

And behind her sunglasses, Bria's eyes stung.

*     *     *

The ancient town of Pavina had no vehicular traffic. The Rolls followed the high meandering wall for several miles outside the town until they turned into large gates and crunched down a shell driveway. The Palazzo, constructed of enormous blocks of dark gray basaltic lava and golden granite, was an interesting hodgepodge of time periods.

Nick frowned as the magnificent car crept up the gracefully curved driveway. At least a hundred people labored in
the manicured gardens surrounding the place. A spiderweb
of scaffolding, holding dozens of workers, dotted the front
of the building. For a man strapped for funds, King Draven
Visconti was spending a royal fortune returning his home to
what Nick presumed was its former glory.

He hoped the guy was spending an equal amount on his
subjects who were attempting to restore their lives, fortunes,
and homes to what they had been before Marrezo was over-
run by terrorists.

The car glided to a stop before a long sweep of curved
stairs leading to massive carved double doors, tires crunching discreetly on the gravel. The original moat had been
filled in and covered with freshly mown grass and flowering
shrubs. Enzo jumped out and held Bria's door open. Nick let
himself out on his side, circling the front of the car to her side.

Standing at the top of the stone steps stood a fashionable
too thin, too blond, too tanned woman in her late forties. She
wore a conservative business suit made of some unpleasantly
shiny material in a weird shade of green, and had accessorized
with enough gold and emeralds to feed the island residents
for a year.

Beside him Bria said *sotto voce,* "Brace yourself," and
started forward, ponytail swinging, back straight. Nick adjusted his steps to hers as they climbed the steps.

Silky blond hair in a simple twist reminiscent of Grace
Kelly, Dafne stood at the top of the stone steps in front of the
open double door, both hands outstretched in welcome.
"Gabriella, *benvenuti a casa mia sorella cara!*"

The queen spoke Italian badly, with a strong Afrikaans
accent. Nick had no trouble placing it. Pietermaritzburg,
South Africa, as a birthplace, several years at public school,
then a social climbing step to what Nick guessed was a good
boarding school in Durban.

Then Johannesburg.

"Thank you, Dafne," Bria replied in English. The woman

had barely moved, just waited for them to come up the deep stone stairs to greet her. She dropped her extended arms, clearly having no intention of anything as emotional or welcoming as a hug. Bria tucked a strand of hair behind her ear. "This is Nick Cutter of Cutter Salvage." Dafne's penciled-in brows rose before she offered him her thin, pale, ring-heavy hand. He gallantly took it in his, brushing a kiss two inches above her cold fingers, because she expected it. Not that he gave a flying fuck that she did. But not doing so would probably cause fallout on Bria. And that he wouldn't tolerate. He didn't care to analyze why that should be the case. "Your Majesty."

Dafne bestowed a serene smile on him as he straightened. "Charmed, I'm sure," she told him, in what Nick figured she imagined was upper-crust British. It wasn't even close. Her low-class South African roots showed through like worn silver plate over a base metal.

She turned less friendly eyes on Bria. *"Tu sei troppo presto. Il re è stata ritardata a Roma."*

As the old guy at the airport had told them, Draven was in Rome. Nick wondered if the woman called her husband "the king" in that annoying, superior way even when they were in bed. Clearly, Dafne loved being the king's wife, and he could see why fiery, joyous Bria didn't like the Ice Queen.

"No problem," Bria told her sister-in-law without any editorial comments, which Nick found refreshing. Most women rushed to fill awkward silences. Bria was gracious and polite, but she didn't jump in to make her sister-in-law look less ungracious. Dafne did that herself. "We'll wait."

Lips pursed, the queen rang a little gold bell. A man in a black suit materialized from behind the twenty-foot-high carved mahogany doors behind her. He looked like a wrestler, short and boxy, overly muscular, with the flat nose of a prizefighter.

His suit, Nick noticed, was custom-fit to conceal the weapon he carried beneath his arm, and efficiently covered his barrel chest, every button done up. He gave the Queen an inquiring look from beneath his unibrow.

"I presume you will want to cohabitate?" Dafne asked Bria with frosty contempt, hard to read on a face that barely moved.

Nick took Bria's hand. He liked holding hands with her. A first for him. But this time it was for moral support and solidarity. She wasn't here alone.

"Of course." Nick's response was immediate and frigid.

"Absolutely," Bria said cheerfully at the same time, making him want to laugh.

"Alfredo will take you to your room to freshen up. I'll see you at dinner." And just like that, they were dismissed.

Bria seemed to take it all in stride as Alfredo shifted to allow them to pass by him to get through the door. Nick was already pissed, and the woman had barely said two sentences.

God damn it. Now he was having second thoughts about leaving Bria among her less-than-friendly relatives. But then, she didn't have to be *happy*. Just safe.

\*       \*       \*

While Bria showered, Nick used the house phone to contact the T-FLAC operative and fill him in on the latest developments.

"The body will keep," Aries told him succinctly.

"That might well be," Nick said with annoyance. "Doesn't mean I want a corpse on board my ship, Aries. Take care of it."

"Head back to Cutter Cay. Before you dock, this situation will be resolved."

"How close are you to doing that?" The shower in the other room turned off. "My people are in danger. The princess was attacked, I have two men dead, and I have a murderer on board. This is no longer *simple*. You have twenty-four hours to resolve this or I'll take matters into my own hands."

"Don't do anything that'll jeopardize this op, Cutter. Three days should have this tied up."

"Strangely enough," Nick voice dripped frost, "as a *salvor* I don't *have* fucking *ops*! Resolve this within that three-day window or I'll sail back to the Cay without crew *or* diamonds."

He replaced the receiver lightly on the cradle, then said, "Fuck," quietly under his breath.

\*          \*          \*

Bria had lasted an hour after they'd been shown upstairs to a newly decorated suite. There were signs everywhere that the place was being remodeled, redecorated, and refurbished. The garish, ostentatious bad taste everywhere she looked made her long for the *Scorpion*'s white-on-white-on, oh-so-*white* décor.

"Let's get out of here," she said quietly, coming out of the opulent bathroom wrapped in a towel. "We can visit my cousin Antonio, tonight, do you mind?"

Nick turned from the window and smiled. "You're the boss."

"Dafne's the boss." Bria mock shivered. "Hang on, and I'll get dressed super quick."

He gave her damp body and wet hair an appreciative look. "Don't hurry on my account."

"Much as I'd love to take you up on that leer, staying here is giving me hives on my hives. Can I take a rain check? Five minutes, I promise."

He rested his hip on the wide stone windowsill. "I'm in no hurry."

"You could come and keep me company while I do my face," she suggested before returning to the bathroom.

"If I can't do you, I'll be safer out here watching a hundred gardeners prune trees into strange and unnatural shapes. Don't be long. I'm hungry, and apparently food is all I'll be getting for a while."

With a spring in her step, and her heart doing the Snoopy dance, Bria went all the way with her makeup. Smokey eyes, glossy lips. Even though she was going to bronze the red dress in memory, since it was the only game in town, she slipped it on over her lotioned, completely bare body.

Let Nick think about *that* all night.

Nobody stopped them as they strolled out the front door. Not that there was any reason they should. This was her home as much as it was Draven's. She might not be welcome, but she wasn't a prisoner.

It just felt like it.

Halfway down the driveway, she called her cousin using Nick's phone, and they arranged to meet in an hour at an out-of-the-way *trattoria* on the other side of town.

They walked through the town, and she bought him a slice of pizza wrapped in paper from a vendor because he said he was starving and couldn't wait for dinner. Then waited until he'd taken his first bite, and they were surrounded by people, to let him feel that she was completely naked under the dress.

"And for some reason," he said darkly, crowding her against an alley wall, "you think that I won't retaliate?"

She wrapped her arms around his neck and kissed him lightly on the lips, feeling wanton and happy. "I'm betting on it."

They shared the pizza as they walked. It was a warm summer night and the streets were filled with people enjoying their evening walk, chatting with friends, stopping for a cold drink. The evening meet and greet perambulation was called *fare lo struscio,* something Bria remembered doing on summer evenings with her parents.

Because she looked so much like her mother, people recognized her; some stopped, most dipped their heads and respectfully kept walking.

"You're a celebrity," Nick observed. He was holding her hand again. Only, as he assured her, to prevent getting separated with all the people milling around them. Bria was perfectly fine with it. No matter the excuse.

She'd never strolled any streets holding hands. It was . . . sweet. Innocent. Lovely.

"Most people who recognize me are my parents' age," she told him, smiling at two elderly women who were bug-eyed staring at her, hands talking at the same time. "So they recognize me because I look like her."

It made her sad, because her parents should still be ruling now. If they had been, the streets would be in better repair, and all the shops would've been open instead of only a handful. "Young people don't want to come and live and raise families here," she told Nick, as he paused to buy a large paper cup of freshly squeezed lemonade, which he handed her first.

"It seems busy enough."

She sipped the tart juice and pulled a comical face, making Nick smile, as she'd wanted to do. "Older people have returned, and they're trying to make a living here." She took another deep gulp of the tangy drink. It tasted exactly the same as when she and her mother used to come into the village on market day.

"But the vineyards won't produce for several more years, and industry as it was has pretty much died out. Twenty years ago, when their parents fled, they would've been young. So this isn't their world any more. They want to be in big modern cities with Internet in their houses and a thousand channels on TV."

"Did you study public relations to help your people?" Nick wrapped his arm about her waist and steadied the cup in her hand, as several people stumbled out of a nearby alley, laughing and joking in English. Tourists. Bria was happy to see them, even if they were tipsy in public.

Nick stroked her bottom through the thin fabric of her dress, reminding them both that she was commando. "Marv encouraged me to do a lot of things in the hope I'd come home one day. PR seemed a good overall way to perhaps encourage tourism or persuade companies to come into Marrezo to start cottage industries to feed the tourism. I did some hotel management, even some travel agency work and international business relations, all in hopes it might eventually make a difference. But as much as I want to help my country, that's not going to happen."

He took the cup from her and drank deeply, his tanned throat working as he swallowed. "You can't tell me that you don't want it." He handed it back empty. "Every move you've made since we've gotten here has shown me how much you love it. Is it because of Dafne?"

"Dafne, is just—Dafne." She paused, looking down and wondering at the hot sting of tears she quickly blinked away. "It's more Draven. You're right. I do love it. But he's been perfectly candid that he has no interest in me coming back here. He doesn't see that I have a place here, which kind of stings a little, since I've spent the better part of my life learning, training, and anticipating the triumphant return and all the good I'd do here."

"You'd be an asset."

She tossed the empty cup into a nearby container. "But that's okay. Things change, and sometimes even if we can't see it, they change for the better. My skills won't go to waste. Second thing is, we—I don't know—we feel awkward around one another. We used to be relatively close considering the age difference, but now that we're older and have led such vastly different lives, we just don't . . . click. I envy you your close relationship with your brothers. Family is everything. Ever since Marv died, I've felt . . . I don't know— adrift, maybe?"

"That's understandable, since for all these years you believed he was the only family you had left, even if there wasn't blood between you."

"I have Antonio. I think you'll like him— Oh, there he is now! Tonio!" Bria let go of Nick's hand and ran across the street to fling herself into her cousin's arms. He lifted her off her feet and swung her around, then bent her over his arm and kissed her smack on the lips.

Antonio was almost as tall as Nick, with black hair and naughty brown eyes. Last time she'd been home, she'd seen the way all the girls gave him suggestive glances, and probably their phone numbers. He was handsome, single, and fairly wealthy as the owner of a vineyard that, while not producing yet, still had stores of his family's famous wines. Hidden from the terrorists during their occupation, the extra twenty years of aging would make some of them more valuable.

She locked hands with Antonio and dragged him across the street. A trick of the light made Nick look a little demonic as she introduced the two men.

"We'll talk English, okay?" Tonio asked, keeping his voice low. "Less people will understand us here."

They walked into the Trattoria Amici, which, at first glance, looked like any corner grocery shop. The fragrance of tomato, garlic, basil, and freshly baking bread made Bria's mouth water, that slice of pizza a distant memory.

The narrow entrance was filled with people waiting for tables. The walls were stacked to the wood-beamed rafters with piles of wooden wine crates, dusty bottles of olive oil, sacks of locally grown lentils and chickpeas, jars of honey, and braided strings of onions, garlic, and bright red chilies.

Antonio walked over and pulled a dusty bottle from the rack, wiped it with a napkin from a stack by the door, and showed it to Bria. *Frutti del dios*. His family's fine red wine. Bria gave him the thumbs-up. Tonight she'd eat wonderful homegrown food, drink lovely red wine, and take Nick home to the Palazzo and give him a night he'd never forget.

She smiled into the middle distance, and felt Nick slide his arm around her waist, then discreetly cup her behind.

"Great minds think alike," she whispered, her voice husky.

"I'm not hungry," he whispered against her ear. "Are you?"

"Starving," she assured him, laughter bubbling up in her voice.

There were a couple of dozen tables in the back, near the kitchen, and the small space was hot and filled with animated conversation and the clinking of china and glassware. It was loud, boisterous, and frenetic. Bria wanted to bottle the whole place so she could take it out to sniff when she felt homesick back in Sacramento.

Nick, standing right beside her, smiled, tucking a strand of hair behind her ear, then ran the back of his finger down her cheek. "You love this, don't you?"

"Table is ready. Come on." Antonio pushed his way through the people waiting, hailed the owner, then led them to a fairly secluded table in the very back near the kitchen.

"Don't bother looking for a menu. Giovanni will bring us the specials." He uncorked the wine and gave it all of thirty seconds to breathe before he poured three glasses. *"Cin Cin!"*

They talked about the salvage business, and Antonio's plans to revitalize the winery he owned. The vineyard alongside the Pescarna/Pavina road was his. "Another year, maybe two. We'll see." Their meal was delivered to the table, big steaming bowls of a fragrant tomato-based broth, spiced with basil and filled with an assortment of cut vegetables and seafood, from small clams still in their shells to bits of calamari and sea bass.

"Nick has generously offered to refund Draven's investment in his salvage operation."

The soupspoon stopped halfway to Tonio's mouth and hung there suspended. "The whole five million euro?"

Bria nodded. "I know you couldn't convince Draven to rethink his strategy, but once the bank loan is repaid, I think we have a chance to make a few strategic short-term investments and put that money to some use helping the people."

Tonio set his spoon down, the contents untried. "Draven's concept of what a good yield is with relation to time spent in the investment doesn't seem to be improving. Neither does his understanding of high-risk versus low-risk investments."

"If you're referring to the money he's obviously socked into refurbishing the palace, I would have to agree."

"I was actually referring to the outrageous high-interest loan that's due shortly. The salvage operation was the only thing he's done of late that's made much sense, speaking purely from a financial perspective. And even that was high-risk, no offense meant, Nick."

"None taken." Nick leaned back in his chair. "But I have to ask, are you suggesting that I not give him his investment back?" His voice was a little cool.

"For the country, maybe," Tonio said doubtfully. "But I can't see that Draven will invest this money in a more conservative scheme. And nothing is going to give him a return on his investment in time to pay off this foolish loan in twenty days."

"But?" Bria swirled her wine in her glass absently.

"But I think he doesn't so much care about the money he invested with Cutter Salvage. I believe he has another agenda that I'm not privy to."

Bria met Nick's eyes over her glass. Draven's Minister of the State didn't have details about the country's finances? "Do you have any idea what that would be?"

Antonio shook his head just as Nick's phone rang. He took it out of his pocket, glanced at it, and frowned. "It's my brother, sorry; I need to take this. I'll go outside." He got up and said, "Hey, Logan—" as he walked between the tables.

Tonio waited for him to stride out of earshot before turning to Bria. "I like him, *Fiammetta.*"

Bria hadn't had anyone call her little fiery one in more years than she could count. It was her cousin's special pet name for her, and because of their closeness in age, he was more a brother to her than Draven was now. "I like him too. But tomorrow he goes back to his ship, and I must stay here. For a few days at least."

"It's not serious then? He certainly seems interested in you."

She shrugged. "Tonio, let me show you a picture." Bria pulled her sketch pad out of her tote. "This man worked on Nick's ship. I thought I recognized him. But I only saw him briefly. Does he look familiar to you?" It was a long shot, but Halkias had been surprised to see her, and he had called her *Principessa.* The idea that she should've known him, and couldn't place him, had niggled at Bria ever since.

Antonio took the sketch pad and turned it to the light. "The Greek? Cappi, I think his name is, *si*?"

"Halkias," Bria said grimly.

"You made a good likeness, especially here around the eyes. Yes. That's him. He was Dafne's personal bodyguard when she and Draven came home. What is he doing on Cutter's ship?"

Put back into context, Bria *did* remember him. Vaguely. Folding the cover over the pad, she shoved it back into her tote, then met her cousin's eyes. "Trying to kill me."

# Chapter 16

It was two in the morning. Somewhere between Pavina and the palazzo, she seemed to have removed her shoes. A sleepy guard had unlocked the door for them, then stood back to let them pass before relocking the massive hand-carved slabs behind them.

"I feel like a teenager sneaking into the house with my boyfriend," Bria stage-whispered.

He grinned down at her. "Were you the type to sneak a boy in?"

"With Marv in the house?" She muffled her laugh against his shoulder. "Hell to the no." She leaned against his side as she padded barefoot across the cool white Carrera marble entry hall. It was a vast, echoing space filled with the smell of fresh paint, which overpowered the scent of the large white Casablanca lilies in the man-sized urn on an enormous seventeenth-century gilded table in the center. The stone walls were hung with huge paintings and several smoke-damaged tapestries. Half the stuff Dafne had around looked familiar and just right. But the rest looked too new, too ostentatious.

The place was nouveau riche grand, and a bit gothic with all the heavy shadows. Only a couple of wall sconces had been left on to greet them.

Rows of pedestals topped with white marble busts lined the walls, empty stone eyes watching their progress as Nick guided her unsteady steps toward the wide, sweeping staircase at the far end. Bria put a finger up to her lips, "Sssh," she told the marble heads. "Ow!"

Nick steadied her as she stumbled over the smooth floor. He had a strong arm around her waist, which was lovely, and kept her steady—steadier—on her feet, which was awesome. His splayed fingers were right under her breast. "I love your hands," she told him, owl serious. She *loved* his hands, large and capable, and hot through the thin fabric of her dress.

She wanted those hands all over her. Now rather than later. The whole evening, while they'd had a fabulous dinner and sipped Antonio's lovely fruity wine and talked, had translated to foreplay. At some point, Nick had bunched up the back of her dress as she sat there eating, then glided his hand across her bare bottom as he explored sight unseen. As they savored cherry cassata torte spiced with brandy, he'd slid his fingers under her dress, and over the top of her thigh. Only Bria's quick action of tightly crossing her legs prevented him going farther. But the devil had danced in his eyes every time he flexed his fingers suggestively.

At some point in the evening, talk of Draven's poor financial choices had faded into background noise and she'd gotten to sip her wine and study Nick over the rim of her glass as he felt her up.

"Would Marv be waiting up there at the top of the stairs with a loaded shotgun?" Nick's quiet voice was laced with amusement. Bria shot a quick glance at his face, to see what was making him smile.

Cutter blue eyes twinkled back at her in the meager light of the sconces. A hint of the smile she heard in his voice tugged at his lips.

She dragged her slightly muzzy thoughts back from his mouth, and what she hoped he'd do with it when they got upstairs, and back to the conversation in the vast echoing space.

"Probably an automatic weapon," she told him, turning in front of him so she was walking backward. A neat trick made possible by the strong tether of his hand. "I *am* his little princess after all. Shhh. Let's take the servants' stairs and fool him. Come on." Laughing was better than remembering that there was no father waiting for her. Never had been through her teen years. Teasing was better than remembered pain.

She tugged him along, walking backward for a while, then snuggling up close beside him, pulling his arm around her shoulders. She was a little tipsy. He was steady as a rock.

Awesome.

As they took detours off the main public spaces, the hallways got progressively shabbier, until they reached the service stairs. One dim light burned at the top, leaving the base shadowy.

"No weapons," she whispered, wiping her hand across her brow. The flares in Nick's eyes made her steps falter and her blood race through her veins. "But if I *am* going to be grounded until I go to my marriage bed a virgin, could you kiss me again?"

"My pleasure, Princess." This time her title didn't sound insulting at all. His tone went smokey, his voice low, and the word sounded like an endearment. He cupped her face, running his thumb across her cheek. Bria shivered deliciously. The look they exchanged sparked with electricity.

"How much of Antonio's fine wine *did* you drink?"

Bria placed her palms on his chest. His heartbeat was steady under her hands. She stood on her toes and lifted her face. "It is most excellent wine, *sì*? You should buy cases of it to send back home."

"I did." He brushed back her hair. "You sounded more Italian with every glass."

"I'm not drunk, just a little tipsy. It feels nice. I don't want to say good-bye to you tomorrow. I think I might cry a little." She brushed her lips against his. His were cool and dry and Bria's lips clung as he wrapped his arms around her waist.

His voice was a little thick as he murmured, "I don't want you to cry."

"No. I know. It's okay." She shivered when he kissed her

eyelid, then his lips moved to her temple where nerves pulsed. He feathered a kiss there.

"Cold?"

Blazing hot. Heart beating fast, she shook her head and slid her hands up his chest to loop around his neck as she walked backward a few more feet. Her ankle bumped the bottom stair. She stepped up. They were almost eye level, but not quite. Bria took another step. "Finally, we can see eye to eye."

His soft laugh filled her with golden champagne bubbles. "You think so, do you?" His hands closed over her hips, bunching the thin red cotton, sliding it up her legs. The cool air from the drafty corridor washed over her exposed skin. "Want to go upstairs?"

She shook her head.

"The place is crawling with servants," he warned, his voice raw. "Anyone can appear any time."

Incapable of speech, she merely shrugged. She didn't give a damn if a horde of armed gorillas suddenly materialized.

Nick nudged her arms, and when she raised them, he slid the dress over her breasts, then over her head, leaving her wearing nothing more than goose bumps. Her hair fell back around her shoulders in a cool whisper.

"Jesus," he said reverently, holding her arms out wide as he slowly looked at her body. "You are so beautiful."

Bria felt dizzy, then realized Nick had lowered her down on the stairs. She stretched her arms over her head, arching her back and was rewarded by leaps of blue flame as his eyes stroked her from lips to knees. His jaw was tight, the skin stretched taut over his cheekbones. There was absolutely nothing stoic about him now. Spock had beamed out of the building.

Standing several steps below where she was stretched out like a virgin on an altar, Nick peeled his T-shirt over his head. She heard the soft plop as it hit the carpeted stairs behind him.

His skin looked like bronze satin in the muted light, his well-defined abs rock hard. The front of his jeans jutted out with what she knew was an impressive erection. Holding her gaze, his hand went to the button.

Bria sat up. "Let me," she breathed, reaching for the front fastening. She managed the button with fingers that shook, then eased down the zipper. One. Tooth. At. A. Time.

He made an inarticulate sound deep in his throat. "You're killing me, here."

Bria wanted, in some crazy way, to imprint herself onto him, so that no matter how far away he went, no matter what sea he roamed, Nick would always take a piece of her with him.

Just as she'd always have a piece of him.

She leaned forward, sliding her hands into his open fly and spreading the edges apart. He shuddered, the muscles of his stomach tightening in response.

She stroked her fingers lightly across his hard belly, his lean waist, feeling the smooth, powerful play of layers of muscle moving and shifting beneath her exploring fingertips.

She loved the heat of him and pressed her mouth to his hot skin, kissing the tender triangle revealed, the place where his skin was paler, and silky smooth. The place where a line of crisp dark hair disappeared beneath the elastic of his black boxers. She stroked her tongue across his navel, exploring the indentation.

And studiously avoided his erect penis curved against his belly.

His hands came up to cup her head, and he guided her gently to where he needed her. Urged her with his fingers in her hair.

She used both hands to push boxers and jeans a little farther down his hips. She ran the tip of her tongue from hip to hip. A shudder traveled through him, and his entire body tensed as she whispered, "Prepare . . . to die . . . slowly."

His fingers flexed tightly in her hair as his erect penis sprang free. "Let's take— Jesus, Princess . . . Up . . . stairs."

"I want to lick you all over." Her fingers explored as her hair trailed over him. She loved the soft, suedelike feel of him, the salty musk taste. God—the sheer size of him gave her pause. She'd never done this before, and wasn't sure if she could handle it. She wanted to try. She licked up and down the thick length, stroking her lips and tongue along the vein pulsing there. The head jerked in her hand.

"Oh, Jesus . . ."

She loved his unguarded response, especially when he couldn't control his heated reaction.

She licked again. Wrapping her cool fingers around his thick hardness, she tightened her grip, squeezing and stroking. Learning him. Loving him. She took him in her mouth, swirling her tongue around the very tip of his penis, and was rewarded when he gave an inarticulate cry and arched his hips.

She ran her tongue up the length of him from root to gleaming tip, and then down again, knowing she was driving him insane, and loving that she had the power to do that to him. The power to shatter that Vulcan control.

She loved the hot, salty taste of him, his musky male smell. All of it called to everything sensual and female in her. She measured his rapid heartbeats against her caressing tongue, and twist-stroked her fingers up and down his length.

"Bria—!" He convulsed and came apart.

\*     \*     \*

Bria passed a servant carrying a vase filled with pure white chrysanthemums. She'd tracked her elusive sister-in-law to the conservatory at the back of the palace. The glass-walled room ran the length of the back of the building with a panoramic view of the gardens and small ornamental pond nestled between gently rolling hills.

She remembered the dizzying delight of rolling down the springy, emerald green grass as a child, her laughter loud and carefree. She dragged her attention away from the sun-bright gardens filled with gardeners pruning and planting, another insanely expensive endeavor just for pleasure of the royal couple that Bria didn't understand.

Golden rays of sunshine streamed through the large French doors and expansive leaded windows in blinding white squares. Crossing acres of marble and soft Persian carpets, dodging islands of gilded furniture, she walked with purpose to reach her sister-in-law.

Dafne wore a gold-toned suit, pantyhose, and medium heels. At her throat, a string of Bria's mother's pearls, on her ears, Bria's grandmother's canary diamond eardrops. To go with the ridiculously formal clothing and jewelry, her sister-in-law was incongruously wrapped in a green canvas apron as she cut and arranged flowers at a marble and gilded wrought-iron table.

Dafne was lucky that Bria had a slight hangover headache and wasn't in the mood for a confrontation.

*"Buongiorno, sorella."* Dafne started at the sound of Bria's voice. She probably didn't much like being called sister, or being spoken to in Italian either.

The other woman paused with the secateurs in one gloved hand and a long-stemmed yellow rose in the other. "You're up early." The Stuart crystal vase already held at least three dozen yellow roses, and more were in boxes on the other side of the table.

Bria had seen them delivered an hour before when she'd come in from her run. Along with enough other flowers to outfit an entire state dinner, or possibly two weddings.

No wonder Marrezo didn't have any money, she thought, annoyed by the extravagance when people were looking for work to feed their families.

Dafne turned back to her arrangement.

Bria shoved stems and leaves off the edge of the table and leaned her hip against it. "Dafne, do you know why Cappi Halkias was working on Nick Cutter's ship?"

Dafne didn't even bother to look up from the rose she was ripping outside petals from. "Who?"

"Your bodyguard?"

Her sister-in-law waved the rose like a wand. "Goodness, Gabriella, how on earth would I know where or why a disgruntled ex-employee works?"

"He doesn't work for you?"

Dafne jammed the rose in the overfull vase. The stem snapped, making the rose hang limply off the side of the arrangement. She plucked out the offending blossom and flung it to the box at her feet. "I fired him for theft and inappropriate behavior years ago."

Bria frowned. "But he was here for the coronation."

"And he was fired soon thereafter." Her sister-in-law picked up another rose, inspecting it. "What's this about, Gabriella? I have the flowers to finish."

"He tried to kill me a few days ago."

The queen didn't even look up. "I'm sure you're exaggerating. Why would he do something so crass?"

Bria wanted to pluck the rose from her heavily ringed hand and smack her with it. "He recognized me—"

"Well there you have it," Dafne cut in smoothly, fluffing the foliage around the roses, trying to make the arrangement look more symmetrical. Which wasn't going to happen. "He recognized you and decided to kidnap you and hold you for ransom, knowing how fond the king is of you. Draven would pay any amount of money for the safe return of his baby sister, in the unfortunate event that you should be kidnapped." She spoke like a detective solving a grand case.

Bria bit back a sigh. "The man wasn't kidnapping me, we were on board a ship in the middle of the Atlantic Ocean. He *strangled* me."

Dafne wasn't paying much attention to the matter. She'd obviously decided that the only fix for the issue was more roses. She picked up the shears and angle-cut another stem. "Well clearly, if he'd wanted you dead, you'd *be* dead," she told Bria unsympathetically. "I'm sure he just wanted to terrorize you."

"He didn't," Bria said flatly, picking up a discarded rose with crinkled petals. "He just pissed me off."

"Gabriella! Please, the servants." Dafne glanced over her shoulder at her personal bodyguards who slept with their eyes open in four corners of the room.

Bria bit back another sound, knowing it'd be as sharp as the shears her sister-in-law was using to devastating effect. "That's illogical, Dafne." Her temples pounded and she strove for calm. "I'd met the man once, and didn't even remember who he was or where I'd seen him until I realized why he was familiar last night. What reason could he possibly have to want me dead?"

Dafne pointed the shears at Bria. "You're asking me the motivation of a servant I haven't seen in years?" She ruthlessly cut the head off a flower that had fallen out of favor. "You always were an impetuous girl, Gabriella."

*Always?* Dafne had known her for one freaking week, two years ago, and for less than twenty-four hours *this* visit.

"If you want answers," she continued sounding bored. "I'd suggest you ask them of Halkias himself. Only he knows his intent."

"I'd love to. Unfortunately he's dead."

Dafne acted as if she'd said nothing more than that he'd left no forwarding address as she carefully put the shears down on the marble table, her rings clinking against the smooth, polished surface. She glanced up at Bria, her mouth a polite smile, but her eyes disinterested and cold.

"Then that puts a full stop at the end of the sentence, doesn't it? Now, I must be off. The king has been delayed in Rome, and has asked that I fax him sensitive papers."

Bria pushed off the edge of the table. "Draven won't be back at noon?"

"Didn't I just say that? He's in an important state business meeting. He can't be expected to come like a puppy when you snap your fingers, Gabriella. You must wait." She flicked her hand at Bria, as if she was some kind of annoying bug, and swept out of the room. Just like that, scattered roses and Bria were forgotten.

Bria stared at the mangled rose head in her palm and tried to remember if there was anything she liked about her brother's wife.

She couldn't think of one damn thing.

\*   \*   \*

Since it was early, and they had four hours to kill, Bria and Nick went to Antonio's house. They woke him at what he groused was the crack of dawn. Nevertheless, Tonio was a wonderful host, and insisted on making them sandwiches and lending them transportation for the island tour Bria had planned. He packed a picnic lunch in an old backpack, grumbling good-naturedly the whole time.

Tonio's amusement only increased at Nick's face as he wheeled out his bike for them to use. A top-of-the-line, lime green Vespa.

Bria grinned as Nick struggled between manners and mockery.

"How about we borrow the family car," he asked hopefully.

He looked more relaxed than Bria had ever seen him, and heart-stoppingly handsome in faded jeans and a teal-colored T-shirt that made his eyes appear even more of a striking Mediterranean blue.

Bria grinned as he eyed the Vespa with dislike. "I think it's pretty. Is it the color or the fact that it's a scooter?"

Nick gave her a pained look and threw his leg over, then patted the seat behind him. "Get on."

Tonio waved them off.

Fabulously satiated after a night of lovemaking, Bria had risen very early and gone for a long run through the streets while he slept. Her headache was gone and she felt energetic, and ridiculously, crazy-happy. Even the talk with Dafne hadn't dampened her spirits. With just a few hours left before his departure, she wanted to show him a little of Marrezo. And since going around the island, small as it was, wasn't in the cards, there was one place she wanted him to see. Because as much as she'd strived the night before to imprint herself on Nick, she wanted to keep special memories of him imprinted on herself too.

Her favorite place from childhood was Grotta Zaffiro— the Sapphire Grotto, a maze of limestone caves carved into Monte Tolaro. It was where she'd huddled, scared and alone, hidden deep inside while Marvin had found the small boat he used to take her to safety twenty years ago. She hadn't been back since.

It was a magnificent day. Bria had decided from the moment she'd woken up that she was only going to think in the moment. She wanted to overlay that old memory, the scar of that place in that night, with the memory of Nick Cutter.

They rode through the picturesque little fishing village of Pescarna, with its houses stacked up and down the hillside, faded salmon, terra-cotta and muted mustard building-blocks one against the other. Black wrought-iron balconies dripped blood-red geraniums, and canaries in pretty cages hung from hooks in the shade.

Old men smoked on rickety benches under centuries-old olive trees, backed by majestic pines that had withstood wind and weather for hundreds of years. Women clustered near the early morning market stalls to gossip, hands painting the story as they gossiped.

As they passed, vendors were setting up their wares in stalls that displayed the brilliant colors of the Mediterranean—sunshine yellow lemons, translucent green grapes, and glossy black olives. Some of the stalls were piled high with fruits and vegetables, others groaned under the weight of the catch of the day.

"Local women used to set up their crafts between the produce booths to tempt tourists," Bria said in his ear, her arms around his trim waist, her cheek against his sun-warmed back. "It's sad not to see them here anymore. Maybe one day."

"You could put all that training of yours to good use here," Nick told her. "Bring the tourist trade back to Marrezo."

It was a nice thought. It was what she'd been trained for, what her entire life had been focused on. But even as everything in her responded to the encouragement in Nick's voice, Bria knew it would never happen now.

If nothing else, Dafne would never tolerate her sister-in-law having any part in what happened to Marrezo. *She* wanted to be the one who brought the small country back to its former glory. She'd never let anyone else steal the thunder she believed should be hers.

Bria told herself she didn't care who did it, as long as it got done. Saying nothing, she leaned against Nick's strong back and inhaled the fragrance of the wind as he drove along the winding vaguely familiar streets, following her directions.

They passed Vaccaro's, a pastry shop she remembered from childhood. It still had the exact same burgundy-and-gray awning and gold lettering on the small window. The same hot, yeasty, just-out-of-the-oven bread smell.

"Want to grab something?" Nick slowed down and pointed.

There'd be time before she left to visit some of the places she remembered from her childhood. "I'd rather wait and eat at the Grotto."

It was cool in the canyons between the buildings, and the air smelled pleasantly of oregano, garlic, and the ever-present tomatoes. Bria smiled happily against Nick's broad shoulders.

A strong smell of fish drowned out the smells of produce and cooking as they approached the small harbor where a few fishing boats were at anchor, their catches already distributed. Seagulls swooped and dived over the nets, their loud calls piercing the air. The sun warmed Bria's head and shoulders. "Draven and I used to play on that little beach over there," she said as they passed it.

"It was our lawyer," Nick said abruptly.

*Lawyer?* She looked at the beach. The penny dropped. "Your call last night?"

"We requested DNA. The results came back." She felt the movement of his chest as he inhaled. "This guy is the real deal."

Frankly, Bria thought gaining a sibling would be an awesome and a fabulous thing. But Nick, being Nick, was hard to read. "How do you feel about it?"

"I think it's interesting that this guy seems to know a lot about us, and we know bugger-all about him."

"You know he's your brother." Bria said gently, tightening her arms about his waist. She lifted her hand off his belt to point, unnecessarily, to the arrowed wood road sign for the branch off to Monte Tolaro.

"Do you want to meet him?" she asked as Nick veered right.

"He's coming to meet us all at Cutter Cay in three weeks."

"That'll be good, right? On your home turf?"

"Logan will have to fly home from his dive. He won't be happy."

They passed a small olive grove of twisted trunks and limbs, dusty-looking leaves hiding their fruit. Bria didn't care about the unknown Logan; she looked at the back of Nick's head. "How do *you* feel?"

He shrugged under her chin. "The *Scorpion* will return to home port by then. I'll be there anyway."

Bria wondered where she'd be.

# Chapter 17

The narrow, barely two-lane, road, curved in death-defying switchbacks up the side of Monte Tolaro. It had been blasted out of the sheer granite cliffs once overlaid by molten lava. On the right, a solid gray-black wall of rock soared thousands of feet above them, on the left was a sheer, dizzying drop to the ocean lapping at jagged rocks at the base of the extinct volcano.

Sunlight dazzled off the oily calm, making the water look like a sheet of silver. Nick pushed away a niggling sense of urgency about what was happening on board his ship while he was away playing tourist.

He wanted, needed, this time with Bria, short as it was. Returning to Pavina, handing her off to her brother's security people, meant saying good-bye.

That could wait.

In the meantime, he had a beautiful woman clinging to him, and a few hours of uninterrupted time, with zero responsibilities. He wasn't going to think of dead bodies, uncooperative T-FLAC operatives, sunken treasure, or prodigal brothers.

The Vespa didn't go fast and wasn't a thrill ride as a Harley would've been, but it gave him a slower, longer ride with her pressed against him. He'd miss her, he realized with a

pang. Miss her quirky sense of humor and zest for life. Miss
the smell of her skin, and the sounds she made when they
made love.

She'd be a tough act to follow, Nick mused, and hard on
the heels of the thought was the knowledge that he'd be celibate for a very, very long time. Well hell.

They reached the caves twenty minutes later and he could
see right away why the dark mysteries would appeal to a
child.

Bria hopped off the back of the Vespa as soon as Nick
stopped just outside the cave entrance. He got off and turned
around to look out over the granite cliff. Beyond the weed-
infested gravel parking lot was a scenic overview of the
sparkling Tyrrhenian Sea. It would be a good dive day, with
a little surface chop, and clear visibility.

"Come on." Bria raised her voice, excited and happy. Dying to share her special place, just as he'd done when he'd
taken her diving. Nick rubbed the middle of his chest where
a heaviness had settled. It'd been there since this morning,
when he'd woken with Bria spread over his body, a lithe,
wriggling electric blanket.

"I want to show you something amazing," she called impatiently, and Nick turned and walked back.

She was wearing a crisp white shirt, open at the throat,
tucked into skinny blue jeans. Gold sparkled at her ears and
throat, and on her fingers and toes. Her gypsy hair tumbled
around her shoulders and down her back, blowing in the
warm ocean breeze.

He held her gaze as he closed the gap. Her dark eyes
danced and laughed, soft unpainted lips curved in a delicious smile. Nick needed a taste. Right now.

He hooked a finger in the narrow red belt around her
waist, tugging her closer, then leaned in and brushed his
mouth across hers. He lifted his head, knowing a taste wasn't
enough.

"Yum," she whispered, eyes dancing. "Should we . . . ?"

No. Not if she ever expected to get anything done today.

"See something amazing?" he repeated, intentionally misdirecting. He took her hand. "Lead the way."

She tugged him to the entrance to the caves. A ragged hole—large enough to drive a train through—opened into the first chamber. It took a moment for his eyes to adjust to the dimness.

"It looks *exactly* the same." Bria stopped, looking around the rough-hewn granite walls, and holding her hair back as the wind blew it over her face.

"Is this where Marvin hid you?"

"Back there." She jerked her chin, busy scooping her hair in a ponytail, holding it in her fist to keep it from blowing. She used her hair as another might a worry stone. Something to occupy her hands while she dealt with something difficult. In this case, the memory of that day twenty years ago.

She blew out a hard breath. "Twenty years," she said, as if echoing his thoughts. "But the smell of the mineral springs and the ocean remind me of happy times too. Picnicking here with my parents. Oh! We had my fifth birthday party here with my friends." She glanced at him, her smile sad. "But it'll always remind me of Marv. Always there, a rock, even when I was too young to know I needed one."

"I think I would've liked him."

Bria's smile warmed and she let her hair go. It floated around her shoulders in a dark, shiny cloud. "He would've really liked you. He enjoyed quiet and deep." Her grin widened. "I was a trial."

"You?" He wanted to slide his hands down her back, over her waist. Feel her, warm and vibrant beneath his palms. Instead, he drew her closer to his side, slanting her a look filled with mock surprise. "A trial, Princess? I'd never have guessed."

She tipped her head back as she laughed. Then tugged him across the sandy floor through an arch that opened into another, larger chamber. It was darker, and the smell of sulfur stronger than that scent of the sea.

"I used to climb up here with a book and a sandwich."

Bria looked around, her slender fingers clasped in his. "See that rock that looks like a chaise lounge?" She pointed. "I'd sit right there, and read all day."

Nick raised a brow. "You were how old, and they let you come all the way out here *alone*?"

"I was a precocious child, but I wasn't allowed to drive ten miles on my own." She grinned. "Marvin was my designated driver. He allowed me to feel like I was here alone if that's what I wanted, but he kept watch from over there." She gestured.

"I have happy memories here. Come on, there's plenty more to see. The deeper we go, the better it gets."

"Odd place to see those." Nick indicated a row of battered-looking portable toilets, the blue paint flaked and rusted, most of them with doors falling off their hinges.

"This used to be a big tourist attraction," Bria told him, combing her fingers through her windblown hair. "Italians, Europeans, and a lot of British visitors used to flock here to see—" She grabbed his hand. "Wait, I'll show you why."

Nick allowed her to drag him farther inside, moving from chamber to chamber through jagged holes, presumably lava tubes. The floor was sandy, and slightly uneven, and Bria slipped off her shoes to walk in the cool sand. The caves started off about twenty feet wide, but each got successively wider the farther inside they went. It got cooler as well.

"Almost there," she told him as they came to a shallow slope.

"We only have a few hours, Princess. How long's this going to take?"

She didn't seem to care. He hid a smile. "Close your eyes," she ordered.

He did so. "I hope this is the part where you tie me up with silk scarves and have your wicked way with me."

Bria led him forward about ten feet. "I didn't bring any scarves."

"So that's a rain check, then?"

Her hand tightened in his, but she didn't say anything for a few moments. "You need to duck a bit here. Okay, you're clear." The cave smelled damp and a little musty, but not unpleasantly so. "You can open them now."

Nick blinked his eyes open. And stared. The ceiling arched cathedral-like a hundred feet overhead, and shimmered with watery, iridescent turquoise light. In the center of the giant natural auditorium lay a placid lake. Mist floated above its surface and draped over the gleaming emerald ground cover and foliage at the water's edge.

The cavern was about the size of two football fields. The sapphire water was crystal clear, casting shimmering waves on the pale walls. "Grotta Zaffiro," Bria murmured reverently.

"The famous Sapphire Grotto. Stunning." But he wasn't looking at the scenery. The expression on her face, the way her whole being lit up, entranced him. Brighter than any grotto. More beautiful than any sapphire.

She was all but bouncing with excitement. "There's enough light in here for all these plants, which is amazing, right? I always thought it was a faery garden." Bria pointed to the lush ferns and moss.

"This is a lot bigger than I thought," Nick admitted. "How far back are we going? I'm getting hungry."

"A couple of hundred yards-ish." They circled around the right-hand side of the lake. "The clarity is deceptive. It might look shallow, but it's spring fed, freezing cold, and forty-five feet deep." Circling around a huge fern that was as tall as he was, he turned back to look at her with a smile. "We won't be swimming then."

"No. But we could eat our lunch right here."

"Hot spring farther back?"

She smiled. "It is."

Decision made. "Okay, let's go."

The sapphire glow of the water faded as they walked. The faint odor of sulfur assaulted his nose as he came across the small pool of steaming water. The underground spring that fed it was several hundred feet away, so the water would be pleasantly hot, the smell of sulfur not too overpowering. The pool was about six feet across and surrounded by water-smoothed rock covered in a thick layer of moss. The bottom was white, powdery sand. Steam drifted lazily across the dampened stone and disappeared up to the ceiling some thirty feet above them.

Bria wiggled her toes for a few moments in the cool greenness, then plopped down cross-legged on the emerald green moss covering the rocks and immediately opened Antonio's backpack. "No wonder it's so heavy, look." She pulled out a bottle of vino and held it up triumphantly. Nick's heart leaped, then did a somersault. God. She was so pretty. Beautiful without a doubt, but today *pretty*. Her hair was gypsy-wild, her lips a sweet natural pink, and her cheeks flushed with a rosy glow. Everything about her was vital and joyous.

She looked young, carefree, and happy.

Big brown eyes danced as she unpacked the rest of their lunch, setting containers and wrapped packages beside her on the moss. "And meatball panini. And oh! Chocolate-covered biscotti. I bet it's his mother's re—"

"I'm not hungry for panini, or biscotti, but definitely for something Italian." Nick cut off her happy chatter. Kneeling beside her, he plunged his fingers into her silky hair, drawing her face up to his, and slanting his mouth over hers.

One hand dropped to the top button of her shirt. After several breathless moments, he lifted his head to look down at her.

"Don't you just love it here?"

His eyes met hers. "Yeah," his voice was thick. "I do."

"Maybe after lunch we can go swim—"

He pressed a finger against her lips.

Bria tugged his hand away, kissing his fingers. She smiled a siren's smile and murmured, "Too chatty?"

He curved his arm around her back and lowered her down. "Way," he murmured before he kissed her.

The soft-looking moss was deceptive, providing only a meager layer of protection from the hard rock beneath it. But after a moment, Bria forgot the discomfort. She let herself sink into the kiss.

Nick cupped her face, his mouth hot and hungry, impatient. As hungry as he was, Bria realized *she* was the one who was insatiable. She couldn't get enough of him. She gasped for air, lips and body begging for more, and twined one arm around his neck.

He ran his open hand from her cheek to her throat, then slid his cool fingers inside the V of her blouse, against her superheated skin. He brushed the peaked nipple with the edge of his nail. Bria whimpered, tightening her hands in his hair, and arched her back. It pressed her breast into his hand.

"You have on far too many clothes," she told him breathlessly when they came up for air. Her mouth felt hot and swollen, and oversensitized. Reaching down, she grabbed fistfuls of his T-shirt, dragging it up over his chest, then tugging it over his head. She tossed it aside and cupped the back of his head.

"Good things come to those who wait," he told her, blue eyes snapping with heat.

She wanted it now. Wanted him, but he resisted her efforts to pull him closer. Systematically, Nick undid each tiny button down the front of her shirt until he reached the waistband of her jeans, then tugged the tails free and leaned away from her to spread the fabric apart to reveal her lace bra.

"Better things come to those who take," she assured him, fumbling between their bodies to find his zipper. Behind the heavy fabric, the hard ridge of his erection jerked against her questing fingers. She got it unzipped all the way and his penis sprang, long, thick, and pulsing with life, eagerly into her hand.

She couldn't believe how soft he was there. Velvet over steel. Bria felt his heartbeat in her palm, and circled his length, running her fingers up and down. His hips bucked.

Still kissing her, driving her slowly insane, he wrapped his fingers around her wrist to hold her hand still.

Bria opened glazed eyes as he leveraged away from her. The skin was pulled taut over his cheekbones, and his eyes blazed blue fire. He used both hands to drag her jeans down her legs.

When he'd yanked her feet free, he rose, grabbing her hand and pulling her up with him. Their bodies collided, skin hot and slick, already dampened by the steam around them. Bria dug her fingers into his loosened jeans and forced them down over his lean hips, taking his boxers with them. Nick kicked them aside.

"You look like Eve." Holding her hand, he stepped over the edge of the pond into the thigh-deep water, then tugged her gently into the water beside him.

Instead of inching in, Bria jumped into the hot water, splashing it onto his chest. Smiling, Nick shook his head as he drew her body flush with his. Crystal clear water, as hot as if she'd just drawn a bath, lapped around her waist. His happy penis caressed her belly, and his hands held her against him exactly where she wanted to be.

"I think there's an apple in the backpack," she managed to murmur through the pulse hammering at the base of her throat.

Nick splayed his hands on her hips, backing her up until the mossy rocks surrounding the pond brushed her hip. "I don't need fruit to tempt me."

Her brain came up with a million rejoinders, clever things, light and teasing and sexy, but he didn't let her get even a word out before his hips pinned her back against the mossy rock and his penis nudged with gentle insistence at the juncture of her thighs.

Her breath shuddered out on a strangled sound of raw lust; her hands tightened at his shoulders as he slid one hand down her side. He drew her leg upward, cupping her thigh and sliding it over his hip. Opening her.

His eyes never left hers. Bria drew in a steam-laden gulp of air, barely able to draw a full breath through the tension he was building within her.

"What was that?" he asked wickedly. "Did you say something?"

She opened her mouth.

Nick sheathed himself in her body in one smooth, incredible motion, and she moaned with it. With him, until their voices merged as totally as their bodies and Bria lost all sense of reason or balance.

There was only him, his body pulling away, pushing back, the muscles of his chest and shoulders flexing as he held her buoyant weight in the hot silken water.

Her legs tightened around his waist, and though she tried to hold his gaze as he watched her respond to every thrust and delicious inch of him, she couldn't. There was too much emotion welling up inside her, too much feeling and heat and intensity that she couldn't risk revealing. At this moment he was the brilliant sun, and she the sea. Together they were liquid light, without end and infinite.

But what would she be when the sun disappeared? Dark, like the ocean at night. And Nick was leaving. Though she was trying to imprint on him, she knew that she'd only succeeded in imprinting every part of him even further on her heart: his smile, his blue eyes, his scent, the feel of his body beneath her hands. Inside her.

She closed her eyes, trying to draw every last ounce of sensation she could from the moment to store in her heart for the years to come. Bria threw her head back and rode the wave of pleasure as it crested.

*       *       *

The noonday sun sparkled on the smooth sapphire ocean far below the mountain drop-off as they headed back down to civilization. Satiated from a spectacular bout of lovemaking, Nick was starting to feel guilty for being absent so long when the shit was hitting the fan on his ship. He knew Jonah could handle anything, from a third corpse to the confession of a killer, but *he* needed, *wanted,* to be there.

Wanted to tie things up . . .

Needed to resolve issues . . .

But for now, he had Bria glued to his back, her arms around his waist, and her warm breath on his neck. Their downhill momentum gave the ridiculous lime green Vespa a little extra speed, and he enjoyed the feel of the hot wind through his hair.

He deserved one more hour of her company. Soon enough he'd be kissing her good-bye.

Bria rested her chin on his shoulder, tightened her arms around his waist, and leaned as he followed the first switchback. "I could do this all day," she shouted, wet hair lashing against his cheek as the wind whipped tendrils around her head.

Nick smiled. He couldn't remember when last he'd done anything unrelated to diving just for the sheer joy of it. Bria had an amazing capacity to enjoy life no matter what it tossed at her—and it had thrown a lot. She'd come from her brutal childhood a strong, vivacious woman unafraid to take life by the horns, and she pulled everyone within arm's reach along with her. She turned the world Technicolor brilliant, and somehow he wasn't sure he could go back to feeling the same way about black-and-white.

A surprising dull boom of thunder had him sending a fleeting glance up at the cloudless sky. "Sounds like a storm is coming." Didn't look like it, however. The hair on the back of his neck lifted.

"We left just in time," she said, pressing close. Nick was hyperaware of her soft breasts pushed against his back and the curve of her thighs around his hips. They'd made love several times, yet he was ready to do it again, and he felt a pang of . . .

Hell, he didn't know what it was. Regret? Relief? Whatever it was, he realized that in an hour or less, his interlude with Bria would be over. But for now, he wouldn't analyze the situation and ruin what moments were left.

Something moved in his peripheral vision, but he didn't dare look away from the upcoming curve. Scudding clouds, or a low-flying bird, maybe.

Except his sixth sense was kicking in. Hard. He risked a glance up the mountain, and saw a very large shadow positioned on the edge above the road. Thunder boomed again.

No. Not thunder. The unmistakable retort of an explosive device. He dragged a quick glance away from the dangerous curves in the road. The dark shadow shuddered on the lip of the mountain and he realized with a sick twist to his gut that wasn't a shadow—it was a fucking boulder. And it had just been blasted, dislodged, right overhead.

"Hold on! Hold on!" Nick leaned low, hands flexed to squeeze down on the brakes if needed, but until then he was gunning the bike for all it was worth.

"What happened?" she shouted in his ear.

A hell of a lot in a split second, but now wasn't the time to explain. "Bury your face against my back!" The precariously balanced boulder above had knocked loose a lot of stones and grit that fell like rocky hail, making the road a death trap of slippery scree. There was no way he could avoid the small stuff. His goal was to avoid getting flattened by the big boulder teetering on the edge and not skidding off the two-hundred-foot drop to the ocean below.

She buried her face against him, her hands tight at his waist, her heart beating a manic tattoo against his back.

With the sound of another thunderclap, the boulder broke free and Nick's heart hammered as he sped down the mountainside. The narrow road wasn't made for speed, and the little moped shook at anything over fifty miles an hour.

Nick swerved to avoid being slammed with shrapnel, using one foot to brace the Vespa as they tilted at a dangerous angle almost parallel to the road. Bria's arms clutched his middle, but she didn't scream, didn't make any sound that might break his concentration as he shifted gears. Pieces of rock pinged off the Vespa and bounced off his arms and thighs, shredding the places that weren't covered. Helmets would've been a fine idea when they'd left, but they were in Marrezo. Italians as a freaking species didn't believe in wearing them.

Second gear. Third. Fourth. Back to third gear. *Boom!* The refrigerator-sized boulder fell behind them, taking one entire lane of the road with it as it cracked the pavement, turned end-over-end, and plunged over the side. Bria molded herself to Nick's back as they heard the giant boulder hit the rocks two hundred feet below and shatter on impact.

"Made it," Nick said grimly. "Can you hang on until we get all the way down?"

He felt her nod and slowed the bike to a mere jaw-shaking forty-nine miles an hour. Slow enough that he was able to hear another blast. "Damn it," he growled. A massive rock slide would come on the heels of that detonation. This was no fucking accident.

The Vespa whined as the engine worked overtime. Zigging. Zagging. He was running when it was his style to stay and fight.

He heard Bria draw in a shaky breath, heard himself roar, "Hang on!" He skidded the scooter as close to the solid granite wall as humanly possible. And then the second barrage jettisoned over them. Crashing onto the roadbed hard. Jagged, sofa-sized blocks of granite, boulders of lava rock the size of cars dumped over them. Gravel flew as the wheels slewed into another spin. A big chunk of mountain crashed to their right and he had to swerve to get the hell out of the way.

Somehow, he had to navigate them beyond the rock slide. *Now.* If he didn't, they'd have to scrape what remained of his and Bria's bodies off the side of the mountain below. Nick cranked up the gas, the Vespa shuddering in protest.

# Chapter 18

Bria clung to him, and he was acutely aware of how much depended on his quick thinking in the next crucial seconds.

Visibility was limited as rocks and rubble crashed down around them in a thick choking cloud, surrounding them with fallout. Assorted debris, dirt, rocks, vegetation rained down without letting up, skittering and bouncing off the road, rolling down like a hellish waterfall over the almost sheer drop to the rocks and ocean below. The majority of the big chunks flew over them, but not all. Bria curved over his back like a protective blanket. Shit.

While he was trying to save her life, she'd been saving his ass from the worst of the sharp rock. Without a word of complaint. His respect swelled in his chest into something he didn't want to name.

He brought the bike to a bone-jarring stop. "Switch places," he shouted. He flung his leg over the handlebars, clearing the bike easily. "Move!"

With a startled look, Bria slid forward. He pulled the backpack off her shoulders. It had taken the brunt of the hits and was a ragged mess. But there was still blood and rips and tears in her shirt. Damn it to hell. He tossed the pack aside, then jumped on the back, covering her body with his as he revved the engine and gunned it. The thin shirt on her back was stained with blood and dirt, and he cursed again. Himself, and the assholes trying to kill them.

She knew automatically not to grab the handles for purchase, and held on to his thighs with a precarious death grip, while he kept her caged between his arms.

He'd been followed to Marrezo. Or Jesus! *Bria had been followed?* One and the same. Fuck. He didn't know. Right then he didn't care. The killer was right here on the island. He hadn't fooled anyone by bringing the princess home, where he'd been sure she'd be safe. He'd been too mesmerized by her in her natural setting to fucking notice until it was too late.

His goddamn fault. A lesson he'd learned well from his father—never let a woman take your eye off business.

But what was a man to do when the woman *was* his business?

Fingers white-knuckled on the controls, Nick squeezed the gas to gain an ounce more speed. Wasn't happening. Instead of more speed, the Vespa dragged slower. Hell! He glanced down and behind him briefly and swore out loud. The rear tire was rubbing on the motor case, which had probably been crushed against it by a bouncing rock; he thought briefly that it could just as easily have been Bria's leg, and shuddered. They weren't moving fast enough to begin with, and now they were moving slower.

Nick knocked it back to third, maneuvered through the crap littering the road, then nailed the throttle again. The bike leaped forward. He maneuvered through the rocky obstacle course—volcanic rock and granite, a black hailstorm of shrapnel that rained down all around them. He jerked the bike across the road in a crazy zig-zag, the small tires bumping and slewing over the rocks and stones littering the road surface. The front tire hit the base of the rock face, where Nick hoped to hell the shit would jettison over them.

Another muffled boom warned of the next onslaught.

The attackers obviously didn't care if they took down the whole fucking mountain, so long as he and Bria were buried alive—preferably dead.

"Nick!" She tipped her head back, her side pressing into his arm as she shifted to look at him. Her face was smudged, her eyes impossibly wide and dark in her pale, set face. "There's a lookout ahead. Right over—Just go!"

Without hesitation he went for it, keeping his head down, his body cradling Bria's as he swerved through the mine-field ahead.

The rear wheel locked, screeching in protest as he pushed the bike beyond its limit. Under the smell of dust and debris was the stink of burning brakepads and rubber as the over-worked tires started melting beneath the friction of metal and pavement.

The clutch cover lifted from the motor, clattering to the roadside.

More boulders thundered down in their wake.

Another distant boom.

The bike started pulsing up and down, indicating a warped front disc. Jesus, what next?

Nick guided the Vespa back to the interior mountain wall opposite the guardrail, engine idling. He swung his leg over the back of the bike and grabbed her arm. "Off!"

White-faced, Bria clasped his forearm with both hands to maintain her balance and jumped off the bike. Nick flat-tened her against the vertical granite wall. Then spun around and revved the engine to a high-pitched squeal. "Give me that elastic on your waist—Good girl."

Nick jumped back on the bike, spinning it to face the other side of the road. He twisted it around the accelerator several times. "Stay put!" If the bastards saw the Vespa go over, maybe they'd fucking stop blowing up the mountain on top of them.

"Nick!"

Ignoring the fear in her voice, and his own gut wrenching with it, he headed at full speed straight for the guardrail and drop-off.

As the front tire hit the edge, he dropped and rolled.

*        *        *

Bria screamed in wordless terror as, through the bombardment of falling rocks, she saw Nick disappear over the edge *with* the bike.

Ohmygodohmygodohmygod!

Her next breath brought a painful onslaught of dust into her lungs and she coughed hard against the assault.

Eyes narrowed against the dust, her gaze never wavered from the spot he'd gone over, even as she couldn't stop coughing. *Please, be okay.* If she wished it hard enough, thought it hard enough, prayed it hard enough—

"Ow!" She flinched as a fist-sized rock struck her shoulder, knocking her off balance and down on one knee. Eyes watering, heartbeat racing, she staggered to her feet, pressed by necessity against the granite mountain to avoid what was crashing down unrelentingly.

He'd driven the Vespa away from the narrow lookout point and over the edge to the ocean below. Maybe he'd hit the water? God, she hoped. But then logic dictated that he'd more likely hit the rocks. Her stomach clenched into a hard knot, part fear, part pain. She'd go see for herself. As soon as she assessed the situation, she'd call for help. Only he had his phone. She had nothing.

For God's sake, *somebody* had to notice the mountain was disintegrating! The explosions alone would have carried into town. Antonio knew where they were . . . When she didn't return, surely he would notify her brother?

She had to get to Nick now and make sure he was okay, then they could wait for Draven to return from Rome. She started across the road, arms over her head. "Crazy man!"

Nick's dark head topped the cliff, his eyes hidden from view, his voice gravel rough. "Get back!" He levered himself over the lip with his upper body, then flung one leg up, pulling himself the rest of the way onto the edge of the road. He paused as a boulder bounced twice beside him, then dropped out of sight. She would have laid out flat as a pancake, exhausted. He rolled quickly, scrambling to his feet, his whole body tense as if braced against an impending collision. He crouched low, then sprinted toward her.

Bria hesitated, torn between following his sensible instructions or dragging him to safety. She darted two more steps away from the wall and got hit a glancing blow on the head for her trouble. Heart beating wildly, she hesitated.

"What the fuck are you doing, woman?! Get *back*!"

Bria backed up, flattening herself against the solid rock face as he ran across the street. Her mountain was trying to kill them. Her island had decided to wipe them off its face with everything it had. Perhaps she just didn't belong here any longer.

Another enormous boulder dropped, missing Nick by what looked like inches. Unblinking, she watched his every move, anticipated every obstacle, every missile, as he ran.

A deafening crash, followed a minute later by an enormous splash as another boulder hit the rocky shore hundreds of feet below.

Her eyes smarted from the dust, her lungs hurt, her chest hurt. She held out her hand for him, even though he was fifteen feet away. "Hurryhurryhurry!"

Her head jerked up as another muffled crack came from high above. The sounds melted into one vast, loud, chaotic blur.

Bria realized she was holding her breath as Nick alternated between sprinting and dodging as he made his way across the rock-strewn road. It didn't seem as though the avalanche would ever stop. "Hurry!" she urged unnecessarily. Nick "I don't exercise" was moving at a remarkable speed.

When he got to her side and straightened, he wasn't even out of breath. "That was fucking stupid!" he said, voice low and steady, but his eyes blazed with temper as his fingers curled around her scraped and bleeding shoulders. "You knew what I was doing. Why did you put yourself in danger like that?"

She unclenched her fists and asked deliberately, calmly. "How will we get down the mountain now?"

He didn't let her go. He didn't shake her, either, and she realized that while she was talking, he'd been checking her over for injuries. "I have a plan," he said, not bothering to answer the question. Satisfied that nothing was broken, he pulled her tighter against the wall, and shifted his body in front of her.

Coupled with the fear that they were going to be buried alive right where they stood, his cool tones when she was scared out of her mind made her crazy.

"Were *you* hurt?" She searched his dusty, torn clothes, his dusty hair, the streaks of blood on his cheek and arms. She ran her hands across his shoulders, his chest, searching for any signs of serious injury.

His fingers ghosted across the stinging cuts on her upper shoulders and he grunted. "We've got a long walk." He reached out and briefly touched a gentle hand to her cheek, then undid the top two buttons of her shirt.

Bria managed a smile. "I don't think now's the right time to undress me, do you?"

"Fucking hell," he said savagely, baring her shoulder where a large dark bruise was already forming. "How bad does it hurt?"

Bria shrugged back into her shirt and briskly did up the buttons. "Don't feel it. We'd better make tracks, don't you think?"

"Liar."

She blew out a long, shaking breath. "If it hurts, I can't feel it. I think my body and brain are numb."

He took her hand and started walking, fast, hugging the roughhewn granite wall. "Sooner than later, whoever's up there is going to come down here to make sure they finished the job."

"Ah." Her voice shimmered with false cheer. "That makes more sense than my mountain trying to kill me." The look he shot her said without words that he considered she might have sustained a concussion, but she waved it away. "Let's get off the road. If I remember correctly, there's an animal trail leading to the beach. It's a dangerous climb, but—"

"Can you do it?"

"Of course." She'd never actually done the climb; her parents had always said she was too young. But Draven had.

She remembered waiting at the base with her mother, watching Draven and her father scale the almost vertical rock face from the beach up to the road.

They'd promised she'd get her chance. Twenty years later, here it was.

They followed a switchback around a sharp corner, and Bria pointed to a shrubby, graveled area on the side of the road about fifty yards away. "The path is that way."

The road here was also littered with rubble, but nothing new was falling.

"I haven't heard another explosion in a while. This is just residue from the last blast," Nick told her grimly. "Which means they're on their way, searching for our bodies. Hopefully the wrecked Vespa will buy us some time." His fingers tightened around hers. "Ready?"

"Yes." They bolted, hand in hand, away from the safety of the wall, running flat-out diagonally across the road toward the guardrail. Stomach in her throat, she felt as though they had targets on their backs. Slipping and sliding, Bria helped by Nick's strong arm around her waist, they came to the small gravel area with its curved guardrail, beyond which was a sheer drop-off to the sea and the rocks hundreds of feet below.

Nick helped her over the metal rail and down the first forty feet, which, while at a fairly steep incline, was crab-walkable as long as they held on to whatever was available—a shrub, a clump of grasses, a protruding rock.

Always, Nick's steadying hand, his strong shoulder, or his iron hard forearm was there to support her as they descended.

Sweat ran down Bria's throat and stung her eyes, making a multitude of small lacerations on her exposed skin itch and sting. Fire ate at her shoulder, causing it to throb with every heartbeat.

"Stop," Nick said in a harsh undertone, suddenly yanking her flat against the side of the mountain, her face pressed to the hot dirt. She heard it too. A vehicle crunching up the road fifty feet above them. It went a mile or so farther up the mountain toward the caves, then after an interminable ten minutes, during which every inch of Bria's body itched or vibrated with tension, the car returned, stopping, she presumed, where the Vespa had taken a dive.

Nick shook his head when she shot him an inquiring glance. She closed her eyes, and crouched still until even the faintest sound of movement disappeared down the switchbacks.

She opened her eyes to find Nick watching her. She raised a brow as she'd seen him do, and he gave her a faint smile. "You're a remarkable woman, Bria Visconti."

"Gee, Mr. Cutter," she said sweetly, but with a note of sincerity she couldn't hide. "You sure know how to show a girl a great time."

His smile deepened, and he reached over to brush the damp, tangled hair from her cheek before pointing back down the path. "The next bit looks tricky. Steady, and deliberate. Don't hurry. They'll have done their job if we take a header to those rocks below."

"Thank you for putting that cheerful image in my head," she told him dryly, then grabbed a sturdy shrub, testing it to see if it would hold her weight. It did, and she lowered herself another five feet. Nick stayed right with her all the way down.

It took them almost an hour to reach the bottom. By the end, she was filthy, covered in more dirt and scratches than she could ever remember from her childhood. Her ankle and shoulder hurt, and she desperately wanted a bath.

A long, hot, forever soak. Preferably with Nick. They never should have left the cave.

Standing on the rocks, the surf shooting up foaming waves nearby, Bria glanced up at where they'd climbed. "I used to wait here while my father and Draven went up." She wiped the grit from her eyes. "I thought they were so brave, and I couldn't wait until Dad would let me climb too. Now I realize my mother must've had her heart in her throat every second."

Her arms and back ached from hanging on to whatever

she could find, and the contortions needed to get from one handhold to another, but she had a feeling her father would have been proud.

Nick brushed a kiss across her dirty forehead. "What am I going to do with you?"

"I can think of a few things," she tossed out lightly. "Beginning with giving me a bath."

But he didn't rise to the easy bait. Instead, he cupped her chin on one filthy hand and skimmed his lips across hers, so softly that her heart skipped a beat.

"Are you okay?"

"God." Bria gave a shaky laugh at his appearance. "Do I look as scary as you do?" He was covered in a thick layer of dust; runnels of sweat had cleared filthy trails down his face and neck. Bloody scratches seeped and made new estuaries in the dust. His T-shirt was thick with dust and had large holes in it, his jeans ripped and torn.

"You look beautiful."

Bria managed to laugh. "Crazy man. You must have a concussion."

There was a narrow strip of beach between the water and the jagged rocks, then the side of the mountain loomed over them. "I think we can walk on the beach all the way into Pescarna," she told him.

"We'll risk it. Hiding between these rocks makes better sense in case anyone is watching for us, but frankly I'm going for speed. We need to get to the airport ASAP. Whoever was after you on the boat has followed us to Marrezo. It's not safe for you here."

She couldn't disagree. She hadn't even gotten to speak with Draven. The last thing she wanted was to bring trouble, especially potentially lethal trouble, to his door.

This time Nick didn't take her hand, and Bria matched her stride to his as he walked at a faster clip through golden sand that was so fine it squeaked under their tennis shoes. Small waves broke a few feet off the beach, and the sun was hot overhead.

She remembered skipping along this beach as a child,

searching for shells that would tell her the thrilling stories of mermaids in the deep. She remembered her kite was pink and Draven's red as the gulls wheeled about in the breeze while her parents napped on a blanket in the sun.

The breeze smelled of ocean and seaweed, and felt good on Bria's hot cheeks, drying the sweat and cooling her skin "What should I tell Draven?"

"I'll have my lawyer contact his, they can work it all out. Don't worry about him."

"But—" She did worry. Other than Antonio, Draven was all the family she had left. By now he'd have returned from Rome, and would worry if she didn't return.

Nick's smile was very white in his filthy face. "Antonio will make sure he pays off the loan, and he's going to try and convince your brother to get better financial counseling."

*But where will I be?* Bria didn't ask.

# Chapter 19

Every time Nick heard a vehicle on the road far above them, he ducked into the shelter of the large rocks beside them, pulling her down with him. Bria never heard a thing until the car was almost directly on them. "You do have ears like a bat," she teased.

He nodded. "One of my many skills."

"I'm quite fond of your bedroom skills, myself."

"Just the bedroom?"

"Steam room," she murmured. "Hot springs. Whatever."

He turned and gave her a sexy wink, but didn't encourage her banter.

She was too tired to try.

They reached the fishing village an hour later. Nick proved he had cab-attracting skills as well. There was one cab in Pescarna, and they practically bumped into it near the docks.

Nick had a knack for getting what he wanted.

She just wished he wanted her. What would it be like to be in a family like the Cutters? Close-knit siblings all in business together? Working together with a common goal? A fourth brother they'd yet to welcome home. It seemed exciting to her. A dream actually, since she'd practically grown up an only child.

The cab bumped along the cobblestone streets and within minutes they were at the airport where the crew waited, playing cards with the ground crew in the terminal building.

A half hour after flagging down the taxi, they had boarded the plane, which immediately taxied down the runway. "Now what?" Bria tightened the seatbelt across her lap.

Nick looked out the small window. "We're going to Plan B."

"Cool," she settled back. Too tense to relax, and too grateful to still be with Nick, no matter the reason. She'd talk to her brother as soon as she could. But not now. "What *is* Plan B?"

He accepted the hot towel the flight attendant handed him with a pair of tongs and a smile. He scrubbed at his face, then dropped her hand to give her a look that made Bria's blood cool in her veins. A second ago she'd been hot from all the running, climbing, and fear; now she was ice cold.

She twisted her hot towel between her fingers because suddenly she had a bad, bad feeling when Nick fixed his blue eyes on her face and didn't smile.

"I didn't know if Halkias's attack on you was sexually motivated, or—" Nick paused. "Something else. Plan A was bringing you here, where your brother's expensive security detail would make sure you were safe from whatever is going down on board the *Scorpion*. I didn't believe that you were the target. But I sure as hell wasn't prepared to take the risk that you *were*."

"I'm not."

Nick cocked a brow. "Really?" he said savagely. "We're here in Marrezo, and some sick fuck just tried to bury you under an avalanche!"

"Maybe some sick fuck followed *you* and tried to bury *you* under an avalanche!" Bria returned hotly. "Why would anyone want *me* dead? It's not like I wrote a shitty press release, or overbilled a client to warrant it. I don't *know* people who kill people."

"Could be an enemy of your brother's. Bria, this looks

political. Others might be aware that Draven is drowning in debt."

"That makes no sense at all." She kept her voice rational and even with Herculean effort. "How would killing me have anything to do with him?"

He looked at her calmly. "Maybe there's a large life insurance policy on you."

"That's absolutely ridiculous!" Bria's pulse raced so fast she felt sick. "First of all, there isn't. Second of all, even if that was the case, who bought the policy? Can you even buy a life insurance policy on someone else? If so, that seems an open invitation to murder every day of the week. And who'd do it, if they could? Draven? That would mean that my own brother wants me dead, which is patently absurd."

She felt hysteria building. She'd never been hysterical in her life. Furious, cranky. Irritated. Annoyed. Hysterical? No. But hysteria was rising like a poisonous tide inside her, making her want to cry. Or throw up. Or both. The thought that anyone—particularly her brother—wanted to kill her was insane.

But if *she* wasn't the target, then *Nick* had a killer after him.

That almost made it worse.

"I agree. It is," Nick said in his cool, calm, rational voice, which should've been comforting, but freaked her out another layer.

"But until all questions have been answered to my satisfaction, and since we don't know if whoever pulled that stunt was after you, or me, I'm not risking leaving you anywhere unprotected."

Bria wasn't foolish enough to tell Nick she could take care of herself. Yes. In a dojo. But someone had tried to kill her twice, either her, or by association with Nick. She wasn't stupid. "Where, then?" *What about you?* She wanted to scream. *Who will protect you?*

"Not back on board."

"Sacramento is a long way away."

"No. I have friends who'll keep you safe until this is re-solved."

"Do I have any say in this?"

"No."

"I don't want to go off with someone I don't know to— Thanks," she added to the attendant who brought her an-other wet towel and took the used towels. "Where will they stick me?"

"Wherever they consider you the safest."

In other words, not with him. Bria twisted the second, unused, towel in her hand. "And you'll be back on the *Scor-pion* with a killer on board." It wasn't a question. And Nick didn't answer. In fact, as he'd wiped the dirt off his face, he'd frozen back into the man he'd been when she'd first met him.

Inscrutable. Cold. Impersonal.

As soon as the plane reached cruising altitude, Bria ex-cused herself and went to the bathroom to wash up. When she saw herself in the mirror she started to laugh, albeit a little hysterically. She was a mess. Dirt she'd missed with the towel, sweat-streaked makeup smeared by her own at-tempts to clean herself, blood from the multitude of cuts, filthy clothes. No wonder the flight crew had looked at them strangely when they'd shown up in the cab. The real wonder was that the cab had picked them up at all.

Turning on the taps to fill the small sink, she stripped off her clothes. She only wished she could wash away the ache slowly building up in her chest as easily as the dirt.

*     *     *

Nick left Max Aries a phone message to call back ASAP. He ordered the counterterrorist operative to have his people meet them in Tenerife the second the Lear landed. The rock slide on Marrezo, coupled with Halkias's attempt on her life, made discounting Bria's risk impossible to ignore.

Even if she was just collateral damage, posing a potential risk to the Moroccans' plans by being in the wrong place at the wrong time, he was damned if he'd put her in the line of fire. He couldn't leave her on Marrezo. He couldn't take her back on board his ship. He couldn't let her travel solo across the globe back to her life in the U.S. Not until he'd transported the diamonds to Cutter Cay, and Aries and his team had gotten their man or men.

T-FLAC had access to safe houses, and people trained to protect. Nick demanded both for Bria.

He didn't know *who* the fuck the target was. But taking Bria completely out of the equation would ease his mind while he found out.

"Hey! Is there a blanket out there?" Bria shouted from the head.

Nick glanced up, waving away the flight attendant who'd stepped through the door from the cockpit at Bria's call. He grabbed a cashmere throw from a pile on a nearby seat, and carried it down the aisle.

Her face was clean, and stunningly beautiful despite the scratches and small bruises marring her smooth olive skin. She was wearing just her red bra and panties. He handed her the lightweight blanket. "Every man's fantasy. Your clothes disintegrated."

"Hold these." She dumped her wet clothing in his extended hand. Wrapping the blanket under her arms she stepped out of the bathroom. "If the flight crew was behind a door *I'd* locked, I wouldn't be wearing anything at all."

He chewed off his smile before she saw that her crankiness charmed him. Sympathetic to what she must be feeling, Nick brushed the back of his fist across her strong jaw. "I could barricade the door."

She moved her head out of reach. "I think that's some kind of National Transportation Safety violation." Her voice was even, but her color was high.

"It's a violation having you *like* this and not *having* you like this." He held up the clothes. "What shall I do with these?"

Walking back to their seats, she took her wet shirt and jeans from him, spreading them out over two leather seats that were in direct sunshine through the small porthole-like windows. Adjusting the overhead air vents, she said, "Hope-fully, by the time we get there these will be dry. If not, at least I'll arrive clean. I'm pretty tired of not having any clothes. I desperately need to go shopping before I go any-where else."

"That can be arranged."

"With no money or credit cards?"

"Still can be arranged. Don't worry about it."

"I'll worry about it—*slightly*." Her smile slipped. "Oh, boy! I have to call the palace and Antonio, as soon as possible. They'll both be worried sick."

"They'll be notified."

"Notified?"

She flopped down in her seat and chewed her lip as she looked up at him. For a moment she squeezed her eyes shut, clearly trying to get a grip on her emotions. "Okay." The light tone was gone. "This is absolute bullshit. You know things, and I have a right to know them too, Nick. You have to tell me everything. I know something serious is going on, but I have no idea what. And since someone has tried to kill me twice, I deserve a straight answer."

His expression closed, so she flashed him her boobs. "I know how to thaw the deep freeze." She waited until he smiled, then rearranged the blanket so it looked like she was wearing a strapless sundress. Jesus. What the hell was he go-ing to do when they parted?

"I need to know what I'm up against."

Nick touched her sore cheek and gave a quick nod, com-ing to grips with something inside himself that he didn't have time to analyze. If it needed analyzing at all. "I'm go-ing to clean up as well. Then I'll tell you what I can. See if they have something for us to eat, will you? I'll be right out."

Nick washed off the dirt and grime, but opted to shake the dust out of his clothes rather than sit around in a fucking blanket. He stepped out of the bathroom, drawn to Bria's profile as she stared out of the little window at the clouds.

She didn't look at him as she said, "Molly is making something for us. Coffee okay?"

He presumed Molly was the flight attendant. Typical Bria learning the woman's name. "Yeah, thanks." Nick settled in the seat opposite her instead of across the aisle. "A few weeks ago, a friend who works for a covert counterterrorist group asked me to do him a favor. An unknown group has been moving conflict diamonds out of Africa and filtering them into the North and South American markets undetected."

Bria's gaze snapped to his.

The marks—bruises, cuts—made him feel feral. When he found the party or parties responsible for those marks, they'd wish it was T-FLAC who beat the shit out of them. He took a breath. Counted his heartbeats. Took another calming breath.

"When it was discovered that they've been using noncommercial vessels—like the *Scorpion*—to move the diamonds undetected, they asked— Thanks Molly." Nick waited until the woman had set up their light meals, and waited until she went back to the cockpit and shut the door before continuing.

"They're very close to closing in on the principals, the man or men at the top. They just needed a little more time, and since they knew the route and method the diamonds were taking, they asked if I'd let the diamonds come on board the *Scorpion*."

She ignored the food, concentrating on his words.

"I followed two men from Rabat to Tarfaya, where we had a meeting in the medina. And the same café where you showed up to ask Asim Nabi El Malamah to take you to the *Scorpion*."

Bria raised a brow. "How do you know I asked for a ride to your ship?"

"*I* was El Malamah. I believe that they saw you there, then someone on board alerted them to the fact that you'd shown up in their business, on board the ship transporting their diamonds."

"I talked to that man. He wasn't you. Different accent, Different gestures—" Her eyes narrowed as he gave her a steady look. "It was you!" She leaned over and smacked his arm hard. "You rude bastard!" Then swatted him again for good measure. "You are one ballsy guy, Nick Cutter."

"As El Malamah, I boarded the *Scorpion* in Tarfaya and hid the uncut diamonds in our bins in the hold where we store our salvage. Then El Malamah disappeared, because dollars to doughnuts, the Moroccans planned to kill him before he got any funny ideas about millions of dollars' worth of diamonds in a location that only he knew."

Snugging the blanket around her shoulders, she drew her feet up on the chair and wrapped her arms around her legs. She rested her chin on one knee. "But how will they know which bins to find them in when you get—where?"

"Cutter Cay. Jonah and I marked the three bins. I called them and gave them the bin numbers and locations. I didn't get paid until their men on board confirmed that the diamonds were indeed on board, and hidden in plain sight."

"What men on board? Halkias and the brownie guy?"

"Fakhir was hired on new in Tarfaya, Halkias has been with us a year, and Jonah and I thought he was loyal. But money talks, and clearly he was paid to eliminate what the Moroccans considered a threat."

"Halkias was Dafne's bodyguard a few years ago. She fired him for stealing, so I guess dishonesty was a pattern of behavior."

"Wait. You're telling me this *now*?"

She gave him a cross look. "We've been a little busy."

Good point. Nick filed away the info to add to the puzzle. "We suspect—"

"Who we?"

"Jonah and myself. That Fakhir was caught trying to help himself to some of the diamonds in the hold, and was killed for his trouble."

"How many bad guys are on board?"

"We start with a skeleton crew, then hire on five or six new people when we're at our closest port of call for the salvage. In this case, we hired on six guys in Tarfaya, knowing that at least a couple, if not all, of them, would be working for the Moroccans."

"Well, we know there were at least three bad guys on board. Someone had to kill two of them."

"Possibly more. And we don't know why someone followed us to Marrezo. If that was some kind of warning, an intent to kill, or a message—I have no idea how to read it. Whatever that was about, I couldn't leave you there unprotected, no matter what I promised the good guys."

"The Palazzo is crawling with security guards and infra whatever beams," Bria pointed out, rubbing her hand up and down her blanket-covered legs. "I would've been safe there."

"You'll be safer with a trained T-FLAC operative, believe me. I won't be able to focus on what's going down on my ship if I need eyes in the back of my head to protect you from a determined assassin."

"They aren't after me."

Nick wasn't willing to bet her life on that. "I believe that ninety-nine percent. The other one percent wants you somewhere where I don't have to worry about you. That's why I don't want you anywhere near the *Scorpion* until this is over."

"Fair enough. Believe me, I have no desire to be anywhere near some spooky phantom killer. You can't even know for sure if it was just the new hires, right? Halkias had worked for you for a year."

"Right." Nick exhaled. "When we get to Tenerife, one of the black ops guys will be waiting. He'll make sure someone is with you every second until they know for sure who's in charge and apprehend him or them. Hopefully the ship won't have to sail all the way to Cutter Cay before that happens. Once the Moroccans and the principals above them are all in the net, Max Aries and his team will come and retrieve the diamonds, and my part in this will be over."

"And I can go back to Sacramento and my new job?"

Nick hesitated. "Yeah."

*     *     *

All things would've been right in Nick Cutter's world, except whoever Aries had arranged to guard Bria wasn't there when the Lear jet landed at Tenerife North airport five hours later.

He stuck his phone into his back pocket. "I'm not fucking leaving you here standing on the tarmac hoping someone shows up. They'll have to transport themselves out to the *Scorpion*."

"I think I'll be safer here, Nick. Seriously. Nobody is going to make an attempt to do anything to me in a crowd of tourists. I'll stay with a lot of people and wait. I'm sure your friend will send someone soon."

"And if he doesn't get those messages for hours? Or days? What the hell will you do?"

"Take care of myself, which is what Marv trained me to do. Go. I know you're worried about Jonah and your friends. I'll be fine."

Yeah fine. Her banged-up, scratched, bruised face was pale, and she rubbed her upper arms as though she were cold. Her shirt and jeans were still damp, but it was a tropical ninety degrees.

Fuckfuckfuck!

"I can't do that, Princess, I fucking can't." He pulled out his phone and left his friend a rude and terse message to get his ass in gear right fucking now, and go pick Bria up on board the *Scorpion*. "Let's go."

The flight in his waiting chopper took an hour and a half on the return trip. Jonah had pulled anchor as instructed. The *Scorpion* was on its way back to the Caribbean and Cutter Cay. Aries better get his shit together and the matter resolved. Nick hadn't been shitting him. The man had two days and counting to resolve the situation, or Nick would put the entire crew ashore and jettison a fortune in uncut diamonds.

Nick circled the *Scorpion* once in a low sweep before heading in.

"She looks as graceful as a white bird skimming across the water. Magical," Bria observed, sounding subdued. She must be exhausted. Hell, Nick admitted, *he* was pretty worn out with all the high drama as well. A shower and a decent night's rest should iron out the majority of their kinks.

Still, the sight of his ship revitalized him.

As many times as he'd flown to and from the *Scorpion,* his pride and joy, the ship he'd helped design and spent six months outfitting still looked beautiful as she skimmed across the deep blue ocean, leaving a delicate trail of froth in her wake.

Nick felt an intense sense of pride as he lightly touched down on the landing pad on the aft deck.

He turned to Bria as he unsnapped his belt. "Promise me you won't do anything foolish? Let me repeat my earlier warning, stick to me like Krazy Glue, and if not me, Jonah."

She gave him a serious look. "No problem."

Jonah waited for them inside the sunroom. "Nothing," he told Nick, who hadn't asked, with a smile. "Hello, Princess, this is a pleasant surprise."

Jonah glanced back at Nick. "I sent the dive team off in the motor launch headed for Tenerife as instructed. They were ecstatic to fly home early from there. I entrusted Olav with the sword and medical kit, to save you another flight."

"Good." Fewer people to worry about, and priceless artifacts secure. Nobody was going to waltz off with the gold coins or silver bars. They were just too numerous and bulky, especially given the conglomerate-encrusted state the hundred-pound silver bars were in.

When he linked his fingers with Bria's, she moved in closer, her shoulder brushing his arm. His friend appeared to wink at him. "Did you just wink at me, Santiago?"

Jonah laughed, rubbing his eye. "Nothing so high school. Have something in my eye. If I was to wink at anyone, it would be this gorgeous woman."

"Save your strength," Nick told him dryly, appreciating Jonah's lack of curiosity as to their appearance. For now. "The fewer people we have on board, the better I like it. I want to send some of the crew off in the tender next."

Jonah rubbed his hand around the back of his neck, then nodded his agreement. "Which ones?"

"Don't care. Since we have no idea about the good, the

bad, and the ugly, let's halve the odds, and send off fifty percent of them immediately."

Jonah raised a brow and glanced from Bria back to Nick.

"The princess is here until Aries airlifts her to wherever," he told his friend, without him having to ask. A valuable trait in a friend, Nick acknowledged gratefully. "But for now, she's with one of us. No exceptions."

"I'm desperate for a shower," Bria said brightly. "Who do I get to do that with?" She looked from one man to the other.

Nick was desperate for a shower as well, but he had things to do, and being distracted by a naked Bria was counterproductive. He met Jonah's eyes. "Do you want to choose who goes and who stays?"

Jonah, sensing his need, said smoothly, "I need some down time with zero confrontation. I'd prefer for you to do it."

Nick smiled his thanks. "I'll take care of it from your office then." Where he could gather his thoughts and grab that shower Bria-free at the same time. "Give her the Bersa in the safe."

\*       \*       \*

"Sorry you pulled the short straw," she told Jonah as they bypassed the small elevator, taking the stairs down to Nick's cabin.

"He's not happy about ditching the crew. But he's worried as hell about—"

"He told me about the extra cargo," Bria said quietly, although there wasn't anyone around.

"Did he now? That's interesting." Jonah blinked his watering eye a couple of times. "Yeah. That. But he likes to look at the log book and charts several times a day. It was nothing personal."

Bria hadn't thought it was anything personal before Jonah had said it wasn't.

"He's pretty self-contained, isn't he?" Bria asked rhetorically, as Jonah used what she presumed was a master key and let her into Nick's cabin, then locked and bolted the door behind them.

"He's . . . reserved." She followed him into Nick's office and waited while he opened the safe, then handed her the Bersa. "He doesn't trust easily. You know how to use this, right? No shooting off strange men's body parts before Nick gets back?"

Bria smiled. God, she couldn't be more tired, more darned confused, and more jumpy. She hoped Nick was right. That his other friend would come and get her, and that, for Nick's sake, this was all over sooner than later, without anyone else getting hurt. Getting dead. She shivered. She needed to get out of her damp clothes and into a hot shower.

"Part of it, I think, is just who he is." Jonah grabbed a few clips, then closed the wall safe. "He's pretty calm and collected most of the time—"

"*Most* of the time?" Bria asked, amused as she sat on the foot of the bed to remove her damp, sandy tennis shoes. "Someone just tried to kill us on a mountain and he barely broke a sweat."

"Pretty much all of the time." Jonah blinked rapidly to dislodge whatever was still in his eye, which was now bloodshot and watering. *Men!*

"Don't keep rubbing it, you'll scratch your cornea! Would you like me to get that out?" Bria stepped forward.

He held up his hand with a smile. "No, I'm good, thanks." Sitting in the chair by the window, he swung his feet up on the ottoman and grabbed one of the magazines on a nearby table. "I'll just wait right here while you're in there. Lock the door, and take your time." Taking out a Beretta, he laid it down on the table beside him.

"You don't really think anyone is going to break in, do you?"

"Doesn't matter what I think, honey. It's what Nick thinks that counts." Rubbing his eye he opened the magazine. "Enjoy your shower."

Bria took her time. A sponge bath in a twelve-inch sink,

while the best she'd been able to do, didn't cut it. She needed lots of soap and hot steamy water to wash away the dust, and to soak out some pretty colorful bruises.

She was sorry Jonah was stuck babysitting her, but with any luck Nick would be in the bedroom waiting for her when she was finished.

Putting on the white toweling robe that was hanging behind the door, she stuck the gun in the deep pocket and unlocked the bathroom door.

Jonah, his back to her, was at a mirror over the dresser across the room. She padded over to him. "Men!" She gently tugged on his arm. "Why do you have to be so damned stubborn? Let me look at that before you poke your eye out."

"My contact has a tear in it I think. I have it."

"If you had it, Jonah, you wouldn't have your finger in your eye," she told him with asperity, tugging at his wrist. "Let me look."

Jonah turned slowly.

One eye was a dull brown. The other, the white red from prodding it, was a startling, bright Cutter blue. Her belly dropped to her toes. "Oh my God, *Jonah*! Does Nick know? He doesn't, does he?"

# Chapter 20

Able to breathe freely for the first time in what felt like a month, Nick opened the door to his office, then strode across to open the connecting door to the bedroom. Half an hour to shower and collect his thoughts and he'd get a second wind. He'd called in six crew members and assigned them to the motor launch to return to Tenerife immediately.

Giving them no time to collect their personal items, or even return to crew quarters, he escorted them to the launch and had seen them off. At gunpoint.

No doubt they'd set foot on dry land and contact whomever they had to contact, and without a doubt there was a possibility that one or more of the remaining men were in fact the bad guys. But the odds were severely shortened.

It was the best he could do.

He anticipated joining Bria for a slower, more exciting shower, then taking her to bed for a few hours before he filled Jonah in on what'd happened on Marrezo.

"Hey, buddy, I'm here to—" His best friend and the woman he— And Bria stood close together. Bria had an intense look on her face, Jonah looked guilty as hell, and she was saying urgently—

"Does Nick know? He doesn't, does he?"

They turned as one as he asked coldly, "Does Nick know—*what*?"

He searched Bria's pale face first. Her dark eyes were large and troubled, and she took a step forward. "Ni—"

"What don't I know, *pal*?" He dragged his attention from Bria to look at his best friend. One look at Jonah's face, and Nick felt as though someone had hit him across the chest with a two-by-four.

Jonah started back. One eye was its customary brown. The other was as familiar to Nick as looking into a mirror. Or looking at Zane or Logan.

"You fucking son of a bitch! *You're* the brother?" he demanded, ice cold to his marrow.

Guilty as hell, Jonah put out his hand. "I can expla—"

One moment Nick felt absolutely nothing. The next, blind rage exploded out of nowhere. His fury erupted like Mt. Vesuvius.

He pulled back his arm and slugged Jonah square in the nose. Idiot didn't even put up a hand to protect himself. He went down without a whimper.

Bria grabbed Nick's arm, holding on to him with both hands. "Don't, oh, please don't. Let Jonah explain."

Nick shook her off, staring down at the man he thought he'd known so well for two fucking years. The stinking proof of his father's infidelity. The proof that shook Nick's trust to its very foundation. Sucker punched, he struggled to shove the anger somewhere manageable.

It wasn't goddamned easy! "I'm not interested in explanations." His voice was filled with icy disdain that cost him. "Are you going to get up? I'm not done beating the shit out of you."

"I think I'll lie here and look at the ceiling awhile," Jonah said, but after a few seconds he sat up a bit, leaning on one elbow. He wiped the back of his hand under his bleeding nose, which was already starting to swell. "I've got plenty of explaining to do. But I guess that can wait." He gave Nick a baleful look from one blue, very bloodshot eye and one brown eye.

"Is your name even Jonah Santiago?"

"Jonah Cutter."

"Fucking, fucking hell. He gave you our name as well?"

"Afraid so."

"You lied on your papers." The least, the very *fucking* least of Jonah's perfidy, Nick thought savagely, but right then the only thing he could wrap his brain around.

"Am I relieved of my duties?"

Nick narrowed his eyes as he looked down at the reclining, traitorous son of a bitch on the floor. Wishing he'd waited another fifteen minutes to send the crew off in the motor launch so he could've sent Jonah with them.

"Do you have anything, I mean *anything* to do with the diamonds?" he demanded tightly, noticing that so far Bria had remained silent. How long had she known about this?

"Nothing. I swear."

"We all know how much your sworn oath is worth." Nick scoffed, his chest tight, and his breathing constricted. He'd never suspected this. Never. Not from Jonah—"You're still captain until we get to Cutter Cay, then your ass is fired, and I never want to see you again. Same goes for Logan and Zane."

"You can't speak for Logan or Zane."

Nick's eyes narrowed dangerously, and his temper slipped its moorings. "You think we don't stick together, you conniving dishonest prick? Think again. The three of us are like this!" He held up twined fingers. "Think that ingratiating yourself to me, insinuating yourself onto *my* ship, into my *life,* will change that? It won't. Get out of here—I can't stand looking at you."

Jonah straightened his shoulders, the muscle in his jaw jumping as he clenched his teeth and stumbled to his feet.

He started for the bedroom door, then turned to address Bria, his voice level and contained. "Check his hand. I think my nose broke it." He let himself out, closing the door quietly behind him.

Nick stared at the closed door. "I didn't see it. How could I not see it?"

His fiery Bria sounded subdued as she said, "He was

waiting until the three of you were together at Cutter Cay. Think about that for a second, Nick. He was waiting until you were on your home turf. Until you had the support of your brothers. He was going in alone. No support at all. To tell you all something he must have known would hurt and upset all of you."

He turned on her, his stomach sick. "You feel sorry for *him*?"

"I feel sorry for all four of you. None of you asked for this. It isn't a situation of your making." He wanted her to shut up, but she kept talking. Not giving a shit that he was twisted inside. "What a wonderful gift this could be if you just went with it. He's your best friend. You already like each other—"

Nick gave her what Zane called his dead-eyed snake look. She took a step back, but kept talking. "Okay, you *liked* each other for two years. I think that once you think this over, you'll realize that Jonah is just as much a victim of what your father did as you, Zane, and Logan."

A victim. He was never a victim. He had to call Logan. Feeling in his pocket for his phone, he realized with a jolt of pain that he'd left it in the pilothouse. "Damn it to hell."

"Is your hand broken?"

Felt like it. "No. I left my phone in his office." He was damned if he'd go there and see Jonah's lying, duplicitous face.

"You can't avoid him until you get home," Bria said gently.

Ten days . . . Hell. "I could ignore him if we were the only two people on a fucking ice floe in the middle of the Arctic. Don't open the door to anyone. I'm going to take a shower."

He took a punishing ice-cold shower, then turned up the heat, letting the water scald the anger from his bones.

His father—Jesus. Nick didn't even have a word in his vocabulary to describe how he felt about his father. Yeah, the lawyer had contacted them and said there was another kid out there—intellectually he knew it wasn't that kid's fault— that son of a bitch *Jonah's* fault.

In spite of his anger, his lips twitched. Christ. His father had named his fourth son *Jonah*? He slapped his palm against the wall. His hand wasn't broken, but it hurt like hell and was starting to swell.

He. Did. Not. Want. To. Fucking be *amused* by *anything* about this whole goddamned mess.

He wanted his simple, *un*-fucking complicated life back. Diving, drinking a beer with a good friend at the end of the day, sleeping with the occasional attractive brunette . . .

Diving was still in. But Jonah had ruined the drinking a beer with a friend. And, God only knew. Bria had certainly put the kibosh on sleeping with any other attractive brunette. Between the two of them they'd fucked up his life in ways he could never have anticipated in a million years just a week ago.

What a clusterfuck. A killer possibly still on board. Killers loose on Marrezo. Fucking Aries AWOL. Bria glued to his side for the duration. And Jonah the missing link. Nick braced his hands on the mosaic-tiled wall, letting the hot water pound his back. Pound on the bruises, nicks, and cuts sustained from the rock fall.

Shit. He lifted his head, water pouring into his face. He hadn't even looked at what Bria must've sustained. He shoved away from the wall, and backed into silky, curvy, wet Bria.

He'd been so engrossed he hadn't heard her come in. And him with ears like a fucking bat.

She put her arms tightly around his waist, laying her cheek on his back. Sliding her hands up his chest, she held him tightly, pouring soundless empathy into him like refilling a well. He felt the soft brush of her lips across his shoulder blade, then she slipped under his braced arms.

"You're not part of my plans," he told her roughly.

Bria placed her cool hands on either side of his face and murmured, "I know, *tesoro,* I know." And she kissed him, so pure, so perfect that it dislodged an icy pain deep in his chest.

The gentle sweep of her tongue felt like a benediction. A man drowning of thirst, he feasted on the flavor of her sweetness, and was warmed by her heat. Wrapping his arms around her because he just couldn't help himself, Nick deepened the kiss.

Hands on her hips, he dragged her against his erection. Her hands in his hair. His on her sweet ass. The pounding water scalding hot. Pounding. Sluicing over their heads. Sheeting their faces. Lips fused.

Her shiver as he ran his finger down the crease of her ass. His shudder as her fingers closed around his length and guided him to her.

Nick cupped the cheeks of her ass, lifting her. Positioning her.

She tightened her arms around his neck, and wound her long silky legs around his waist.

The thump of her back as he pressed her to the cool mosaic wall.

The hot wet glide as he slid inside her to the hilt. So exquisite neither could bear to move. Her body tightened inexorably around his length.

"Gabriella . . ." He flexed his hips, his climax close. Intense. Earth-shattering. Once more. Pounding into her unbearable. Perfect. Heat.

Hope. Again. Harder. Deep. Faster.

Bria taking every bold stroke. Her gasps. His. Wordless communication, drenched in need. Head thrown back in wild abandon. Teeth sharp on his shoulder. Nails scoring his back. Heels drumming at his waist as she arched for deeper contact.

"I love you. I love you I love you." Her cries echoed through the steam-filled room. Echoed and reverberated deep in his chest.

Limp, exhausted, he carried her to his bed, tumbling her on the crisp white sheets. He was still inside her, and they fell asleep that way, the sunset painting the white room in spectacular Technicolor.

*        *        *

He wasn't asleep this time; Bria could practically hear Nick's brain working. They'd fallen asleep like two puppies.

But they hadn't slept long. An hour maybe. Then he'd rolled her over and started kissing his way down her body.

He'd been insatiable, and in the past hour they'd made love twice, desperately, and almost wordlessly.

She got it. For Mr. Spock, this had been a day filled with far too much emotion. She stroked his hair. Poor baby, he just wasn't equipped to handle it.

Her lips curved. He'd learn. She'd teach him.

And she had faith that he and Jonah would work it out.

He was lying on her arm, which had gone to sleep, but she combed her fingers through his hair, loving the silky feel of it drifting between her fingers. Loving petting him. God, she mentally rolled her eyes. Loving *him*. How on earth had that happened?

"You don't have to stay. I've got the Bersa, and there's a solid lock on the door. I'll be fine by myself if you have places to be."

"I want my phone. But I'll call for it." He rolled off the mattress and got to his feet, unconcerned about his nudity, which was awesome for Bria because he was deliciously sexy to look at. All bronzed muscle and hairy chest. Her eyes lowered to his penis, which was semi-erect and still happy to see her. "Oh, no you don't, woman," he said, not smiling even though little bright blue flares sparked in his eyes. "If you had your way we'd be in here until morning. Stay put, take another nap."

He was back to Spock. Unemotional and detached. The only way he knew how to handle things.

Bria stretched her arms over her head and arched her back. Oh yeah, those flares smoldered. "Extremely rude, Cutter. Snap out of your pissy attitude when you have a naked woman in your bed. A naked willing woman."

The strain around his eyes lessened as she'd meant it to do. He pressed a quick, hot kiss to her lips, then picked up the phone by the bed. His Bluetooth lay right beside it. But he wasn't communicating with Jonah.

"Khoi? Oh, Basim. I left my cell phone on the chart table

in the pilothouse. Yeah. Right away. While you're at it, bring a pot of coffee—"

"And brownies."

This time he did smile. It was strained, but his lips curved as he sat down beside her hip, then muttered, "To hell with it," and rolled over on top of her. "And brownies." He reached out and tossed the phone on the bedside table with a clatter. It bounced onto the floor

"That'll take at least ten minutes. What do you wanna do while we wait?"

It actually took the steward twelve, but they were still rolling around on the bed when there was a brisk knock on the door. "Tell him I changed my mind. Brownies. Later."

Nick cupped her cheek. He was still hard inside her, and her body was clenching around him as the last orgasm faded. Easing out of her, he threw his legs over the side of the bed and stood, leaving Bria in a very vulnerable position.

Still aroused.

She closed her legs and sat up to grab the sheet.

"Leave the tray outside, I'll get it in a minute." Nick called, grabbing the robe she'd left on the floor when she'd gone into the bathroom earlier.

She shot him an inquiring look.

"I'm not taking any chances. The Sig and Bersa are both in the office." He held up a hand, and they listened to footsteps retreat down the hall outside.

Nick went into his office, and returned with both guns. He placed the Bersa on the bedside table, picked up the dropped house phone, then went to open the door with the Sig pointed into the corridor.

Stacking the pillows behind her, Bria waited for him to lock the door and come back to bed.

He looked distracted, and she figured he'd had enough calisthenics for the day. She tossed back the sheet and stood beside the bed. "I'm going to grab another quick sh—"

The phone in his hand rang once. "Cutter. Jesus. About time! Where the hell— Yeah. Fine. Good or bad?" He walked to the window, bracing his shoulder on the glass. "You're positive?"

Bria strolled into the bathroom, leaving the door open. Just as she turned the water on, she heard Nick say. "Draven Visconti. You're positive?"

Oh, God! Now what the hell had Draven done? Her brother was a damned menace to society. She tiptoed to the door, even though Nick's back was turned, and he couldn't see her. She used her fingertips to push the door so it closed a few inches.

"Wait. Just wait a second," Nick plunged his fingers through his hair in such an atypical gesture that Bria's entire body went on red alert. "Draven Visconti? The king of Marrezo is the linchpin for the diamond smuggling operation?"

Bria grabbed the edge of the door as her knees buckled. No. No. No.

*       *       *

"That's ins— Yeah. I'm sure you are," Nick said tightly, as he went to the closet and yanked out jeans. A dark blue T-shirt. Socks. Boxers. He switched the phone from ear to ear as necessary as he dressed. "You found him in Rome?" Nick paused. "Then where the hell *is* he? Someone tried to kill me on the island. Was he responsible?" Another long pause. "Then goddamn find out. And while you're doing that, send someone to get her off my fucking ship. You have an hour! *Three!* You're shitting me!" He paused, then snarled, "I don't give a flying fuck. You got me involved in this screwup. *Do* it."

He hung up.

Bria couldn't breathe.

"Come out of that bathroom, Princess."

She opened the door and stepped into the bedroom. Unlike Nick, she was naked. She'd never felt more exposed and vulnerable in her life. She lifted her chin, and met his eyes dead-on. "I had no idea."

"Is that so?" his voice was soft and measured, and didn't

fool her for a second. Beneath that ice-thin veneer, Nick Cutter was simmering on a roiling boil. He shoved the phone into his back pocket. "You show up at the café where two of your brother's associates are negotiating with me to bring seventy-five million dollars of uncut, conflict diamonds on board—"

"Diamonds that I knew nothing about until you told me a few hours ago!"

"How long have you been involved in this? How fucking long, *Principessa*? They sent you precisely because you're exactly the type I fuck. And they chose well, didn't they? You seemed to enjoy your work, didn't you? Or was that all part of the con? Were all those moans and little sounds you made genuine, or learned responses for the mark?"

"Do you hear how irrational you sound? *Think* for a second, Nick. Why would Halkias try to kill *me* if I was involved?"

"Because you recognized him."

"I agree. But not for the reason you think. I think he was shocked to see me here, because I'm *not* involved."

"Convoluted as hell."

"The truth frequently is. Now that I know Draven is the one who's behind the diamond smuggling, Halkias trying to kill me, the landslide—neither made sense before. But now that we know it was my *brother* who instigated you bringing the diamonds on board, it suddenly does."

"Not to me."

"Draven didn't know I was coming on board to ask you for his money back. Draven had no idea I was on board. When Halkias saw me, he must've panicked. And when I took you to Marrezo, Draven must've believed that we were on to him. He was determined to stop us—you—from telling the other people involved."

"Very neat." It was. Almost too neat. But that might be emotion trying to control reality. He wanted to believe that she wasn't involved. But his knee-jerk right now was blind fury, and a gut-deep sense of betrayal. He had to get away from her pale lips and big beseeching eyes to think rationally.

"Nick. Stop. *Think*, please! My brother is an idiot, but just because we're related doesn't mean *I'm* involved in his machinations!"

He picked up the Bersa from the table beside the bed.

"God. Are you going to shoot me?"

"I wish I could be as cold-blooded as you are. Unfortunately, even *I* can't be that reptilian. Get your shit together—only the things you brought on board. When Aries's people get here, I want you gone."

"Nick—"

"Aries will debrief you. Unfortunately for me, they're five hours away. You've got that much time to get your story straight. If you leave this cabin, I *will* shoot you." He didn't slam the door behind him, but the air around her felt the percussion anyway.

Bria sank onto the foot of the bed. The sheets were half stripped because they'd rolled around, and smelled musky.

She believed that if not for his unnatural control, that Nick would've shot her, he was so mad.

Her heart was pounding so hard her vision was pulsing with every hard thump. "I'm going to kill you, Draven Visconti!" She lunged for the phone beside the bed. Nick and his spy-type friends might not know where her brother was, but Bria had his cell phone number. And if this frigging phone got international—she dialed before she finished thinking it through.

*"Sì, quello che è, adesso?"* Draven demanded impatiently.

"What have you done?" she shouted into the phone.

"Who is this?"

"Your *sister*! Draven. I'm on Nick Cutter's ship, and he says you're smuggling uncut, conflict diamonds on board. Is this true? Did you do this? Did you purchase the blood diamonds with Marrezo's money?"

"This is men's business, *sorellina*. Do not concern yourself."

Her vision faded from red to pink as she got a grasp—barely—on her temper. "Answer me! *Are* you responsible for transporting blood diamonds on Nick's ship?"

"It is a viable revenue to bring Marrezo back to its former glory."

Her stomach lurched. "It's criminal. It's criminal to— Damn it, Draven! It's against the law in every country I can think of! What in God's name were you thinking?"

"I'm thinking," he told her briskly, "that in a few weeks I will have in my possession over seventy-five million American dollars."

"No, *grande fratello,*" Bria told him tightly, her fingers white on the phone. "*You* do not. Possession is nine-tenths of the law. *I* am now sitting on seventy-five millions American dollars in uncut diamonds." She slammed the phone down, then, because her legs gave out, collapsed onto the floor beside the bed, and screamed her frustration into the mattress.

# Chapter 21

The headset he'd picked up out of habit buzzed in Nick's ear.
Jonah. He ignored him. For the first time since he'd bought
the biggest, most expensive toy of his life, not to one-up his
brothers as Zane teased, he wanted to be somewhere else.
*Anywhere* else.

Except that his rage, his feeling of betrayal would go with
him like a fucking tick buried in his *head*. Buried in his
brain where he couldn't shake it.

To Nick, the *Scorpion* was home. His sanctuary. Other
than Cutter Cay, this was where he was happiest. Now he
couldn't find anywhere on board he wanted to be.

Thanks to the two of them, right then, he couldn't imagine *any*-fucking-where he wanted to be. He was in the gym,
where nobody would think to look for him.

He sure as shit didn't want to be here either. Everywhere
he looked he got a strobelike image of making love to Bria.
By the treadmill. Against the wall. He gave the double doors
to the steam room a dirty look, then stalked over to stare
unseeing out of the large windows.

The *Scorpion* cut cleanly through the plum and magenta
ripples of the tail end of the sunset. The sky, streaked with
brooding black clouds, looked exactly like he felt. Bruised.
Battered. Pretty fucking bleak.

Mr. Spock.

Didn't he wish he were that right now? He had a reputation for being soul-deep cold. Yeah, he was frosty on the outside, he just wished the feeling went all the way through to the bone, because even though it was hard for him to show it, he felt deeply. His inner nature had always been maintained at a well-suppressed boil. Emotions firmly under lock and key. He made a low angry sound deep in his throat.

*That* box had been chainsawed in half. He had no idea where to fucking start.

Jonah? Yeah. He prodded that one like an abscessed tooth. Logan said he had trust issues. No shit! Nick knew he had *father* issues. Daniel Cutter had been a liar and a cheat. Idiot Zane had spent his younger years trying to emulate him. Lucky Logan had zero feelings for their father as far back as Nick remembered. And he'd been squarely in the middle.

Loving his father, hell even worshipping him in some ways. His ability to sail a ship like he was walking on fucking water, for one. Daniel had had an uncanny knack for discovering the richest wrecks, the most newsworthy artifacts. On the other side of that coin was that Daniel Cutter had been a shit father, as well as braggart, a show-off, and a womanizer.

Nick had spent his life proving to himself, if not others, that he was *nothing* like his father. Not in deed, not in temperament.

Suppressing emotion had become second nature to him. Maintaining a stoic calm was an essential part of his survival. It had worked, and worked well. After his mother's death, Nick had basically closed down. He'd been seven. Who he was, what he was, was ingrained. He let no one other than his brothers in.

Until Jonah.

Until the princess.

And look what it had gotten him. Fucked. Over.

Keeping a tight lid on his emotions wasn't working so well for him now. The tightness in his chest was that lid about to blow.

And Jonah, Jesus.

Presenting a secret sibling was his father's final sucker punch. The kind of low blow that proved everything Nick had always thought about the man who'd fathered him. Daniel had screwed his family even from the grave.

And the man—the jack-in-the-box brother for God's sake—had the gall, the fucking unmitigated *audacity,* to wax poetic about *his* father.

His. Theirs. The same goddamned man. Yet so totally different in description that Nick didn't recognize that it was the same person.

Jonah not telling him right away was a different kind of betrayal. How long had he known about the connection? How fucking long had he planned to do a stealth attack and catch Nick unaware? At least the two years since he'd hired on to captain Nick's ship. At *least* that long.

He pressed his throbbing, slightly swollen fist to the cool glass and stared sightlessly out to the horizon as he joined the dots to try to make a whole out of the mess. He and Jonah were mere weeks apart in age. While Nick, Zane, and Logan were anxiously waiting their father's return for whichever salvage he was on, Daniel had had a whole fucking other life somewhere. A whole happy family somewhere.

Nick hadn't trusted his father, so while this was a shock, he wasn't exactly surprised. But God damn it, he'd trusted Jonah as he did only a handful of people.

His brothers. *That* was the handful. And Jonah.

And now Jonah had stabbed him in the back without a goddamn blink.

And Bria—

Jesus. Nick flattened his fist, pressing his palm against the glass, ready to jump out of his skin with—frustration. Anger. The deep aching hole in his chest burned. Beyond the window clouds boiled angrily over the dark water. He didn't even know where to begin with *her* betrayal.

She'd deceived him from day one as well. The princess had lied with every whispered word, with every breathy moan. She'd lied with her lips, she'd lied with those big brown doe eyes, she'd lied with her eager body. God damn it, he'd almost fallen in love with her. Thank God he could turn *that* off like a light switch.

The Bluetooth and his phone both beeped at the same time. Expecting—praying for Aries to call, he answered the phone without checking. "Tell me you're about to land on my deck, Aries!" *Take the princess away so I never have to look at her beautiful, duplicitous face ever again.*

"Don't cut me off," Jonah said urgently. "I think I've joined the dots."

Dots? All Nick felt were holes. "I have fuck-all to say to you," he growled.

"It's life and death, Nick. Two minutes of your time."

Fuck. "I'll meet you in my off—" Not with the princess there. "No. I'll come to the bridge," Nick told him tightly. "Two minutes is all the time you're worth."

He took the stairs and strode into Jonah's office two minutes later without knocking. He was pleased to see that the man's nose was swollen to twice its size, and that he had a painful-looking shiner. Most excellent, he thought with vicious satisfaction.

Unfortunately, Nick's hand hurt just as badly as he suspected Jonah's nose did. And the livid bruising only made Jonah's blue eyes even more predominant. "What do you want?" Nick didn't go farther into Jonah's office than necessary. He gave him a dispassionate look. "Make it quick."

"Close it behind you," Jonah ordered. Nick raised a brow. "Jesus, Nick, this is sensitive information. I'm not just being an asshole, here."

Nick shut the door behind him, but remained where he was.

Jonah raised the sheet of paper he held. "Before signing on a year ago in Vietnam, Halkias worked for Draven Visconti."

Nick put his hand on the door handle. "Old news." Br— The princess had claimed that her sister-in-law had told her the man had been fired. It didn't surprise Nick that she'd lied about that, too.

Jonah cut him off mid-turn. "Alfonso was also hired on

in Vietnam one year ago, same time, same place. His stepfather works for Visconti on Marrezo."

Hired as chef's helper, the Italian had been promoted to chef six months ago when his predecessor had unexpectedly died of a heart attack. He'd been a "loyal" crew member for two year.

Two years. That seemed to be the fucking cutoff for loyalty on his ship. Halkias, Alfonse, and Jonah had all been hired on then.

"Basim was in Rome two weeks before I hired him in Tarfaya," Jonah continued levelly. "Isaac Vanderpool spent seven months in Italy last year."

"All roads lead, literally, from Rome." Nick slid his fingers in the front pockets of his jeans instead of clenching them into fists. "This means Visconti planned this more than two years ago."

"At least."

Nick shot him a cool look. "*You* were hired in Vietnam."

"Coincidence," Jonah assured him, blue eyes unflinching. Christ, in that moment he looked like Zane at his most earnest. "I had absolutely no knowledge of *any* of this. I just wanted an opportunity to get to know you."

"Then you know me well enough to know you're dead to me." Before he opened the door, Nick said coldly, "Secure Basim and Isaac. Then we're done—"

The door at Nick's back was shoved hard, and he took a step forward as it swung open and struck his shoulder.

"Nick? Oh my God, is Nick here?" Bria's voice filled the cabin, high and shaking. "I've been looking for him *everywhere*!" She was crying and the words were barely intelligible. "I have to speak to him right away! I lost my tem— I just d-did something *incredibly* stupid!"

Nick pulled the door wider, revealing himself. "I already know *that*. There's not a damn thing you have to say that I want to hear, *Princess*."

She turned on him, her face blotchy and her eyes waterlogged. A damn fine show, he thought bitterly. He wouldn't have believed her if she'd looked creamy and beautiful as she cried. Tears ran down her cheeks, but she managed to look him dead in the eye despite the welling tears. "I just talked to Draven."

She'd hastily pulled on a powder-blue T-shirt, but had it on backward and inside out. Her jeans were unbuttoned. Barefoot, she carried a bright red striped beach bag over her shoulder. Her hair looked as if it had been combed by an eggbeater. Tears streaked her face, and her nose was pink and swollen.

She was so beautiful Nick's heart hurt.

"Nobody knows where he is," he told her curtly. Now what was she up to?

"I'm his sister." She dashed the back of her hand at the tears dripping under her chin. "I have his private number."

This new sucker punch made Nick's chest squeeze so bad he could barely breathe. "You tipped my hand? Jesus, you really are a piece of work, aren't you?" He swore in Arabic. "Blood *is* thicker than water. Nothing we shared in the last week had any impact on you whatsoever."

"No, I—"

"What did your darling brother instruct you to—" His phone rang. "God damn it." Noting it was Aries, Nick sliced a hand across his throat to shut her up as she opened her mouth to speak again.

"Are you landing?" he demanded without greeting. Of course not. There was no sound of an approaching chopper, and God only knew, he couldn't be that lucky. Not on this trip.

"I and my team are three hours out," Aries informed him shortly, not sounding happy about it. "You have a more immediate problem, Cutter. Your princess made contact with Visconti. I gave strict orders no fucking calls in or out remember?"

Both his captain and the princess listened to his half of the conversation with tight expressions. Nick glanced away. He couldn't look at either of them. "I don't work for you, Aries," he told him, his tone flat and grim. "You seem to forget that this was a 'low-risk' *favor*."

"Because all the calls from the *Scorpion* are being monitored." Aries talked briskly as if Nick hadn't interrupted.

"Your girlfriend just claimed possession of the diamonds, Cutter. She says she's holding them hostage until her brother turns himself in."

*"What?!"* She'd planned to take her ruse all the way to Cutter Cay? Which didn't make sense since, as far as he knew, she didn't even know where they were.

"You heard me," Aries said irritably.

Nick turned to stare at her, but she was talking quietly with Jonah by the desk, her hands darting expressively with every shaking word. "It works as long as—"

"Not only did *we* intercept that call," Aries cut in, "so did the Moroccans. Bad enough as it stands, but as we speak, Visconti is about to double-cross his partners and has a hit squad waiting in Tenerife for Najeeb Qassem and Kadar Gamali Tamiz to arrive for an impromptu meeting. Who in turn are planning to send a team to the meeting and do the same to him."

"They kill each other." Seemed like a fine plan to Nick. "A win–win. What's the problem?"

*"Visconti* has a hit team, the *Moroccans* have a hit team. And instead of offing each other, they're all headed *your* way to take possession of the diamonds. Winner takes all."

"Winner *kills* all," Nick said his voice feral. "Is that what you're *not* saying, *buddy*?"

"ETA ninety-seven minutes."

"And you and your firepower are three hours away."

"Two hours and forty-three minutes eighteen seconds. Hold them off until we get there."

Nick's jaw tightened. "I have a Sig, a Beretta, and a Bersa, and enough ammo to last about thirty fucking seconds, Aries." And nobody he trusted at his back. "How the hell am I supposed to do that? How many are there?" Not that it mattered.

"Twenty plus on each side. Don't let anything happen to those diamonds." Aries disconnected. Nick stared at the phone as if it were an alien life form. Ninety-seven minutes. What the fuck was he supposed to do? He wasn't a super spy like Aries.

Hold them off? With fucking what? Card tricks?

"Talk to me," Jonah demanded as Nick stood there with the phone in his hand. He stared through the window at Jonah's back, watching the black clouds scud across the sky, as his mind raced with the ramifications. Beside him, the princess gave a shuddering sniff.

Nick blinked Jonah back into focus. "Thanks to their inside woman here, I have two factions closing in. Forty and change, well-armed, determined men, on their way to secure their diamonds. Aries is three hours out. The bad guys are due in just over an hour and a half. I guess I should be grateful that I have a heads up."

As far as Nick was concerned, Max Aries was also on his shit list. And was now another person he didn't trust. The son of a bitch had left him holding the bag, with zero fucking backup and no goddamn options.

No good deed went unpunished.

Jonah snarled, "Shit!"

"Oh, God, Nick." The princess looked at him with tear-drenched big brown eyes and long spiky lashes. Her lip trembled. "I'm so, so sorry! I was so mad at him, I just wasn't think—"

"Payback's a bitch." He looked dispassionately from the princess to his captain. "There's a pretty damn good chance that we'll *all* die in the next couple hours. I consider everyone on board an enemy. Next time I see so much as a glimpse of either of you, I'll shoot to kill you myself." If either of them knew him at all, they'd be wise to believe him.

\*   \*   \*

Bria glared at a sober, silent Jonah, who had his back to her as he stared at the darkness outside the window. "We have to fix this."

"Really?" His tone was flat. Defeated. "You gonna call that deadbeat brother of yours again and give him our exact coordinates?"

Her temper spiked. "Come on, Jonah! Give me a break

here. I made a colossal mistake. I'm the first to admit I did something incredibly stupid. It was knee-jerk. I lost my temper and wanted to give my brother hell for what he's done. It was stupid telling him I was keeping the diamonds. Really, really stupid. And God only knows, I regret it. But this isn't about us, it's about helping Nick."

Hunching his broad shoulders Jonah ran a hand over his battered face, looking out the window. Bria saw his reflection there as he asked grimly, "Haven't you helped him enough?"

She flinched, but strode across the room to stand beside him. "Can we discuss my thoughtless culpability and your well-meaning deception another time?" she demanded, grabbing his hard forearm to hold him there when he looked like he wanted to be somewhere else. He didn't shift under her hand, but he didn't push it away either.

"Let me ask you this? Did you hire on with Nick to cause him harm?"

His jaw tightened. "Of course not!"

"Did you have anything to do with smuggling the diamonds on board?"

"Hell no. I told him I didn't."

"Well *I* didn't either. I knew nothing about them until he told me about them this afternoon! But, God, Jonah, he thinks we did, and right now that's all that matters." Bria wasn't normally a crier. She'd thought she was done crying. But tears stung her eyes, and her heart ached for what she'd done. "Have you ever seen such a bleak look on his face?"

He shook his head, fingers tightening on the sill.

"*We* did that. Nick believes he has to fight this alone."

Now he looked at her, and Bria had to catch herself as Nick's eyes stared out of Jonah's face. "You think he was joking about shooting us?" he asked dryly. "Trust me, he wasn't. I've never seen him that angry."

"How can you tell?" Bria returned, just as dry. Stepping back, she slipped the strap of the beach bag off her shoulder and set the heavy canvas bag on Jonah's sleek black desk. Upending it with a clatter, she asked, "Colder than usual? Arctic ice or just more frigid?"

Jonah shook his head, eyes hard. Damn those Cutter blue eyes. "Then you really don't know him at all," he said, trying and condemning her all in the same breath. "Get out of here, Princess. I have to figure out how to fight Nick and the bad guys, and keep *you* alive while I'm at it so he doesn't kill me twice for not taking care of you."

None of that made much sense, but she didn't try to unravel it. "I already had this fight with your brother," she said firmly, ignoring his swift inhalation at her casual familial connection. "Don't worry about me. Here. This should help." She handed him a Sig Sauer and picked up what she considered *her* Bersa from the stuff she'd dumped on his desk. "Take these." She slid a box of bullets toward him.

He stared at her, aghast. "You broke into his safe?"

"I watched you open it this afternoon, remember?" He wouldn't believe her anyway. She sighed. "Who *cares*? What matters is that we're both armed. Now, what's the plan?"

The eyes he leveled on her weren't quite so chilly as he hefted the weight of the Sig in his hand. "Which of us is going to sit on him while the other talks, and talks fast? Because believe me, when he sees the blue of my eyes, he's going to use his allotment of bullets to blow my head off."

Bria shook her head. "Not on my watch. You sit on him, I'll do the talking. But first, is there anyone we trust on board right now?"

"No."

She blinked. "Comforting. If that's the case, that means we have to lock everyone up somewhere before the other bad guys get here, right?"

He cocked a brow, his resemblance to Nick, now that she knew they were brothers, uncanny. "How do you propose getting six men to gather in one place?"

She hadn't thought of that. Quickly, her fingers deft, she checked the clip in the Bersa. "Just tell me where you can lock them in," she said. "I'll get them there."

"Locks are *inside* cabins, not out," Jonah pointed out. "And if there's a lock on the door on the outside, it's because there's something critical to the ship inside that I don't want people messing with."

Bria's brow furrowed in exasperation. "Help me out, here, Jonah. We need a padlock of some sort. A big one. Do you happen to have one of those?"

His eyebrows shot up. "Hang on, yeah. I do. And oh, God—I have somewhere we can stash six people. The old walk-in refrigerator in the hold."

She gave him a dubious look. "Will they be able to breathe in there?"

"The only person in there right now doesn't need to breathe." He opened and closed several cabinet doors. "No. And I guess we don't want to kill them, although God only knows it would make this a whole lot less complicated."

"What about the steam room?" Bria gestured toward the door triumphantly. "Easily can handle that many. They'll even have somewhere to sit, and access to water."

"Access to—" He pushed his hand through his short hair, slanting her an incredulous look. "What are you, in with Amnesty International? These are terrorists we're talking about."

"Maybe not all of them." She set the Bersa back on the desk, her jaw set. "And *we* aren't."

He held up both hands. "Okay. Steam room."

"Good. How long to get the padlock?"

Jonah slid the Sig in the front of his jeans and rounded the desk. He opened a cabinet nearby and dug around in a plastic tub. After a moment, he pulled out a giant padlock, then went back in for a length of sturdy chain.

"I don't want to know why you have that in your office," Bria said with a crooked smile.

"Hey, you ask, I deliver."

"Okay, put that in here." She held out the canvas bag. The chain clanked and made a hell of a racket as Jonah coiled it in the sack, and made it heavy enough that she had to use both hands just to hold it. That and the big padlock filled it to capacity. Jonah took it without asking. He was a Cutter all right.

"Let's go up and make sure this will hold them. Then we'll call everyone to the sunroom for a staff meeting." Bria yanked open the door. "I have a degree in bullshit. If you can get them there, I can get them to the steam room."

He searched her features, and she read in his eyes his worry. Hell, he was just as anxious as she was, just as concerned for Nick. No matter what the idiot had said to them both. She squeezed his arm. "Let's get the party started."

"I hope to hell we don't bump into Nick," he said grimly. "Our relationship is strained enough as it is. It'll be damned inconvenient getting blown to hell by my brother at this stage of the game."

"Won't happen," she said firmly, and hoped her forced optimism was right. Nick wasn't a cold-blooded killer. No matter how icy he seemed. He'd avoid rather than confront, just like he did by concealing his emotions and locking them away.

"Weapon?" Bria tucked her Bersa into the waistband of her jeans where she could grab it quickly.

They took the stairs at a run.

Basim and Isaac were bringing in the cushions on the sundeck, stacking them neatly, ready for the next morning. The head steward, Khoi, had been sent away in the lifeboat earlier. Jonah called to Basim, who gave him a startled look when he took in his black eye and distorted nose. "Make an announcement that I want to talk to everyone in here. Everyone, no exceptions. Five minutes. Come on, Princess," he added smoothly, "I have something to show you in the gym."

A padlock, a chain, and two loaded guns.

She prayed it was enough as she accompanied Jonah across the room as Basim's voice came over the PA announcing the captain's request, and ordering all hands to assemble in the sunroom *immediately*. No exceptions.

They passed through the doors to the gym, letting them swing closed behind them, and Jonah immediately pulled the chain and lock out of the bag. He looked at the gracefully curved, solid brass handles. It was a swing door with no locking mechanism. But with the chain threaded through the handles, and padlocked in place, it would hold, leaving a gap of a few inches.

"There's the advantage of them getting a sliver of fresh air," Bria thought out loud as Jonah tested the fit and function of the chain through the handles, then slid it free and coiled it behind the Bowflex machine out of sight. "I really didn't want to be responsible for killing anybody. Now my brother, on the other hand . . ." Bria trailed off because just thinking about what Draven had done, what he was responsible for instigating, made her furious all over again, and right now she needed to be as cool, calm, and collected as Nick Cutter to get through this.

Beyond the panoramic curved windows was nothing but black now, and the reflection of the two people as taut and tense as bowstrings. Bria felt the weight of the Bersa pressed against her belly as she dragged in a deep breath before turning to Jonah. "Ready?"

He gave her a narrow-eyed look. "I think you should go to the pilothouse and wait for me."

"I think not."

"I'm going to have to herd all those possibly pissed off men in here at gunpoint," he argued. "Nick will kill me twice if I add you getting hurt or worse to my infractions. This could get ugly."

Bria loved the understatement. She had no doubt it *would* get ugly. "Then we'll get ugly back. Come on, Jonah. Time's a-wasting. Nick needs us. We can't screw this up."

He didn't have the time to keep the debate going and he knew it. She marched to the doors, forcing him to swear as he hurried to catch up. The downsized crew was already assembled in a tight knot in the middle of the room. The men turned as one to look at their captain.

# Chapter 22

"We've had a breach in security," Jonah told them. The men glanced at each other nervously. Bria thought they also looked guilty and ill at ease. The level of tension in the room was thick as a gathering thundercloud. She tried to read their expressions. They knew something was up, but she suspected they weren't yet aware that whoever they worked for was sending in reinforcements.

Or maybe they did.

"The princess is missing a valuable family heirloom. I'm not accusing anyone," Jonah added as mutters rippled through the crowd, "but this is a serious issue. The princess assures me that as long as she gets the piece back, there will be no charges filed."

"What is missing?" Basim demanded, his eyes narrow dark slits, his anger palpable, his handsome face ugly with contempt.

The look he gave her made Bria's skin crawl. "The person who took it knows." Bria made no attempt to straighten her clothing or mess with her hair. Both were a lost cause. Straightening her spine, she transformed her features into a mask of righteous, *royal* annoyance and pretended she was wearing silk and a tiara. It was going to be honey as long as they complied, and until they were secure in the steam room.

Frankly, she'd rather shoot a few body parts—to encourage them to do what was asked—than go through the motions so they didn't become alarmed and start fighting back.

The fact that she was feeling so bloodthirsty didn't shock her at all. One or all of these men would kill her, Jonah, or Nick without a blink.

She was here to make sure that didn't happen.

If there were any strange men on board in the next hour, the three of them would know for sure *they* were the bad guys.

This situation was not up for debate.

She braced her hands on her hips as Jonah stirred beside her, and pitched her voice to carry over his whispered, "What are you—?"

"*I'm* not required to give *you* an explanation," she said waspishly. "I demand you empty your pockets, right now." Easier to say than—*Hey! Any of you guys armed to the teeth?*

There were loud cries of indignation until Jonah held up his hand. "Guys, you know how I feel about stealing." Bria admired his quick recovery, even as she continued to tap her foot impatiently. "And we can't afford an investigation, especially not in international waters. Cutter Salvage takes accusations of theft seriously, so empty your pockets as the princess asks so we can all get back to work."

She tried to read which of the men were scared they'd lose their jobs if accused of stealing, and which were afraid they'd have their weapons removed and worse. Problem was, none of them looked particularly scared, but they all looked angry.

A glance at Jonah and she gathered he felt the same way.

To avoid a bloodbath, they had decided on this ruse to get the men to comply without tipping their hand. But damn, Bria just wanted it to be over!

Where was Nick? How was Nick? She wanted to be with him. To let him know that she and Jonah were there to help.

One by one, the men filed past Bria, emptying their pockets. They were silent, but that silence was thick with churning, escalating anger. The looks they gave her told her what they thought of her. Like she gave a damn. She gave each a cool appraisal.

As soon as the crew lined up, pockets turned inside out, Jonah withdrew the gun from his waistband, his hand steady as he trained it on them, his own expression turning from fake annoyance to deadly intent. "First man to move loses a limb. Princess, pat them down just to make sure." Sure they weren't concealing a weapon.

Bria used the Bersa to motion to the first man to raise his arms. The German did so, his face mottled, the cords in his throat bunched. Keeping the gun inches from his back, she used her free hand to pat him down. Ew. His T-shirt and shorts were both clammy with sweat as she ran her hand over his clothing.

"What is going on?" Basim demanded from further down the row. "What is this? First half our associates are sent back to Tenerife so our work is doubled, now this indignity!"

This was taking too long. Bria could practically hear a metronome ticking in her head. "On second thought—strip." The men turned as one to gape at her. Bria kept her eyes steely. "Take off your clothes, all of you. You can keep on your skivvies. Do it. Now!"

Silence flipped to a series of loud indignant protests. Bria raised her voice to carry as Jonah trained his weapon on the knotted group. "You have one minute to get those clothes off," she said tersely. "Then I start shooting what I can't see."

A few of the men hastily pulled off their shorts and T-shirts, bent to unlace their tennis shoes. The others refused to comply. Basim was one. "This is an outrage!"

Jonah motioned to the steward to do as he was told. "The order is nonnegotiable."

"I won't do it," Basim said angrily. He strode purposefully toward the exit, his lanky legs carrying him quickly. Bria raised the Bersa a few inches and fired directly in front of him. The wall fountain shattered, scattering marble and river rocks like buckshot. Some of the men ducked, others screamed. Everyone stripped faster.

She held the gun steady as Basim spun around, a look of

fury coupled with shock on his face. It didn't bother her in the slightest to see blood was streaking his temple and cheek where a sliver of rock had grazed him. "Get back with the others, and *take off your clothes*. I won't ask again. The next shot will be in you."

Cursing in Arabic, he strode over to the others and yanked off his clothing.

When they were all down to their underwear, or in a couple of cases, bare-assed naked, Bria and Jonah herded the men into the steam room and shut the door on their angry questions. Jonah affixed the chain and padlock, and Bria, because she felt as though a bull's-eye was now painted on her back, rammed the chin bar from the Bowflex in beside the chain to reinforce it.

"How much time do we have left?" she asked over the noise of raised voices and body slams to the door.

Jonah yanked on the lock to make sure it was secure, then motioned they get out of there. "Under forty minutes."

She looked around for the time, but didn't see a clock. "How do you know?"

"One of my many skills," he answered as they crossed through the sunroom, now littered with clothing, and shards of rock and granite and spilled water. "Now let's go find Nick."

"And then?" Bria asked, hurrying to match his long-legged stride.

Jonah's Cutter blue eyes flicked to her. Hardened. "We sit on him until he accepts our help."

\*      \*      \*

Down in the hold, Nick was excruciatingly aware that every second was crucial. The shit was about to hit the fan.

He was calmer and more in control than ever. But he could see how another man might feel the savage urge to put his fucking fist through a wall.

His heartbeat was a little fast. Just a tad.

Bria.

Jonah.

*Scorpion.*

Fucking, *fucking* hell.

Move bins. Transfer and consolidate the diamonds from three containers into one. Attach marker. Shift the most archeologically interesting artifacts into a central location, attach more markers, move heavy water-filled bins containing gold and silver coins.

Same same same. Faster. Faster faster.

One man. One and a half hours.

Attempting to move what *six* men had taken three months to accumulate. And then— "Take care of the diamonds?! Fuck you," he muttered without heat to the absent T-FLAC operative who'd gotten him into this clusterfuck in the first place.

"Three *hours* away? Screw you, twice, you son of a bitch."

His first thought had been to consolidate the diamonds into one smaller container, and fly out on his helicopter. The bad guys would show, they'd tear his ship apart to find their diamonds, and they'd be shit out of luck. By the time they figured out their uncut gems were gone, Aries and his team would be on them like a shark after chum.

It was a good, solid plan.

*Except* that there was a good chance they'd intercept him midair en route to land. Not to mention he wasn't leaving either the princess or his captain behind. No matter how pissed at them he was. Getting the two of them on board the chopper was simple enough. But risking being shot out of the air was out of the question.

And that would still leave half his crew behind.

He didn't know how many of them were really bad guys. So he'd have to take the bad and the ugly with them. *If* he had room on the small helicopter. Which he didn't. There was one lifeboat—but pretty much the same issues applied. They'd be spotted from above if/when the bad guys flew over. Or picked up by a fast boat.

Because, unless the Moroccans and the king's thugs were

all complete morons, they'd realize that he was making off with their loot the second they saw him.

They might have all decided to take opposing sides, but in this, they'd once again be united.

Anyone sitting in that open lifeboat would be easy pickings. The bad guys would shoot first, and ask questions never.

All of which left him with an unpalatable last-resort solution. Scuttle the *Scorpion*.

"Fuck."

Buy time until T-FLAC arrived to clean up their mess.

Drown the diamonds so no one could get to them.

Cause enough chaos and mayhem that no one would notice that a lifeboat was making a getaway while they were on board.

It didn't even sound good in theory. But it was all Nick had.

He went for it.

He'd had found two rounds of underwater explosives; they rarely had to blow shit up on a dive. Two would have to do.

First order of business before coming down to the hold: Set a charge inside his brand-new, million-dollar state-of-the-art chopper, which was neatly tucked belowdecks. Once the power went off, the special elevator lift to take her up on deck would be inoperable. For a few hopeful seconds, Nick had considered raising the helicopter onto the helipad. But concluded *that* would give the bad guys either one more way to get off the sinking ship, or another opportunity to sabotage her so they couldn't be followed when they fled.

Either way, the Robinson was toast.

His second order of business had been the small explosive he'd set off in the engine room's sea chest, the scoop-like device that brought in the system's cooling water.

As he worked, water was pouring into the hull. Fast. Soon the generators would short as it rose. Until then, he had light to work by and the incentive to work *fast*.

He'd also removed the panels over the diver access holes.

The water had immediately gushed into the hold. Was still pouring in. It lapped at his ankles as he moved bins.

More to come, but he'd started the ball rolling.

He'd scuttled his own multimillion-dollar ship.

The thought made Nick's gut twist unhappily, but he was still feeling too numb from the day's revelations to have a physical reaction to murdering his ship.

He worked grimly, knowing this would hurt more when the shock wore off.

Bria—

Jonah—

*Scorpion*—

The knocks kept on coming.

There'd be no insurance claim for this act of sabotage. And if what he was doing right now didn't work, he'd be well and truly screwed.

Nope. Well and truly dead.

Lift. Move. Open. Remove. Transfer. Lift. Stack.

He shoved Jonah and the princess into a mental freezer deep in the To Be Ignored recesses of his brain. And he'd leave them there. Forever, if he could. Until his ship went down, if he couldn't.

There was only so much a man could take.

Lift. Move. Open. Remove. Transfer. Lift. Stack.

That mental freezer wasn't nearly strong enough to keep the thoughts at bay. As his body worked, his mind raced.

The princess had taken some hard blows from the rock-slide, yet she hadn't complained once. Because she had an agenda more important than physical injury? Or because she didn't want him worrying about her with everything else he had on his plate?

She must've known the inherent risks when she'd agreed to work for her brother on such a dangerous scam. And yet . . . Her stunned surprise when he'd told her had seemed so genuine. So sincere.

Nick didn't know up from down and port from starboard anymore. "Fuck them." They'd made their beds. Let them lie in whatever crap was about to go down. They were going to have to take their knocks with the imminent boarding parties.

The thought was in no way comforting. Or true, he realized. Damn it to hell! He'd *never* leave Bria or Jonah to fend for themselves. Couldn't. Wouldn't. The thought only added to the weight on his shoulders.

T-shirt sticking uncomfortably to the sweat on his back, he stripped it off, wiping his face with it before tossing it aside. It floated away on the false tide now washing around his ankles.

Lift. Move. Open. Remove. Transfer. Lift. Stack.

As he worked he listened for out of the ordinary sounds. A chopper. A fast boat. Gunshots. Voices. But other than the water pouring into the compartments belowdecks, there was just the slightly elevated flub-dub flub-dub of his own heartbeat in his ears.

Lift. Move. Open. Remove. Transfer. Lift. Stack.

Six inches of water and rising.

Aries had said the ETA for Visconti's men and the Moroccans was ninety-seven minutes. Make that well under an hour now. The T-FLAC operative hadn't specified how each group would transport from Tenerife out to the *Scorpion*. The ship was traveling at the maximum sixteen knots, but a smaller and faster craft would catch up easily enough.

The *Scorpion*'s generators would short. Shut down by the rising water. The supply of power to auxiliary equipment that ran the engines would kick in briefly, but those too would be severed. The ship would then float adrift. Easy pickings. A free-for-all.

Lift. Move. Open. Remove. Transfer. Lift. Stack.

Water lapped at his shins.

A plane would be fastest, Nick knew, but the helipad wasn't big enough for a plane that size. The men would have to be dropped either into the water, or on the deck. A complicated and tricky maneuver, especially at night onto a moving target.

The other option was a fast boat, large enough to hold the twenty or so men Aries claimed were assembled in each group. If that were the case, it would necessitate the men scaling the sides of the moving *Scorpion*. No easy feat either, day *or* night.

Twenty minutes earlier, the public address system had crackled to life and he'd heard the call for the crew to assemble on the sundeck. Basim. Nick recognized the layers of inflection in his voice. For him, better than a fingerprint for identification.

What was Bria doing? Where was Jonah? They'd better damned-well be together. Watching each other's backs . . .

He didn't want the son of a bitch dead. He wanted to kill his new brother/ex-best friend himself. But if Bria got hurt on Jonah's watch, Nick would kill him twice.

Zane wouldn't like that. Nick would bet his last dollar that his gregarious younger brother would be over the moon to find himself with another brother. Logan, for all his gruff protest, was all about family, so Nick suspected Jonah wouldn't get a hell of a lot of opposition from him either.

Hell. If Jonah hadn't conned and lied to him, Nick had to admit he wasn't a bad choice in the brother department. But it would be a damned long time before he admitted that to Jonah. Let him sweat bullets for a while.

Lift. Move. Open. Remove. Transfer. Lift. Stack.

So where were they? Worried now, Nick rubbed the back of his neck. If Jonah had been incapacitated by one of the turncoats on his crew, where was his— where was the princess?

He tried not to let his imagination run the hell away with him. But damn it, the situation *was* dire, and bound to get a lot worse as the night progressed. He'd feel a lot better if he had both the princess and his captain nearby so he could keep an eye on them.

He couldn't stop what he was doing to go from stem to stern looking for them. The die had been cast. He wasn't done in the hold yet, and there was still more he had to do to scuttle the ship quickly and efficiently before he could go topside.

One lifeboat and the motor launch were gone. The chopper was no longer an option.

Basim paging the crew could mean the men were gathering to aid their partners in crime the moment they boarded like the fucking pirates they were. "Yeah. Probably."

Half the crew was out there in the dark in a lifeboat, keeping a low profile until they got picked up by the late, great T-FLAC team.

Three fucking hours away! "Thanks for nothing, Aries."

The PA crackled. "Cutter, contact the bridge. ASAP."

*As if.* Annoyed by the surge of relief he felt hearing Jonah's voice, Nick ignored the terse page. He had neither his phone nor the Bluetooth on him because there'd been no one he'd wanted to talk to. Now he wished to hell he hadn't tossed both aside. With Jonah's help this would've been done in half the time, and all three of them could be floating out to sea in a dry boat waiting for safe pickup.

He shouldered another bin, moving it to the new pile.

Jonah was still around. Great. That meant Bria was too.

Which meant she was still on board and vulnerable. Nick's sense of urgency intensified as the image of Bria's bullet-riddled body tightened the knot in his gut. With conscious, *conscious* effort, he shoved the picture aside, drawing a veil of ice over the hot swell of panic the image produced. He wasn't an imaginative guy, but picturing her injured turned his blood to ice and made his heart knock uncomfortably.

If she had so much as a scratch on her, he'd kill Jonah himself.

As pissed at her as he'd been, he'd had time to cool down, and his rational brain kicked emotion to the curb. His gut told him she hadn't known about her brother's plan to use his ship as a mule to get his illicit diamonds bound for the States and South America. Bria was a lot of things, but now that he'd had time to process, Nick knew that she didn't have the capacity to do what he'd accused her of doing, and adding fuel to that dead fire was counterproductive.

As for Jonah, his new brother was a lot of things, but Nick believed him when he said he had nothing to do with the diamonds.

*Kumbaya,* he thought savagely.

But right now none of that mattered. Innocent people would die tonight, and there wasn't a damned thing he could do to change that.

Nick lifted a seventy-five-pound tub of water and artifacts out of his way. It was hard work, and hot and stuffy without air-conditioning. His muscles strained as he moved dozens of heavy containers from one side of the aisle to the other in a measured, orderly, carefully thought-out pattern.

Water lapped below his knees.

Lift. Move. Open. Remove. Transfer. Lift. Stack.

He figured he had maybe fifteen, twenty more minutes to mess with this before he had to get out.

His muscles burned. Sweat dripped in his eye and he used his shoulder to swipe it away.

The knee-high water made it slower going to wade through to his next bin location.

He realized he'd cut it really fine as he looked around at what he'd accomplished in the last twenty minutes. He'd done all he could here. Time to go topside and make a stand.

He started between the rows of bins, then heard Jonah's voice from the doorway. "Hey, asshole? Need some hel—" And then his voice strangled on his own incredulity. "Did you *have* to?"

"Oh, God. Have to what?" Bria demanded just as the emergency alarm sounded a bleak, frantic shriek. A death knell.

"Scuttle my ship," Nick shouted above the noise. He rounded the end of the row to see them waiting for him. Bria raised her gaze from the dark water lapping at her legs, her eyes bleak and unhappy. The profound relief—the overwhelming joy—he felt at seeing her almost brought Nick to his knees.

Everything in him wanted to close the gap and wrap her tightly in his arms. He stayed put. This wasn't over yet. Not by a long shot.

"On paper," Jonah said, taking in the scene at a glance.

The rearranged bins, the water flooding the floor and rapidly rising. "Officially, she's still *my* ship."

"Scuttled—?" Bria stared at the water around them with dawning horror. "As in *sink*?"

"It's the only thing I could come up with that'll foil everybody's plans," he said, his voice calm. "And give Aries what he wants."

"God." Jonah rubbed his chest. "This hurts my heart."

"You'll get over it," Nick told him briskly, grabbing Bria's upper arm as she was almost swept off her feet by the moving water. He kept his fingers around the cool skin of her arm, in case she fell. Damn it. Because he couldn't *not* touch her.

"Heard the explosion," Jonah braced a hand against the bulkhead for balance. "Where're we at?"

"What do you care—"

Jonah moved so fast, Bria beside him yelped in surprise. Suddenly, Nick was wedged in the doorjamb, the edge jammed into his back and Jonah's fingers closed not that gently around the base of his throat. Staring into Jonah's eyes was like meeting Zane's in a temper. Or Logan's when the Wolf meant business.

"Look, you jackass," Jonah yelled over the bleating of the alarm. "She's my ship and I love her too! We're in this together because, surprise! We're all on the *same* fucking side!"

Nick grabbed Jonah's wrist, as Bria pulled on his arm. "Jonah, stop, this isn't helping!"

"You lied to me," Nick snarled.

"Yeah, so I lied. You'll get over it. But to do that, we've gotta survive the next twenty fucking minutes."

Pissed as he was, angry as hell at *both* of them for a mess he now believed they didn't cause, Nick could only stare at Jonah's fierce blue eyes and swollen nose.

Bria's attempt to keep them focused made him realize that it was relief filling his chest now. Relief that Jonah was at his back one last time. That Bria could be protected better when she was with both of them. Hell, he was pleased to see them.

He pushed Jonah's hand away from his throat, and straightened. "Ventilator pipes removed," he said tightly. "Valves open."

Jonah looked pained. Nick knew how he felt.

As they stood there, water was rising steadily, flowing through the hole in the bulkhead and into the waste disposal tank. Without check valves in the holding tank, the water was coursing through the main drainage pipes, rising like a tide within the ship.

Every waste disposal unit, every sink, toilet, shower, and basin on board was now hemorrhaging water as the enormous pressure of seawater rushed into the sewage system.

Jonah scanned the vast space. Nick could see him calculating how long it would take the hold to fill—about thirty minutes, maybe less. "I'll disable the doors," his ex-best friend told him briskly. The watertight doors that, if automatically closed, would contain the water on the lower level. Now they needed just the opposite. "What else?"

"Took care of the diver access holes—" Another opening that was currently hemorrhaging seawater at the rate of hundreds of gallons a minute.

Water now lapping at their hips, he and Jonah quickly did a checklist of every conceivable way they could fill the *Scorpion* with even more water, and faster.

"And, yeah, turn off that alarm," Nick ordered. Jonah waded out to do so. Half a minute later, the alarm went silent, leaving Nick's ears to throb in the quiet.

"Are you okay?" he asked Bria gruffly. Her hair was a wild tangle of gypsy curls, the water came up under her breasts, and her inside-out, back-to-front T-shirt clung to her skin, showing Nick every curve and valley.

Her sweet nipples peaked under the thin cotton of her T-shirt. When had seeing a woman's erect nipples caused his throat to close with emotion?

Her eyes were dark and shadowy, and her lips pale as she nodded, then added, "I had nothing to do with—"

He cupped her cheek. "Yeah. I figured."

"We should head up," Jonah said loudly from the doorway.

"Can we run like hell?" Bria shouted over the sound of rushing water as she waded toward the door. The lapping water was cold and he saw her shiver. But she didn't complain. "Don't just *stand* there, Nick! Come on! If you go down with the ship, I'm going down *with* you. And then I'll haunt you and make your ghostly afterlife a living hell."

"I'd die before I let anything happen to you," Nick told her grimly, then scowled when Jonah shot him a knowing grin. "Wipe that smile off your face," he added blackly, splashing forward to extend his hand to help Bria. "I'm not even close to being done with you." *Either of you.*

The water was already darkening her shirt over her breasts.

Good. Water was rising faster than he and Jonah had estimated. Not good if they didn't move higher ASAP. Bria's cold palm slid into his hand, and her fingers curled around his. Her hand felt ridiculously small and fragile in his.

She wasn't fragile, he knew. She had admirable tensile strength and grit. "When we get topside—" He steadied her as she swayed toward him as the water surged in the narrow corridor. "I want you to get in the lifeboat." It was the safest place he knew. Faced with a sinking ship filled with their diamonds, no one was going to be looking inside a seemingly empty lifeboat. The lights blinked out, leaving them in stygian darkness. Bria gave a little squeak of surprise.

"We'll join you as soon as we can," he finished, tightening his grip on her hand. When the ship sank, the boat would break free. If anything happened to him—

The lights flickered back on at half power just in time for him to see her shoot him a glare sharp enough to cut through steel. "When this is over, Nick Cutter, you and I are going to have a long, *long* conversation."

"If it gets you out of my—"

"I don't care if you threaten to shoot me yourself," she

said over him. "I'm not leaving your side until we're all safe!
Deal with it."

"Coming?" Jonah yelled from the stairs.

"Bad guys?" he yelled, ignoring the surge of warmth her
words elicited as he held tightly to her hand and waded toward Jonah.

"Secured in the steam room."

Where he would've put them, Nick thought, satisfied.
"Let 'em out at the last second. At least give them a fighting
chance."

Jonah's lips twitched as he walked up the stairs backward. "Another member of Amnesty International, huh?"

Jesus, he looked like Zane at that second. Nick couldn't
figure out how he hadn't seen it the second he'd met him. He
shot his ex-best friend/brother a disgruntled frown. "They'd've
heard the alarm. Bad guys or not, we're not murderers."

"I hear you, but shit, the temptation—"

The wall sconces flickered again, but held, the golden
light playing on the ripples as they moved down the corridor
to the foot of the stairs. Nick intended to keep Bria between
Jonah and himself, but he wasn't letting go of her. No matter
what.

The force of the rushing water tugged and pulled at his
body, strong and insistent. Every time Bria staggered off balance, his firm grip kept her on her feet. He grabbed at whatever
he could to keep her from being swept from under him.

They reached the stairs, the bottom three already submerged. Jonah grabbed Bria's free hand to help her up. As
soon as he was sure she was steady, he let go so she could
grab the hard rail.

Water cold-kissed the back of Nick's leg as he took the
stairs two at a time. God damn it. It was keeping pace with
them, rising at a rate that, while satisfying for the situation,
was alarming because there were still people on board. He
had a gut sick feeling as the *Scorpion* listed slightly to starboard under his feet.

The lights flickered again, but the auxiliary generator
kicked in and they came back on. That wasn't going to last.

In a short time that generator too would be covered with water and inoperable. "Jonah, head directly for the lifeboat. We'll be right behind you. With any luck we can be a mile away when they show up like a bad guy convention."

Bria glanced back as Nick prodded her to move faster. She was several steps ahead of him and at eye level. "Nick, I—" Her attention flickered from his face to something behind him, and the color drained from her skin. Her fingers tightened in his. "All your treasure—"

"And the diamonds. All one hundred feet under when this is all said and done."

She winced. "What a horrible waste!"

He didn't point out the obvious. One hundred feet below was where Cutter Salvage operated best. It was their hallmark in the industry. Jonah had their location marked, and Nick had transferred all the diamonds to one bin, attaching beacons for later retrieval.

Halfway up the stairs Nick pulled the Sig from the small of his back. Jonah followed suit. *"Yes!"* Bria took the Bersa from her waistband, checked the clip, then held it like she meant business. "About frigging time!"

Nick gave a nod of approval before glancing to Jonah. "Anyone on board that shouldn't be yet?"

"No."

"Won't be long." One lifeboat then, Nick motioned the others to move faster up the stairs and out onto the deck and the hell out of the rapidly flooding ship. One lifeboat would be enough. If they could get to it in time.

Or not.

On the landing between decks, he stopped, touching Bria's arm to get her attention. She turned to look at him, and he yelled, "Yo! Jonah! We take the shortest route and get to the lifeboat." Nick's voice was low and dead serious. "There's absolutely, and I repeat, abso-fucking-lutely *no* reason to engage *anyone* boarding. This isn't our fight. They'll want the diamonds, we can't give that to them. There'll be guns and knives, and people with nothing to lose by killing us stone-dead. We're sure to be outnumbered and out-gunned. T-FLAC won't be here to save our asses in the nick of time, no matter how appealing that sounds."

"You saying kiss our asses good-bye?" Jonah inquired politely, glancing up the stairs, head cocked, body braced to run like hell.

"Trying to defend the ship would be pointless. Odds are stack—" Nick held up a hand, sensing sound before he heard anything. He strained his ears to hear anything other than Bria's breathing, and the lap-slosh of the water. "Pointless and suicidal."

The plan had been flawed from the get-go. But it was the only plan he'd had. Factor in greed, betrayal, and revenge, and one had the recipe for disaster. "Counterproductive to get involved in what's coming," he added, feeling a sense of foreboding he couldn't shake.

Yeah. *There.* Now he heard it.

"Shit. We have company!" Hard to miss the whop-whop-whop of a fast-approaching chopper. It was an ominous heart-beat under the watery, pulsing sound of the water inching insidiously up the stairs behind them.

# Chapter 23

"Starboard lifeboat!" Jonah yelled. They increased their speed, taking the stairs three at a time. Bria found herself almost flying as Nick scooped her up, one strong arm tight around her waist, as if afraid she'd be wrenched out of his hold at any minute. Even though they'd be able to run a hell of a lot faster if they weren't attached, she was more than happy to be his Siamese twin. She didn't want to be parted from him for even one second.

The lights, already dim, blinked, then flickered out. Her steps faltered at the absolute darkness, but Nick didn't hesitate, just kept running, making sure she didn't fall. Bria wasn't sure if she really felt the dragging weight of the *Scorpion* as the ship sank lower and lower into the water, or if it was just her imagination. The strong briny smell of ocean and the sound of rushing water were unnerving enough without going the extra mile to envision the large ship sinking like a rock beneath their very feet.

She suspected there was suction involved, and she really, really didn't want to go there.

They reached the landing on the main deck just as the lights flashed on. Then off. The illumination settled into a disorienting, irregular on-off, on-off flicker that was a little—okay, a *lot*—unnerving.

"Take Bria to the lifeboat," Nick instructed urgently, pausing to pass her to Jonah like a feudal lord handing off a chattel. Jonah automatically grabbed her hand and held on. God, they were more alike than either realized, Bria thought as Jonah reeled her in closer.

They were all soaking wet, their clothing sticking to their chilled skin; she couldn't remember ever being dry. The men's shoes squished as they moved, but she was barefoot. "I can get there on my own." She held up the Bersa. "Do whatever, and meet m—"

"No fucking heroics," Nick cut her off as he glared from Jonah to Bria and back to Jonah. "From *either* of you," he had to shout over the sound of the water, which was rapidly ascending the stairs behind them and starting to insidiously pool on the landing. But there were other ambient sounds she couldn't identify.

"You take Bria to the lifeboat," Jonah told Nick flatly. "I'll get the men out of the steam room and meet you. Back in five."

Nick hesitated. "Make that four. Watch your back."

Jonah gave him a mock salute and disappeared back into the dark corridor.

"Move it." Nick pulled her through a doorway into a shadowy room. The library. The side deck ran alongside the room, and she froze as dozens of men, dressed in dark clothing, ran past the picture windows in the darkness.

She spun around to whisper a warning, but Nick was right behind her. Ears like a bat.

"See them," he assured her. "We have eleven minutes before that second charge goes off." His voice was raised, although it was still hard to hear him over the noise of what sounded like approaching boats, planes, and helicopters. And running, shouting men just outside the window. Subtle they weren't. No shooting yet, so she presumed this was just one side. The real fun would start when the other side showed up. She hoped like hell they'd be long gone by then.

A gunshot sliced through the noise. They froze, pressed

against the bookcase as it was followed by a succession of short loud retorts.

Both sides *were* on board.

Bright lights circled overhead, and men started dropping from the sky like black spiders shimmying down gossamer-thin spider webs.

"Good or bad?" Bria pointed, hoping the new arrivals were friends of his.

"*Bad!*" Nick grabbed her hand and started running across the room. They raced past ceiling-to-floor bookcases, a long table, and groupings of chairs, ghostly in the shadows. It was as loud as a frat party outside.

Concealed inside the dark room, its tinted windows affording at least some cover, Bria prayed they couldn't be seen and that the auxiliary generator Nick had mentioned didn't decide to kick in, illuminating them like goldfish in a bowl.

The doors to the side deck were only about twenty feet away. She saw the lifeboat hanging right *there*. But men ran past it, and Nick put his hand across her chest to hold her until they disappeared around the corner. What did he think she'd do? Run out there and engage them in conversation? The grip on the Bersa was damp from nervous perspiration. Bria reminded herself that she'd been trained well by Marv. She knew how to shoot. How to defend herself. How to survive.

She knew it *academically*. Marv's relentless lessons were about to be put to the test. Her heartbeat pounded crazy fast. Sweat ran down her temples, and she had that jittery too-much-caffeine feeling as high-octane adrenaline surged through her bloodstream. Something brushed her ankle under the water, and she almost screamed; instead she bit her lip and forced herself to regulate her breathing and get a grip. This was not the time to get spooked, or to give in to fear.

On this deck, the water was barely ankle-deep, a plus after wading up to her armpits down below.

She looked out at the Uzi-wielding men running around like black ants outside. The bastards were between them and the damned lifeboat. So near and yet so far. The chaos outside was getting louder and brighter. Big, brilliant lights strafed the decks. More men scaled the sides of the *Scorpion* as small craft came alongside.

The ship was crawling with men. Lots of men. Through the darkened windows she saw dozens of them inside now, heard their running footsteps on the deck overhead. They all wore dark clothing. How did they know who was on their side, and who was on the other? And how were she, Nick, and Jonah going to get into that damned lifeboat? With this much illumination, and this many men, they'd be exposed for as long as it took to lower the boat all the way down, and then once they were in the water, they'd literally be sitting ducks with anyone looking down able to see them quite clearly.

The bright lights outside bled through the windows, illuminating a wide expanse of shiny wood floor a foot from where she and Nick stood in the shadows.

The cluster of ominous human forms outside melted from eight to four, then two. Then none. Bria held her breath watching Nick for a signal.

He shook his head.

She took shallow breaths, although no one out there could possibly hear them inside.

After several tense moments, Nick yelled, *"Move,"* and gave her a push. Needing no urging, Bria broke into a run, splashing through the cold water, feeling the slip and slide of the wood floor, then the squishy pile of the area rugs beneath her bare feet.

Behind her, Nick yelled unnecessarily, "Go. Go. Go!"

Men shouted, and the pounding of running footsteps on deck was muffled by the closed windows. But the pirates—because, God only knew, that's what they were—were trading gunshots in a hail of bullets, muzzle flashes, and loud splintering crashes of parts of Nick's beautiful *Scorpion* being blown to smithereens. Bria's heart was beating so fast, she felt dizzy.

She reached the doors just as a group of black-garbed men stopped right outside again. Nick grabbed her around the waist, pulling her into deep shadow against the back wall.

The Sig he was holding brushed her breast. His bare chest felt hot through the thin wet cotton of her shirt as he held her tightly against him.

"They're not going to give us time to lower that boat, are they?" Bria whispered, her harsh breathing sounding far too loud to her own ears.

"Doesn't look like it." Nick absently rubbed her arm with his free hand. She wasn't sure he was aware he was doing it, but it helped. "Head to the dive platform. There's an inflatable life raft there."

She kept her attention on the men moving about near the lifeboat. "We can't get there unless they move."

"Right. Give them a minute."

They didn't have a lot of minutes to spare. But then Nick knew that as well as she did. She relaxed in his hold, and concentrated on regulating her breathing. She scanned the deck beyond the windows, measuring how many steps it would take to cross it and get to the ladder down to the dive platform.

Probably thirty feet. But with that many armed men, the obstacle course would be lethal.

The clump of men outside the door broke up, melting into the shadows. But Bria heard the roar of more powerful engines, and the eggbeater sound of a large helicopter overhead. The bright flashing lights strobed onto the wood paneling just feet away from where she stood. She didn't so much as blink.

Nick kept his arm around her waist as the brilliant light slid slowly across the wall. "*Wait. Wait. Wait,*" he whispered.

Bria's mouth was so dry she could barely swallow. Her soaking wet clothing clung uncomfortably to her skin, but she still felt the tickle of perspiration between her breasts as she waited for Nick to say the word.

She felt that half-scared, half-excited feeling she'd experienced when she'd run track in high school. Ready. Set. Wait. Wait . . .

"*Now!*"

Go!

They raced across the library. Bria, a nose ahead, threw

out a hand and slammed through the door, letting in a rush
of warm night air, a faint acrid smell, and a stronger stink of
sweaty male.

It was much, much louder outside. She blocked it out. Run.
Run. Run.

Through the door, turn left, run like hell, bare feet slap-
ping against the teak deck, heartbeat knocking hard against
her chest. An enormous helicopter, blades whipped to a blur,
engines throbbing, lights strafing, hovered low on the starboard side of the ship, half a dozen ropes swaying in the
wind the rotors caused. The high-beam white light shining
down cast black shadows where they ran close to the wall.

Nick wasn't letting her slow down. For now, and Bria
knew the respite was merely temporary, they were the only
ones on the side deck. This was their window of opportunity
to get to the dive platform undetected.

Something banged loudly against the side of the *Scorpion*. A *boat*? They stayed where they were. Bria wanted to
keep running so badly she could taste it. Things were going
from bad to worse, hesitation wasn't going to get them across
the deck, down the ladder, and anywhere *near* that damn life
raft. Nick stopped her with the steel band of his forearm
across her midriff. Half a dozen men swarmed over the side
railing on the far side of the deck. He put a finger to his lips,
and pointed up.

God! *Now* what? It took a moment over the other loud
noises to hear the altercation breaking out on the sun deck
directly overhead. The three men must be standing against
the railing, and their rapid-fire Arabic, while low-pitched,
carried easily to the deck below.

She had no idea where the men who'd rappelled down
from the helicopter were. The group who'd just boarded ran
as one, disappearing inside. Not for long when they saw the
flooding inside. For this nanosecond there was no one in
sight. She started forward. Nick's arm tightened across her
middle.

The unexpected/expected *bang!* of a gunshot seemed to
come from inches away, and Bria's heartbeat responded by

charging into overdrive. The loud retort was immediately followed by a scream. A few seconds later, a man's body came hurtling from above. He landed, with a hideous crunch of bones, on the rail, a few yards in front of them. Half his head was missing.

Bria watched in horror as his broken body hung there for a moment, then slipped overboard, spinning off down to the black water below. A moment later she heard the splash.

Her heart was beating so fast it felt as though a wild animal was trapped inside her. Her body practically vibrated with the need to move. The ladder to the dive platform was only ten feet away. She glanced up at Nick. He shook his head.

The argument seemed to be the signal because a split second later all hell broke loose. Shouts and gunshots from various weapons suddenly drowned out the overhead helicopter. The stealthy movements became loud running footsteps. And everyone seemed to be shooting at everyone else.

"Go!" Nick said urgently.

Bria went.

A few more feet and they'd gain clear access to the ladder down to the dive platform where the small inflatable was stored. There was enough noise and confusion on board that there was a chance, slim as it was, for them to get into the raft undetected.

Bria stopped short. "Keep moving, damn it." He grabbed her shoulder as the *Scorpion* gave a massive sigh, and the deck tilted dramatically. "Don't sto— Fuck it!" A small group of black-clad men were dead ahead, guns leveled on them. He tried to maneuver her between his body and the wall.

More men filed in behind them, semiautomatic weapons raised threateningly.

Trapped.

Nick tightened his fingers on her shoulder, grinding out her name in warning as he felt her shift her center of gravity.

"Seven," she said matter-of-factly in a low voice. "I'll take the two on the left."

Like hell she would. He squeezed her shoulder harder, his will more than his strength holding her in place.

"Drop your weapon."

Nick hesitated. "Do it," he ordered calmly.

She hesitated, then dropped the Bersa to the teak deck. Nick followed suit.

"You are Cutter?" The strafing lights painted Kadar Gamali Tamiz's expression black and white as he strode forward. "There are three bins in your hold, Mr. Cutter. The contents belong to me."

"Well, that's going to be tricky," Nick told him mildly. "Since the hold is ass-deep under water." Where the hell was Jonah? Footsteps thundered overhead, a burst of gunfire cut into the shouted orders, in both Arabic and Italian. The helicopter swooped lower, then lifted in a hard throbbing beat to do a wide circle around the *Scorpion*. Out on the water various boats bobbed against the waves his ship was making as she sank deeper and deeper.

"You are a professional scuba diver," Tamiz said coldly as Najeeb Qassem closed in from behind himself and Bria. He too had a phalanx of armed men surrounding him. "This should not be a problem for you."

Nick saw muzzle flashes reflected in the windows, heard the chatter of gunfire all around them as the two factions killed each other off on other parts of his ship.

"True," he said dryly. "I'll just suit up."

"There's a really nice sunroom one deck up," Bria offered sweetly. "Why don't you wait there?"

Ignoring her, Tamiz gave Nick a narrow-eyed look. "How long will it take?"

"To suit up? Five minutes. To dive the hold? 'Bout fifteen. Grab a beer and I'll get back to you."

"You don't even know what you're looking for, Mr. Cutter. Or do you?"

"Whatever it is, I have no desire to be in the middle of some international incident. Tell me what it is, and where to find it. I'll bring it to you quickly. I don't want any of my people hurt."

Was Tamiz buying this? Nick searched the Moroccan's

features. Not really, but right then Nick was the only game in town.

"You do not need to concern yourself with the contents." Tamiz handed him a business card with the three bin numbers on the back. "This is what I want."

Nick raised a brow. "Each bin weighs upwards of a hundred pounds."

"Then I suggest you work quickly, Mr. Cutter."

"I suggest," Nick snapped, "that you fuck yourself, pal." He lifted Bria clean off her feet. "Brace yourself and roll!"

He threw her over the edge of the deck, then followed her over the rail to drop onto the dive platform below.

Hopefully the men would believe that they'd gone over the side into the water.

The platform was a foot underwater and they landed with a splash. Immediately he rolled to cover Bria's body with his. She gave a muffled cry, but stayed put, even though she was half submerged and the weight of his body pinned her down. "Okay?" he demanded harshly. Not willing to get off her unless she couldn't breathe.

"Peachy," she managed ironically. Nick felt the ragged rise and fall of her chest beneath his as he rolled her tight against the wall near the ladder where it was pitch dark. He shot out a hand and grabbed the bottom rung of the ladder for purchase as the ocean poured over the platform.

"Find them!" The cry was peppered with the ear-shattering ricochet of bullets and men's screams. Bright lights moved across the water beyond where they lay. Shit. The illumination was close, too damned close.

Bria's dark hair floated like a mermaid's, framing her pale face. Nick curved his arm protectively around her head. As if that was going to stop a fucking bullet. Sweat and seawater ran down his face. To reach the locker where the inflatable was kept, he'd have to stand and walk about seven feet. With those lights searching for them, he didn't dare. "Stay put!"

The froth and churn of white water beyond the platform picked up the high beam. Back and forth. Back and forth. A

slow, methodical search. With any luck, the men above would
think they'd drowned and eventually give up the search.

Better be fucking soon, Nick thought as he had to brace
the back of Bria's head to keep her face out of the water.

It wouldn't be long before someone smarter than a monkey realized that there was a dive platform covered with
water, just a few feet below where they were gathered.

He heard the throb of a powerboat fast approaching. Nice
if it were the cavalry, but he suspected not. The men above
them had a quick discussion, and decided to move off, rather
than wait to see if it was their own men, or more of Visconti's.
Nick took a breath as the sound of the engine was drowned
out by the renewed, escalating gunfire. Added to the hard
pounding of running feet and bullets was the cringe-worthy
sound of splintering wood, fiberglass, and teak decking as his
ship was shot to hell.

She was dying anyway, Nick reminded himself, but Jesus,
the death rattle was made worse by the wholesale destruc-
tion wrought by two opposing factions who had nothing
better to do than destroy a magnificent work of art.

Several loud shots were instantly followed by an almost
musical avalanche of fragmenting, crashing plate glass. Bria
sucked in a shallow breath to whisper, "Sorry," in his ear.
Filled with an unnamed warmth, Nick moved his head the
fraction of an inch necessary to brush his mouth against
hers.

"*You're* safe. I can always build another ship."

"Oh, God," she whispered, dark eyes gleaming. "*Now*
you tell me?"

Booted feet thudded on the deck six feet above them. So
close, Nick heard the heavy breathing of the men standing
there. Visconti's men this time?

Did it matter?

Do *not* look down. Do *not* fucking look down.

A shot. A scuffle. The thud of fist hitting flesh and bone.
*Go for it*, he thought savagely as the men resorted to fists.
A nearby splash.

The splash was what looked like an Uzi. Fuck it. So near

and yet so far. And sinking perilously close to the edge of the platform out of reach.

Nick's fingers curled around Bria's rib cage. He couldn't wait. "Grab the ladder."

Obediently she reached up, fumbling for a grip on the rung beside his hand. "Where're you going?" her whisper was low and harsh.

"Inflatable." He measured the few feet between where they lay and the locker containing the raft. He'd have to belly-crawl out of the deep shadows through water sheened with lights from above.

He calculated the odds of being seen. High.

Calculated the chances of survival staying where they were. Low.

He shifted his fingers to make sure Bria had a good grip, just as there was a double thud and two men landed with noisy splashes a yard from where they lay, half submerged. Damn it to hell.

The black-garbed men staggered to their feet, locked in mortal combat. A Moroccan and one of Visconti's men from the random speech clues.

Nick had one hand wrapped around the bottom rung of the ladder, the other tightly around Bria's waist. She was staring intently at the area where the Uzi had vanished moments before, as if she could somehow summon it to the surface.

Their legs were entwined, anchoring them to each other like lovers. The movement of the water made it impossible to remain still. The sea surged violently over the dive platform, sucking and pulling at them. They were practically floating in the ebb and flow as the *Scorpion* sank.

Arms straining, Nick maintained his death grip on both Bria and the ladder with difficulty. Something slammed into his hip.

"Loosen your hold a little," Bria whispered urgently against his throat. He eased his grip around her waist. Slightly. She wriggled a bit, twisted, leaned sideways bent double. While she wriggled in his hold, Nick kept his attention on the men nearby, praying they didn't see the movement. "What the hell are you—"

She pressed hard and ridged against his side. "Uzi!" Bria mouthed triumphantly.

Hallelujah! The strap had caught on the raised handles that bookended the platform so that the divers could more easily climb aboard. "Can you—" She managed to slide the weapon between them so he could grab it barrel first. "Perfect."

The men fighting were finding it impossible to remain on their feet as the deck tilted and water washed violently around their legs. A shot went wild, another ricocheted off the metal band securing the dive tanks to the wall.

Shit! If it had hit, the explosion would've taken them all out.

Grappling, holding on to each other for balance, the men staggered upright, let go, and started swinging. The blows rained hard and heavy, but they had to fight gravity as well as each other on the steeply angled deck. Their boots—dragged down by twelve inches of water—made their footing even more precarious.

Nick let go of Bria's waist, locking his legs even more firmly around hers, and fumbled to get the Uzi in position to fire while he still had one hand tethering them to the ladder. Bria said, "Give it to me. You get the raft."

It was a good plan. Except Nick didn't want to let go of her. Didn't want to risk getting separated. The surging water was incredibly strong. One wrong move, and she could be—

*"Go!"*

He double-checked that she was holding on, untangled their legs, then released his fingers. He was instantly swept several feet away. Close enough to the men that Nick was struck in the shoulder by a heavy boot. He looked up in time to see the man's eyes gleam as he suddenly saw him there. His weapon swiveled from his Moroccan opponent to point at Nick instead.

Nick wrapped his hands around the guy's ankle and yanked hard. Already staggering under the nonstop blows

from his oblivious opponent, and surprised by an attack at
foot-level, the man cursed in Italian as his arms windmilled.
He fell back, crashing into the lashed scuba tanks nearby.
Over the clatter and crash of the tanks, the sound of the ac-
companying shot was all but lost as the Moroccan put a bullet in his chest.

The man rolled off the sloped edge of the dive platform
and disappeared into the churning water behind him.

Spreading his feet, the Moroccan bent his knees to balance on the tilted deck and swiveled to point the business end
of his semiauto at Nick's head. The man squinted against
the sudden blinding glare of a light shining directly in his
face from a boat that suddenly appeared against the dive
platform. Ignoring the new arrivals, he yelled in Arabic,
"Where—"

The distinct sound of a discharged bullet was instantly
followed by the Moroccan's head exploding like a ripe water-
melon.

\*   \*   \*

Bria had fired. But it wasn't her bullet that hit him. Or at least
she didn't think so. Not that it mattered. Dead was dead.
"Nick!"

The bright light, positioned on the deck of the small boat,
shone directly in her face. She couldn't see a damned thing.
Not Nick. Not the boat, not who was *on* the boat.

Terrified she'd hit Nick instead of some unseen bad guy,
Bria pulled herself upright, the Uzi cradled against her chest,
one foot hooked around the bottom rung of the ladder as the
water tried to suck her across the platform. "Nick, answer
me, damn it!"

As he emerged from his prone position in the water, raising his hands over his head, he morphed into a blurred backlit shadow. "Stay put." It was hard to hear what the hell he
said; pandemonium was reigning all over the *Scorpion*. Bria
figured most of the bad guys were suddenly realizing that
they were on a sinking ship, and wanted off. Fast.

Since they were on a small square of rapidly submerging dive platform, with the stark white paintwork behind them, she thought Nick's suggestion to stay put was pointless. Whoever was behind the light was in the catbird seat. She swiveled, aimed at the light, and fired. A man screamed like a girl.

One light went dark. "Turn off the other light before she hits someone! Namely me, you assholes!" Bria immediately recognized the furious voice—Draven! How had he gotten there so damned fast? She'd only spoken to him a few hours ago. Not enough time to fly all the way from Marrezo. Which meant he'd been close by when she'd claimed to be in possession of the diamonds. Oops.

The platform dipped, and Bria staggered. Nick grabbed her arm to steady her. But they both knew that it was just a matter of minutes before the *Scorpion* gave her last hurrah and sank. Then everyone and everything standing too close was going to be sucked down to a watery grave.

"Bria," Draven said smoothly, "drop the weapon. I'm here to help you."

"Let's see you drop yours first," she told her brother. She had no intention of letting go of the Uzi.

\* \* \*

Five minutes eighteen seconds.

"I suppose," Nick said mildly, moving his grip from her arm to her waist as she splashed over to join him in the middle of the platform, "it was a foolish dream to think you'd obey an order?"

"Oh? Was that an order?" she asked sweetly, losing none of her sass and fire no matter what the circumstances. "I thought it was a suggestion."

The bright light was suddenly turned off, leaving them in relative darkness. Relative because his ship was lit up like Christmas with the fucking hovering chopper and half a dozen boats with spotlights surrounding the *Scorpion*. The noise had quieted down to just intermittent chatter of gun-

fire as small vessels converged beside the *Scorpion* and men
bailed over the side. Pretty much everyone seemed to be
determined to be the next ones off the sinking ship. It was a
fucking three-ringed circus.

He'd heard the mechanism, followed by the splash, as the
lifeboat was lowered into the water a few minutes earlier.

"Bria! Throw down your weapon, and put your hands
where I can see them!"

"Oh, for—" Bria threw up her hands, one of which held
the fully loaded Uzi. A quick glance at her face showed Nick
she knew exactly what she was doing. Any male with a pulse
seeing her right then would be eyeing her with nervous anticipation. They'd be keeping a wary eye on an unpredict-
able, bra-less woman in a wet T-shirt with a loaded gun.

She got top marks for misdirection.

The platform dipped a few more inches to port. Water
sloshed up his legs. He tightened his grip around Bria's waist.

"Draven, you idiot!" Bria shouted over the noise. "What
if I'd hit you? Although God only knows you deserve it!"

"Where are the diamonds, you stupid bitch?"

She swept her arm wide to encompass the water surrounding them, the helicopter swooping overhead, the men
shouting, the boats converging. "Trading insults with you
while standing on a sinking ship isn't what I'd imagined for
my final hour," she told the man sarcastically. "Look around,
Draven. *No one* is going to win here!"

Nick had a bigger problem than sunspots burned into
his retina. Because the man standing on the deck of the
smaller boat *wasn't* Draven Visconti. Wasn't Bria's brother.
Couldn't be.

His accent, his tone, his inflections. All *wrong*.

She made a sound of pure female anger. Nick could practically hear her temper sizzle. "Damn you! Look around you,
Draven! *You're* responsible for all of this!"

The man standing on the deck of a fast luxury boat was
in his mid-thirties, morbidly obese, and appeared to be un-
armed. Unlike the *very well-armed* men with him, he wore
a shiny dark business suit, and a white shirt and red power

tie. He was as out of place in the middle of the ocean as a hooker at a church social.

The four thugs with him carried semiautomatic weapons just in case someone got the crazy idea of trying to push past them and lay claim to their boat. A fifty-foot Sessa. Low, sleek, and fast.

Nick wanted the craft, and he wanted it *now*. Five minutes four seconds.

"If you hadn't meddled and put your nose where it didn't belong, I wouldn't have had to come all the way out here to deal with the situation." The man dabbed his sweating face with a white handkerchief, then waved it to indicate to his men to secure the boat to the platform.

*Great idea, pal; you might notice she's sinking.*

One of the men threw a line to another who'd jumped down onto the platform and was splashing around looking for somewhere to tie the boat. Nick didn't bother telling them.

Nick figured the two on the platform would be relatively simple to eliminate. But the two on board were hardened professionals. Bria, Nick saw, got that memo too.

Five minutes. They were trapped. "What in God's name is the *matter* with you?" Bria looked like she was going to go and haul the guy over the railing of his boat down onto the dive platform with them. Nick tightened his fingers like a vise around her waist, holding her back. Hell, trying to maneuver her behind his body. He ground out her name in warning as she strained against his hold.

Bria wasn't going to hide behind anyone, and she shifted aggressively, giving the guy the evil eye. "Stop this before people get hurt."

Nick almost laughed out loud. Get hurt?

The man-who-wasn't-her-brother, his florid skin greasy with sweat, didn't even acknowledge, let alone *look* at her; all his attention was fixed on Nick. "Where's my merchandise, Cutter?"

Two launches put on speed, the sound of their engines retreating, twin white wakes showing their progress. Out of the corner of his eye, Nick saw several men floundering in the water, having jumped overboard.

The *Scorpion* was dead. He had actually felt a physical reaction surge through his own body as his ship's heartbeat stopped with the last hurrah of the auxiliary engines shorting out minutes before. The millions of gallons of seawater inside would finish the job. The cherry on top would be the explosion below decks as the fuel in the full tanks of the helicopter blew.

Four minutes forty-nine seconds.

"Najeeb Qassem and Kadar Gamali Tamiz are both here," Nick told him coolly, fighting the slope of the platform and the wash of water around his lower legs. "Why don't we discuss just how the three of you want to split your diamonds?"

The weapons lifted.

"Fine," Nick said smoothly, his heart beating fast, his nerves stretched to the limit. There were things he'd be willing to risk if he were alone. But nothing he'd risk Bria for. "Let Bria get off the *Scorpion* safely. I'll take you to your diamonds."

Gunfire erupted on the other side of the ship. How soon before any number of those men glanced down, saw the Sessa? They'd take it from there.

Four minutes forty seconds to detonation.

He wanted the Sessa with her sleek shape and fast engine. That would put a nice distance between her and the *Scorpion* in minutes. Nick calculated the odds of the two of them taking the faux Visconti and his thugs.

The armed men stood with their legs braced against the tide that the sinking *Scorpion* was causing. Off balance, yeah. But at this close range, they couldn't miss hitting one or both of them.

One of the men spoke in rapid Italian, and the fat man smiled unpleasantly and replied in the same language. "Look how she holds it like a baseball bat. Do you think she will club all of us to death one by one? If *he* gets it, shoot it out of his hand. Knowing it's there will keep you on your toes!"

Overconfidence *and* stupidity.

"Both of you stay put. Tell my men where to find my merchandise, and do it quickly." The man wiped his face, holding on to the rail on the Sessa as it rocked with the slap of the waves against her sleek hull. The guy was oblivious.

Nick gave the men clear and specific directions to the hold, and the three bin numbers, in fluent Italian. "Want me to repeat that in English?" he asked politely.

They shook their heads, and were told to hurry by the man pretending to be Draven Visconti.

The good news was that the immediate threat was cut in half. The bad news was that he'd better come up with a way to highjack that Sessa, because they only had four minutes thirty-one seconds more to play with.

The two men on the narrow deck lifted their weapons, keeping them covered, Nick presumed, until the other two returned with the diamonds. After that, they'd be toast. Not that the other two guys would make it down to the flooded hold and back in the time remaining, especially without any diving gear. Idiots.

"You're going to regret this, Draven Albion Hilderprad Visconti!" Bria snarled. "What's *happened* to you? Have you lost all sense of honor that our father taught us?"

"Shut the *fok* up, *teef*." His eyes all but disappeared in the fat of his cheeks as he leaned against the pilothouse wall, flanked by his men. "I *will* have my men *foking* shoot you!"

"Oh, for— You wouldn't shoot your own *sister*!" she told him furiously.

Nick held on to her so tightly he was afraid she wouldn't be able to breathe. "You're going to be the fucking death of me, woman," he hissed under his breath.

Fighting mad, she struggled to free herself.

Nick kept his eyes on the Sessa and bent his head, his breath harsh in her ear. "He's not Draven, Gabriella. This man's an impostor."

It took a moment for her to stop trying to break free him. She went dead still. Her head dropped back against his chest. "What?!"

"He's not Visconti." Suddenly, Nick could hear the faint

sound of powerful engines approaching from the north, barely audible over the susurrus of the water, which was now up to Bria's knees.

Nick prayed that he was hearing the fast approach of Max Aries and his team. Unfortunately, he suspected the Moroccans and this guy had beat out the good guys by a good half hour or more. It was more likely to be backup for one or both sides.

Two against a horde was shitty odds. And where was Jonah?

"Who the hell are you?" Bria demanded hoarsely. "Where's my brother?"

The man smiled. "It's too late to mourn the king, you stupid bitch. He died ten years ago."

Bria froze. He could only see the top of her head, but he knew the news shocked her to the core. "You killed Draven?" she demanded, sounding bewildered and shell-shocked. "Why?"

"He was thrown from a horse—" He smiled. "But someone might've seen to the bridle . . ."

Nick met the fat man's eyes. "Who are you?"

Had Jonah managed to secure the other inflatable? If so, he could very well be on his way back here right now.

Or not. Nick couldn't count on Jonah or Aries saving the day. Shitfuckdamn.

Three minutes and change.

The impostor dismissively waved a ringed hand with fat sausage fingers. "Where are my men? Why aren't they back?" Sweat and splashed water rolled down his chins as he seemed to suddenly notice that the dive platform was submerged, and that Nick and Bria were knee-deep in rising water.

He scowled. "Shoot the girl if the men haven't returned with the diamonds in five minutes. Shoot his kneecaps if they're not back in six." He turned to go inside his craft.

Out of the corner of his eye, Nick saw a small glimpse of red just beyond the white water froth. If that was Jonah ready to save the day, he had two minutes to get into position.

Nick wanted the faux Visconti on deck where he could

see him, where his men *couldn't* see one another because his bulk was a massive wall between them.

"Parents Afrikaans speaking," Nick told him coolly, buying seconds now. The man paused at the door, then turned to look back.

Three minutes forty seconds. Nick squeezed Bria's waist in warning, then angled her slightly so she could see what he was looking at. A slowly moving inflatable raft hugging the swirling waters around the hull of the rapidly sinking *Scorpion. Jonah?* Jumping overboard at the wrong moment could, hell, *would* prove fatal. Nick knew he'd only have one opportunity. He had to time this perfectly. Jonah knew exactly where they were. He'd navigate the inflatable boat as close as possible without risking detection. Now all Nick had to do was be walleyed so he could observe both Jonah and the faux king at the same time. And any minute now, the second act would begin and then he could just kiss his ass good-bye because that would be all he wrote.

Three minutes twelve seconds.

"You lived in Jo'burg most of your life." A light strafed the water. Damn it, now he didn't see the inflatable. Had he imagined it? "Educated at an expensive private boys' school. Durban?" The guy's flat brown eyes sparked with surprise. "Yeah. Right on the mark. What happened? Did you go to school with Visconti and decide to assume his titled position?" Nick heard the soft clatter of a boat striking the hull of the *Scorpion.* Then another. And another in quick succession. Not the soft sound of a rubber boat. Fiberglass. Wood. Not Jonah. The arrival or departure of more bad guys.

The whop-whop-whop of a military helicopter sounded like a faint heartbeat in the darkness of the night, getting closer, but not nearly close enough to help them—if that was their intent.

Three minutes.

The ship moaned a low mournful death rattle that made the hair on Nick's body rise and his chest constrict in mourning. His goal had been to be gone before they got caught in the crossfire. But it was already too late. Had Jonah managed to survive the firestorm? *Was* he the one in the inflatable, or had Nick just fucking wished it was? He could see Bria out of the corner of his eye. She still hadn't moved. "That's it, isn't it?" he prodded. "Visconti told you all about his idyllic childhood on Marrezo. I bet the more you heard, the more you wanted it. It wasn't hard to remember a mere thirteen years of his life there. What did you do? Kill him when you were in school, or did you wait until just before he planned to go home triumphant?"

Out of time. It was now or never.

Under his breath, barely moving his lips, Nick whispered, "Let's prove what a good marksman you are. Three seconds. Three o'clock. One!"

Two minutes thirty.

"Two." Nick grabbed up a filled oxygen canister, swung back his arms, and with every ounce of strength he possessed, flung it up and out, as far over the deck of the Sessa as he could. Then yelled, "Now!"

Bria fired a burst from the Uzi.

The tank exploded over the small boat in a fiery eruption and with an ear-splitting bang.

That was all the distraction Nick needed. Grabbing Bria up in a bear hug, he threw them off the dive platform into the midnight black water.

\*       \*       \*

Bria barely had time to suck in a breath before Nick catapulted them sideways off the edge of the dive platform. How he'd known where the edge *was*, when it was under several feet of churning, frothy water, was a mystery. How they missed hitting the small boat that carried Draven and his men was also hard to wrap her brain around.

But she had more urgent concerns as they sank beneath the water.

Black.

Cold.

All-encompassing darkness.

Nick's arms, wrapped like steel bands around her, were literally her lifeline in a world gone crazy.

Bria let herself go. To fight the water was impossible, and she allowed her body to sink. Eventually, please God, they'd pop to the surface some distance away. Because the suck and pull as the *Scorpion* sank would drag them under if they didn't get out of range.

How far? Her lungs were already bursting. She let out a small breath to relieve the pressure, part of which was Nick's death grip around her waist. That was okay by her, and she tightened her arms around him, gripping the waistband of his jeans.

After what felt like hours and was probably seconds, Nick start to kick. She couldn't see him, but she followed suit as he guided her by some internal radar to the surface.

"Grab a breath," he said, steadying her as the water pushed and shoved them as they crested the chop. His pale eyes, all she saw, picked up some of the light behind her. "You okay?"

Nodding, Bria let out the breath she'd been holding in a gasp, then breathed in, coughing and choking on a mouthful of salty water. It slapped her in the face, and stung her eyes.

The sound of shouting was drowned out by a series of explosions that sheeted the water in brilliant red and amber light and made her squint against the intermittent brilliance.

Bria tried with everything in her not to give in to the panic and fear filling every cell in her body. God. They were only twenty or so feet away from the *Scorpion*. Nick's ship was circled with foamy white as the sea churned and frothed angrily around her. Only the sundeck and atrium were now above water.

There was no sign of the small boat attached to the dive platform.

Men screamed as they dived overboard. And yet—other morons were still shooting at one another!

Her own erratic breathing was louder to her ears than whatever was happening on the *Scorpion*.

Nick spun her around and gave her an ungentle shove. *"Swim!"*

She swam. As fast as she could. Arm-over-arm-over-arm. Every stroke felt as though she was swimming through water as heavy and viscous as cement. Another explosion rent the air, making her flinch. The water around them turned a bright metallic orange, then went dark again.

"Don't look back. Move it! *Go! Go! Go!"*

She went. Arm-over-arm-over-arm. Bria's lungs heaved with exertion, and her arms, legs, and back burned like fire as she put every ounce of energy into getting as far away from his ship as they could in the shortest amount of time.

Arm-over-arm-over-arm. Saltwater stung her eyes and dozens of small lacerations on her skin, her breathing was labored, and her mouth was dry. Heartbeat a frenetic thud-thud-thud, she put her back into it and swam as if her life depended on it. It did. Breathing when she could, holding her breath when she couldn't. Her lungs burned, and her breathing was labored and erratic. Nick stayed one arm-stroke to her left the whole time.

It felt like several hard-laboring hours later that he shouted, "We're good." His breathing was rough. "Float and rest a bit. Good job, Princess." He held out his hand to draw her close. "Hell of—"

"Ahoy!" An amplified voice came across the water. "Cutter?"

Nick started to laugh. "The cavalry has arrived."

"A day late and several millions of dollars short," Bria said crossly, so relieved to see the large, powerful motor launch approaching them as they bobbed in the middle of nowhere that she almost cried.

Nick wrapped his arm around her to keep her afloat, and yelled, "About fucking time you got here!"

The next few minutes were surreal as she and Nick were pulled from the water by black-garbed men.

Aries and his team arrived just in time to see the end result of Nick's handiwork. Several other launches had moved into position to pick up swimmers. Overhead, the large helicopter she'd heard approaching circled the area, its light strafing the water. Wrapped in blankets, they were handed steaming mugs of coffee and encouraged to go belowdecks.

Nick refused, and Bria wasn't about to leave his side for an instant. She used the cup to warm her hands as they stood at the rail and watched the bright flares across the water.

"Took you fucking long enough." Nick turned his head as a tall man strode toward them. Bria presumed this was Max Aries.

"You should go below," the guy said in a reasonable tone that got Bria's back up. "Grab a shower . . ."

"What do you see?" Nick pointed.

The man came up beside him, curling his large hands around the rail as he watched what was happening. "God, I'm sorry, Cutter."

Standing on board the motor launch, one arm around Bria, Nick watched his *Scorpion* sink in a churning, frothing foam of white. He rubbed his hand up and down her blanket-covered arm as she shuddered. Her wet hair danced around her shoulders like Medusa's snakes in the wind kicked up by the helicopters swooping overhead.

Nick didn't say anything, and she slipped under the arm he had braced on the rail and leaned against his chest as the remnants of the *Scorpion* went up in one last fireball, then sizzled as it dragged everyone and everything under the water with it.

Countdown complete. Game over.

\*     \*     \*

Nick tightened his arms around her as they rode the swells.

The illumination lasted seconds, then they were plunged into intimate darkness.

Aries shifted away from the rail. "I've gotta—"

"Go," Nick told him, hearing the almost imperceptible chatter on the other man's headset. There were bad guys to apprehend. More men to fish out of the water.

"Is it over?" Bria asked softly.

"Yeah." His voice was hoarse as he rubbed his chin on her wet hair. Over.

Dozens of human lives, and millions of dollars' worth of ship and equipment. More millions of his salvaged treasure, and a boatload of uncut diamonds. Yeah. Over. He didn't give a rat's ass.

Nick adjusted the blanket around her shoulders. He was bare-chested, his pants wet, he wasn't cold. He felt . . . nothing.

"I'm so, so sorry."

"Why? None of this was your fault."

"Maybe not initially. But if I hadn't called him in a temper, he wouldn't have come . . ."

"Maybe. People like that have trouble following them wherever they go. Your faux brother. The Moroccans. I'd rather sink the *Scorpion* out here in the middle of nowhere than have them follow me to Cutter Cay. She was just a ship, Bria. Just a toy."

"A pretty expensive toy," she murmured, turning to wrap her arms around him. "And what about your treasure that you spent months finding and cataloging?"

He shrugged. "It's not going anywhere."

For several minutes she remained still as the waves swirled and eddied beneath the boat. Nick felt the warm kiss of her breath, and the soft press of her breasts against his bare chest. She stroked her palm over his chest.

"I presume that was the late Max Aries?" She stood on her toes to brush a kiss to his rigid jaw. "Can I be the first to punch him in the nose?"

"Bloodthirsty, Bria." Nick smiled, tightening his arms around her. "Be my guest."

"Jonah's all right, right?"

Nick didn't know. He didn't like not knowing. Damned fool.

Aries came back to join them. "Jesus, buddy. Wasn't that extreme?" he asked, sounding pained, as he stared out at the dark water.

Bobbing in the water were men clinging to the flotsam and jetsam of his ship. Was Jonah one of them? "Only way I could come up with at short notice that leveled the playing field."

"It certainly did that," Aries said dryly, his dark hair blowing around his head. "Must say, the pyrotechnics were impressive." He paused. "I don't suppose the diamonds are on you?" And when Nick shot him a "Fuck you" look, Aries grunted in response. "How much is it going to cost us for you to head the salvage op?"

"I don't have a ship, remember?"

Aries winced. "That'll cost us."

"Ya think? Try upward of two hundred and fifty mil. Yeah, that would be *million*. Better break into the T-FLAC piggy bank, pal."

Nick was already figuring out what he wanted on the *Scorpion Two*. T-FLAC was going to pay, and pay dearly, for the "small favor" he'd performed for them.

"As for heading the salvage, Cutter Salvage doesn't take on private salvage jobs. I'll let you know if we're interested."

They both knew he'd be right there to do the job. Not just to retrieve the fucking diamonds that had caused so much death and chaos, but for his own treasure, retrieved and then sunk. Yeah. He'd be back to bring both to the surface.

But he'd let the counterterrorist operative sweat for a while.

"Shit, Cutter. I'm so fucking s—"

"I'd rather hear a lengthy apology over a beer. Later. Much later."

"You got it. We arrested Prunella Baumgartner a few hours ago, and—"

"Who?" Nick asked blankly.

Tucked against him, Bria laughed. "Please tell me that's Dafne's real name."

"It is. The fake Visconti was her husband, Roland. Both from Johannesburg. I'm sorry to inform you, Princess, your brother died ten years ago in a riding accident."

"We don't believe that was the case," Nick told him as he

watched the motor launch closest to them pick up half a dozen men from the water. It was almost as bright as daylight with all the searchlights. He could see that none of them was Jonah.

"Yeah. Too coincidental. My people are looking into it. Baumgartner was into petty larceny from a young age. He and your brother attended school together and became friends. This crime of the Baumgartners' was years of painstaking attention to detail in the making. Certainly it started in Johannesburg when he encountered your brother. He got deeply involved with the conflict diamond trade several years ago. According to his wife, he saw an article about Cutter Salvage in the paper, decided one of your ships would be a perfect mule to transport the diamonds to the Americas."

Nick raised a brow. "Are you telling me he planned to use the *Scorpion* as early as my arrival in Vietnam almost two *years* ago?"

"He knew how and when you hired on new crew. Many of the men working for you reported directly to Baumgartner."

"Jesus." It was hard to comprehend that kind of cunning and patience. "What happens should he be out there alive?"

"Impersonating royalty is considered treason. If Baumgartner is still alive, he'll get the death penalty for that alone. After the United Nations and T-FLAC are done with him, he'll be begging to tell us all his sources and connections in his blood diamond–trafficking operation.

"The rest—the Moroccans et cetera—will be prosecuted by several countries to the full extent of their laws." Aries glanced out over the water, and his tone hardened. "Those of them that make it."

"Good!" Bria said with alacrity.

"We figured that Halkias saw the princess and panicked. Baumgartner had already been unpleasantly surprised when you showed up unexpectedly for his coronation two years ago. You were one of the few people who knew him well enough to suspect something was wrong. He didn't want you around. When his man saw you on board, he must've panicked and tried to get rid of you."

"My bodyguard taught me how to protect myself." Bria slipped her arm from beneath the blanket to wrap it around Nick's waist. "But I never for a moment suspected that he *wasn't* my brother when I went home. He played his role really, really well."

"Only thing I don't get," Aries said to Nick. "How did he fool *you*? Accents are your superpower, why didn't you hear that he wasn't who everyone thought he was?"

"I'd never spoken with him. Logan does all the investor relations. And he wasn't on the island when Bria and I went."

"The landslide on Marrezo was set by cousins of your chef, Alfonso. We believe for the same reason. They believed that the princess was about to blow the whistle. Baumgartner promised all these men a large cut of the diamond payoff."

"Apparently everyone was getting a large percentage payoff," Bria pointed out. "The Moroccans, the people working for Drav—for the *Baumgartners*."

"Which was why Baumgartner went to Tenerife to kill the Moroccans so he'd have *their* slice of the pie, and why they in turn were going to off him." Bria rested her head against Nick's chest. "Greedy."

Aries looked up from Bria's profile and met Nick's gaze. "Want to be airlifted, or stay put?"

She turned her head to give Aries the evil eye, then said firmly, "Stay put if there's a hot shower to be had. I think taking a helicopter to dry land would give me the bends."

"The bends?" Aries asked, puzzled.

Nick got it. "She needs time to adjust to being safe."

"Take the main cabin. No one will disturb you."

Nick shifted Bria in his arms. She felt solid and real and, thank God, blessedly unharmed. Other than the whop-whop-whop sound of the rotors, and the powerful beam from the low-flying chopper, the excitement was over. Aries and his team would scoop up everyone clinging to whatever they'd been able to find in the water. He didn't give a shit what happened to any of them.

"Don't leave the area until I have confirmation that you have my brother."

Aries shot him a look of surprise. "Your brother? Hell, how did *he* get involved? Logan or Zane?"

"*Jonah*. Let me know when you have him. Alive and well. *Not optional*. I'm going down to get Bria into a hot shower. Clothes?"

"In the cabin."

"Where are we heading?"

"Tenerife," the counterterrorist operative said absently, watching his men hauling bad guys into their vessels. He glanced over at Nick. "After everyone is picked up. Give or take a couple of hours. Sure you don't want the chopper to take you in?"

Nick cocked a brow at Bria, and when she shook her head, told Aries, "We'll be below."

Nick took Bria to the compact cabin. The bunk took up most of the floor space, which suited him just fine. He turned her, nudging her back against the locked door. The blanket dropped to the floor. He indicated she raise her arms, and when she did, pulled the wet, inside-out T-shirt over her head.

As soon as he tossed it aside, she pressed her cool breasts against his chest. "How come you're so warm?" she demanded, nuzzling his chest.

"I'll have you toasty in no time." He undid her jeans and unzipped them, then shoved the wet denim down her legs. "Step."

He made short work of his own jeans and nudged her into the tiny head, then turned on the shower; there was barely enough floor space for the two of them to stand toe-to-toe.

She slid her arms around his waist and met his eyes. "Aries will find Jonah."

"He'd better." He stuck his hand under the spray. Tepid.

"How long—"

"It's pitch dark. I have no idea what, if any, equipment Jonah might have." *Or none.* The thought chilled him. "With any luck he grabbed the other inflatable and is bobbing about, ready for pickup."

She shivered, stroking her hands up and down his back. "That's what I think too."

He shifted her under the tepid spray, hoping it would warm up soon. Nick could hear the chopper out there, flying in a low search pattern. He lifted a strand of her hair, then brushed his lips with it. He could act as casually as he needed to, but he found he wasn't as cool, calm, and collected inside.

He poured shampoo from the tiny bottle into his palm and lathered her hair while she soaped his chest with scrupulous attention to detail. She didn't need to work so hard; he already had an erection. But God, he loved the way she petted him.

"Will your cousin, Antonio, be king?" He'd never wanted a woman as much as he wanted Bria. Not just sexual want, although God only knew that was a constant driving force. Nick slicked back her soapy hair, then nudged her under the spray.

Eyes closed, she shrugged. Foam slid in a maddening glide down one gleaming breast as the water sluiced over her. Steam drifted to the ceiling. "He's a vintner. I don't know if it's something he'd want to do. But he loves Marrezo, and would do anything to bring it back to its former glory. So yes, maybe. I think he'd be good for the country."

"Yeah." He exchanged shampoo for soap, lathering it between his hands. "I do too." He soaped her shoulders, and curved his palms around the globes of her breasts, then down the gentle indentation of her waist.

He had no doubt Bria would help her cousin, utilizing her education and experience in public relations, as Marvin Ginsberg had intended her to do. "With this turn of events, will you consider going back to your island to live?" he asked casually, maintaining his distance with sheer, bloody willpower alone. His dick was a heat-seeking missile, and she was the target.

She shook her head, then took the soap back from him. His entire body braced for contact as her palms filled with lather. "I'll help Antonio if he asks. And it's somewhere that will always hold a piece of my heart. But I'm not that princess. I haven't been for a long, long time. My life is elsewhere."

"Sacramento?" he said lightly, as he took back the soap. Her hands glided down his chest, around his back. Soapy and slick. "They probably held that job for you."

"Maybe."

"You like islands." Nick felt a little desperate. He had no idea how to read a placid, and cool, princess. "And extinct volcanoes, right? We have both at Cutter Cay."

Her soapy hands stroked across his ass. She murmured, "We have other things in common, don't we?" She tasted his shoulder with her open mouth. Despite her wandering lips, frustration of a different kind ate at him.

He turned off the water and reached behind her for a towel. They both still had soap all over them. He didn't give a damn. "I'm more interested in our differences."

Lifting her head, she laughed, then punched his chest. "I'm in love with you, Nick Cutter. Madly, crazily, insanely in love with you. I didn't plan this—*any* of it. But I'm not sorry for any of it either."

In spite of everything that had happened that day, and the catalog was long and hellishly eventful, Nick smiled too. Her words made him feel ridiculously euphoric. He wrapped the towel around her hair, and shifted her out of the shower stall. "That's my Gabriella! Cut straight to the chase." Thank God. His frayed nerves couldn't have handled this much longer. They were both dripping on the carpet. Nick toppled her backward onto the tightly made-up bunk.

"I was seeing just how long it would take you to beat around the bush."

He felt her smile against his throat. "Life's too short to waste time dancing around what I really, truly want. You. I understand that emotions are anathema to you, Nick." Her dark eyes were luminous as she put her hand over his heart. "But give us a try. Please give us a try. I can live without you if I have to. But God, I don't *want* to." Her fingers played in his chest hair when he was silent for several long seconds. She smacked her palm on his chest. "Say something. Damn it."

Nick pressed his lips against her forehead, inhaling her unique salted-peach fragrance, which he'd recognize anywhere.

"I wasn't looking," he admitted softly, his heart swelling with emotion that felt as bright and effervescent as champagne. "Wasn't even thinking about meeting someone— *anyone* like you. But there's a moment in a man's life when he stops and says: 'There she is,' " he told her softly. "I saw you walking toward me in the medina, and subconsciously I thought—Ah! *There* she is."

"Ha!" she laughed, wrapping her long legs around his hips, her arms around his neck. "You *really* thought—*there's* a sneaky, devilish spy, out to have her wicked way with me."

He smiled against her wet hair, his heart filled to bursting, the sensation becoming more and more familiar. "That too," he murmured against her mouth as he slipped into her wet, welcoming heat. "Crazy that I agreed to help Aries because I was becoming bored. I wanted, needed, a little excitement in my life. I could have come straight to Sacramento and found you."

Had he ever in his life had a rational conversation in the middle of sex? Nick thought, amused, turned on, and blindingly, ridiculously happy.

"That certainly would've saved time," she told him cheerfully, her inner muscles clenching around him. Neither dared to move. It would be over in a second. Nick was grateful that she wanted to hold the sensation as long as possible. "But look at the adventure we would've missed."

"Ninety percent we could've done without."

"Which made what we did have that much sweeter," she argued. And Nick realized that fiery arguments with Gabriella Visconti for the next fifty years were definitely conducive to his continued good health.

"I'm sorry you lost your brother," he told her gently, sliding his hands beneath her sweet ass. "We'll find out what really happened so you can have closure. But I have brothers to spare. I'm happy to share. You'll love Logan and Zane, and I know they'll adore you. Jonah certainly does already."

She started to move, slowly, as if they had all the time in the world. "You're okay with him?"

"It'll take some adjusting, a lot of filling in the gaps . . . but yeah. I think we'll be good." No matter what had happened before they met, Jonah was still his friend. They'd build on that. If— No. They'd find him. Jonah Cutter had already proven he was a survivor.

There was a sharp, loud rap at the door. They both froze. Hell, had he remembered to lock the door?

"Nick?"

*Jonah*. Nick let out the breath he hadn't realized he'd been holding. "Get lost," he yelled back, and grinned down at Bria when he heard Jonah's laugh as he walked with loud purposeful steps away from the door.

"I'm glad." She rubbed his chest in maddening circles that made all sorts of exciting promises. Her hips picked up the pace too.

Nick anticipated—Joy. Laughter. Exasperation. And makeup sex.

He imagined his life without her. And the image was a blank white canvas. He imagined life with her, and everything was in glorious, vibrant color.

"Family's important," she told him.

"So I've been told."

"We'll be good for each other," Bria assured him, nibbling a path across his jaw.

"You think so, do you?"

She nodded, her hair brushing his throat, her still-soapy, wet breasts sliding maddeningly against his chest as she moved. "I'm fire to your ice. You make me more—" Her voice was filled with the humor he loved. "Temperate, let's say. And I make you more— temperate as well, I guess. You cool me down, and I fire you up." She kissed him tenderly on the mouth.

"I don't want to cool you down. I love you hot and fiery

and standing toe-to-toe with me." He decided that Bria quiet and methodical wasn't who he wanted her to be right then. He drove inside her to the hilt.

She took up the rhythm, her heels pressed against his flexing ass. "Did you just say you love me?"

"Want me to repeat it in Italian?"

She put both hands on his face, and stared at him, her heart in her eyes. "*Sì.*"

Turned out, she *was* his princess after all.

The Cutter Cay trilogy continues . . .

Look for

# VORTEX
ISBN: 978-0-312-37195-1

From *New York Times* bestselling author

# CHERRY ADAIR

Coming in summer 2012
from St. Martin's Paperbacks